I0667289

Georgia's Rebellious Heart
Sweet McKenna Book Twelve

Christine Young

Published by Rogue Phoenix Press. LLP
Copyright © Christine Young 2025

Names, characters and incidents depicted in this book are products of the author's imagination or are used fictitiously. Any resemblance to actual events, locales, organizations, or persons, living or dead, is entirely coincidental and beyond the intent of the author or the publisher. No part of this book may be reproduced or transmitted in any form or by any means, electronic or mechanical, including photocopying, recording, or by any information storage and retrieval system, without permission in writing from the publisher.

ISBN: 978-1-62420-888-1

Credits
Cover Artist: Design by Ms G
Editor: Sherry Derr-Wille

Chapter One

London 1758

Rain sluiced from the dark-clouded sky. Chandler would be here soon. She did and she didn't want to see him. After his last ultimatum more than two months ago, Georgia acknowledged the fact she would never be able to trust the man...her person forever...her mate for now and into the future.

She loved Chandler. Many days wished she didn't.

She would never confide in or rely on the man. Would never be able to trust him with her heart or her person. He was not a good man. Chandler was a horrible person.

He insisted she stay the remainder of her contract after she gave birth to their little girl. Maintained she owed him. In her mind, Georgia didn't believe she owed Chandler anything. He threatened her. Told her he would give her to Bertram, a man she despised, for his personal entertainment if she didn't continue to work the nightly shows. She would be Bertram's plaything. His little doll to toy with as he pleased. Also told her he would auction her to the patrons of his shows. If he sold her to the highest bidder, she would find herself on her back in the rooms on the third floor entertaining different men. Her favors would be sold to any man who had enough money as if she was a common whore. At the thought her stomach cramped. She was no whore. The only man she'd ever been with was Chandler.

Never, would she ever go back to the brothel. Her future along with her daughter's and her unborn child lay ahead of her.

Giving into his demand was a lesser evil than the other choices he presented her with.

She endured the month and a half left on her contract. Escaped him. Now, she owned a home. She was beginning her career as a professional caterer. She did enjoy cooking. Loved to visit with her clients while they planned menus for their gatherings. With this job, she could bring her daughter along with her bodyguard Hollis to work. They did make an eccentric trio.

The situation was peculiar. Chandler insisted she hire Hollis. She smiled thinking about this man, who wanted to see to her protection even though he didn't love or respect her. Chandler would never love anyone except himself.

Hollis was the largest man she'd ever known. His dark black skin glistened, while the muscles of his forearms bulged. Each and every time he smiled, the white of his teeth gleamed against the background of his face. If Hollis wished, he could lift her with one hand. His thighs were the size of tree trunks. Dark, very dark brown eyes, gifted his handsome face. He always treated her with respect. When Chandler visited, Hollis remained close. Surprising Georgia, Hollis was loyal to her, not the man who hired him.

Once she arrived in this small cottage just outside the busy city of London, Chandler would attempt to convince her to return to the fold. Her return to that decadent lifestyle would never happen. The five-month-old daughter she cradled in her arms was too important to spend her formative years living in a high-priced brothel. Maeve was the most important person in her world. Her hair was as black as midnight, her eyes the color of a vibrant summer sky. The little girl resembled her in every way. Didn't look at all like her father. Georgia was pleased about the fact.

Chandler didn't like the name she gave her daughter. Wished she called her something less Irish. Too bad. That was alright by her as long as he never abused the baby or the girl as she grew into womanhood. While he never hurt her, Georgia acknowledged the fact he harbored a mean streak. Recalled when he hurt his sister-in-law. Resented his immediate family for disavowing him. Promised revenge. He no longer sought vengeance. His business was too much fun as well as lucrative. By seeking revenge, he could lose everything.

Now, even though she was free of the brothel where he made his money, he continued to attempt to bring her into the world she left behind. A world she wanted no part of. Maeve would never see the inside of Chandler's whorehouse. Would never learn about her mother's participation in the debauchery within. With Chandler, she never cared who watched them while they were intimate. Didn't even mind the participation of Jimmy along with Johnny when they fondled her breasts. Sometimes the scenarios excited as well as pleased. When he brought his best friend, Bertram, into the mix, she drew the line. Bertram disgusted her.

Now, her future lay ahead of her. She intended to make the most of her prospects. Their daughter's potential would never be compromised by the filth of her father's world.

Georgia let out a slow breath of air. She loved Chandler with all her heart. After some time, she came to realize he would never love her back. He was too enamored of himself to give his love elsewhere. This egotistical nature of his actions blurred anything that was good in him. He was unable to give of himself even though he was her mate.

The loud boom of thunder startled her. A tiny noise of surprise escaped the baby. Within her arms, she rocked Maeve. The noise frightened the child. Tears filled her beautiful blue eyes. The babe let out a thin wail of distress, her head bobbing against her as she searched for something that would give solace. Georgia brought her little love to her shoulder, smoothing her hand along her back to calm the infant. Maeve's entire hand found its way to her mouth as she tried to soothe herself.

"Hush, little one, this is just a terrible storm. Lots of noise that's all. The dark clouds will pass then the skies will be sunny as well as clear again. Nothing for you to worry over. You must get used to the tempest outside as well as the ones that will be brought to you because of your father. Your papa is not a good man."

A long slow breath of air left her. She should never prejudice her daughter against the man who sired her. Time would explain to Maeve who her father was as well as what he was not.

Setting her hand on her stomach, she thought about the tumultuous days as well as nights with Chandler. She was pregnant again. Georgia wasn't positive about how she felt about another pregnancy so soon. It would be difficult to raise one child by herself let alone two. Now she would have two little ones to be responsible for. The man made certain she conceived before he allowed her to set out on her own. She still didn't believe he would, in truth, give her to Bertram. Mates didn't treat each other in the manner he threatened. They were possessive as well as demanding of their partners.

Humming to Maeve, she strode around the room. Stopped to peer out the window. Set her forehead on the cold pane of glass. Maybe the storm slowed the man down. Perhaps he had a change of heart. Maybe an accident. The thought caught in the back of her throat. While she didn't wish to have anything more to do with Chandler, she didn't want any harm to come to him.

She hoped the storm would slow his progress. Maybe the wheels of his carriage would get stuck in the mud. A quagmire might serve to keep Chandler away for another night. Perhaps he would turn around, return to London. She wasn't looking forward to the argument that would ensue upon his arrival. Chandler argued they should marry. Told her she should return with him so they could be together. The new Winter Snow was not the same caliber. His audience wanted her. She opposed a marriage between them. Never wanted him to own her.

Never!

Never say never too often. What you don't wish for might come to pass.

Gritting her teeth against the thought of being under his thumb, she forced herself to stay strong. When she pushed her chin in the air then stiffened her back, the act would help. Considering this scenario, being weak would do her no good. Shivers pounded down her spine when she thought of those last days of her contract. Fear of what he could do to her or Maeve if she protested held her at his whim. That last month and a half, she did all he asked. Some of those nights, he would leave Bertram to stay with Maeve as a reminder of the command he held over her.

Maeve's daddy was not a nice man.

She never did understand why he forced her on stage when she didn't wish to be there. The audience witnessed her reluctance. That fact brought in more groats than the previous performances. Forced her with threats. Bertram was always close. Always nearby to carry out Chandler's wishes if he asked. To her disgust, sometimes Bertram participated.

Until she arrived on the scene, the two men always shared their women, their conquests. To her knowledge, she was the first female Chandler and Bertram didn't share. Well…that fact was one point in his favor.

"You are Winter Snow, the ice maiden," Chandler told her with a grin that didn't reach his eyes. "Your fans want to see you with me. Once, you enjoyed the lovemaking in front of an audience. You will again. Your unwillingness is an aphrodisiac to my audience. They wish to see you struggle against my attentions, to hold back your pleasure. Perhaps I should tie your hands above you. Leave you open to whatever my audience asks of me. We could allow them to write the script for us to play out. I am certain the production would be titillating. The pounds would pour into my coffers."

She didn't enjoy the last days of her contract. The different scenarios she found herself forced to endure were horrible. Her mind would be with Maeve, sheltered upstairs. While she never believed he might hurt the child, she could never allow herself to trust him or Bertram. Must take care to give into all his dictates. The time would pass. If anything happened to her, Chandler would become the child's guardian. As soon as she escaped Chandler, working the ensuing weeks of her contract, she would set about making her father, Cormack O'brien, Maeve's guardian.

The knock on the door startled her. Her stomach turned over while her heart pounded hard against her ribs. Before she walked to the door, she swallowed the huge lump of fear lodging in her throat.

Chandler...

A long deep breath helped for a swift moment. He was here. Would insist on staying the night. Could hold the horrific weather as the reason to remain. If he stayed, he would expect to share her bed. Chandler needed to realize she wasn't going to change her mind about their future together. While she would never stop him from seeing his child, soon to be children, she didn't intend to share intimacies with the man. She couldn't bear to have him in her bed. Didn't wish to be reminded of the intense feelings she had for the man.

Taking her time, she brought Maeve to her crib then set her inside. Kissed the baby's forehead before drawing a light cover over her tiny body.

"Sleep tight, my darling. I won't let anyone hurt you." Beside the crib, Georgia lingered. "Your father is here now. I'll check on you as soon as possible."

The knocking on the door became more insistent. "Open the damn door!" The uttered words sounded frantic.

Father!

Georgia rushed to the door, unlocking then flinging it open. So thrilled to see him, she was in his arms before he could step inside the door. She heard the strong, steady beats of his heart. With each breath he inhaled, she felt the movement of his chest. His strong arms locked around her. As she pressed herself against his large frame, the moment was not much different than when she was a little girl. She wished she could keep him here with her forever. Wished he could protect her from Chandler. No one except herself could manage the feat. She needed to rely on her wits as well as her strength of will.

"Fáilte!" she cried out in welcome.

Cormack O'brien set her back to look at her. His smile was just as she remembered. "That was a nice welcome." The ensuing pause seemed significant. His brows furrowed together. "Are you alright? The bastard hasn't hurt you? Has he?"

She couldn't stop the cringe at the label her father gave her mate even though the name was true. "I'm fine. Can I take your coat? Get you something to drink? You do know I wasn't expecting you. You didn't write." She sounded as if she lectured her father even though she was certain the surprise visit was meant to be just that…a surprise. "You're a long way from Belfast."

"A nice hot cup of tea with a *wee* splash of brandy to help warm my chilled body would suffice. For the time being, I intend to take up residence in London." Cormack shrugged from his coat. "Where's my little Maeve?"

"Asleep in her crib. While I get your tea, you can look in on her." Georgia smiled at her father's back as he made his way to the nursery. "Don't wake her. If she is awake, bring her out to the front room."

Cormack was such a loving grandfather. What happened to her broke his heart even though he understood finding her mate was a necessity along with the claiming. After she discovered her mate, there was no backing down. She realized proceeding with her plan was a necessity. Well, Chandler, with his father's help, learned the ceremonial words that would result in his ability to mark her as his.

While he claimed her, she did experience past lives together.

Acknowledged the fact they would continue. Some of what she saw was turbulent. Other times they were so in love the sight of them together made her shake with longing for those long-ago years.

Forgetting what happened between their meeting and the claiming would never happen. Nor would she ever regret her experiences with him. Some of those moments were wild. At times exciting. Chandler understood all her weaknesses. She would never regret the twelve months, the good along with the bad. Maeve was the result of her first few encounters with Chandler. In less than five months, God willing there would be another child, a boy now.

The teakettle had been on the stove warming. It would not take much for the water to boil. She pulled cookies from her cookie jar to set on a plate. Arranged the teacups along with the plate on a tray she would bring to the front room. Brandy, lemons and sugar were included to add to the plain drink.

Before everything was ready, Georgia heard Cormack. When she brought the tray into the room, he was staring out the window at the pelting rain. His hands were behind his back. When he heard her walk through the door, he turned. Gifted her with a smile she realized he didn't feel into his heart.

"Thought you might wish for something to eat as well." Walking into the room, she set the tray on a table.

She poured the tea then handed her father the bottle of whiskey while she doctored her tea with a bit of lemon and milk. To sweeten, she added a spoonful of sugar. Wasn't eager to tell her father she was expecting Chandler. Since he'd yet to arrive, thought the storm might have made him change his mind. Chandler was a man who loved his creature comforts. To be out in a night such as this one went against his natural behavior.

"Always thinking of others." He tested the temperature with a small sip. "Good, glad you remembered the whiskey. Warms my innards on this cold November day." With his look of concern, he seemed to see into her soul.

"I know you, Father. Understand your likes along with your dislikes. Try a cookie. Baked them yesterday. It's a new recipe I'm trying out for my business. You can tell me what you think." Her attempt to keep his mind off her relationship with Chandler wasn't going to work. She could tell by the way his eyebrows drew together.

"You plan to go forward with this foolishness? I can't believe you are going to cater to the rich and arrogant in the city." He quirked a graying eyebrow to the ceiling appearing to test her mettle with her plans. "This is too much work. Maeve is only five months. There is another on the way. You will over tire yourself." He paused again, tapping his finger while he appeared to be thinking.

"My ideas are not foolish. I need to support my daughter. While I've put some money away, the two of us will go through those funds if it's not supplemented. Before my eyes, she is growing, sprouting up so fast. Every time I turn around, seems she needs larger clothing."

"I will continue with your allowance." His voice was so stern she brought her head up to look into his eyes. "There will be no need to supplement your income with work outside your home." Cormack bent over, his forearms resting on his thighs. "I will see to all your needs."

"I understand. I will accept your kind offer if I need money. Don't mind if you continue to put my allowance into the account you set up in London in my name. The only coin I intend to use unless there is an emergency is what I've added to the account."

"Stubborn girl…" Cormack muttered under his breath. "What did I do to make you so willful you won't listen to good common sense?"

Yes, she was stubborn. Meant to forge a life along with a future for her and her children. "Thank you for being here for me. Having you in my home makes me feel less uneasy. I also need to find a nanny for Maeve. Any suggestions?" Even though her father had many negative opinions, he could be helpful. Cormack had her best interest in his heart. Helping out his daughter was his role as he saw it.

He grumbled for a few ticks of the old clock on the mantel above the fireplace. "A grandmother, yes, she lives too far from her grandchildren. Met her just the other day while she was shopping for groceries. Doesn't enjoy living in the city. With you in mind, we had a nice long chat. She would treat Maeve as one of her own. Lives here in London. Doesn't have much. Certain there is plenty of room for her in your little cottage."

Georgia didn't repress the giggle on the tip of her tongue. "The cottage is not so little. Did you know it had a name? Of course, you did. Orange Blossom Cottage is not what I intended. I assume you put a hefty downpayment on the home. Otherwise, I doubt if I could have afforded the monthly dues."

The extra money her father had a way of dropping on her was both appreciated and was not. If she were to make a go of this independent life she saw for herself, this was something she needed to accept. "I do intend to pay you back at some time in the distant future."

Cormack looked up, surprise registering in his vibrant blue eyes. With a slight tilt to his head, he began with a snort. "No...no I didn't place a downpayment on this Orange Blossom Cottage you bought. Doing so did cross my mind. Nor did I negotiate the price down. As you asked, I stayed out of the affair. You did tell me you intended to do this on your own. I accepted your wishes even though I disagreed with the concept."

So startled by the revelation, the teacup she held slipped from her hand. Hot tea splashed around her. She stood to shake the water from her skirts then picked up the broken cup. With some of the napkins on the tray she wiped up the mess she created. Dazed by the revelation, walking into the kitchen she mulled over all he told her. Nothing made sense. If he didn't, who did?

The man didn't lie. If he told her he stayed out of the picture because she wanted him to do so, his words were the truth. What was left was something she didn't like. Didn't want to owe Chandler anything. He was not supposed to have stepped into the negotiations or paid even a single penny for this home. She stuck her chin in the air while she poured more tea into her cup. Her back stiffened while she thought on the repercussions of her new discovery.

Bloody eyes, Chandler was trying to buy her! The man meant to orchestrate her return to the brothel by putting her in debt to him. Seemed he would stop at nothing. She sipped in a deep breath of stuffy air. Tried to stiffen her backbone against her mate. He wasn't going to succeed. With a fresh cup of tea in hand, she sat down across from her father. Her fingers shook, the cup rattling on the saucer. She set the China back on the tray, unnerved by the revelation.

Rubbing his jaw, Cormack stared at her. "Chandler? Do you think he discovered who our agent was? I didn't tell him."

"Through the Wolcott name he has unbreakable connections. Through his business he has the ability to blackmail any number of important people. Besides you, he is the only other possibility. No one else would toss money my way." For a few moments, she fiddled with her skirt. Looking up, she tilted her chin. Her gaze focused on her father, "I'm not certain what I should do at this juncture. I cannot give him funds I don't have. I'm certain he…well…he would not take the money from me even if I had the needed amount. His intention is to use this situation to bend me to his will. The man wants me back in the brothel performing with him. He intends to have me under his thumb."

"I will see to this problem. Don't wish for you to worry. With the child along with the new baby on its way coupled with the business venture you wish to create, you've enough on your mind. I'll also see to the hiring of the nanny for you. The lady is wonderful. Positive you will appreciate her skills."

"The woman will be a godsend. I will look forward to having female company. While Hollis is a dear, he doesn't talk much. Do you think the woman will enjoy coming with me when I cater? I'm still…" Georgia wasn't certain if she could speak of breast feeding with her father. She didn't feel comfortable addressing the subject.

"You still need to feed Maeve. I get that. Of course, she will wish to follow along with you and the child. If you are agreeable, your new nanny might also wish to help with the cooking. She told me she is skilled in the kitchen. However, I believe she was hoping to invite me to dinner. We were interrupted before she could issue an invitation."

The loud wail brought both their attention to the nursery down the hall. "Speaking of feeding the babe. Maeve must be hungry or frightened. The storm is still loud, booming all around the house. She doesn't like thunder or loud noises." Wind howled around the eaves. "Excuse me for a moment. I'll feed her then bring her out. You can play with her."

Georgia took her time changing Maeve's diaper, then sitting down with her while she nursed. Her father gave her a great deal to mull over in her head. She wasn't certain how to proceed with Chandler other than to continue on this same course. Everything she decided on was difficult. If she didn't love the man, none of this would matter.

Debating with herself, she couldn't make up her mind whether to confront Chandler about the downpayment or ignore what he did. In any case, Georgia didn't believe her decision would change the outcome. She didn't need to decide this instant. Part of her evaluation would be made when she discovered his motive.

After she finished feeding Maeve, she brought her out to see her grandfather. Cormack held out his hands to her while Maeve gifted him with a huge smile then a little squeal which sounded much like pleasure. It was obvious to her Maeve loved her grandfather. When he visited, he always made time to play.

A thick wool blanket was spread on the floor for Maeve. Cormack lay down beside the baby, handing her different toys for her to peruse. Everything he handed her found its way to her mouth. She seemed to like the cloth doll the best. She was propped in a sitting position. It would not be much longer before she would be able to sit by herself. She was growing up way too fast.

While the two played, Georgia tidied up the front room before heading for the nursery to rinse out the diaper. Once she thought this type of work would not suit. Now, she found everything, even diaper-duty, was something she could do without complaint. Humming to herself, she left the nursery. Wandering to the front room, with her arms crossed she leaned against the wall and watched. Maeve reached for the wooden toy. Started to topple. Her grandfather caught her then lifted her high above his head. Georgia thought she could watch these two forever.

All this time, she forgot Chandler was supposed to arrive. He was late. Tardiness was not something unusual. Chandler did what he wanted when he wanted. Didn't care for time restrictions. She acknowledged the fact her father would not leave just because Chandler showed up. Cormack meant to stay. Tonight, because of the storm, she would have two men under her roof. Two men who despised each other.

Chandler would want to occupy her bed. His doing so was not going to happen. Not in this instance. Keeping him from her bed when he visited was difficult. He knew just how to seduce. Never stopped with the word, no. Thought he had *carte blanche* with her body. In some ways he did.

Once, one time, he managed to seduce her. He made love to her, carrying her to her bedroom. He set her with gentle ease on the bed. The mating was hard…messy. In this instance, she felt shame at what they did. Felt dirty. After he finished, Chandler grinned at her. Believed he made his point clear. Whether or not she lived with him, she was his. After the one and only episode, she tried harder to remain strong. Attempted to stay away from him. Let him play with his daughter. Watched. Was always amazed at the tenderness he showed their baby. He never left the cottage without making love to her at least once.

With the new pounding on the door, Georgia realized this small period of tranquility had come to an end. Chandler was here. He would attempt to dominate everything. His wishes would be made clear. The rest of the evening would become a battle of wills between her father and Chandler. This evening, she was glad there would be a buffer between them. Chandler would stay more than one night. If her father knew, he might also choose to remain at the cottage. Feeling the stress, she pinched the bridge of her nose. Tried to breathe.

Before she could reach the door, Cormack with little Maeve in his arms, tugging on his ear, opened the door.

"Chandler." There was no emotion in his voice. A cold chill enveloped each word. "What are you doing here? Don't believe you are welcome."

"Cormack." Chandler was just as frigid. "I'm here to see my daughter along with her mother. You can't stop me. Both are mine." He pushed past her father, shoving him aside. Stopped when he spotted her. "Winter…you are looking lovely tonight."

Her father could be a cold man when the purpose suited him. Cormack was unforgiving for the time she spent with her mate in the brothel. Intolerant about some of the things Chandler orchestrated during those months. Though she told him less than nothing, he heard tales of what went on behind the closed doors. She signed a contract saying she was willing. The contract for a year was binding. What Georgia would never forgive him for was what happened after she gave birth. Would never pardon him for the threats he made to her person along with the threats to their daughter.

Chandler could be even colder. Could be mean as the devil. Georgia recalled what he did to Harris, his brother's wife. That was all before he made his first fortune with the whorehouse. Now, he was among the wealthiest men in London, possibly the richest.

"Came to see Winter," Chandler nodded toward her. "My mate," he added with emphasis for her father.

"Her name is Georgia," Cormack ground out through clenched teeth. His hold on Maeve tightened.

"Not to me," Chandler pointed out as he stepped into the room. "Winter Snow is the woman I've known in so many different ways. I've seen as well as touched every delicate, white part of her." Chandler's insulting gaze traveled the length of her then settled on her face. "She is the woman I claimed. If you've any doubts, all you need to do is look at her shoulders. Those are my claw marks. Winter is mine. The babe is mine. I own them. Their fate rests in my hands. If I want Winter to be my playmate again, she will."

"Don't elaborate, Chandler. What you said to father should not have been expressed," Georgia pushed away from the wall. Walked toward Chandler but stopped before she reached him. "I'm not going anywhere. There is no need for the two of you to argue. Maeve won't like the loud voices. You'll scare her. If the two of you continue in this manner, the both of you will make her cry." Just within the few minutes while the two males bristled for superiority, her nerves stretched. She set her hand on her somersaulting stomach. The stress was almost too much to bear.

"Why is your father here? Had plans to have a discussion with you…an important one. Can't speak to you with company. Send him away." He looked her over. Once he perused her from her head to her toes, Chandler stopped at her breasts before lifting his gaze to her eyes.

Georgia understood he would have made some other comments if her father wasn't in the room. She wasn't positive why her father's presence would stop him. Though she did appreciate the small effort he made.

"Hollis has made up a room for you if you wish to stay the night. The storm is still howling. Father is staying here also. You are welcome to spend the night in the guest room." The words of welcome caught in her throat even though he always stayed at least one night.

Dinner would be a tense affair. Already, she felt the pressure building between her father and Chandler. What she didn't say was that he wasn't welcome in her bed. Couldn't say those words in front of the man who sired her. Even beginning the night in a separate room, she would not be surprised to find him beneath the same covers by morning. She would think of a way to keep her distance. Chandler thought of her as his possession. Her deflection from his brothel, infuriated him. Tonight, she intended to sleep in the nursery. Hollis would have her bed. If he did seek her out in the middle of the night, he would find the huge black bodyguard, not her. The thought brought a smile to her lips, one she needed to hide from Chandler.

She hoped given enough time he would begin to understand this was the right thing to do for their child. Ignoring the babe, he stepped up to her. Placed his hand on her belly. Grinned. Caressed. Smiled again.

"A tiny bump…a promise for my future. Do you think this one is a boy?" he asked as his fingers moved across her. "I hope so. A son I can mold to be like me."

"No!" Georgia moved away from him, surprised by his words. She had prayed for another girl. Wasn't to be. "Never…you won't have the opportunity." She knew as a shifter, Chandler should know the gender. His powers were weak.

The fury in Cormack's eyes was undeniable. "Leave off. You've no right to touch my daughter. Didn't hear her give you permission to set your hand on her stomach," he growled, his voice low and deep.

"You can't stop me, old man," Chandler spoke with an air of superiority. "You can't stop me and neither can your daughter. If it's a boy she is carrying, he will live with me. Perhaps, Winter will return to me so she can be near her second child."

Maeve let out a tiny whimper at the harshness of her grandfather's voice. Georgia paled at Chandler's words about a son. Her breath wobbled in the back of her throat as she tried to grasp the new threat. Cormack's retreat from his building anger was undeniable. Her father would do nothing to cause her more discomfort. Chandler's look of victory was also undisputable. He was filled with himself. Caught up in the moment. He would use the baby any way and any time he could.

Hollis, bless his heart, seemed to understand what was happening. He stepped between the two men. She found she could breathe again.

"Father, would you put Maeve to bed. She is tired. Sing a song to her. She loves the sound of your voice."

The two men needed distance between them. She needed to make certain her father never showed up here unannounced again. Two bristling male peacocks were too much for her to deal with. Her head ached.

Her bodyguard sat on a large chair near the fire. His hands were folded in his lap. His legs were stretched out in front of him. He didn't say anything. His size alone would intimidate most men. She walked to the kitchen. Dinner was roasting in the oven. Vegetables were ready to steam. She hoped Chandler would sit down in the main room. Wasn't surprised when he shadowed her to the kitchen. Set his hand on her shoulder. She flinched away from him.

"Why is your father here?" Chandler's harsh voice reverberated behind her.

His hands were set with possession on her shoulders. She tried to shrug them off even though she understood the attempt would be useless. He brushed his lips across the back of her neck. Bit with a light touch meant to tempt her to his wishes. The contact gave rise to a shiver she needed to ignore. He understood how to touch her as well as where.

Stiffening, she cut vegetables. Chopped hard as if she was cutting into him. To answer him would give him more questions. Not answering him would enrage the man. She didn't wish him to be angry. He was hard to deal with when he was calm. This was not how she planned the evening before her father showed up unannounced. Catching her lip with her teeth, she tried to keep her mind focused on preparing their dinner. Realized Chandler wasn't about to let up. He would continue until he got what he wanted from her.

"Why is your father here? You knew I was visiting. Tell him no next time or I won't be responsible for what happens. Not willing to share my time with you. Hollis living here is bad enough. Though I do acknowledge the need for a man to protect you when I'm not here to do so."

"Don't need protection except from you."

She swallowed her anger along with her fears. "To see Maeve, I believe my child is the main reason my father arrived here during this storm. I had no idea he intended to visit. He never wrote." She also thought he would try to make her see everything from his point of view. Every time her father visited, he spouted new examples as to why she would return to their home in Ireland.

~ * ~

Chandler slipped his hand around her to cup her breast. Heard the tiny hiss of pleasure. Ran his thumb across the tip. Since she was nursing Maeve, she wore only a chemise beneath her gown. He held on to the taunt crowns, twisting. Bloody eyes, but he missed her. Missed all of her. Needed to feel her sultry heat surround him, kiss his length with sweet pulses. It didn't make a difference that her father was here. He meant to sleep with her tonight. Would do so.

"What do you want?" she asked, her words clipped while she placed the chopped vegetables into the pan.

"Shocked you need to ask. Thought what I wished for in this cottage was you…or did you think I came to see the baby?" Chandler didn't care much about Maeve. Girls had one reason to be on earth…for a man's pleasure. Otherwise, females were worthless. When she was old enough, he would choose her husband. Find a rich titled man for her. If she didn't accept his choice, he would find a role for her to play in his cast of characters.

His thumb continued the lazy path across her nipple. Felt some moisture as he touched her there. Some of her milk leaked. He liked the sensation. Was different from what he was used to. Sucking on her, he would taste her milk.

"Sit down, Chandler. Burning the dinner would not be pleasant." She tried to twist away from him. His hands slid to her hips. Held her still. Brought her against the hard length of his arousal.

"Ah, you can't concentrate on two things at once?" Chandler bit the back of her neck again before moving one hand back to her breast, squeezing the hard tip he'd been massaging. He did as she asked. "Don't like your father. You do understand my feelings about the man. He wants to take you back to Ireland with him. You comprehend I would never allow you to leave me. I would follow. Bring you back."

He sat down at the small kitchen table. They'd eaten breakfast in here each time he visited. Did so once a week. Georgia brought him a snifter of brandy. He studied her. She was always so bloody cool. Her emotions were like ice.

"Join me?" Chandler asked. He held up the glass. Knew she would decline. The few times she drank, she didn't hold her liquor all that well. Wouldn't mind if she became a bit fuzzy-headed before bedtime. He would never feel one moment of guilt. "Sit down. Have some wine."

Remorse was lost on him. As far as he was concerned, the feeling was a waste of time. Thought of the show in London that was going on right now. Ah...it was Summer along with Autumn who would be on display this evening. When he wasn't participating, Jimmy was the one to play with his little school girl. Summer played other parts with him, all virgin parts. After a year she was not the virgin who came to him. Though he was working on a new script for the woman. Wasn't surprised when she signed on for a second year. Her family still sacrificed her for his entertainment. They needed the money. Summer didn't like the work. Didn't enjoy the auction where men bid on her for their personal use. Didn't enjoy being a whore. His clients loved her. Paid top dollar for her charms. Most of the men who bought her, loved to bring her to heel.

"No. Don't want wine tonight."

She stirred the vegetables. Seemed she was trying to keep her distance from him. Her ploys would never work.

"I think you will." Chandler found the bottle of wine. Splashed a good amount into a glass. "Drink."

He didn't know if she would comply to his wishes. If she didn't, he had ways to make her drink.

He was pleased with his efforts when he saw her chin tilt and her back stiffen. He liked it when she thought she could get her way. Winter understood he would insist then continue to insist until she drank the wine. He eyed the almost full bottle then Winter. She would down the bottle before the evening was finished. He would see to it. Maybe begin on a second one.

"You realize I don't like to drink." Opening the oven door, she bent over to check the meat. Her delicious rump was presented to him. He didn't think she would bend over in front of him if she understood what the sight did to him. Chandler imagined thrusting into her from behind. He could set her face down on the little kitchen table. Toss her skirts…ah… So swollen with lust for her, he had to adjust himself.

"Drink the glass of wine." His voice held a hard edge as he confronted her disobedience. Insubordination was not something he would allow. She would do as he wished. "Drink, then I'll pour you more. You do understand I'm not giving you a choice. I still own you."

Winter nodded. Drank half the glass before she wiped her mouth with the back of her hand. After she swallowed, he smiled while he watched her body shudder. It was obvious she didn't enjoy the taste.

"The rest of it…"

He pointed to the glass while he held the bottle up to her. Winter would understand, she would finish the bottle before the night ended.

He hooted his laughter when her brows drew together and her lips thinned with her burgeoning anger. While he didn't hold all the cards tonight because her father was in the house, he still had the winning hand. Their daughter was vulnerable. Winter understood he could do what he wished. Told her if she disobeyed, he would find the worst workhouse in the slums of London. Almost the moment Maeve was born, he made the fact clear to her the baby was expendable. If she behaved, he would grant her some leeway. Nonetheless, Maeve's future rested in his hands.

Finishing the glass, Winter slammed it on the table. "Are you satisfied?"

Her eyes blazed with fury. She was passionate. He'd felt her passion many times. Watching the rise of anger now pleased him.

His grin turned into a chuckle. "Not yet. No, not satisfied at the moment. By tomorrow morning I'm certain to be feeling better…more than quenched by your fire."

Again, he laughed at her. Saw the look of defeat in her sparkling blue eyes. With Winter he would always have his way. He allowed her to leave the brothel. Didn't think he could ever be so generous. The feeling he would gain more sway over her if she wasn't with him every day of the week was a top priority in his mind. The more he granted her the more he held over her head. The more she would owe him. Chandler wished for Winter to owe him the world then more.

"You are not coming to my bed." She pointed the serving fork at him, her brows drawing together as if her scowl would stop him. The one she tested the roast with. "Not while my father is in the house. I swear..." Turning her back to him, she pulled dishes from the cupboard then silverware from the drawer clattering around her.

"We shall see."

He grinned at her stiff back. Decided she needed more wine. The sooner she felt the influence of the alcohol the easier it would be to seduce. She would still tell him no. He would say yes. As always, she would melt around him. Chandler knew just the right places to fondle then to massage with serious concentration.

In one lithe cat-like move he rose. Chandler was beside her before she could step back. Pulling her to him, he pressed her length against him. His hands cupped her sweet butt. Her large breasts pushed against his chest. When he brought her closer, he knew she would feel his arousal. He wanted to be snug within her. Intended patience.

"No, Chandler. You cannot have me anytime you wish. I don't want you in my bed. Do not threaten me with our daughter. You would never do the things you say just to get yourself into me. You are not as ruthless as you wish me to believe."

Winter didn't struggle against him. No, she held herself very still. Frozen, just like the ice queen she was. She would not give into her passion as long as she was fully clothed. He wanted to change the situation. With her father as a house guest, he didn't intend to mortify her to the tips of her toes if Cormack entered the kitchen.

"I know your ploy, Winter. Doesn't make a bit of difference if you act frigid. Nor does it matter to me if you say no. Your no doesn't mean a bloody thing to me. I will have you tonight. Understand how to make you want me." Chandler kissed her hard. He needed to savor the taste of her. Thrust his tongue deep into her just as he wished to thrust his sex inside her small body. Wanted to become part of her while she moaned and heaved beneath him. She didn't move. Her hands remained limp at her sides. There was no response from her. He groaned at the quick rise of sexual power he experienced. Tugging on her bottom lip, he sucked the sweet flesh inside.

While he continued to kiss her, he slipped his hand inside the bodice of her gown. Held his hand against her where he could feel the rapid stamping of her heart. Swept his hand across her hard-tipped nipple. Delicious feminine sounds floated from the back of her throat. His smile was one of victory. She was not as immune to his seduction of her as she tried to make him think. She couldn't freeze him out of her bed. He wanted to kiss her again. Decided against another one when he heard footsteps. There would be more time to grant her the pleasures of the flesh he knew she craved. His Winter could never remain frozen against him for long.

"Finish dinner," he left her side to return to the chair along with his brandy. "Believe I'll watch you. Love to see your breasts move when you do small things. They are so large. Firm ripe melons meant for our pleasure. The small damp spots on your shirt are such a delight. Those two beautiful globes are so much larger now that you've given birth and Maeve is suckling on your tits. Think about me sucking on each one. Pulling your breast so far into my mouth that you scream with the pure delight of the ecstasy I give." After filling her wine glass again, he stretched his legs in front of him. Sipped on the brandy. Gazed.

The next ten minutes, he studied her. Sought a way to get her to admit she wanted him. Bloody hell, Chandler knew she loved him. Begged him to claim her. They made love the night of the claiming. He'd taken her several times before they fell asleep. He never believed she would leave the brothel. Never realized she was serious until it was too late to keep her where he wanted her. That's when he made his threats to give her to Bertram. She detested his best friend.

Winter refused to marry him. Refused! Told him she didn't want him to own her. Said now that he claimed her as his mate, she didn't need marriage. All that needed to be done to secure their passage through time together had been completed. Had the gall to tell him, she hoped he would be a better man in the future.

The table was set. Would Maeve sleep for most of the night? Chandler wondered how often Winter fed the little girl. She was five-months-old now. Surely, Winter didn't get up more than once. Maeve was eating some solid food. Maybe she slept through the night. The last few times he visited, he didn't pay much attention. Every time Winter allowed him to seduce her, she swore to him sex with him was the last time.

"Dinner is ready," she stood in the main room wiping her hands on a towel. Hollis along with her father rose.

The meal was eaten in silence. Chandler continued to fill her glass with the red wine. She drank. He was content. Acknowledged the fact she would never argue with her father in the room. Would be compliant to his whims. With dinner finished, Cormack settled in a big chair facing the fire. For his further amusement, Chandler decided to help Winter with cleaning up. Well, he wasn't going to help. He meant to fondle all those beautiful body parts of hers he adored as well as missed during the long week. Meant to caress her breasts, her hips, the soft damp parts between her legs. Her breathy little sighs of pleasure would lend encouragement to his plans. By the time he finished, she wouldn't be able to refuse him. Winter would come to him warm as well as willing.

Opening another bottle of wine, he spilled more into her glass. By the expression on her lovely face, she wasn't pleased. Her hands were in the sudsy water. He held the glass to her lips. If she didn't open her mouth then drink, the liquid would spill down to her lovely breasts. The thought of sipping the wine off the tips gave him something to think about. Another time perhaps, when there weren't so many people in the house. He saw himself pulling her corsage down to her waist while her hands were immersed in the sudsy water. Seducing Winter would satisfy him. For him, she was an easy mark. Perhaps he didn't wish to wed Winter. The woman could be a demanding shrew. She always had a plan contrary to his. This arrangement almost suited him. As soon as he could convince her she wanted him in her bed, he would be more than pleased. Perhaps she would return with him to the brothel. No, he doubted she would give into his whim.

She drank. He didn't put the glass down. When Winter gasped, wine slipped from her mouth to run down her chin. He followed the path of the drops with his lips, touching her chin then sipping wine from her long slender neck. He paused at the racing pulse at the base. Sucked then nibbled. Felt the shuddering rush of pleasure from her slender body. As he charmed those evocative places, he knew they would bring her to the point where she wouldn't snub his efforts. He would continue this until she begged for more pleasure.

Ah, but the evening would drag on before he could climb into her bed. Before he could have his way with her delicious body. He missed her.

Was used to having her every night, showing her off to the lecherous people who paid to watch him give his ice queen her pleasure. Loved to see her reach that beautiful pinnacle more than once in the evening.

"Don't…" Winter's eyes were closed. Her shoulders stiff. "Please don't. I don't want anything more to drink. I'll get sick. The wine can't be good for Maeve. She is such a tiny little thing. Chandler, no…"

"Open them. Open those pretty eyes of yours. I want to see what you're feeling. Do you realize you are an open book for me to read?"

He watched the slow move of her lashes. Gazing into her eyes he saw her anger flare along with fear of him. Chandler didn't like seeing distress in her eyes. Though he understood at one time he enjoyed seeing terror in the eyes of a woman. He shook his head. He wasn't like that anymore. Found he liked to see desire in a woman's eyes, in Winter's eyes. Winter wasn't afraid of him. She loved him. Had said the words the night of the claiming. If she loved him, why didn't she want him in her bed? That was a question to befuddle his mind.

Chandler scrunched the fabric of her gown in his hands while he brought the material higher up her legs. With his boots between her feet, he pushed hers apart. Felt the fine shiver of desire rush through her. He teased her soft flesh. Rested his hand on her belly. Cursed the fact the house was filled with people.

"I don't want you to touch me there."

Her muted voice told him of her arousal. The words she spoke weren't true. Soon she would beg for him to bring her to the point where she lost command of her body.

"Where?" He didn't care what she wanted. He told her the fact numerous times. "Where is it you don't want me to touch you? Here? Or there? Maybe over here?" His hand roamed. Scorched her flesh with its presence. For about the hundredth time tonight, he wished they were alone and she was naked.

The wine glass at her lips stopped her from replying. She drank more. Swallowed the potent liquid. She was on the second bottle of wine. He smiled with thoughts of desperate pleasure rumbling around in his head. She might have a raging headache when she rose. What did he care for her morning comfort if the wine gave him better access to her feminine endowments?

He wanted to come into her from behind. With her father sipping brandy in the front room, she wouldn't let out even a squeak. She would hold the yell of ecstasy inside her mouth. After setting the glass down, he ran his hand along the inside of her leg. Touched her. Fondled the softness welcoming his attention. Found her dampness delightful. Thrust two fingers through the soft welcoming folds that were even now pulsing, milking his fingers with her need. Her body was crying out for him.

"You want me."

"No." In defiance of her word, her head was thrown back. Rested on his shoulder. He watched the frantic tick of her pulse at the base of her neck.

Stroking her, fondling her with intimate precision, he understood if he continued, she would climax in a matter of seconds. Not wishing for her to reach her pleasure, Chandler brought his hand away. Heard the tiny noise of disappointment. Touched her cheek with his wet fingers. Sipped on the back of her white neck. Thought to travel lower. He did. Tested the flesh along her shoulder. Unfastened several buttons as he slid the fabric aside.

"You want me," he repeated. "You can deny with words all you want. Your beautiful woman's body is telling a different story. If I allowed it to happen, in another second you would have screamed your pleasure."

"No."

"Come, finish the dishes. Believe I heard your father retiring for the night. We can go to your room as soon as you..."

He paused while he looked her up then down. She must be blocking her thoughts from him. He wished to listen to what was in her mind. "I'll undress you. You can do the same for me. We will sleep naked after I've given you more pleasure than you deserve for denying yourself what you want."

"You're not going to sleep with me," Winter continued in the same vein. "You are not going to sleep with me or give me pleasure."

While he wasn't known as an easygoing man, he felt as if he exhibited a great deal of patience where his ice queen was concerned. A bit of standoffishness was alright. Winter carried the aloofness to an extreme.

"We will see," his soft murmur surprised him. His feelings for this woman shocked him. Chandler denied to himself the tenderness he felt for her. He didn't love Winter. Acknowledged the fact he was a man incapable of love. Lived on the seedier side of life which he enjoyed to his immense delight. Every day of his life there were women vying to gain his attention. He was a man who thrived on sex as well as female attention. Since Winter surged into his life, he'd not wanted any other woman. He forced himself to play with a few he employed. Couldn't stand the thought he only wanted to have Winter in his bed. When he returned, he would take Celine to his bed while Summer Passion watched. Next, he would give Summer more pleasure than she merited. The girl was too standoffish though her act was part of her charm. The men loved to bring her down a peg or two.

Winter turned on him. Her hands pressed against his chest. Her eyes blazing with emotions, she told him again her thoughts on the most prevalent topic on his mind. He'd gone without her long enough. She wasn't going to escape his attention tonight. All he meant to do was give her the sweetest climax.

"You are not..."

Chandler held up the glass that was still half full. "Finish this. Once I'm done with your lovely self, you will sleep soundly." All tolerance with her denials fled. "I will come to you as soon as the house is quiet. Though your father should understand I belong with you. He knows I claimed you. With that said, Cormack would also comprehend you are mine."

Winter shook her head. She tried to push away from him. Her breasts shimmied across him. He groaned his delight. "No. Don't come to me. Can't you understand? I don't want you. You need to comprehend. Stop coming here. I want nothing to do with you. You don't care about Maeve. You won't care about Colin."

Chandler didn't wish to admit to the emotion. He was hurt by her comments by her denial of him. Retaliated to her negative words. "Yes." He helped her finish the wine. Held the glass until she drank all the liquid. Set his hand at the small of her waist. "Come, you look tired. You need to rest."

He steadied her when she missed a step. She was just where he wanted her to be. Winter would be pliant as well as willing when he came to her in another hour. He loved waking her from a deep sleep. Would kiss her closed eyes, the tip of her nose. After that he would fondle her mouth with his lips then his teeth. He would caress those sweet parts of her that were his favorite places. She would be warm and wet. Ready to accept his full arousal. When her eyes opened, he'd thrust inside. Would fill her to the brim then more. Would accept her cry of pleasure into his mouth. No one in the home would be the wiser.

"I don't," she swallowed her words. "Don't…no…in my bed. Can't." She leaned into him, pressing her weight against his chest.

On his shoulder, her head lolled. She stumbled again, steadied herself with her hand. "Yes, in your bed, Winter. That's where I belong. In time you will see things my way." They walked past the nursery.

"No."

"Do you need to see to Maeve?"

He wanted her to be done with the nursing then waiting for him. She would unveil her breasts. While he watched, he would see his little girl suckling at her breast. It was a fine sight. Though he threatened her with Maeve, he would never do anything to harm the baby. In the present, the child made Winter vulnerable. He appreciated that aspect of his little girl. If he would mold Winter to his wishes, she needed to be defenseless.

"No."

At the door to her room, he gave her a gentle push before walking away. He was going to have a few words with Hollis then retire to his room. Thought he should have helped her out of her clothing. Did enjoy disrobing her. Before he sought Winter's bed, he would wait until the house quieted. Until there were no sounds disturbing the cottage. He stepped into the front room, lighted with a few lanterns. Outside the wind still howled. It was a miserable night for anyone to be outside. Inside the fire warmed the home. He stuck his hands out to receive some of the heat generated.

"Hollis," he said as he settled into a large chair with a glass of brandy in his hand.

He held it with both hands, warming the liquid as he rolled the glass between his hands. Watched the amber liquid catch the warmth of the fire.

"Chandler. You will behave yourself tonight."

Hollis' sigh after the words held a wealth of meaning. Hollis would understand his words meant nothing to him. Hollis was a good man. He was glad he protected Winter. He was loyal to her as well as Maeve. Tonight, he wished him to be gone.

"You should remember who pays your salary." The big man would never stop him from seeing to Winter. Winter Snow was his. He created her. Gave her work when she came to him with a willing as well as an open mind. By God, she signed a contract then thought to renege. Her act of defiance forced him to threaten her. "I always behave myself," he returned as he chuckled at the humor those few words produced.

"I remember," Hollis said in what sounded like a snort of disgust.

Hollis understood what he would do. What he wanted. Winter in his arms. Damn, but he just couldn't keep away from the woman he coveted. After she left the brothel, he intended to do just that. Stay far away. Why did he want a woman who didn't wish to have anything to do with him? Supposed this mate thing was what drew him to her.

He wouldn't allow a woman to control his desires. There were plenty of women who wanted him. He could have his pick of all of the women at his unique whorehouse. Crook his little finger at whoever caught his eyes. The girl would run to him. Would want him to do anything he chose to her female parts. At one point, he thought to take Summer to his rooms upstairs. Summer could never replace Winter. Sitting back in the big chair he closed his eyes. All he could see was Winter's breasts. Her other wonderful female endowments. She was so beautiful. Made for his enjoyment. Made for his use. She was his doll, his plaything, a bauble meant to be his personal toy. Thoughts of her naked and in his arms caused his stomach to cramp with need. Bloody everlasting hell, she was his! Only his! She forgot that small fact. Forgot they were a couple through all eternity. She bedeviled him.

The groan stopped in his throat. Didn't want the big man to see his obvious need. Hollis rose. Appeared he meant to retire for the night. The big man rubbed his hand behind his neck. Seemed to start to say something then didn't.

"Good night. If you can behave yourself, know the little mama doesn't wish for you to be in her bed," Hollis said before he left the room to walk down the hall to his room. All was going as planned.

Chandler couldn't see him. Heard his door open then close. He wondered how long he should wait until Winter slept. She drank so much wine. Must be asleep by now. In her room, lean against the wall so he could watch her sleep. He could go see her. Slip inside the bed then into her. That all sounded just fine to his way of thinking.

He quenched all the lights before following Hollis down the hall. In his bedroom, he rested against the door. Closed his eyes imagining Winter on his bed. His dream was for her to come to him. Her hair down and with no inhibitions. Naked. Realized he needed her the way they used to be. Didn't wish to pursue her this diligently. They had another child on the way. Before she left, he made certain she was increasing. Took her both night and day as well as any time he felt a need for her.

Sitting down, he removed his boots then the rest of his clothing. Just thinking about Winter made him ready for her. His body tightened. He slipped on a dressing gown before lying down on his bed. His hands were behind his head. Rain pelted the window. Trying for patience, he counted the beats of the clock. Time crept by with the speed of a slug.

Fifty-five minutes passed. He was about to rise. The sound of footsteps caught his attention. A gruff clearing of a man's throat told him either Hollis or Cormack was awake. He cursed. Swore out his frustrations while he was forced to wait for the house to grow silent again. He closed his eyes. Awoke with a start to a loud wail from the nursery. Would nothing go his way tonight? Was beginning to doubt he would have his wishes fulfilled. Cormack would leave tomorrow. At least he hoped the man would return to London. After her father left, he only needed to deal with Hollis. The bodyguard held no sway in what he did. He didn't hear the light fall of Winter's footsteps headed toward the nursery. The crying stopped. Winter must be in the room nursing Maeve. Another half hour passed. He didn't hear her return. Realized her steps must be so silent, he wasn't able to hear them.

Another few minutes ticked by. Chandler decided he was out of tolerance. He rose, strode to her door. Opened it. For a few seconds he propped himself against the doorframe studying the form lying on the bed. The body was way too large.

Bloody eyes!

Hollis turned over then sat up. He grinned at what must be his startled expression. "Looking for someone?" he asked with nonchalance that surprised Chandler. "Georgia's not here."

"You damn well know I am! And it's not you!" Chandler exploded into his surroundings. "Where is she?" He stalked into the room, his fingers tightening into fists. Looked in all the corners as if he could conjure her from shadows. The truth was obvious she wasn't in the room. Winter played him for a fool.

Hollis let out a long deep breath of air. "Won't do any good to keep the truth from you. If I don't say, you'll wake the household looking for her."

"She's in the nursery!" Chandler remembered the single bed in the room. Winter must have slept there when Maeve was sick. He knew she had the crib in her room for the first few months. "Damn her lily-white hide!"

He didn't slam the door even though he wished to do so. Winter wasn't going to get away with avoiding him. If she didn't know this now, she would. The bed in the nursery was big enough for both of them. When he opened the door, she was sitting in the rocking chair, Maeve in her arms. Maeve had her fist stuck into her mouth, her eyes closed tight.

"Chandler," she said, her voice all quiet and serene. He wished he could shake her. "Maeve is frightened of the storm. If you wish, you may sit on the floor. If not, go back to bed. I will be here all night. Believe this will be a long night for both of us." Winter brushed a soft kiss on the child's forehead.

"Why was Hollis in your bed?" he gritted out, asking the question even though he knew the answer.

"Believe you know the answer to the question. I did tell you I didn't want to sleep with you. The fact you didn't listen to my wishes doesn't surprise me." Winter yawned, placed her hand in front of her lips. The very ones he needed to kiss.

"You intend to sleep in the baby's room every time I visit?" he asked again, knowing the answer. "You don't sound muzzled any longer." Chandler was furious with her. Should have made her drink all of the second bottle of wine.

"I'm sitting. If it's any consolation to you, I had a terrible time walking to the nursery after you left me at my door. My mind is hazy. Not hazy enough to let you fondle me. That's not ever going to happen again."

"You understand sleeping in the nursery won't deter me. You are dead wrong if you think I won't ever again be deep inside you while I take you to the amazing place you so love."

His words didn't have the ring of truth. Sleeping with a baby next to him, held no appeal to Chandler. He would be forever conscious of any sounds they made. Winter's little feminine, throaty purrs delighted. A baby's cries repulsed.

"Go to bed, Chandler. As you must be able to tell, I'm staying in this room while you are visiting. You will just need to get used to this arrangement."

There were other times to make love with his mate. Didn't need the night. Nor did he need a bed. She wasn't a damn virgin. The hell of it was he wanted her now.

"Put Maeve in her crib. She's asleep."

"No."

~ * ~

"Bertram!" Chandler bellowed when he arrived at the brothel three nights later. "Get over here!" He slapped his riding gloves on his leg. "I'm out of stamina. What the blessed hell are you doing? Bring me Summer."

The show featuring Summer and Autumn was about to begin. Bertram looked up at the bellow of rage he heard from his friend of fifteen years. He was seeing to last minute details. Chandler would understand the fact. The women keeping the body cooling fans going were positioned in strategic places wearing see through gowns. They were all beautiful women. All signed contracts giving the patrons permission to have sex with them. The fan maidens were next in line to be auctioned at the end of the night for any man's pleasure who had enough coin to buy them. The bodyguards were situated around the room. One night a fight broke out. It was then Chandler decided they needed a few men who would protect the women from someone who lost control. At times the audience became frenzied with their frenetic desires. Bertram loved watching men lose themselves in a woman's soft body. He never could believe his good fortune when Chandler derived this idea.

He chuckled when he looked at Chandler. His smile was broad. The reason behind Chandler's bad mood could only be credited to one small woman who always bedeviled him. "You're in a bad mood tonight. Did nothing go as planned?" Bertram asked as he watched his friend pace the floor. "The little harlot refused all your advances. You don't need her permission to take her any damn way you wish. You do know that? Of course, you comprehend you are bigger as well as stronger than Winter."

He wished for his old friend to return. Liked him better before Winter changed him. Looked forward to the nights they shared their women.

"Horrible. She wouldn't…hell she worked everything out so it was impossible for me to get to her. The devil knows I tried. She outwitted me, damn her soul. She believes she can set rules as well as boundaries. I won't allow her to dictate what goes on between us. Next time, I will win. I'll push her up against a wall right in front of Hollis if she doesn't give me an alternative." He circled the room before stopping at a window that looked down at the street below.

His chuckle at Chandler's distress bought him a scowl from the man. Bertram frowned. He wondered about Chandler's intentions for tonight. "Do you wish to perform tonight? Summer always gives herself as much as is possible to you. After her first time on the dais the woman understands her place. We do need to think of some other script for the pretty lady. Believe our audience is tiring of the little girl act. All realize she is no longer a virgin or a little girl. What do you think she should become? Perhaps a nun. The role of a nun might be fun for a change."

"Believe I'd like to let off some steam. Hot air seems to be all bottled up inside me. Yes, I want Summer. Need to punish her for her naughtiness. We will put our heads together to come up with a unique scenario for a new role. Maybe we could reenact how we discovered her. Pushed her up against a store just to talk to her. Do you recall the day? We brought her to her parent's home. Made her father a proposition he couldn't refuse. Her being a nun sounds intriguing." He turned, his fingers beneath his chin while he tapped them. "I'll think on the two scenarios. Perhaps both roles in one night. Doubling the fun would put a new twist to the script."

Bertram nodded. "Oh yes. Love new kinks."

He rubbed his hands together anticipating the pleasure. The two left the rest of the evening's details to Jimmy and Johnny, the twins they had with them from the beginning. The thought of watching Chandler take Summer multiple times in different scenarios appealed to all his sexual fantasies.

Once the new thoughts were mulling around in his head, Chandler poured them both a glass of whiskey. Bertram spoke from the heart. Worried about his friend. He wasn't acting normal. Hadn't been since Winter gave birth then left the brothel. Chandler had not been the same since.

"Tell me everything. You can't keep going to the cottage then returning in a royal snit. You become a bore for the next few days. Bring her back with you. You're stronger than she is…bigger…overtake her…bind her."

Chandler rubbed the back of his neck. Winced as if the movement caused him pain. "You realize, I've thought about hauling her home more than once. I just have to find a means to deal with this obstinance of hers. She is only a woman and thus inferior. A female doesn't have the wit to outsmart a man."

While he listened to the beat of the clock on the shelf, Bertram wondered if Chandler believed what he spouted. Though he never enjoyed giving a woman the credit of possessing a brain, he was well aware of the fact many were smarter than some men. They did possess a different way of thinking about things. Some managed to have their way over a man's desires. Seems Winter had Chandler wrapped around her fingers as well as twisted in knots.

"I believe we should drink to male prowess…to their competence in all things. To outwitting all the females of their knowledge."

Bertram held up his glass in salute. Grinned at Chandler. He enjoyed women with no ability to think for themselves. A woman with a mind was dangerous to his wellbeing. Twits were convenient. They were easily molded into the woman Bertram wanted at the time. Never wished for an intelligent woman beneath him unless he could subjugate her.

He tossed the remainder of his drink down his throat then grimaced. "Winter blocks her thoughts from me. She doesn't have the right to do so. I'm her mate!" He splashed more brandy into his glass. "I'm supposed to know what's in her mind. Need to get inside so I can understand if she is in danger."

"You are too new to shifting. Have some tolerance. Together we can work on that point. Make you stronger. Does she read your thoughts?"

Bertram decided he was just the man to teach Chandler how to best his woman at her game.

"She must read my mind. Winter seems to know what I'm going to do before I've cemented a plan. Most of the time she is two steps ahead of me, if not more. I don't like that fact. Not right for her to have so much power over me."

Bertram watched Chandler pace the room. What he needed was a woman to ease the ache between his legs. He must have spent two days in a state of arousal she wouldn't let him relieve. Chandler didn't appear to be in any shape to perform tonight. Not even with Summer playing the school girl. He thought about Summer as a nun. Perhaps he could arrange a costume before they came on stage. A new script would be just the thing for Chandler to come out of his snit. Would put bounce back into his step. Would give him the confidence he needed to confront Winter in another week or two.

He heard the chime of the clock. It was eight o'clock. No, there wasn't enough time to set up the new script. Next time…for tonight, he could send her to Chandler after the show. Summer would lose out on the auction. Would not gain the extra blunt. Her loss didn't disturb him. His friend's sexual health mattered.

"I must go. Why don't you watch through the viewing room you had built. Might get you aroused enough to make an appearance. Could send you Celine or one of the other girls."

-

Chapter Two

Georgia met with Lady Estelle Laughton to plan the dinner party to be held this next Friday evening. Hollis would drive them all into London first thing the morning of the party. It would take the majority of the day to create the dishes. The new nanny her father sent to her was a delight. The older woman loved playing with Maeve. She also helped with the preparation of the delicacies that would be served up to the guests attending the evening entertainment. She was excited. This was her job. What happened tonight would set the stage for further engagements. This was her new business. She wanted her plans for her new life to succeed. Success would give her a measure of independence.

Together they tried out new recipes while Maeve played with the measuring cups and spoons in the kitchen. Her highchair was the perfect place for her curiosity to thrive. Winter understood she needed to make herself scarce during the evening's pleasures as she was positive some of Lady Estelle's guests might have seen her at the bordello…would have seen her naked…with Chandler deep inside her. She didn't enjoy the notion. Felt her cheeks heating. Now, there was nothing to do about her past. She could never take back that part of her life. If anything needed to be seen to in the ballroom, Bea would do the honors. She would remain in the kitchen with her little girl.

An apple crumble was top on her list to show off. Also, a caramel cheesecake would be presented to the guests among a few other desserts. For the people who needed more than sweets, they made sausage rolls and pigs in a blanket. There were other foods for the more discriminating tastes. Simple items such as various breads, cheeses and meats. This was not to be a sit-down dinner. For that she was thankful. A formal dinner would have entailed a lot more work as well as planning.

The day of the party, Georgia's nerves seemed to snap. She received a missive from Chandler telling her he would stop by the townhouse after his show. If she wasn't there, where he wanted her, he would come looking for her. She wouldn't enjoy the consequences of her disobedience. Hah! He couldn't force her. She always wanted him. The trouble with the truth was she was no longer going to allow him to use her for his sexual pleasures. Standing firm on her conviction was the only way to go about stopping Chandler. If she gave no response to his fondling, the act would frustrate him. Put him off his game. She was, after all, Queen of the Ice. She could manage.

After she read the note, she snorted her contempt. He couldn't order her around. All of them had plans to stay with her father this evening who remained in London. She wasn't going to cave to Chandler's wishes just because he thought he could order her around. All he wanted from her was her body. She didn't intend to change her mind about sex with him. If she could stop him, sex with Chandler wasn't going to happen again.

She wondered who would be the featured seasons of this night. Wondered too who he found to replace her. He asked her to come watch the show every time he visited. Told her he built a viewing room where one could watch without being seen. Georgia shuddered at the thought. Told her his new Winter Snow was quite clever.

"Oh…everything is wonderful. The food tastes absolutely divine," Lady Estelle whisked into the kitchen beaming from ear to ear. "You have done a marvelous job with this being your first time and all. After the first samples I had a week ago, I knew you would work magic in the kitchen. I would introduce you to everyone before my guests begin to leave. It will be so good for your business."

"No." Introductions could never happen. While she'd been almost honest with Lady Estelle about her past, she'd failed to tell her everything. Couldn't explain the nudity, the sex or Chandler. If she told her how she worked that she was indeed Winter Snow, the ice queen, the lady's mind would weave all the rumors she ever heard together to form the right conclusions. The woman understood she played some part in Chandler's establishment. She could never tell the poor lady she sat naked on his sex while men fondled her breasts, while she climaxed more than once in front of all the people who paid outrageous sums to watch the decadence Chandler orchestrated for their viewing pleasures. Didn't wish to confess even women fondled her feminine endowments. A shudder tore through her.

"No?" One of Estelle's eyebrows lifted upward. "No?" she questioned. "Why ever not? Making you known to everyone here, would be good for your business. Doubt it not." She shook her finger at her. "What you've done is nothing to be ashamed of. You've left the establishment to start a new and better life. Now, you are making your way with an honest job. No one should judge your past."

Georgia packed some of the unused supplies she brought with her while she spoke, her heart racing within her chest. She had trouble getting the words to form. "What I've done...I am ashamed of, mortified to the tips of my toes. I haven't told you everything I did. Can't. Won't. Would be humiliated if you ever discovered the depravity that was once a part of my life. I've come to respect you too much. Rest assured. I do value your business. There might be someone you introduce me to who will recognize me. Won't risk that."

She hmphed. "As I have respect for you, I will back off for now. Great admiration. When necessary, everyone deserves a second chance at happiness. You've traded in a bad job for one that will prove your worth. You're keeping your baby girl safe. I'd never ask how you got started in Chandler Wolcott's awful business. It's none of my business. All I can guess is the horrible reality you must have been down on your luck."

Down on my luck...no I wasn't. Can't tell her I entered into Chandler's domain because I was a shifter and Chandler was my mate. There was no choice for her. What she did was more than necessary. So, she supposed one could say she was down on her luck. Once, when she first met him, she thought perhaps he would change his way of life for her. She was soon dissuaded of the notion. Chandler was all about making money along with holding power over women in the guise of sex.

"Lady Estelle," Georgia held out her hand. "As I said before, I appreciate your business. Hope if you ever need a caterer again, you will call on me. No, I can tell you no more than you know already. Don't ask it of me."

Nerves seemed to control her stomach which was rolling with fear. She caught a glimpse of Chandler's mind. Chandler was walking down the stairs of his establishment. He was on his way to Laughton's place. He meant to confront her. Chandler wanted her under his thumb. Would insist on having a one-sided conversation. Given a chance, he would ruin everything for her. He was trying to get inside her head. Bertram must have been helping him learn how to read her mind. Chandler was more powerful than ever before. She was having trouble blocking him.

What to do.

"I need to go. Now!" She turned to Hollis, ready to run if necessary. She could barely get the words out. "Are we all packed? Bea?"

Chandler was talking to her. Telling her how much he wanted her. No, he wasn't leaving yet. The new Winter Snow was sitting on him. Even as he fondled Winter, he was saying all he was going to do to her to give her the pleasure she so enjoyed. Seemed once he found his way into her head, she couldn't toss him out.

Hollis spoke. Diverted her. "Believe we are. Just gather up the *wee* one here and we'll be on our way. I'll carry this last box. You carry Maeve. As I said, Bea is already in the carriage. We'll be at your father's home in less than ten minutes. You will be safe there."

"Mother...?" The young man stopped. Appeared to freeze midstride. His mouth worked but no words came from him. He rubbed his jaw as he looked her up then down. Stared into her eyes then his gaze drifted to her bosom.

Seemed he was imagining her the last time he saw her several months ago. If she didn't get out of here fast, all would be lost. He would tell his mother everything he saw, all she did. She thought her knees would give way.

Georgia turned away from him shielding her face from his view. He'd already seen enough of her to recognize Winter Snow. Though the young rake had seen her wearing nothing at all. She cringed. Reached for Maeve. Cradled her baby next to her breasts. Oh, God, if he'd seen her perform pregnant, he would realize, Maeve was the baby she carried.

"Douglas?" Lady Estelle asked her son as she frowned. "Whatever is wrong with you? You look as if you've seen a ghost. What is it?"

"Maybe I have," he said while he rubbed his chin. His gaze fixed on her. "Maybe I..." He stopped short as if he knew what he was about to say might not sit well with his mother.

Wrong? Douglas recognized her. The young man frequented Chandler's little whorehouse. He was a regular every Wednesday night. Came with three other young rakes. He'd seen her perform as Winter Snow. Would also recognize the fact she belonged to Chandler. Chandler never shared her nor was she ever auctioned off for the evening. The only good thing about this uncomfortable situation was the fact she didn't believe he would reveal who she was to his mother. In doing so, he would have to explain to his doting parent why he frequented Chandler Wolcott's little whorehouse. The one known as the most decadent in London.

"Nothing." He scratched his chin again. Set his finger on the cleft there. One more time he undressed her with his gaze. He did know what she looked like wearing nothing at all. "Just thought…never mind." He waved his hand in the air. "Wanted to meet the lady who made all this deliciousness. One of my friends thought his mother might like to hire her for an occasion coming up in about two weeks."

Georgia let the air she'd been holding inside her lungs out in a rush. She didn't wish to accept the job. Needed to think about this catering business. Though she enjoyed the work, it seemed dangerous to pursue.

"We'll be on our way then."

With Maeve in her arms, she picked up her skirt to hurry from the room. This was not alright. The man was behind her.

"Wait, I'd like a word with you." He started after her, waving his hand. "You and I need to talk about…"

Pretending not to hear him, she continued, neglecting to put her hood over her head. Georgia needed to escape. She cuddled Maeve closer. Didn't wish to have a word with the young man. Didn't need to talk about anything. All she wished was to leave. Hollis stood at the carriage waiting to assist her inside.

Douglas caught up to her. Grabbed her arm, swinging her around so they stood toe to toe. His face was inches from hers. He stared into her eyes. She remembered another time when they stood together. The boy fondled her naked breasts. Sucked on each one. That night Celine led her around the room so the guests could touch her, caress her if they wished.

"I know you," his voice was harsh. Penetrating. "How dare you come to my home on the pretense of being respectable?"

"Never seen you before in my life." The lie stuck in her throat. She didn't feel one bit of guilt. If necessary, she would lie again. "Let go of me."

She jerked away from him. Hollis took Maeve to hand the baby into Bea's waiting arms.

"Is the boy bothering you?" Hollis asked as he took on the protective nature, he displayed any time she was distressed. He straightened to his full height. Clenched his fists. "I will take care of the lad."

"No, the young man will be on his way. Douglas just mistook me for someone he thought he'd seen before. Didn't you Douglas?" Crossing her fingers she was hoping he would agree with her. Praying, he wouldn't take this notion of his any farther.

"Suppose I did make a mistake." His hands behind him, he backed up still watching her while Hollis helped her inside the waiting vehicle.

By the time Hollis started the carriage moving, she'd yet to stop shaking. Maeve was touching her cheek. Tears slipped from her eyes. "Ga?" she asked, too perceptive by far.

It was one of the only sounds she made. Maeve could also say, 'B' for Bea. Hollis was a different story altogether though the little girl did love the big man. When he held her above his head, she giggled with delight. Sometimes she drooled. When the drool hit him in the face, he would bark out his laughter. The two were quite the pair. Hollis would always protect both of them.

Georgia held her hand, kissed the tiny fist. Realized Maeve was curious about her tears. "Mama is fine now that we've left. Just had a little scare. That's all. It's nothing for you to worry over."

She didn't understand why she spoke all those words to Maeve. Perhaps she was speaking to Bea instead. Perhaps the baby understood more than she expected. If the baby was a shifter, she would understand her thoughts along with her emotions. With two parents who could change form, Georgia would be surprised if Maeve didn't inherit the ability to shift. Maeve would also understand she was terrified.

Bea knew most of her past. Georgia felt the woman should know as much as possible about what she did in the name of securing her mate, not all. Bea learned she had sex in front of an audience. She could never tell her why. Hollis didn't know either. When Chandler hired him, he told him nothing. In time, Maeve would begin to test her abilities. Both Hollis as well as Bea would learn the truth. Most likely they would both be shocked. She would need to trust them with her secret.

Where are you, Winter? I need to find you. You are not where I told you to be. Don't like the disobedience. You are mine. Yes, mine through all eternity. Your job is to obey. You will never tell me no. I won't allow it.

She jerked, startled by the words. Acknowledged the fact that whenever she could, she would do as she pleased. So distracted by the young man, Chandler found his way into her head. It wouldn't do. She threw up a block. Discovered he was still there. Damn! His power was growing too fast. She didn't understand. He only learned to shift a few months ago.

Woman, you are supposed to be at my brothel, at Chandler's Little Theatre. Now! I'm not pleased with this defiance. If you go to your father's home, I'll drag you out, damn your white hide. You forget you belong to me.

Just left work. Not going to father's home. I'm going to the cottage. If it pleases you, you may follow. The hour is late. You're, perhaps, too tired from playing with your new Winter Snow.

A grimace on her face that Bea saw, looking down she smoothed the fabric of her gown. Tried to hide her expression. Traveling the country roads late at night was a horrible idea. Chandler would realize she lied. Maybe she didn't. She would need to have Hollis stop so she could explain her change of mind. Seeing Chandler tonight was not something she wanted to deal with. Douglas' role in her possible future was enough of a problem for her to contemplate. Didn't need Chandler playing in her mind confusing her.

No, you're not. Don't lie to me, Winter. Lying to your mate is not acceptable. I need to see you. Do as I request. Must hold you. Fondle your beautiful lady parts.

Hah! That was no request. It was a demand. Don't want to see you, Chandler. My feelings count. Can tell you're in the devil of a mood. Take the new Winter Snow to your room. She will satisfy all your needs. I'm certain of it. If not, drag Summer to your room. You enjoy Summer.

You're right, of course. I could have sex with both women tonight. You're also correct when you say I demand for you to be where I direct you. Expect my mate to obey me. When she doesn't the fact makes me angry...no, furious…more than annoyed. Heard the young pup talking to you. Douglas Laughton is a regular at my place of business. You recognized him. He recognized you. Every time he comes, he buys one of the girls to spend a relaxing…stimulating evening above stairs. Right now, his favorite seems to be Summer Passion. What do you think? If I brought you back to the auction block, would he buy your services? You would go to the third floor with him.

No! You wouldn't. Your words are just an idle threat to make me cower at your feet. I don't tremble, Chandler. I'm not afraid of you or Bertram for that matter. You should understand the truth by now. I would never sign the consent. If you forced me, I'd ruin you. Go to the devil!

As if she could stop the pounding voice in her head, she put her hands to her ears. She closed her eyes. Listened to the sounds around her. No…she wasn't going to let him inside again. She was stronger than Chandler. Bea looked at her with a strange expression on her face. A few minutes before, she'd taken Maeve into her arms. That was good of her. Bea had an uncanny ability to sense her needs. Maybe the woman was a shifter. That fact might be why her father hired her. At first, she thought Cormack might be falling for the woman. They were of an age. Now, she believed there might have been another reason

She didn't know what to do. Couldn't tell Bea that Chandler insisted on her coming to his townhouse. No, that wasn't what he demanded of her. He wanted her at the whorehouse. She didn't intend to go there again…not ever. Compromising might be a good idea. If she went to the townhouse and not to the cottage or her father's home the diversion would be fine.

"My dear, whatever is wrong with you?" Bea asked, tender concern etched in her voice. "You look…frazzled."

The air she doused her lungs with smelled of fear. Each time she saw Chandler it was getting harder for her to resist his insistent pressure. He teased her with innuendos along with caresses that left her trembling with need. Never stopped to give her a breath of air. He told her he wouldn't take her now unless she begged. Always left her aroused. Nothing could stop him from the seduction plans he made. He wanted her to be strung so taunt, she would beg. She would never plead with him. Never!

"Never!"

"Never what, my dear? You are so distraught. Was it something the young man said to you? Do you know him? Did he threaten you in any way?"

Georgia didn't realize she said the word out loud. Bea was far too perceptive for her likes. Chandler prying into her head affected her more than she wished to admit. Yes, she was frazzled, beyond frazzled.

"I don't know him. Douglas is his name. He thought he'd seen me somewhere before." That much wasn't a lie. She didn't know him. What she was distraught about was Chandler slipping into her head. There wasn't any way she could hide from him. She couldn't go to the whorehouse nor to her father's place. It would be folly to drive home in the dark of night.

There was only one decision she could make. She tapped on the roof. Hollis slowed the carriage to a stop.

He opened the door to peer inside. The man looked concerned. "What is it, Miss O'brien is there a change of plans? Thought we were to go to your father's place."

"Yes. There has been a change of plans. Take me to Chandler's townhouse. You know where it is located. I know he wants me at the brothel. Can't go there. Won't bring Maeve or Bea into his horrible establishment. Take me to his place. You recall where his other home is?" she repeated as much for herself as for Hollis. She was running but she didn't know in which direction to go.

He nodded. "I know where it's located. Don't like this plan of yours. You're not thinking clearly. Don't like taking you anywhere near the officious man. You do understand he will send us, your only protection back to your father's."

"Yes, and you will need to keep my father from running to the rescue. I have ways of holding off Chandler. I won't allow him to do what he wants with me. He has no control over what I will and will not do." Georgia placed her hand on her belly, growing rounder each day with her second child. She could use this ploy…the baby ploy. He would still want her. With her first child, Chandler enjoyed sex with her up until the day she birthed Maeve. They performed in front of his audience while she was nine months pregnant. She would never go in the same direction again. Standing firm was the only course for her.

"If that's what you wish. I'm remaining firm on my opinion. Do you wish for me to take you to Chandler's first?"

"Yes, Maeve needs to be put down. Must feed her then change her. There will be no problems I cannot handle. You do understand he's been at the cottage several times. I've been able to keep him at bay with your help. I will again then again as long as he persists in this stupidity. There is also help at his residence." She didn't know if she could stand strong against him. She did love him. Love had nothing to do with their relationship.

I know you can't keep me at arm's length forever. You love me. Just said so. Your feelings toward me are simple. You enjoy sex...all types of positions as do I. You want to reach that coveted pinnacle where you lose command of your body. I like to see your eyes glaze over with the pleasure only I can orchestrate in your little person.

She groaned. It would take all her strength to keep him out of her head. *Go to the devil, Chandler.*

His hoot of laughter rocked her. *Did you realize yet that I love to be inside your head. Bertram taught me how to avoid the blockage you put up. You are only a woman thus inferior to a male shifter. I am stronger as well as more intelligent than you. Thus, I am the one who will control what we do.*

I don't find anything amusing about all this. You can laugh all you want. Nothing will change. Go away, Chandler. Let me have the life I want. Without you.

Not going to give into your little whim.

Why?

Not about to tell you why. Let's just say you are the woman I need as well as want in my bed. A man needs to ease himself once in a while. While I've enjoyed the girls in the brothel, none of them hold a candle to you. Summer has come to my room several times. I want her to watch me come inside you. She won't like watching. That's too bad. The new Winter is with me now. She's not you.

You are insatiable.

You used to love my unquenchable appetites.

Never again!

She gritted her teeth then closed her mind to his perverse words. Didn't want him to hear her thoughts, all her worries along with her fears. Every time he was with her, he came closer to breaking her. Her restraint balanced on a hair's edge. If she was alone with him at the house, he would have *carte blanche* with her. She needed to freeze him out of her mind. Needed Hollis along with Bea to run interference. The presence of Maeve had little to no clout regarding his desires. Responding to him would be the death of her future dreams.

She didn't intend to beg.

When they arrived at the door, the butler greeted them. His name was Philipot. He issued her into the big front room that looked out onto the street.

"Miss Snow," he greeted her. "I wasn't expecting you. Will Chandler be coming along later?"

No, of course, he wasn't expecting her. Chandler would never tell him she was coming here. Stiff with her anger, she spoke. "Chandler wanted me at the brothel. His lascivious whorehouse is not appropriate for a child. I chose to come here. He won't be pleased with my decision. Could you show me to my room? I'm tired. Maeve needs to nurse before she ends up in a crying fit of exhaustion. It's too much."

"Yes, of course." He reached out to smooth a finger on Maeve's soft pink cheek. "She is very beautiful. Looks more like you every time I see her. Glad she doesn't look like her father."

He turned then headed up the stairs to the bedrooms above.

Georgia trailed after him. In this house there was no bed for her in the nursery, only a rocking chair. If need be, she intended to make use of the chair for the rest of the night. If Chandler was entertaining the new Winter in his chamber. It would be a while before he came to her. Chandler would never allow her to sleep in the nursery.

After she finished with Maeve, gently tucking her in for the night, Georgia sought a blanket to cover herself. She'd expected Chandler by now. Closing her eyes she drifted to sleep. Was thrust awake by the bang of the door against the nursery wall.

Maeve let out a loud wail that sounded more like anger than fear. The dark shadow of a large man stood in the doorway. Philipot hovered behind the huge shadow, twisting then turning in an attempt to see around him.

"You're coming with me!" He stepped into the light.

She sat up, pushing hair from her eyes, blinking the sleep away. "Bertram, whatever are you doing here? No, I'm not going anywhere with you, not this instant, not ever." Georgia didn't understand. She frowned. Looked at the clock on the table next to her. It was well past two o'clock in the morning.

"Chandler needs you," Bertram gritted out as he stepped inside the room looking ready to toss her over his broad shoulder if she didn't do as he wished. "You must come with me."

"I need to see to Maeve."

Georgia picked up the wailing child. Acknowledging the fact, she would need to allow the baby to nurse. She didn't like baring her breast in front of this man. He'd seen her naked enough times. One more time should never make a difference. She heaved a deep breath of air into her lungs.

"No, the little brat can do without your tits tonight. Philipot can feed her milk. Chandler needs you more than the baby." He stepped farther into the room. "Don't argue with me. You won't win."

He didn't need to be crass. That was Bertram, tactless. If he took Maeve from her, she would never be able to retrieve her without hurting the baby. "Maeve is a baby. Chandler is a grown man. He can wait a few minutes for this much needed attention. If you didn't barge in here banging the door against the wall, she would still be sleeping. I wouldn't need to attend to her fears. Besides, I'm not going anywhere near that whorehouse of his."

Ignoring the man hovering over her, she put Maeve to her breast. Maeve latched on as if she hadn't been fed in days when the last feeding had only been four hours ago when she put her to bed. Now, she was whimpering while she nursed, still terrified.

Hovering over her he was clearing his throat. "Chandler's been hurt. He's in a bad way. You have to come with me," Bertram said, his voice a bit calmer than before. "He's asking for you. Wants only you."

When he first said the words, her heart lurched. She found, despite her feelings about Chandler perhaps because of her true emotions for him, she was ready to follow Bertram even to the brothel. *Stand firm, I can do this.* Bertram was lying. She knew the tale Bertram projected was a lie. She sneered. "How very convenient of him. I would not go to the brothel. So, he pretends to be hurt so he can lure me there. How very arrogant of the bloody bastard. Don't give a damn about the man. Why would he think I would come with you? I dislike you more than Chandler." Georgia wasn't having anything to do with this outlandish pretense of Chandler's. Chandler must have realized from their brief conversation she would never back down, never come to that place with a willing step.

"You don't know what you are talking about, Winter. During one of the scene changes, a man knifed him. Cut his thigh." Bertram was pacing the room, looking at her then the door. "I'm not lying."

Of course the man lied. That was one of the things he did best. Georgia shook her head. "I don't believe you. It's a ploy of a little boy to get his way. I'm not going to Chandler's little playhouse. Bring him here if you must. If he is indeed hurt, I will see to him here. Philipot will help me with him." She didn't wish to be left alone with Chandler.

"I can make you go!" His hands were fisted by his sides. "Except for your amazing bubbies, you're just a tiny little thing. You have no say in this process. I'll toss you over my shoulder. Haul you kicking and screaming if that's the way you want it to be."

"Now, wait a minute," Philipot stepped into the room, defending her. "If Mr. Wolcott has been wounded, I'll send for the physician. Miss Snow should not be at the brothel with the little one. She must never leave the baby alone in this home. Especially if there has been an attack on Mr. Wolcott. Either one of them could be hurt. No, Miss Snow will remain here in this household. A place where it is safe for her. You will bring the master to the townhouse. Take care of it now. If he is hurt badly as you say, he will need the doctor."

Georgia let out a swish of air, relieved Philipot thought along the same lines. "I won't go there. Philipot's idea is a good one. The ambience here is more conducive to a sick person if he is indeed hurt." She spoke to the butler. "Do send someone for a physician."

Then to Bertram. "Fetch Chandler here! Go get him. We'll see if he's faking the injury. Seems you've wasted valuable time. When you are here, take him to the bedroom. I can look after him better here where it is not so noisy. I gather the evening is not over. There are rooms on the third floor of the brothel being used for further entertainment." Georgia paused for a breath of air. "What happened to the man who attacked Chandler?"

Bertram was quick to answer. He sifted in a huge breath of air. "He was waylaid. Seems his daughter was part of the show tonight. He took exception to the fact she was having sex in front of fifty people. She is the new Winter Snow, Queen of the Ice. Despite all her efforts to the contrary, he discovered where his daughter went missing. Came after her. Although there is more to the story than meets the eye. Miss Snow told Chandler her father had been abusing her since she was ten. She is only eighteen now. The girl signed all the legal papers. Told him if she was going to have sex, it would be more than nice to profit from the act. She is quite enthusiastic. Ready as well as eager to show off her female endowments to anyone who will pay her."

So, Chandler was hurt. She calmed herself. Needed to keep a steady head on her shoulders. "How bad is he hurt?"

She needed to go to him. Told herself, she must stick to her resolutions. His employees would bring him here.

"In and out of consciousness. Has a fever. Lost a great deal of blood. Whenever he comes to, he asks for you." Bertram was talking fast in a hurry it seemed to make her believe. "I'm worried about Chandler."

That must be why he wasn't in her head the last few hours. Georgia was positive he would have woken her to taunt her more about his male prowess. He would intend to tell her what he was going to do when he was with her. How he would take her to his bed. Now, she was worried about him. After setting Maeve in the crib then blowing out the candle, she herded the men from the room.

In the hall, she stopped to speak. Meant to take charge. Repeated herself. "Philipot, send for the physician. Tell the doctor this is urgent. He must come here. The brothel is no place for Chandler to recover. I'm not going there. So, he must come to his townhouse. There is no other alternative. If I could take him to the cottage that would be for the best. It's too far away."

"Yes, ma'am."

After she finished with Philipot, she spoke to Bertram. "Have Jimmy and Johnny help you with Chandler. I assume you've stopped the bleeding."

Bertram looked to the stairs then back. "He's not going to be pleased with this arrangement. You not coming to him. It's what he demanded." Bertram paused in thought. "Yes, the bleeding has stopped. Celine wrapped the wound as best she could. He's going to need a few stitches. If a fever doesn't set in, he'll get well…"

Thought he'd said he had a fever. Another ploy to get her to do his wont. "Go with haste. I'll have everything ready when he arrives. Philipot will help. Hurry!"

Georgia shooed him from the hall. She followed him down the long stairway. All the while she prayed. Said prayers from her childhood, she thought she'd forgotten.

~ * ~

Chandler enjoyed being in her head, hearing all her thoughts. Winter was both furious as well as annoyed with him. He was a horrible patient. He felt her squirm then tense. Realized her heart speeded. Her body responded to his words of seduction. Heard the sharp pants of air she inhaled. Bertram taught him well this act of getting into his mate's head. He found he learned fast…was an apt student.

While she angered him by not coming here, he would seek some type of revenge when he followed her through his townhouse. Might find a nice corner to taste her sweet charms. At the moment he was enjoying his new Winter Snow. She also was an apt pupil. Quick to adapt to whatever happened. While she wasn't as intriguing as the first Winter, her breasts were almost as lush as his favorite's.

Ah, he sighed with bliss as he watched the audience focus on the sway of Winter's breasts while he pumped into her. The girl had an uncanny ability to seduce with her body. Even Celine wasn't so natural with her passions. She told him her father abused her. Fathers should never abuse their daughters. Winter was right in her assumption; he would never do anything so crass with Maeve. Was surprised he held a few moral values close to his heart.

Chandler was enjoying taunting Georgia with this pleasurable moment. Told her he was going to bring his lady to his room tonight so she could watch them have sex. Also told her Summer had taken her place in his bed. Ah, Winter pretended she didn't wish to have anything to do with him. He knew different.

Winter loves me. She told me so.

Georgia told him so more than once. So, it had to be true. Her words made her vulnerable. Chandler liked her, susceptible to his every whim. The baby also made her defenseless in so many ways. Had threatened her with their child a time or two. If need be, he would do so again even though he never intended to hurt the wee tyke. He was looking forward to the end of this evening's entertainment.

Winter's head was thrown back with the raw passion she was feeling. She cried out her pleasure while he emptied his seed into her. Both Jimmy and Johnny were beside her caressing her large breasts. Bertram had taken up a position in front touching her feminine endowments. That hard little jewel that left her mindless with ecstasy. She was panting in her need. He was certain her eyes were closed. Teaching her to keep them open when she reached that sought after pinnacle would heighten her appeal to his audience.

The commotion at the entrance brought his attention to the large man stalking toward him. His bodyguards lurched toward the intruder to stop the man's forward progress. They were too late. He yanked Winter from him. The knife slashed across his thigh, missing his heart because Jimmy deflected his aim.

Chandler bellowed with the pain. Blood spurted from his leg. The room was screeching. People were running. The bodyguards pulled the man away before he could cut him again. After those first harried moment, he didn't remember much. He fell into a deep black pit. While he couldn't see anyone, he heard chatter all around him. His head pounded while his leg throbbed.

When he came to, he was on his bed. Celine was wrapping his leg with a bandage. Winter was off to the side wringing her hands as well as moaning that she didn't want him to die. Bertram sat on the other side of him.

"Winter…? Where is she?" Chandler moaned the pain making him incoherent. He needed Winter. "Get her…" he grabbed onto Bertram's arm. "Bring her to me. Have to see her. Touch her."

"I'm right here." Winter stood beside him smiling down at him. "I'm not going anywhere. I'll always stay by your side." She bent over and kissed him on his forehead.

He didn't want this girl right now. Needed his mate by his side. "Not you, Georgia. Where is she? Get her, Bertram. Bring her here. No excuses from her. She needs to be by my side."

He knew he was repeating himself. The way his head pounded, he didn't know how long he would remain conscious. "Want Winter here when I wake up next time."

"Thought Hollis was bringing her to the brothel. Shouldn't she be here by now?" Bertram asked, his voice filled with worry.

She told him several times when he was in her head that she would never come here again. He didn't believe her. He never gave Bertram the pertinent information. Meant to get inside her head again before he tossed her over his shoulder then brought her to his rooms at the brothel. "At the townhouse, bring her to me. She didn't want to come to the brothel. Says it's a bad place for Maeve. I don't give a damn what she thinks. Don't give a second thought about Maeve."

The pain of it all, he closed his eyes, trying to sift in as much air as possible. Tonight was not going to be fun. He'd planned for more fun and games with his mate. Thought he might shift to his cat. He could tease her, rub across her, lick her until she moaned with delight. Chandler found he was beginning to fade. The room was starting to disappear, the walls moving.

"I'll get Winter. Be back as soon as possible." Bertram backed away from him. "She'll come with me. Won't give her a choice. If you want the little whore, you get to have her. I will bring her."

Chandler watched Bertram spin on his heel to leave. By the time Bertram reached the door he was running down the steps. For a few beats of his heart, Chandler closed his eyes. Tried to get into Winter's head. He didn't have the strength.

"Celine…?"

His throat felt parched. Needed a sip of water. His body was so weak he couldn't think straight. This night started out with so much potential. The bloody sod knifed him. At least he would live to have sex with Winter again.

"Yes?" She held his hand. Stroked his palm. Pushed a lock of hair away from his face. "I'll do whatever you need."

"Take Winter to her room. Don't want her here when Georgia arrives with the baby. You understand?"

Chandler closed his eyes again while he tried to maintain long enough to tell Celine his wishes. The lady had been with him from the beginning. No, before the beginning, he liked to have sex with her. She was always cooperative as well as eager. Liked to try new things. Different things. Never minded when he and Bertram shared her charms.

"Of course, anything else?"

"Come back here. Need company to help keep me awake. Want my eyes wide open when Winter arrives. She won't be happy."

Chandler felt hot. He didn't wear anything except the stark white bandage Celine wrapped around his thigh. He was hotter than Hades. Felt sweat run down his forehead then into his eyes. "Hot."

Heard the ladies' footsteps when they left the room. Wondered how long it would take for Celine to return. Acknowledged the fact he'd hurt Winter. She'd been enthusiastic. Eager to please him. She wasn't his Winter, his mate. Heard Celine return. She walked to his bedside then sat on the edge. Chandler felt the mattress dip with her slight weight.

"Winter is settled in. She is very sorry for what her father did to you. Hopes you won't blame this on her. Winter told me she doesn't want to go back to him. He's likely to kill her if she does. I like the girl. If you have any doubts, she will prove herself as well as make as much money as possible. She can also be auctioned at the end of the evening unless she has a hold on you. Does she?"

"The girl can do whatever she wishes. Stay or go, the decision is up to her. Give me some water."

He pointed to the pitcher. His voice cracked with his last words. His throat parched so bad he could barely talk. Didn't understand why he was so hot. He felt feverish.

Celine lifted his head, held him up so he could drink. He smiled. Celine was also naked. Her breasts pushed against his back. Felt the hard pebbling of the tips. Blessed hell, he did enjoy women. Didn't understand why he was so possessive of his first Winter. Should have sold her to whoever was the highest bidder. Kept her all to himself for nine months until she gave birth, until she left him. All those months he never entertained anyone else in this room or theirs. The scenario was going to change. As soon as he could, he would take the second Winter to his bed. Once inside her head, he would tell her about what he was doing detail by detail. Hoped she would burn with jealousy. He tried to slip into her head again. Failed.

After she left him, he did see other women in his rooms. The women he took during the shows didn't count. Had needs to ease. He realized shifters always stayed with their one true mate. He deviated from the normal routine. Planned to continue on the same path he traveled before he met his Winter Snow. Resented the fact Winter left him to fend for himself. A man had needs.

The door in the front room opened. He heard Jimmy and Jonny speaking with Bertram. What the devil? He should feel her presence. She should be here, tending to him, stroking him. Georgia didn't come with Bertram. Where the devil was she? He reached out to talk to her with his mind.

Bloody eyes, where are you?

One more time, she didn't answer. Damn her lily-white hide! He wasn't about to allow her to block him from her head. He needed to know everything she was thinking. Concentrating, he closed his eyes. As the minutes ticked by on the clock, he found he was growing weaker. He didn't know how much blood he lost. The room seemed to swirl faster with each time he opened his eyes. Pain surrounded him, incapacitated him.

"Celine? You still with me?" Tried to move his hand to reach out to her.

Chandler thought he said the words. Didn't hear them. What was going on? He tried to frown. Fingers moved with gentle ease along his face. She was here with him.

"It's me. I'm here for you. Won't leave until Bertram brings Winter. She won't wish for me to be in the room with you. I do know her. I will leave when she arrives."

Again, everything seemed to turn dark. He reached out to Winter and didn't find her. Weakness engulfed him. Tore himself back to the light. Celine wasn't sitting by him. For a beat, he panicked. Where was everyone? They wouldn't leave him alone.

"I'm here." Celine sat beside him. She pushed hair from his forehead. "You're hot. Is there anything I can do?" Touched the back of her hand to his cheek. "I should do something. Just don't know what."

She sounded worried. Good, he liked the sound of concern in his friend's voice. Celine cared what happened to him. "Water," he sounded like a croaking frog.

"Just a sec."

She was off the bed. Listened to her footsteps.

He heard water splash into a glass. One more time, she held him up so he could drink. The cool liquid tasted so good as it slithered down his throat. Didn't feel the delightful press of her breasts against his back.

"You dressed," he managed to say. "You shouldn't have. Like to feel you against me even though I can't do anything with you."

Her light trill of laughter reassured him. She placed his hand inside her dressing gown. Moved his palm across the tips. "Even when you cannot speak or move, you're a randy man. There might be even more people parading through this room before you get better. Didn't wish to embarrass anyone."

"Liar…"

With that one word, he blacked out again. Even though he wasn't awake, he felt Winter's anger.

"Maybe…maybe not," Celine said with the easy lift of her shoulders.

How are you, Chandler? Blast you for not talking to me. Bertram told me you were hurt. He's going to bring you to the townhouse. Told you I wouldn't ever go to that den of iniquity you call a whorehouse again. He would need to bind and gag me to get me there. You are better off at your townhouse. Bertram has agreed to fetch a doctor. I'm not sorry either. No regrets.

Drifting between the conscious world and the unconscious, Chandler was pleased he heard her voice, damn woman. He didn't have the strength to tell her what he thought about her insubordination. He supposed he should turn her over his knee. Spank her as he did his little school girl, Summer Passion. Right now, he didn't have the energy to open his eyes let alone seek retribution for wrongs done to him by his very naughty mate. He wouldn't indulge her whims. Given time, she would learn to do all he demanded.

Next thing he knew he was awake and staring into Winter's beautiful clear blue eyes. He didn't say anything. Now that he was awake, he couldn't think of words. He wasn't in his room at the brothel. No, she had the nerve to bring him to his townhouse. He saw the soft blue and yellow Aubusson carpet. Dark blue drapes hung on the window of the master chamber that overlooked his garden. While he liked the townhouse, he preferred the energy of the brothel. Something was always happening in his decadent home.

Winter stood beside the bed; her hands clasped in front of her. The dress she wore was a deep dark blue. The neckline reached her chin. He much preferred her wearing nothing at all. Since she left him, she changed. Always when she was in his rooms, she either wore nothing or a simple dressing gown. Now she covered herself from her chin to the tips of her toes. He didn't like it. No, he didn't like this new Winter at all.

"The doctor is going to look at your leg, Chandler. He will tell me what to do so you don't die on me. Don't wish for you to die." She pulled his covers up to his chin. "You have a fever. A man can die from one of those."

Hah! She probably wanted him to die. No, Winter told him she loved him. He was too damn hot. Needed the covers off.

"Tell me you understand."

Unable at the moment to form words, he nodded. Tried to reach out to her in her mind. She blocked him. He would have to ask Bertram for more help.

"Ah...believe I appreciate the fact you can't speak. Wonder how long it will be before foolish words tumble from your mouth. If you wish to drink some more water, nod to the pitcher." Winter stepped back giving room for a man he didn't know to step up to the bed.

From the corner of his eye, he saw Bertram hovering behind and to the left of the man he assumed was the physician. His friend appeared worried. He was sweating. Winter looked a bit concerned but nothing that would scream out uneasy. He wondered where his daughter was. She was too young to be apprehensive.

Bertram must have dressed him in his dressing gown before bringing him here. Beneath the fabric he was naked. The carriage ride would have been cold, frigid. Last he looked this evening light flakes of snow were falling. Maybe the snow changed to rain. Usually did.

"I'm going to look at the wound. Bertram says you were slashed on the thigh. The cut was deep. Told me you lost a lot of blood. Must unwind this bandage. Want you to drink all the water Georgia gives you. Very important. Will help keep the fever down."

The doctor moved the dressing gown aside then unwrapped the stark white bandage Celine wrapped around his leg. Made little noises while he examined him. Touched the slash. Felt his forehead with the back of his hand just as it seemed everyone else did.

"You are hot. The wound is infected. That's to be expected. Whoever cleaned you up did a fine job. All I'll have to do is put a few stitches on the injury. When I'm done, you will be almost as good as new."

What the bloody hell does that mean? Almost as good as new? Chandler didn't shout out the questions. He kept the words inside himself. Was pleased when Winter answered. She would do for a nurse. He liked the idea.

You still have a fever, Chandler. Quit complaining so much. Believe you are lucky not to have had someone attack you sooner given the nature of your business. She stopped for a moment to gain a breath of air. *The doctor says you will need to be bathed with cool water in order for your temperature to go back to normal. While Bertram assured me he could do a fine job, I told him I would do it.*

He knew if she saw him grin the expression would reach his eyes. He was pleased. *If you're doing the bathing, that's fine by me. You can touch any part of me you like. Don't want Bertram's big hands on me...or Philipot's. Want those soft white hands of yours stroking me from my toes to my head. There are other places you can bathe I would never object to. Give special attention to my man's endowments. If you caressed while you bathed me the sensations would be more than pleasant.*

See you must be healing. Your mind is spinning in all the directions that make you, you. A few minutes ago, you didn't even possess the strength to talk to me this way. I am allowing you inside my head by the way. You will no longer be able to invade my privacy at your whim. I will allow you access only when I deem it right.

We shall see.

With the first stitch going into his leg, he shrieked. Howled loud enough to wake the dead. The pain was unbearable. Thought the doctor gave him something to lessen the pain. He wondered how many stitches this would take. The slash was long as well as deep. Didn't understand how this could hurt so bloody much. Thought he remembered the doc giving him laudanum earlier. Told him the drug was for the pain as well as to sleep. He wanted to be asleep right now. Didn't wish for the pain to continue. His fists tightened on the bed covers. He gritted his teeth, tensing for the next slip of the needle through his skin.

Don't be a baby, Chandler. Be stoic. A man should never give in to the pain. I remember when I gave birth to Maeve. I didn't cry out or yell. Pain from birthing a baby is worse than anything you will endure. Your pain will be over in about another five minutes. Mine went on for eight hours. Again, I tell you, don't be a baby.

You're enjoying this.

Of course I am. I always enjoy your pain.

Don't become sarcastic, Winter.

Call me Georgia.

No!

The terrible pain stopped, to be replaced by a dull throbbing ache. He was either asleep or in hell. For the time being, he didn't care. Must be only half asleep. The cool cloth floating across his heated flesh felt too good for him to be in hell. Doubted if he went to heaven or anywhere close. If that was the case, he must be alive. The big guy up there would never allow him to get through the pearly gates. Chandler knew he wasn't a good person. This last year his character did improve. Winter had that effect on him. He no longer sought revenge against his younger brother and his wife. If he was willing to admit to himself, which he wasn't, he wished them well.

With his eyes open now, Winter's face was fuzzy. She was still beautiful even with an unclear face. Chandler realized Winter was stroking him with the cloth again. Knew he felt cooler. He thought this treatment was very nice. If he'd not been wounded, she would never be caressing him.

Your hands on my body would be nicer. Dip them in the cool water first. Dribble some of the liquid on me. You can hold my sex if you like. Fondle from the base to the tip with the cool water. I'd even smile if you put your mouth on me. Taste the tip as you used to do during the shows. Allow me to come inside your mouth.

Don't want to touch you with my hands or my mouth. You don't deserve pleasure. All I'm doing is bringing your temperature down so you don't die. My mouth would be hot. Would work to do the opposite. If I touched you with my mouth you might succumb to the fever. You do understand.

Being mean to a sick man is not well done of you, Winter. I would know your... Chandler stopped speaking. She wasn't in his mind any longer. Wasn't stroking him with the cool cloth. He felt hot again. Didn't understand why she stopped.

She was also gone from the room. He couldn't see her. The rise of the mattress told him she left him. Winter was back, helping him sit. Felt the curves of her lush full breasts against his back. Wanted to get better so he possessed the strength to suck on them. She would no longer allow him close enough. *Thank God.* The cool liquid slipped down his throat. She let him lie back on the bed. Stood beside the bed staring down at him.

The doctor told me to give you more laudanum when you woke. You will sleep again. That way you can heal faster. In the morning, you can have some of your cook's porridge. Do you wish to have honey or dollop of butter in the gruel.

Chandler heard her laughter. The sound rippled across him. She was laughing at the situation he was in. He realized she was pleased with his weakness. Happy he was miserable.

Wish for real food... How long has it been? How many hours have I been gone from this world, sleeping?

You're pouting.

Wouldn't you if you couldn't eat? How long?

Two days, Chandler. You can't have real food until I know you can keep something soft in your stomach. Don't wish for you to toss your meal all over the clean sheets. Bertram has helped me change your sheets four times to date. You've sweated like a pig. Peed on them. Even Bertram commented on your sweating as well as the peeing.

You've been here all that time? I'm shocked. Thought you would have wished to return to your cottage. Was certain while I was unable to act, you would have left me high and dry. What made you stay?

Winter didn't answer a single one of his questions. He saw her stiff back as she walked away. He did feel better. Still had a fever. When he felt even better, he would see what would happen between them. Damn, he missed her. Blasted woman. She shouldn't keep herself away from him. She was his life mate.

As I said before, Bertram has been here helping. He told me Celine wanted to come stroke you with the cool cloth. I told Bertram no. Celine's coming to attend to you wouldn't be wise. Wasn't going to allow that woman in your townhouse. There would be more scandal. More gossip. Your new Winter also wanted to caress you. All your women, Chandler, it's truly too much to handle. I could never have done this by myself. Hollis and Bea have visited. I think they came just to make certain you weren't pretending as I thought at first. We both know it would be just like you to fake an injury to get me to come to you. Your fever is almost gone. I won't remain here much longer. You no longer have need of the cool water on your skin. I'll be leaving for Orange Blossom Cottage soon.

Believe I'm going to sleep again. Your constant harping is getting on my nerves. Did you drug my water again?

Didn't seem he slept very long. When he woke, he was groggy. Dazed as well as lethargic. Chandler opened his eyes to see Bertram at his bedside, not Winter. Deep inside he understood she left. Must have gone back to the cottage as she told him. Her scent was no longer hovering around him. He didn't feel her presence. He felt empty inside.

"Damn!"

Bertram seemed to guess he was distressed because Winter left him. She would always leave him. He felt betrayed again. Over then over again she betrayed him. There was no loyalty in her heart. "Yes, Winter left early this morning. Said I could take care of you now that you were out of the woods. You no longer needed a tender touch. One of your other ladies could come take care of you for all she cared."

"Damn her white hide," Chandler muttered, wishing he could strangle her for her impertinence. "I'm going to get her then bring her back to the bordello. Don't care that doing so will set me back. She won't leave me again. I'll keep the door to her room locked."

He knew that wouldn't happen. If he tried, all hell would break loose. Winter had him by the balls and what was worse she understood her power. All she needed to do was squeeze.

"In a few days maybe, you will be able to make good on your words. Doubt if you have the ability to stand let alone fetch an unwilling woman to do your whims. Concentrate on getting your strength back. After you're strong again, I'll applaud all your efforts to bring Winter to heel. She has been a constant thorn in your side since she gave birth then thought to renege on the contract she signed. It was good of you to keep her with us for those extra months. Needed to show her you owned her."

Chandler bristled at Bertram's words. He could be angry as well as frustrated with his mate. No one else could.

"Winter is not a dog. You cannot think to bring her to heel," Philipot muttered beneath his breath but loud enough for him to hear.

"No," Chandler paused, surprised he could talk without croaking like a frog. "Winter is not a dog."

He was beginning to think she was a very precious person. One he had no idea how to handle. Because he wanted her, he would learn. She would teach him what she needed. It was obvious sex with him wasn't something she cared about. He needed to figure out a way for her to see life his way. For certain, he would never be able to change nor did he want to do so. If there was to be a future for them, Winter would need to undergo a transformation. Chandler wanted her as she came to him that first day, ready as well as eager to share sex, to feel their bodies joined.

She still didn't wish to wed him. If he asked her today, she would tell him no. Wondered what it would take to alter her mind. Maybe good sex…amazing sex…better sex than she'd ever had before. Chandler paused to wonder if she was getting sensual gratification from someone else. No, she was a shifter through to the tips of her very pretty little toes. Toes he wished to play with again. She would never dally with another man. Doing so would go against her stubborn hide. Winter was the most obstinate woman he knew.

"Did the doctor say how long I would be in bed?" Chandler asked as he stretched his legs thinking to swing them to the floor.

Barely able to move, he doubted his ability to walk. He needed to relieve himself. Was pleased Winter wasn't here with him instead of Bertram. She would have taunted him. Damn woman! Would have been mortifying to ask her for help in this small endeavor.

"No, told me you would figure it out on your own. Never gave estimates on something like that. Knew you would rush things," Bertram told him. "Suppose you are hungry, thirsty as well. What can I get for you?"

"Yes…I want to go to the brothel then to her cottage. How is my second Winter doing? Is she performing with the others? Are you taking my place or one of the twins? Surprised they haven't been here, Jimmy along with Johnny."

"No, I figured you would only wish for her to take the stage once a week. She wants more time in front of your audience. You never gave permission for her to be auctioned. Our second Winter wishes for everything. She sees the money exchanging hands. Wants her share."

"Our new Winter wants to make money. Believe she should get to choose when she performs as well as if she is part of the auction in the evenings. If she expresses a wish, tonight could be her first in the rooms upstairs. I'm certain she will please her buyer."

As if thinking about his words, Bertram tapped his fingers beneath his chin. "I'll ask her as soon as I return. Tonight's show is starting in a couple of hours. Will have to leave you to Philipot's tender hands."

"Tell him I wish to eat something besides gruel. Not in the mood for something so tasteless. All I've had since I can remember is broth and gruel. Need something substantial. Want to get my strength back. Want to make love to my Winter."

You should behave yourself, Chandler. Obey…isn't that what you spout to me all the time? The doctor is knowledgeable. He knows what will help you recover. If you can't keep the porridge down, why then you will throw the horrible stuff up all over your covers. Philipot will need to change them again.

I miss you.

He heard the hiss of air. Knew he didn't expect any tender words from her. She came into his head with the sole purpose of provoking him. Silence. She wasn't thinking about anything. Chandler understood Winter couldn't block him from her head if he wished to be inside. What happened?

You only miss torturing me. Tempting me to change my mind. I won't change, Chandler. Not for you or for anyone. By the way you are wrong about me. I've seen two men since I've left you. They are much better in bed than you, better lovers. They do satisfy me. After all, a woman has needs too.

Damn woman! You lie!

Suppose you will never know. If you see other women, there is no reason for me to restrain my base needs. I do enjoy the end result. The place where I shatter into thousands of pleasure filled shards.

I don't believe you.

More silence echoed in his head. She left him and he couldn't get her back. She lied to him. He knew she lied. Told him falsehoods just to cause him distress.

Yes, I do like for you to realize some confusion.

Ah, you're back. Couldn't stay away from me. Believe that's a good sign.

I can stay away.

He chose to ignore her. Didn't wish to think of her staying away from him. So, he went back to her earlier comment. *Torture? You mean my gentle kisses on the back of your neck? The wild pinnacle of release I bring you to with my man's body? Is that what you mean by torture? I would beg to differ.*

Beg all you want. Won't get you anything or anywhere. I must see to Maeve. She's hungry.

We both comprehend you can talk to me and feed our daughter at the same time.

My daughter.

You want me to transform into a different man.

Yes and no, you can't be altered. You are who you are. That's why I won't marry you. Can't live with the person you are.

You love me.

True. Makes no difference. I loved you when I left you. I also despise all you stand for.

~ * ~

The next morning Bertram rode to the cottage. Confrontation was what was in his mind. He needed to speak with Winter. Understood Chandler needed her. Since she left him, he was a shadow of himself. Granted, once he joined the new Winter Snow on stage he became more like his old self.

This new lady was good for Chandler. He wanted the first Winter to leave Chandler the hell alone.

When he knocked on the door, Hollis answered. He frowned. "Bertram," his voice held a wealth of disgust. "What do you want? As if I didn't know. Did Chandler send you to kidnap Georgia? I won't allow you to seize her. You will have to go through me as well as Bea. United, we are a formidable pair."

Bertram nodded as he stepped past Hollis to enter the room. If he changed to his cat, Hollis wouldn't stand a chance of stopping him. If he did, Hollis would know what he was. Would comprehend more about him than he wished.

"I'm not here to haul her back to where she belongs. On the contrary, I only wish to convince her to stay away from Chandler. I'm on her side. Yours as well."

Hollis snorted then shook his head. "You do realize it is Chandler who contacts her. Georgia doesn't wish to have anything to do with the man. As soon as he's recovered from the unfortunate accident, he will show up here. Don't doubt it for a moment. You do need to convince Chandler coming to see Georgia is contrary to his purposes."

"I still wish to speak with Winter. Want Chandler back the way he was before she sunk her claws into him."

Bertram realized as he spoke with Hollis that he was wasting his time here. If the woman wanted to remain with Chandler, she would have stayed with him. Hollis was right. Winter was doing all in her power to hold Chandler at bay.

Bringing back Chandler to the man he used to be would lie on his shoulders. Winter appeared from the kitchen drying her hands on a towel. She didn't smile at him. Her back stiffened. It was obvious she wasn't pleased to see him.

"You're not going to claim Chandler has been injured again. Now, are you?" She tossed the damp dishtowel over her shoulder.

"No…" Bertram lifted his shoulders uncertain of his next words. "He is much better than when you left him. On the mend, he is."

"Why are you here? Did Chandler send you?" Her voice was crisp, filled with a hard edge. She sounded annoyed. "I don't wish to see the man though he doesn't care a fig about my wishes."

"Chandler didn't send me. Needed to convince you to stay away from my friend." Bertram meant to make a point with her. "Stay the bloody hell away!" His patience waned with each incredulous look Winter sent him.

Her mouth gaped open with surprise. She shook her head. "I trust now that your message has been received, you will go. Don't want you in my home. Don't like you. Never did. While I tolerate Chandler because he is Maeve's father, I have no reason to give the same concessions to the likes of you." She turned to her protector. "Hollis, will you see him out?"

"Be pleased."

Not too much later, Bertram found himself back at the brothel. The trip was a waste of time. When he entered Chandler's room, he sat down opposite his friend for too many years to count. He didn't know what to say. Chandler would continue the way he wished. There was naught he could do to change the reality.

"Where were you?" Chandler asked, seeming to understand Bertram had been nosing into his affairs.

"Not going to lie. Went to talk Winter out of seeing you. Looks as if we are on the same page. She doesn't want you."

"That's just the thing. The damn woman doesn't know her mind. She tells me she loves me in one breath then the next she says she doesn't want to see me. Contrary woman."

Chandler sat forward sifting his hands through his hair. When he looked at him, Bertram saw the dissolution in his eyes.

"Do you love her?" Bertram was certain Chandler's answer would be in the affirmative. "The two of you could try to make a go of it...a marriage. Could live part time here and the other part at her cottage."

"I've asked." Chandler stood.

Winced at what must be the pain from his leg. Sat back down. "Damn, just when is this leg going to be healed?"

"Give it time," Bertram advised. "Give Winter time. If she loves you, she will want you soon. She's only a woman with a woman's needs. You taught her pleasure. She will come to crave more of the same."

Bertram acknowledged the reality. Winter was stubborn. The most immovable person he'd ever known. Even though he gave the advice, he didn't expect Winter to cave to pressure.

"As soon as I'm up to snuff, going to start my campaign to win her over. Now that I can't go to her, I'm having a bit of a setback. The second Winter has been helpful as has Summer Passion. They both come to see me. Talk to me. Tell me all will be fine. Don't have the same kind of confidence. My first Winter won't let me into her head. You've got to help me get through the block she puts in front of her. She's a bloody woman. Shouldn't be more powerful than me. Don't like it."

"Okay, if that's what you would like. I can give you some advice on fighting the hindrance. You're right. You should wield more power than a female."

Chandler didn't have enough experience. Bertram had been surprised when he picked up on the task with such ease.

Bertram had confidence in his friend. If he wished to have Winter Snow in his bed as well as his wife, he would win her over.

Chapter Three

Georgia held the short letter on her lap. She read it three times before she began to understand what James Wolcott wished for. It wasn't because the words weren't clear. They were. It was because she couldn't credit Chandler's father with wishing to meet her. Each time she read the words, she was just as surprised as the last. James Wolcott wanted to visit. Wished to meet his granddaughter as well as the mother. She looked at the paper again.

Dear Miss Snow,

I, along with my butler, Smith-Jones would like to come to your country cottage for a visit. I've never met you or my granddaughter. Would love to change the situation. Do appreciate the little ones. You should realize I will always be here for you. If you need anything, anything at all, let me know. Don't hesitate to send a message. Heard via the grapevine you started a catering business. As I am having a small dinner party in two weeks, I would also like to hire your services. You were recommended by Mrs. Laughton, a delightful lady. While my cook is efficient, he is far from innovative.

Could I call on you in two days? Tuesday the twenty-six at say one o'clock. This is not a business call though we could talk some about what I would like as well as some of your ideas for an appropriate menu. This visit is for the sole purpose of meeting my granddaughter. Chandler announced her birth to me shortly after she was born. Maeve is a grand Irish name and I'm certain she is everything precious.

Please write to me to let me know if this time suits you. If not, perhaps we can come up with a different day which would be better for both of us. Looking forward to hearing from you.

Sincerely,

James Wolcott

"What is it?" Hollis asked as he focused on her. His gaze centering on the paper she was holding. After that, moved back to her eyes. He was holding a rattle in one hand and a doll in the other. Maeve was sitting on a blanket in front of her feet. "You look as if you've seen a ghost. What has Chandler done now?"

"Nothing. I feel as if a ghost…oh I don't know. Never expected to hear from Chandler's father. He wants to visit with Maeve. Don't understand his motives. Says the little ones are precious. Suppose he is speaking of Ash's child also."

"Will you allow him to see her? To come here?" Hollis appeared very concerned. He sat down on the floor next to Maeve then offered her the two toys.

The man was loyal to the depth of his soul. Hollis would always stand by her side, protect her from anything that threatened. She'd expected Chandler to show up here since he'd been knifed. He stayed away for two months. Maeve was almost eight months old now. She didn't know why he stayed from her mind as well as from the cottage.

What was Chandler up to?

Seemed she effectively blocked him from her head; either that or he wasn't trying to listen to her thoughts. He must not care about her any longer. If true, she got what she wanted. Was it? Needed Chandler to keep his distance if she was to remain sane as well as far from his bed.

"James disowned Chandler because of who he was. Chandler had always been a reprobate, skirting the right side of the law. The man must realize I was part of that decadent show his son created. Must understand I had sex with his son in front of an audience. He won't think I'm good enough for his granddaughter though there is nothing he can do about the small fact. I won't hand Maeve over to him or his son to raise. Maeve is a bastard as well as his grandson that I carry now." She paused thinking, trying to calm her breathing along with her racing heart. "He wants to hire me to cater a small dinner party in two weeks." She had misgivings about doing anything that involved James Wolcott. Decided she would reserve her decision of the job until she met with James.

Hollis ruffled the little girl's hair with one big hand. "That is nice. The senior Walcott wants to meet Maeve."

Her hand to her chest, she couldn't breathe. "Why?" Were there other motives he didn't explain? She could not be certain. She was afraid for herself as well as Maeve. "What am I going to do?"

"Write him back. I'll deliver the letter for you this afternoon. See if…" He paused, seeming to wrestle with words. "See if I can gain insights into ulterior motives. Tell him he may come for a short visit. You can always change your mind." Hollis tapped his chin. He always did that when he thought. "Write two letters. If I don't like the look of things, I'll give him one that says no to a visit. If he seems to be the nice gentleman I've heard about, I'll give the man the letter that says you'd love to meet him. Does that sound as if it might work?"

"You always know what to do. What would I do without you?" Georgia felt both relief as well as gratitude for her friend. He'd been with her since Chandler hired him to keep her safe. At that time, she had a lot of hopes as well as fears. She had no idea the depth of the depravity of Chandler Wolcott. When she entered Chandler's establishment, she knew real fear. Nonetheless, she needed to go through with her plan. For her there was no choice. Even with Maeve playing on the floor with Hollis along with another baby in her womb, she held no regrets. In this, their lives would go on and their future was saved.

A few minutes later, both letters were written. Hollis took off for the city to give James the appropriate letter. With Maeve in her arms, Georgia found Bea in the kitchen. Bea was experimenting with a new desert, lavender cakes, a special recipe. Sitting down at the table, Maeve in her highchair, she poured herself a cup of tea then helped herself to the desert. Handed Maeve a little sippy cup of juice. Maybe if she catered James small dinner party, she would serve these cakes.

"They're delicious," Georgia said with a mouthful. Between bites, she spoke, "This is perfection." Chewed, swallowed then sipped the hot tea still giving into her thoughts about meeting the grandfather. What would Chandler think of the pending visit? She couldn't be certain. She didn't want him to be in her head again. Was afraid if she reached out to him to ask, he would discover a way to get back inside her thoughts. He'd been absent for a very long time.

The long sigh she emitted startled her. Chandler had undoubtedly moved on to another woman. She didn't like the thought of her mate being with someone else even though she didn't intend to allow him into her bed. As she wasn't accommodating his desires, she could not complain.

"Heard you speaking with Hollis about James Wolcott. The older man is nothing like his firstborn. More like Ashton, his second son. They are both responsible and outstanding members of the ton. Believe you should let the man into your daughter's life. He will be good to her. Might be able to protect her from any plans of Chandler's as well as your unborn child."

Needed to be blunt with herself. State the situation as it was. "I'm a whore. How could a man who is titled want anything to do with a woman like me?"

Georgia didn't have regrets about the year she spent with Chandler. She did what needed to be done. Now, she would move on with her life continuing to do everything possible for Maeve. If James Wolcott wanted to be a part of Maeve's life, his doing so might be a good thing. Bea was right. James could help protect her children.

Maeve was a bastard. Her mother was a whore. She set her hand on her belly. Her son would also be a bastard. Would live with that stigma for his entire life. She couldn't allow Chandler to make them legitimate. If he legally gave them his name, he would own her children. Could make all the decisions concerning the two precious souls. She might not be able to stop him from carrying out his plans. Perhaps she did need the senior Wolcott to go to bat for her.

While she loved Chandler, she didn't trust the man. If either one of them was different, they might have been able to make a marriage work. As it stood now, she would never allow a child of hers to be brought up in a brothel.

"Now don't you be calling yourself names. You've only been with one man. To my knowledge, that's not the definition of a whore." Bea waggled her finger at her before shaking her head as if exasperated. She popped a lavender cake into her mouth. Rolled her eyes at the pleasure. "You had to be with him, convince the man to claim you... What you did for your future was right and tight. What's done is done." Bea looked startled by her heartfelt declaration. "Oh, my..." she wiped her hands on a dishtowel. "What have I done now?"

"You know about me? About Chandler? What we are?" Georgia wasn't certain what to think about the surprising revelation. She was both relieved as well as fearful. Knowledge in the wrong hands was dangerous. "You know I can shift? Change forms? Know Chandler can too?" She would never need to worry about Maeve practicing before bathtime. Didn't need to worry at all. She didn't believe Bea would betray her. No, Bea would understand what was going on. She would never condemn anyone as freaks. "Hollis?"

Bea lifted her shoulders in a half-shrug. Bit one more time into the cake she was holding. "Suppose as long as the cat is out of the bag, I can tell you everything. Hollis and I are both shifters. Your father hired me because he acknowledged the fact you would need protecting. Would need help from those who understood what would be going on with the little one. Hollis has been with your family, from what he tells me, forever. For what it's worth, most likely knows all your secrets. Even though Chandler hired him, your father made the arrangement without Chandler knowing."

With muffled thoughts she sipped on her tea. She set a piece of toast on Maeve's highchair. The toasted bread landed on the floor. "Mama! Toas!"

Concentration still in a muddle, she put it back on the table. Her mind drifted to Chandler. Wished her life could have taken on a different twist. It hadn't. She would deal with each day as it came.

There you are. Been listening to all your thoughts. Been hearing you talk to yourself for the last half hour. Believe I'll come see you when my father does. Haven't seen him for a long time. The visit might prove interesting. I've a legitimate business now. Though, Father wouldn't agree. I'm above the law. Nothing illegal goes on under my watchful eyes.

What do you care if your father visits Maeve? I assumed you were tired of me. You did tell me I acted like a shrew. You do realize you're not welcome in my home. Don't wish for you...just stay away!

I know. Bertram convinced me to give you some thinking distance. Also gave me more pointers on listening in on your thoughts when you try to block me. Been there for weeks. Just haven't chosen to speak to you. More fun to hear you wade through all your confusion. You just don't know how to come to terms with the way you feel about me.

No...no you haven't. You're lying.

Yes…and I'm not lying. It's just…you are delusional. One minute you want me the next you don't. Winter, you don't know whether you are coming or going. I want you to perform with me again. We can come up with a new name for you.

Georgia felt a blush heat her from her cheeks to her toes. Remembered all she'd been thinking about Chandler. Some good. Some not so good. He was right about everything he said. Right about her feelings being in shambles.

Thought you washed your hands of my shrewishness. Go away. Just go away. Leave us alone. It will be what is best for both of us.

Never. As I told you, I will come to you in two days. Want to meet with Father. Need to make certain he doesn't take something away from me that is mine. You are mine, Winter. Maeve is mine. The boy inside you is mine. I also like the fact you are jealous of my other ladies. All of these thoughts are important to me. You knew from the beginning, I'm not a one-woman man. Love diversion in all I do. All I have known. Will never change.

I don't wish for you to be here. It's not right of you to intrude on the visit. As for all your other women, I don't care a fig about any of them or you. Georgia heard his sigh of displeasure. Acknowledged the fact he would know what she said was untrue. She did care more than she wished.

Winter, you're my mate. My children will know me even if you want them to remain bastard's. My son will be part of my life, more so than Maeve. I'll make him legitimate even if you don't wish to marry me. Even if you protest my involvement. My son will not be a bastard! I've more wealth and power than you. However, the girl will remain a bastard. I will never acknowledge her unless you come back to me.

Georgia didn't want to show him the fear she felt at his words. Understood no matter how she protested, he would do as he pleased. He would take Colin, for that was the name she meant to give her baby, away from her. First, he would threaten her with the loss of her children. Chandler knew how important they were to her. Then he would tell her if she wished to marry him, she could have her child close by. She would need to live at the brothel. That would be the only way he would allow her to see her son. Chandler even told her Maeve would become a whore in his establishment at the age of thirteen if she didn't obey him.

Don't want our son following in your footsteps. Don't wish for him to have sex in front of an audience as you do. I will do everything in my power to stop this from happening. Everything. If necessary, I will elicit help. Your brother told me to come to him if I ever needed anything.

As his mother had sex in front of an audience. As his sister will do the same.

She hissed in a huge gulp of air. What could she say to the truth? *I see. No, I don't wish for him to follow in my footsteps either. I am away from the brothel, changing my life for the better. If he remains here, he will not see that seamier side of life you live in. I earn a decent living with my catering business. Pick my clients with care.*

I can ruin this so-called business of yours with a few well-placed comments. Money under the table. Suggestions about who you were. Did you know Douglas came to me? Told me what a fake upstart you were. Once a whore...always a whore, he told me. The arguments about our children will never change. Colin will be my son. I will make decisions about him, not you. He already speaks with me.

She caught air in the back of her throat. Having guessed as much she wasn't completely surprised by the revelation. That fact could be the reason why he was able to get inside her head with such ease. She never knew he'd been listening for the last couple of months. Never understood his duplicity.

Fine, come meet your father. I will write to him. Tell him you intend to come uninvited. He should have the choice as to whether or not he will encounter you in my home. By the way, he said he is bringing his butler, Smith-Jones. Do you know the man?

A thorn in my side. Always has been.

Ah, you are feeling a slight change of heart? With the butler's presence, this will not proceed with you in control I gather. How amusing. Is this Smith-Jones a formidable opponent? Ah, I suspect he has bested you more than one time.

Bite your tongue.

No, don't believe that would feel too good. You could bite yours instead. If you did so the deed would please me.

You should know better than to go in this direction you've charted. I would love to bite yours for you. Suck on it until you moan with the ecstasy

I gift you. There are other places on your delicious body to bite too. All would give me pleasure. Believe I'll stay the night then maybe the next. I'll sleep with you this time. Hold you in my arms. It's been too long. Has Maeve begun to play with shifting. She is almost eight-months-old. Would like to watch her turn into a tiny kitten.

Not yet though I'm certain she will soon.

I should speak with her too. I'll approach later tonight. Maybe when she's asleep, I'll surprise her. Need to see how much she is like her mother. Maybe when she's old enough she would enjoy being part of the entertainment in my modest establishment. I might not need to force her to my will. Never forced her mother. She might come along as a willing participant. Whoring might be in her blood. What do you think?

No...

Georgia found herself shaking her head, trying to put him outside her mind. He was right. She could not get rid of him. Her heart sunk. A few minutes ago, her life seemed to be on an upward climb. This was not what she hoped. Acknowledged the fact Chandler changed the game plans on a whim. She could take the children, run. He might not be able to find her. Too much was at stake if she ran from him. As things stood now, she had a tiny bit of power. Who knew what he would do if he couldn't find her or his children? He would overturn everyone's life.

"Has that wretched man been in your head again?" It was Bea talking to her, startling her from her thoughts. She should have paid more attention to Maeve and Bea. "He has no right. Just because he is the father of your children, doesn't give the man *carte blanche* with your babies. You cannot let him have his way."

"You knew."

"Yes...wish I could do something more for you. Wish you didn't feel the way you do about that horrible man."

"Nonetheless, he is my horrible man."

I heard that. Kind of like your new way of thinking. I do love debauchery. Scandals in life are all quite fun. They make everything titillating. Don't mind being atrocious. Do you realize how many wealthy men with titles participate in my nightly shows? Right now, all in the audience have a partner for the night. They can have sex with that partner anytime the mood hits. I miss you, Winter. My audience misses you. Nothing has been the same since you left me.

Summer Passion's new role is one of a nun. She doesn't appreciate the irony like you would. Would you like to play a nun? Dressed in a wimple. Nothing more except a tiny collar around your neck. Right now, that is who you are, a nun. Nothing pleasurable for you, my mate for life. I would change this horrid situation if you get down on your knees in front of me praying then beg. I'd let you pleasure me. Summer must get down on her knees. Pray to become a better person. While I have sex with her, she will scream out her pleasure. Don't you think that is a fine idea? The thought was Bertram's. My friend does have original ideas.

"'Olis…Olis!" Maeve clapped her hands together when she saw the big man enter the kitchen.

Georgia felt a moment of great relief upon seeing Hollis' grin. "The meeting went well? The smile tells me you like him. He will come?"

"James Wolcott is a very nice older man. He does have a few health issues that appear to have improved over the last year. Seems he had a stroke over a year ago. That was when he disowned his oldest son, Chandler. James needed someone in charge of the family businesses he could trust. Chandler wasn't the man for the job. He wants to hold all his grandchildren while he still can. James, he wants all of us to call him James. Smith-Jones is his butler, another very nice man. He is not just the butler but James' protector. They are both shifters. Yes, we had a nice visit."

Georgia felt the disappointment in Chandler to the tips of her toes. It wasn't the fact she coveted a title. She didn't. The problem was with her mate. With all her heart, she wished he was a better person. Wished she could live with the man instead of without him. Wished they could laugh as well as have fun together. Needed a good man by her side while they brought up their children. Chandler would be hearing her now, laughing at her thoughts, mocking her. Perhaps she did care more than she should.

She looked at the clock in the kitchen. No, right now, he would be playing with Summer Passion. Bertram would be dallying with Autumn Bounty. She didn't want to feel jealous of Summer or all his other women. She did. If he was listening to her, he wasn't taunting her with the information. No, he was in front of his audience, laughing and seducing

Summer. She knew he would always covet other women. Felt his betrayal to the tips of her toes. Shifters were not supposed to have sex with anyone but their mate. Chandler went against everything she understood to be true.

Again, she found herself in his head. Chandler let her in so she would understand he could not be swayed from his purpose. He was fondling Summer's breasts with his mouth. Jimmy along with Johnny joined him in the endeavor. Now he was deep inside her. Summer didn't like Chandler. Georgia felt Summer's emotions to the tips of her toes. Summer didn't want to be part of this script Bertram along with Chandler wrote. Didn't want to be paraded naked around the room or have sex with anyone in front of the audience. Didn't wish to be auctioned to the highest bidder for the rest of the evening.

Summer had been sold to Chandler, bought and paid for because of the needs of her younger siblings. Seemed Summer's father might sell his other girls for the same greedy purpose. Summer detested Chandler as much or more than she disliked Bertram.

Maybe she should help Summer get away from the brothel. No, her family still needed the money. There was nothing to be done for Summer. She still had at least several months left on this second contract. Georgia wasn't certain about the number of months. Chandler would hold her to her agreement just as he had with her. From a few discussions with Summer, her younger sister would be seventeen this year. The same age Summer was when her father sold her. She wondered what role she would give the young virgin.

"So, they are coming in two days. Less, more like a day and a half now that we are about to eat dinner then go to bed. We need to let James know the fact that Chandler told me he meant to be here when James arrived. Told me he would arrive a day early. He will be here Monday. Can you send someone with a message to James?" she was asking Hollis. "Chandler's father needs to learn about his son's intended intrusion."

"First thing in the morning," Hollis said. "I'm worried about you though. If Chandler is here, he will try to get to you. What will we do then? Doubt if he will care if you are sleeping in the nursery. The man hasn't been with you in months. He will crave you. Force you if necessary."

"I don't know."

Georgia lifted her shoulders, afraid about the upcoming visit. Chandler wouldn't force her. He wouldn't need to do so. Once he kissed her, caressed her, she would fall into whatever plans of his he'd made. She only had so much resistance inside her. "Would assume I just need to wait and see what course Chandler decides to take."

"I'm not liking this. Don't like this turn of events. Here in your own home, you should be safe from the likes of that horrible man."

"True enough. It's unfortunate. My worst enemy is me." The stiffness in her spine would be evident along with the stubborn tilt of her chin. She decided at that moment if Chandler tried to seduce her, she would play the Ice Queen to perfection. If she held back all emotions, she might be able to win the challenge Chandler would set forth. Giving into her love for the man along with all the raw passion he could create would not do. She needed to be strong.

~ * ~

Monday through Wednesday nights were always slower than the others. Sunday, most of the time was the busiest. Busier even than Friday along with Saturday night. Seemed the pious church goers loved to visit the brothel after they said their prayers at church or confessed to their sins. Their reasons made no difference to him. Loved the fact these good Samaritans paid him excellent money for their entertainment. In more ways than one, his shows were always pleasurable.

Two weeks ago, he and Bertram bought Summer's younger sister. She had two more sisters waiting in line to make their father rich. Thinking about the future brought his hands together. He rubbed them thinking of all the delight. He would have to designate a few more nights for special consideration. Jimmy needed a night all his own. Jimmy's delight held a nice ring to it. He'd run his new idea by Jimmy. Maybe the evening should be for Jamie's Delight. He wanted to initiate a night reserved just for virgins. Friday Night Virgin also had a nice sound. He and Bertram would need to go in search of virgins. Summer's little sister could be the first one.

All he needed to do now was bring Winter back into the fold. While he didn't know what to do with the second Winter Snow, he felt certain he would figure something out for the girl. He also thought he should make Summer's sister a star. He had players for all the seasons. They performed once a month. As he thought before, expanding would also be a possibility.

He'd think on his ideas.

At the moment he had better notions in his mind. Standing on the doorstep of Winter's cottage, he walked inside. He felt as if he should have the privilege. Should never be expected to knock. After all, Winter belonged to him. No one was in the entrance. As he strode through the home, he was struck by the quiet. Wondered if anyone was here. Bile rose in throat, thinking Winter betrayed him. She was no longer loyal to him.

Wondered where the bloody hell Winter went. He told her he would be here at three o'clock sharp today. He was here. Where was she? He was even five minutes late.

Chandler tried to breach the block in her head. Found it necessary to hear why she wasn't in the cottage to greet him. Winter was getting better at keeping him outside her mind. Realized he needed to work harder on that little bit of scheming. Needed to fix the error. If necessary, enlist Bertram for help.

Not that I need to answer to you, I'm shopping for the meal Bea will cook. Bea is with me as is Maeve. You should find Hollis somewhere in the cottage or on the grounds. Make yourself at home I'm certain you will.

You should be...

Chandler stopped the diatribe he was forming in his head. The words he was going to lash her with. Winter wasn't listening. She tuned him out. He didn't know how she was able to get rid of his thoughts with such ease. She hadn't been able to for a long time. Winter has Maeve. That was a dangerous thought. Winter might not plan to return until tomorrow when his father was due to visit. No, she said she was shopping for his dinner...with Bea...along with Maeve. She would arrive here soon. They would have dinner. He would have sex with her. What more could he wish for?

"There you are," Hollis stood beside him. Seemed to have appeared out of nowhere. "Should I show you to your room? It's the same one you always use. Surely you must know the general direction to walk."

"Did Winter lie to me?"

"Who?" Hollis's strides down the hall left him no choice except to follow.

Chandler needed answers. "Winter! You damn well know who!"

"Who?" Hollis continued on the same vein. Didn't seem he wished to let up. "Don't know anyone named Winter. Who is this lady to you?"

Fury commanded Chandler's words. "You know damn well who I'm talking about! Where is Winter Snow, my ice queen? Need to speak with her. She said she is shopping for dinner; the one Bea will cook. Where the devil is Winter? Tell me Hollis and don't play me for a fool."

"Believe her plan was to go to London today. She left early this morning with Smith-Jones. If she is shopping for a meal, it is not to prepare one for you. You do realize Georgia doesn't wish to have anything to do with you. You cannot command her to be where you wish. She is not and never will be your wife. You must come to grips with the notion you will never have her. You lost the chance by your less than stellar actions."

"I'll strangle her pretty white neck!"

Disobeying him was not acceptable. She needed to do what he commanded. Blast her lovely soft hide. He needed her right now. All his plans were thwarted. He wasn't going to stand for her disobedience. This would be the last time.

"I wouldn't try that ploy if I were you, Chandler." Hollis' voice was harsh so gruff it made Chandler have second thoughts. "If you touch one lovely hair on Winter's body, you will have me to contend with."

"Will you be more specific as to where my mate has hied herself off too? Would like to know so I can see to her well-being."

Chandler wasn't expecting an answer to his question. If Hollis told him where she was, he would go get her then drag her back by her hair if she refused to come along on her own.

"Believe I told you. But I'll repeat myself. Why," he paused for a blink. "She paid your father a visit this morning. He was agreeable to seeing them in his townhouse a day earlier than expected. Smith-Jones picked her up this morning. Believe the meal Bea and Georgia are shopping for is for your father along with his butler. They have a job to consider at his request."

"Bloody eyes!"

Unable to stop himself, he paced. The habit was his whenever he was frustrated or angry. Pacing helped him think. Pacing calmed his nerves.

"James says he's planning a dinner party in two weeks. Imagine they are trying out recipes." Hollis grinned at him, appearing pleased at his loss. "This visit is both business as well as pleasure."

"My father is having a dinner catered by Winter? He must be out of his mind. This could end up a disaster of enormous repercussions. A man of his position can never allow a whore into his home during a party. Who is he inviting?"

"You would ask the most obvious of questions. Your brother along with his beautiful wife, Harris. Seems her mother and father are visiting in two weeks. They all thought it would be fun to get together in London before they move on to Harris' home near Dover. Seems, Ash did like your mate. He thought she was a lovely person despite her circumstances. I do believe I heard that her three older brothers would also be in attendance. In case you have thoughts of crashing the dinner, best you get them out of your head."

Chandler reminded himself this gathering was still two weeks away from the present. He didn't intend to drive back to London this evening. He meant to spend the night here. Trying to reach out to Winter, he found himself once more stymied by Winter. He couldn't grasp her whereabouts. Damn, he needed to learn if she was alright. He didn't like her in London alone and unprotected. Didn't appreciate the fact he couldn't get to her in a matter of minutes.

Unprotected, hah! Smith-Jones would be her protection. The butler picked her up at the cottage. He would be with her shopping. The man wouldn't allow her out of his sight. Winter didn't mention that fact. She did lie. Left out pertinent information he should know. A lie of omission was just as bad in his opinion.

Once inside his room, Chandler set his valise on the floor. Looked out the picturesque window to the ground below. Set his forehead on the cold windowpane. The fact irked him that Winter could afford this large cottage. She was a woman. Should be dependent on him for her livelihood. Her catering business was doing well. He had the means to stop it cold. Could if he wished, humiliate her to the tips of her sweet and very tasty toes. His clientele would all fall in with his plans if he asked.

Why hadn't he done so? A headache brewing, he began to pace again. Tonight, he didn't intend to sit idle waiting for her generosity that wasn't to be. He needed release. Had expected release.

Because he never thought she could succeed, he didn't pay attention to her endeavors. She might be able to cook. What she couldn't do was run a successful business. Accounts needed to be taken care of. Money spent versus money received needed to be put in the proper place. What did Winter know of anything like that? Something like tallying numbers would take skill. Hell, he didn't know what extent her education entailed.

I'm very adept with numbers, Chandler. Suppose you didn't know that little fact about me. I have the ability to read a recipe as well as create new ones. Hope you enjoy your dinner. Hollis is an excellent cook when he doesn't burn the food.

Winter you are to return…

Frustrated beyond belief, Chandler threw his hands in the air. The little harlot, how dare she cut him out of her life! He wasn't finished talking to her. Damn her. This wasn't going at all the way he imagined and planned. He plotted to have her in his bed tonight. His mate wouldn't even be at home this evening. How the devil was he going to win this game of wills if she wasn't around to cooperate? Decided rather than risk dinner with Hollis he would go to a tavern in the little village. He could find a pretty little piece to enjoy the night with. Who knew, he might discover a new talent for his establishment…possibly a virgin he could use for Friday Night Virgin?

Deciding to look his gentlemanly best, he changed his clothes. Except for the white silk shirt coupled with an immaculately tied cravat, he was dressed all in black. When he studied his large, masculine frame in the mirror, he was pleased with the reflection. Let Winter get jealous again. What did he care? This evening, he would entertain a woman. He didn't need Winter in his bed. He could have sex with any woman he chose.

To enjoy the night out by himself was his intent. Didn't have Bertram with him to share whatever woman he picked out. It would be Bertram's loss. Tomorrow night after James along with Smith-Jones left the cottage, he would enjoy Winter just as he used to do. He would give her pleasure. She would scream his name when that heavenly pinnacle of no return was penetrated.

Feeling better about the outcome of this evening, he swept past Hollis. With a quick nod and a few curt words, he said, "I will see you in the morning. If I don't come back tonight, don't worry about me, not that you would. Just experiencing some of the local talent. Don't usually stay the entire night with the woman I choose for my entertainment. We shall see."

Chandler felt beyond eager to sample what this little village had to offer. On his way to Winter's cottage, he passed through the main street of the town. Saw a tavern that looked inviting, called The Devil's Own Place. The name of the tavern fit his mood. Chandler would find a woman to have tonight. He needed to comfort himself in a woman's warm soft flesh.

Inside he took a seat near one of the windows that faced the street. On the table one candle was lit. The Devil's Own Place was clean. The bar glistened with the lemon oil used to keep the counter clean. The ambiance was nice. A young girl with pretty blond hair came to take his order.

She smiled at him, the blue of her eyes twinkling with what appeared to be desire coupled with innocence. Her well shaped bosom rising then falling with each movement. "What can I get you?"

Her voice was soft, soothing, a bedroom voice if he ever heard one. He was pleased with the prospect of bedding this lady. He intended for her to be his tonight.

"An ale along with you would be nice."

Thought he would cut right to the chase. Working in this type of establishment, she would know what he suggested.

She blushed a pretty shade of rose then lowered her lashes, the gesture seductive. Brought an ache to his groin he didn't intend to deny. He wondered again if she understood the exact nature of his request. "An ale coming right up. Any food?"

Yes, he was hungry. Hungry for a woman along with food then a bottle of wine to savor with the sex. "What's the special tonight?"

He would have loved it if she said she was the featured girl of the evening. She couldn't be more than seventeen or eighteen. Her experience would not be much. Might even be a virgin. In that case, Chandler thought he should hunt in a different direction. Didn't think he was up for taking a virgin. Experience from a woman was up front in his plans. Fun coupled with pleasure was on his agenda. He needed to scorch Winter from his brain for the duration of the night.

"Fresh rainbow trout, caught just this afternoon by my big brother.

Baby potatoes that my mother grew in the back yard. A chocolate custard that is divine to the dining palate. Does anything appeal to you, Sir? We also have some potato soup coupled with fresh baked bread and cheese." When she smiled there was one tiny dimple at the corner of her mouth. "Sir? You are staring."

Yes, he was focused on that tiny indentation. Virgin or not, imagining kissing the dimple when she wore nothing at all had a certain appeal to him. Maybe she possessed other dimples needing to be kissed. "I'll have the rainbow trout. You also if you wish."

She cast him a sideways glance. "I'm not part of the menu."

"No, I suppose you are not."

His long sigh left him wondering if he'd lost his sensual appeal. This didn't usually happen. In his experience, women lusted after him. He was never rejected.

He wondered if she had an older sister. One who would understand all he wanted. They could have a threesome along with the trout. The thought appealed to him. Shared with Bertram, rarely with another lady or sisters. The idea intrigued. Another thought for his show.

Leaning back, the front legs of his chair off the floor, he saw another woman, older than the pretty blond. She too had blond hair, a bit darker than this young woman. Thought she might be a better candidate for what he needed to relieve his swelled member. His ale arrived via the little blond lass. He sipped while he stared across the tavern floor.

"Who is the lady…" He pointed in her direction. "She is older than you?" More years would be better.

"Oh, that's my sister. The whole family works here. Did you wish to meet her? Her name is Mackenzie." She stepped back from him, looking between him and her sister.

"What's your name?" while he asked, he was staring at Mackenzie.

Noticed all her curves. Her hips flared provocatively while her breasts were large enough to fill his hands. He did appreciate huge, soft jewels on a woman. Mackenzie's were not as abundant as Winter's. Close enough to take the place of what he was missing.

"I'm Mara." She curtsied. "The tips go to me," she blurted, catching her lower lip between her teeth.

"Of course. Any other sisters?"

Chandler held the feeling he would need to proceed with caution around these girls. Didn't wish to give away all his cards if they weren't receptive to his plans. Tonight, he meant to taste one or the other if not both.

Mara and Mackenzie have three older brothers. All are very possessive of their little sisters. Don't believe you'll get what you've planned. Might find yourself with a black eye or broken ribs if you get caught with your hand in the cookie jar or some other part of your anatomy where it wouldn't please the brothers. These honest, country folks don't take kindly to strange men deflowering their women.

Her laughter while she drew away from him again, irritated. Challenged him to defy Winter's warning. He could still try for one or both of the girls. Two women would undoubtedly please better than one. Blast her hide if she didn't annoy him. Over the years he'd learned to fight dirty. Knew a thing or two that could bring a man down to his knees. Would be nice to have Bertram by his side as backup or as a partner to delightful sex.

The meal arrived. The trout was delicious. Chandler kept his gaze focused on both girls attempting to decide which one would please him best. Watched as they served the other customers. Mackenzie waited on the other side of the room. Mara his side of the room. When she brought his bill for what he owed, he searched her pretty blue eyes to see if she might be receptive to an advance or more. They were brilliant, the dimple growing as she smiled at him. Mara bewitched all of him. Decided he needed to sample her. This girl would do for tonight.

Thinking about his sensual desires along with how best they could be served, his voice soft as well as beguiling. "Does your family rent rooms for the night?" he asked, hoping to get her alone in an upstairs bedroom where he could see if she was willing. In this case her willingness didn't make a bit of difference. His plotting was coming to fruition if her family did rent some of the upstairs rooms. "I'd be interested in seeing what you have to offer. I'm passing through going on to London. Don't wish to continue in the dark. You know the dangers. Highwaymen and such." He shrugged his shoulders, feigning indifference.

"We do. Would you like me to show you what we offer? I'd be pleased to let you look at what is available."

Bloody eyes, she was falling into his plans with ease. He wished to see what was available too. "Show me the best you've got to offer, sweetheart. I'd like to sleep in comfort this evening." His gain would be her loss. He had no doubts, she would keep him warm through the night once he introduced her to the pleasures of the flesh.

You're playing with fire, Chandler. You need to reconsider this ridiculous scheme of yours. If you don't you might come to regret the outcome of this evening.

This time he wasn't even going to try to answer. He sensed she'd tuned him out already. He supposed he should appreciate the warning. Might take heed if he wasn't hard as a rock. Believed the words came from her jealousy not her concern for his person. Didn't comprehend why she warned him.

"The best room?" She lifted her eyebrows as she was thinking about the rentals. Seemed she waited for a reply. "Very well, follow me. The best room in this house awaits your perusal." She stopped at the bar to explain her destination to a woman who was wiping down the countertop. The lady nodded, appearing to consent to the showing.

Walking behind Mara, he watched the gentle sway of her hips. The slender turn of her ankles when the gown she wore moved as she walked. Wished he could see if her breasts swayed when she took each step. They weren't large but they were noticeably curved in a memorable way. Thought about how the tips would taste when he suckled them…bit. A flash of lightening seared his groin, rocking him hard. He seemed to be swelling with all his carnal thoughts. Mara would please him, yes, she would be a pleasure to his male endowments. Would sooth his urgent need for her sultry heat.

She walked down the long hallway where lanterns lit the passage. Chandler thought they were now at the back of the tavern. The window in his room would look out at the grounds behind the building, not the street. The room would be quiet. The fact suited his strategies. He didn't want anyone to hear Mara's yells of excitement when her sweet body shattered in ecstasy.

"Do you have a room up here on this floor?" He noticed at least twelve doors as they walked down the corridor. "Which one?" Chandler would keep the location in his head for future reference.

"No, my sister and I live on the third floor. We quite enjoy the privacy the third floor provides. My brothers have their own places nearby. Mother and father live behind the tavern. After we each turned seventeen, our parents gave us a choice as to where we'd like to sleep. None of us are ever very far from each other. We all look after each other."

That was a nice fact to learn. Chandler stored the locations of her family away for future use. Mara pulled a key from the pocket of her apron. Unlocked the door then stepped inside the chamber. Holding the door open, she waited for him to enter.

His body tensed with excitement. The room was nice, large as well as airy. He heard the sound of the door closing behind him. Turned. Mara lit one of the lanterns on the bedside table, then another. She wound her fingers together in front of her.

"What do you think? This one has a nice view."

"Yes."

When Mara walked to the window, Chandler joined her. Wanted to see if the view would confirm his assumption. The scene before him was what he thought.

"This window looks out behind the tavern. The room is the quietest room in the tavern. The chamber is above a storage area so it gets no noise from below. You will sleep well. Everyone who has stayed here has complimented my family on the room. Just how quiet it is. What do you think? Is this chamber acceptable? If not, would you like to see another room?"

Chandler leaned against the wall near her, his ankles crossed in a negligent pose. He would enjoy his stay in the room. "Very nice." He studied Mara from her sparkling eyes to her small but well-rounded bosom, lingered on her hips then made their way back to her smiling mouth and the single dimple. Thought he could bring her pleasure and, no one would hear her screams of delight. "I'll take it." He walked back to the door. Turned the lock on the door. An interruption would never be appreciated. Tonight, neither were going anywhere except the big bed.

"Good." She stepped toward him, holding out the key. "Will I see you in the morning?"

"Without a doubt."

He was an agile man despite his size. In a flash of a second, Mara was in his arms. Jammed against the door. Chandler held her hands behind her back. Her sweet breasts pushed against his chest. His lips found hers, stroked with finesse. Bit with a light taste of the plumpness of the bottom lip. He swept his tongue across her mouth leaving moisture behind. The sip of his mouth was relentless.

"You shouldn't…Sir!" She wriggled then twisted. Mara bucked against him telling him how much she adored the pleasure he was giving her.

His tongue slipped inside her warmth. Tasted her sweetness. Needed more from her. He groaned with the pure sensual pleasure speeding through him. Exploring, tasting her pureness, learned of her inexperience. She didn't understand how to kiss or what he needed from her. Bloody eyes, she was magical, a virgin as well. Should offer her a position as an entertainer in his establishment. Wouldn't be a virgin. Bloody eyes, he didn't care. Needed her. Urgent to see her.

"I should like to have you naked. Should we take all your clothing off then lie down together on the bed?" He brought her hands above her head. Kissed her hard with the deep hungry yearning of his pressing need to possess this delightful creature.

Sweet enchanting sounds came from her. He didn't understand what she said. She pushed her breasts against his chest, certain indication she loved the attention he gave her. He spread her legs with his feet.

Against him she squirmed. As his sex would do the same in a different part of her sweetness, he thrust his tongue deep into her mouth. Penetrated then retreated. Entered into the warm sultry depth to explore. To keep her mouth where he wished it to be, he held her chin with one hand.

Leaving her mouth behind, his kisses trailed along her neck passed across her collarbone. With his teeth, he pulled at the string holding her bodice tight against her breasts. The fabric fell away, leaving her white cotton chemise still covering her beautiful treasures. The aroused tips of her breasts pushed against the fabric. If he didn't see her taunt buds soon, he would expire from desperate need.

"I want to see…all of you, sweetheart, all your lovely secrets. Don't wish for you to keep mysteries from me. You are too precious. Beautiful." With his teeth he tugged on one of the ribbons holding the fabric of her chemise together. Pressed his mouth in the valley between her breasts then pulled back to watch the unveiling. When the ribbons came loose of the eyelets, he moved back a step to see what he uncovered.

"No…I don't want this. Let me go…!" She wasn't screaming. Her voice was a thin wail of enjoyment. She wanted him as much as he needed to be deep inside her. Her words meant nothing.

"I'll give you pleasure. After we finish you will thank me. That pinnacle of splintering enchantment will be a delight to all your senses. You are a virgin?" He asked though he was positive he comprehended her answer.

No, she was panting hard. If she wished to scream out her pleasure, Chandler was positive from what she told him no one would hear. With the unveiling, her breasts danced with each breath of air she inhaled.

"I must taste every sweet inch of you." His mouth closed over the tip of her right breast. He sucked then laved. Heard her moan. Bit hard. She arched.

"No! Stop!" Her cry was one of a whisper. No one would hear. Chandler understood her soft protest was a yes.

Breathing hard, Chandler picked her up then settled her on the bed. He fell down on top of her. The weight of him covered her. One hand slid along her leg. Found the softness between her legs. Probed then slid his fingers between the folds. Found the small jewel of deliciousness. Mara would remember this evening forever. Chandler was pleased when she bucked against him. His sex swelled more. Harder. Burning with need. Her tiny hands hit against his back. She lurched upward. He imagined his rod deep inside the heat of her small body. Soon.

The crash of the door didn't stop him from exploring. He didn't have time to register the noise before he was ripped from Mara's deliciousness. Cool air caressed his aroused body. Chandler didn't realize what was happening. A heavy fist hit his jaw. He stumbled back. Light flashed behind his eyes. Saw Mara scrambling to cover herself. He registered the obvious cold hard facts. These three men must be her brothers. The same men Winter warned him about. Damn woman, the night was not going to end the way he imagined.

One of the three brothers swept Mara from the room. Held her tight against him, protecting her naked breasts from anyone's sight who they might encounter. "I'll be right back. Don't want the two of you to kill him before I get my chance at the bloody sod. Must take some of my anger out on the bastard."

I warned you. You didn't listen. Too bad. Sometimes you are too arrogant for your own good. These men will beat you to a pulp for what you did to their little sister. Since you didn't yet violate her, the men might allow you to live. Think on that.

The bitch will pay!

The second brother pummeled his ribs while the other held him. After Chandler could no longer stand, the two men switched places. The beating continued to his ribs, his face, back to his stomach until bile burned in the pit of his throat. He heard himself moan.

"We're not done with you. Not by a long shot," one of the brothers said. "By the time we're finished, you will wish you were dead."

"My turn." The third man was in the room. "Let me at the bastard. He hurt Mara. Thank God we got here before he raped her. Though what he did to her under protest, yells of force. She fought him with what little strength she possessed."

"You were going to rape our little sister," he snarled. "We don't take kindly to men the likes of you. No we don't. If you succeeded, you would be a dead man. Now, you'll just be a dead man walking. When we are done, weeks will pass before you can move any part of you again."

He sagged against the man holding him. His legs could not bear his weight. At this moment, he did wish he was dead. No, he wouldn't die until he got his revenge against these three brutes. He could have held his own in a fair fight. By the time he was finished with Mara, they would regret beating him until he couldn't stand. Didn't think to shift until he couldn't. Vowed, Mara would be his for the rest of her life. His eyes were swollen to the point where he could see a dim outline of the men hitting him. Still the beating continued.

Chandler closed his eyes. The world turned black. There was no light he could see. What he remembered before nothing clouded his brain, was that every part of him was in pain.

When he opened his eyes, the sun was beginning to turn the outline of the hills a soft shade of rose coupled with amber. Chandler closed his eyes. When he opened them again, the sun was too bright. Pain roared in his head. He groaned. Slid into oblivion. Darkness surrounded him. He didn't know how much time passed when he was awakened by water falling on him. Rain sluiced from the skies soaking him through to his skin. His shivers made him colder than the ice in his Ice Queen. Wind tore at him as he staggered to his feet. Unable to stand, he crumpled to the ground. Passed out. By the time he opened his eyes this next time the sun was higher in the sky. Didn't want the brothers to come for him again. He needed to get the hell away from here. Should have heeded Winter's advice.

Understanding the need to leave the premises before they beat him again, he gave another valiant effort to stand. Found the wall of a building to prop himself against. Staggered for how long, he had no idea. Must have been where they dumped him. All of them would pay. The little bitch would disappear from their lives to become an intricate part of his entertainers. She'd be deflowered as well as used by multiple men before they caught up with her. Mara would never be the same sweet innocent again. He would see to her demise. Needed revenge for the wrongs done to him.

At the brothel, he'd be untouchable. His bodyguards would surround him. For the moment though, he had to get himself back to the cottage. Hollis would tend to him. He found the hack he drove here. After several aborted tries, managed to hitch the horse to it. Succeeded to climb onto the seat.

When the cottage came into sight, Chandler drew in a deep breath of relief. Falling from the hack he made a painful effort to reach the front door. Unable to walk, Chandler crawled forward. Hollis opened the door as if he anticipated his arrival.

It hurt too much to speak. Knew there would be no sympathy coming from the big man. Also understood the man would help him because for no other reason, he was Winter's mate.

"Well, well, well, what did you do to bring this on? I can imagine you must have attempted to seduce a tender maid. See your efforts didn't pan out the way you anticipated." The man's smug look of amusement infuriated him. His eyes laughed at him. "Do you need help getting to your bed chamber? Of course, you do. Lean on me. I'll take you there. I believe Georgia realizes what happened. Doubt if you have sympathy coming from her. Even though she will most likely be here to tend to your shortcomings."

With concentrated effort, panting as well as sweating, he was lying on the bed with his swollen eyes closed. He needed to get rid of his sodden clothing. Didn't have the energy to move. Tried to suck air into his lungs. Every breath hurt the broken ribs.

Serves you right!

You could at least feel sorry for me.

I feel so sorry for you, I'm going to allow Hollis to look after you rather than see to you myself. I did warn you. Hollis does have a tender hand where you are concerned. You did hire him even though his loyalty belongs to me.

Winter vanished from his thoughts. He couldn't seem to hang onto her. Hollis stripped him of his clothing. He was naked, lying on the bed. Vulnerable as well as cold. Defenseless as a newborn babe. Chandler didn't like being so powerless. It was not in his nature. He didn't have a choice. He needed Bertram.

"Must see the damage to your ribs." Hollis muttered with a slight sneer in his voice while he tested the ribs. Ran his hand along each one until he seemed satisfied with his diagnosis. "Two are broken. The rest are bruised. You have two black eyes that will turn startling colors soon. Your lips are swollen with cuts that are still bleeding. As to your nose, why it is not broken is beyond me. Who did this to you?"

"Her three brothers," Chandler managed to grit out.

His tongue was swollen. Felt as if it stuck to the top of his mouth. He needed water.

"Who?"

"Mara's," he got out despite the pain. Despite the fact he didn't wish to speak to Hollis. What he wanted was to strangle the girl. Damn bitch!

"You deserve everything they did and more. The lass is too young for the likes of you. She's an innocent. Did you force her? If they find out you did, those brothers will kill you. There is not a doubt in my mind. They protect their family." Hollis showed no tenderness while he cleaned his face along with his ribs of the dried blood. "If you can sit, I'll bandage your ribs."

"Believe I'm going to die."

"Dying would be too easy for you. You're going to live with the pain."

~ * ~

"We are about there," Smith-Jones said to James as their carriage rolled around another corner. They passed through the village about five minutes earlier. "I understand you are worried about your mate. Don't be worried about Chandler. He is a cat with nine lives. I'm certain Hollis took good care of the bleeding sod. From all you told us, he deserved what was doled out to him in payment for his treatment of their sister."

"I'm not worried about him. I'm furious. You're right about the number of lives he has," Georgia shot back while tapping her fingers on the window of the carriage. "The man...damn him! He was going to have sex with that little girl! How dare he? Even though the man has no morals, I love him. Try not to even care about him. He meant to make me jealous, so I would do things his way. I won't."

James set his hand on her arm. "Calm yourself. You can take all your fury out on my son in a few minutes. At least you don't have to worry about Chandler sneaking into your bedroom tonight. He won't be able to force you to his way," James told her with his smug satisfied tone. After a few seconds, he wondered more about her feelings. "What are you thinking? You're not going to forgive the bastard. Are you? Even though he is my son and I wish I felt different, Chandler doesn't deserve a pardon."

"Won't ever forgive him. This time Chandler has taken his never-ending quest for sex too far to forgive. No, he wouldn't force me. Wouldn't need to. When he caresses me, I melt like warm honey all over him."

"You realize, I am thinking you are an absolute delight to all my senses. You have proven you are a strong woman. A good mother for my granddaughter. Hollis told me the child you carry now is a boy. With your guidance, the lad will grow up strong, not like his father. I spoiled Chandler which is the crux of my son's problem. Gave him everything he ever asked for. Taught him he didn't need to work to get what he wished. You my dear are making him work. Maybe the fact will build character. Who knows? Building his character could be too late."

"He doesn't want me, not really," Georgia muttered with a whispered voice. "He loves the sex. That's all I am to him, a vessel for his use. He might have learned how to shift but he still doesn't understand shifters. In spirit as well as mind the man is no shifter."

Smith-Jones lifted a heavy dark brow while directing his question at James. "You certain about what you said? Even with your protection, Chandler can still get to the baby once he is born. Teach him…teach him to be the way he wants him to be. Chandler will be able to mold the child to his whim. Even if he wishes, he wouldn't dare take the boy away from his mother. Raise him in the brothel. What the hell kind of life would that be?"

"He can. Chandler is much stronger than I am. I'm frightened of his power. Don't intend to admit my fears to him. He has told me he will take the boy as soon as possible. Told me he wishes to mold his son to his father's ways. He's told me many times since he learned this child of his was a boy."

"Georgia is correct. My son, who is no longer my son, won't wish to have the lad grow up with our values. I understand this truth better than anyone. For so many years, I overlooked Chandler's proclivities as well as made excuses for him. I spoiled him with whatever he wanted believing he would be my heir."

James repeated his earlier statement knowing he was at fault in Chandler's upbringing. Wishing he could rectify his mistakes.

Smith-Jones cleared his throat then looking at Chandler's mate then back to James. "As long as Georgia insists on living in the country, there is little to do for her by means of protection. She should return to London and live with us. I can safeguard her along with her children just as I protected you when you were as weak as a newborn kitten. I did speak with her father, Cormack O'brien. He told me both Hollis, the man who brought the message to us, as well as Bea, the nanny, are shifters. That fact will help defend your children against Chandler's whims. If she stays in the country, who will protect Georgia? That's my first question. O'brien said Chandler isn't pleased with the fact Georgia walked out on him. He means to get her back by any means possible. If what he has in mind. involves snagging the children, I would never be surprised."

"My son has always needed to have his way. Doesn't much like to lose what he wants or considers his. It's obvious he desires Georgia. He won't stop until he has her back. He's confident and always ruthless. Chandler is a dangerous man."

"I can protect myself," Georgia said, her voice soft. "Even if I fail a time or two, he won't get what he wants from me. In the end, he wants me to marry him so he will have complete control over me as well as our children. I'm not going to let him control my every action. To me, after what occurred last night, it's obvious he won't ever change from this course of debauchery he is set on. Even though I'm his mate, there will be countless women in his bed. I'm thankful Mara's brothers got to her in time."

"Who do you think Maeve looks like," Smith-Jones asked as if searching for a change of subject. His gaze focused on the baby in James' arms. "I for one believe she looks just like her beautiful mother. She has her deep black hair as well as her sparkling blue eyes alight with deviltry." He looked at Georgia, winked, "Georgia is an incredible beauty."

"True, Chandler would never pursue a woman who was not beautiful. Even the servants in our home who he seduced are beautiful women," James said as he turned his attention to the scene outside.

The day was windy. There would be rain later on if the dark clouds hovering above the hills were an indication. Last night a veritable tempest ripped through the town as well as the countryside. Chandler had lain in the open while the rain and wind lashed at him. His body must have been chilled to the bone. He would be lucky if he didn't get sick from the results of his failed deflowering of the innocent lass.

"There might also be turmoil in the cottage. Since Chandler did arrive yesterday and was attacked for his hideous behavior. Who knows what the ambiance would be like. Could be brutal," Smith-Jones said. "Could be as stormy inside as this threat of a tempest we are driving into."

"For the time being, Chandler will not be able to leave his bed. In his state, he cannot create havoc when he cannot move without pain. Bertram will need to take him home. He will linger under heavy doses of laudanum. Sleeping is what he will need to heal."

"Chandler's friend must be told of his condition along with his needs," Georgia said, her hand fluttering in the air for a beat as if she wasn't certain. "I know Bertram will come for him as soon as he hears the news."

"I sent a message to Bertram before we left. The man could be at the cottage before us," Smith-Jones remarked. "Wouldn't be surprised."

"Could be true...all our assumptions could be accurate. This man, for one, is looking forward to the tempest. Need some small excitement in my life." James looked to Georgia as if seeking the truth. "Georgia, you will not succumb to my son's blustering. I won't allow you to give in to his demands. Will you, my dear?"

"No, in certain circles, I'm known as the Ice Queen. I can be frigid if the moment warrants. Chandler won't like the chill. Won't wish to have sex with a woman who refuses to respond to his ardent endeavors. He will swear, curse me to the devil but he won't want to touch a cold woman."

"I understand you love him. If it's true, that fact makes you too vulnerable to Chandler's easy ways. You will have little power to gainsay him even if you can maintain an icy facade." Smith-Jones sat back, tapping his fingers on his hard belly. "Is Ash willing to help guard this small family? She could spend some time in Dover."

"If need be. Believe both Harris and Ash like her."

"Ash told me to come to him if I ever needed help. However, I don't wish to live in Dover. I have my life here…a life just beginning."

Chapter Four

At Winter's insistence, Bertram brought him back to the brothel the next day. From all the rain the roads were wet, untidy. Even with the well-sprung carriage he could not keep from jerking with each turn of the wheel. With his broken ribs, the drive to London was the most painful of his life. He cursed Mara along with her brothers for his circumstances. He wanted to strangle her white neck. As soon as he healed, he'd be back to The Devil's Own Place to orchestrate his revenge. The foursome would regret their rash behavior. Mara would be his to do with whatever he pleased.

After Bertram helped him to undress then settle under the covers, he called for Celine. At least the woman possessed a tender touch. Hollis never cared if he complained. He remembered the first time he had sex with Celine as well as the first time he shared her with Bertram. They'd moved on from that point. All of them were rich. Chandler was good to his employees. After all, he now had more money than he could spend in a lifetime. With each new show, the coins poured into his coffers as if the sky rained money every day of the week. He could afford to be generous with his friends as well as his coveted cast of characters. Chandler wanted all to prosper.

The coloring over his upper torso and face became vivid greens, yellows along with other shades of blues and purples. He looked a sight. Felt worse. His entire body ached with every breath, each tiny movement. He couldn't turn over without cringing. Opening his eyes was a painful experience. Eating was unpleasant but necessary.

In the evenings, Celine read to him when she wasn't performing. There were enough actors in his small group so she wasn't on stage every night. The days were much more enjoyable than the nights when he was left alone. Sometimes the ladies would alternate sitting beside his bed when they weren't on stage. It wasn't the same as participating. Not as exciting. The second Winter Snow was with him as much or more than Celine, seeming to feel sorry for him.

Chandler plotted with Celine, telling the woman what he wished to have done to Mara. How they would go about kidnapping her from the tavern. There would be a day of reckoning for the chit. After he took her virginity, Bertram could have her then both Jimmy along with his twin, Johnny could enjoy her seductive charms. After they all sated themselves with her, any man who wished to pay for an evening with her could do so. She would be given as a gift to his audience the night Summer Passion performed. Every man and woman who wanted a turn at her would have the opportunity. The auction that evening wouldn't be held until everyone in attendance was finished with Mara. The girl would be a broken shell.

Thinking about the evening to come brought a sigh of contentment to his lips. Even with the pain bombarding him, he was able to smile. His imaginings for Mara overshadowed what occurred at the tavern. Yes, he'd been overconfident, stupid too. In hindsight, he should not have ignored Winter's warning. The past no longer made a difference. The future would matter. Mara would have no choice in what her prospects would hold. He would never allow her to use protection. She would find herself heavy with child within the month. Would never know who the father was.

Chandler understood her brothers would find her. By then Mara's discovery would be too late to save her virtue. After she was used by so many different men, no upstanding gentleman would want to have her for a wife. Mara would be his to use anyway he wished for the first year of the contract he would see her sign. The second year then the third until she was so depleted, she wasn't good to anyone. The bitch would be his into eternity. His until she passed on to another life. She would pay tenfold for what her brother's did to him. Crossing his hands over his chest, he closed his eyes, relaxing. Enjoying his thoughts about Mara's comeuppance. He recalled the taste of her breasts. The way her mouth fit snug against his. He would savor the moments with her before he gave her to Jimmy.

He learned the brother's names, Michael, Morgan, then Mathew was the youngest. The smile on his face hurt all the way to his eyebrows. Still, he would allow his bodyguards to give back to the brothers everything he received plus even more. They would be in more pain than they could ever imagine. Every rib would be broken. Kneecaps shattered along with all ten fingers. The brothers would have to plead for him to cease the beating. If they fainted from the pain, the beating would cease until they woke. He would stand over them smiling from ear to ear. Mara would be with him to witness the assault on her brothers.

The payback for what the men did to him would be sweet indeed.

As the days passed, he grew strong as well as more determined on his path of vengeance...an eye for an eye was his constant recital. He was impatient to bring his plans to fruition. He and Celine, coupled with Bertram, plotted the scenario. Jimmy and Johnny tossed their thoughts into the mix. All asked to be part of the raid on the tavern. The plan was cemented. After the passage of two weeks, he was ready to endure the drive to the little village. Rubbing his hands together he imagined the next few hours. Soon Mara would be at his feet and in his control. Her life as she knew it would end the day he brought her into the fold.

He wasn't going to participate in the foray. Would never show his face in the tavern. However, he would be there when Mara was bound hand and foot then tossed into his waiting carriage. He needed to see terror in her vibrant blue eyes. Eyes that would no longer be animated with joy. Needed to see the blue dim until they were a shadow. Acknowledged the fact she would shake with terror. The thought pleased him. He relished the idea of her fragility. Would capitalize on her weakness.

The three carriages stopped in front of the tavern. The afternoon threatened more rain than the morning. What the weather did or did not do had no bearing on the next few hours. They wished to be away from this place before the downpour began. His entourage which included the twins and Bertram, along with Celine and Sasha entered the tavern with lively chatter. Their entry was all he saw. When he closed his eyes, he imagined their plans unfolding with perfect precision to each minute detail. In a matter of minutes, Mara would be his. His body jumped to life while his breath quickened with anticipation. Chandler remembered the taste of her delicious breasts, the tips so hard with her arousal. This time he wouldn't go easy on her. She would need to learn the duties of a whore. He could be gentle as well as rough. Whatever mood suited him.

They planned the abduction down to perfection. Nothing would go wrong. Each member of his cast had a significant part to play. They were all magnificent actors. He was disappointed he wouldn't be able to watch this production come to the proper conclusion. Given the first opportunity, Bertram would fill him in with all that transpired. Celine would add new particulars. Jimmy would elaborate on the characters.

Minutes ticked by with the slowness of a slug. He twiddled his thumbs while he waited. Whistled a licentious ditty he heard on the street below the brothel one afternoon. Set his head on the backseat with closed eyes. Counted each breath entering his body. Several times, he held his breath when he caught movement from the tavern. After what seemed an eternity, Celine glided around the corner of the building arm and arm with Mara. The girl stumbled. Celine caught her, held her up. Appeared to speak to her in a whisper. Mara leaned against Celine, her head lolling. Good, she was drugged. He would keep her drugged for as long as necessary. Not impaired so much she couldn't walk or talk but enough to make her a bit more compliant.

The girl, Mara, was beautiful. Even before she filled out to a woman's body, she would bring top dollar at auction. He might gift her with a room all her own on the third floor. Some men preferred younger maids. That's how he would present her. Mara seemed to struggle against Celine who held tight. With startling speed, coming from behind the two women, Bertram grabbed her. Wrestled with her until he rolled her in a blanket to toss her over his shoulder. Chandler heard a shriek before the fabric closed around her head. Bertram rushed with his victim to the waiting carriage, Celine close behind Bertram. Chandler knew the others would follow quick on his heels. There were three carriages that would take them all away from danger. They needed to move fast. As soon as anyone noticed her missing, the brothers would be right behind. Chandler didn't want the three men to know who kidnapped their sister too soon. In a few months, once she was pregnant with some man's brat, he might send a message. By that time, he would own her for at least five years.

Tossed into the vehicle, Mara lay at his feet. She struggled to rid herself of the blanket she was encased within. Chandler tugged on the blanket. Mara unrolled. She sat up spitting mad, her eyes blazing fire. Bertram launched himself inside the carriage after he helped Celine climb in beside him. With a tap on the roof, the carriage raced away. Stunned, Mara sat up pushing her long golden hair from her eyes. Groped to keep from falling at the lurch of the carriage.

Realized her abductor. "No! What are you doing? You can't just take me. My brothers will kill you. Count on that fact!"

Her shoulders shook with rage or fear. Chandler didn't care. He had her now. She was his forever. He would never allow her to leave his dominion.

"Oh, yes," he grinned, looking down on her. Saw the rapid rise and fall of her beautiful bosom. Enjoyed her terror…the fear clouding her eyes. "You didn't think I'd let your family get away with what they did to me. Did you?"

He felt incredulous at the idea that was just what she believed. Chandler paused, studying the girl struggling on the floor. "Ah, I see you never gave my condition a second thought."

His grin was wide, amused by her look of desperation. He leaned forward, almost nose to nose with her. He tasted her terror. Witnessed the horror in her eyes. "Mara, you are mine now to do whatever pleases me. Don't ever forget the tiny truth. Your time with me as your owner will go easier for you if you remember I own you. You will be my plaything…toy for my every whim. If you obey me, as I said, life will go much smoother." Chandler felt the first twinge of vindication. Mara was just as beautiful as he remembered. More so with the terror in her eyes. "Your family won't find you until you are ruined. Until you've been used by more men than you can recall or count on both hands as well as your feet."

Wide eyed, desolate with fright, in a last-minute dash for freedom, Mara scrambled for the door, her fingers closing around the handle. Bertram caught her around her waist before she could escape. He hauled her back to sit on his lap, his arms beneath her breasts, pushing them up, exposing the rounded tops for his inspection. The move was calculated. He cupped one protruding globe with his hand, fondled the softness while she struggled against his possession. Her movements brought her bodice lower. The rose tips revealed. She shrieked. Yelled at the top of her lungs.

Chandler witnessed enough for the time being. Found he was exhausted by the day's events. Had not yet fully recovered from the beating. There would be more fun when she was tucked away inside his rooms. "Tie her. Bind her tight then put a gag in her mouth. Don't wish to hear her cries of abuse on the way to London. Don't wish to hear her shrieks of outrage. Need peace along with quiet to think." He leaned forward, his forearms on his thighs. Smiled at her even though the grin still hurt. "You are well and truly caught, my dear. Do you want to learn what is going to happen next? No? I'll let you worry, fret over all the possibilities. What we do with the tenderness of your young body will be a surprise. Relax now, there is nothing you can say or do that will change your fate. I love revelations or perhaps shock would be the right word. Your imagination won't come close to the things awaiting you at my brothel. Yes, my whorehouse." He watched her horror twist deep inside. Her back stiffened. Realized she wasn't going to cower. Adored the fact her chin went up in defiance.

She was shaking her small head, her eyes wide while she pushed against Bertram's arms surrounding her. Tried to pull his hand away from her breast. His fingers squeezed the soft flesh until she let out a soft whimper of pain. Her corsage dipped lower. Bertram brought the fabric to her waist.

"Instead of finding yourself tied and gagged, would you like to sit on my lap? I could begin to introduce you to your new duties. You will be… Leave her the way she is. I enjoy looking at her beautiful white jewels sway with the movement of the carriage." No, Chandler changed his mind again. Making her wait and worry was what she deserved. What he wished for was more suffering. She was a damn woman. Worthless except for one use. To his surprise he wasn't in a hurry to sample what her body offered. He blamed Winter for his unusual feelings. After Winter left him, he was insatiable with his need. Had sex with every available woman.

Shortly, Mara would find out what her use was to become. Her family could no longer coddle the baby sister, a baby no longer. Once she caught his eye, Chandler understood one night with her would have never been enough. Now, weeks later he no longer cared if he had her. If he plowed through her virgin's shield, he didn't care as long as Mara was broken. Mara would need a new name. He was glad Bertram was going to gag her. She would be spitting mad if she was left free. Would curse him with words as she was doing now with her eyes.

The next few minutes were spent securing Mara, binding her hand and foot then tightening the gag. She was naked to her waist. The bodice torn in half. Bertram continued to hold her, fondle her beautiful jewels. Held her breasts in his hands. Passed his palm across the hard crests. Nothing more.

Chandler found he was exhausted from the trials of the day. He was still frail from the beating weeks ago. Closing his eyes, Chandler listened to the carriage sounds coupled with those of the night. He heard the labor of Mara's frenzied breathing. Knew she struggled to no avail. Felt her fear penetrate from her small body. He tasted her horror. When they reached the brothel, Bertram hefted her over his shoulder, her butt in the air. His hand beneath her dress, fondling the warm silken flesh.

"Where do you want her?" Bertram asked, the smile forming on his face gave pleasure to Chandler.

If he didn't want her for himself, he'd let his friend have her right now. There was no question as to the fact. When the plan was first formulated, he intended to be her first. At the time, he relished the thought of breaking through her virginity then hear the following cry of pain. For her initiation to sex, he never intended to give her pleasure. He shrugged his shoulders uncertain. Where he wished for her to be placed, Chandler tapped his finger to his chin.

He needed to think about this for a few beats. While he would have her first, he thought Jimmy deserved a personal female slave. A woman who would be special to him and to him alone. Cater to his every whim. His loyalty would be rewarded with the possession of this girl. Yes, Jimmy earned her. Mara would belong to Jimmy through eternity or for as long as Jimmy wished. He did have Winter. His first Winter would be back with him shortly after his boy was born. He had only a month to wait for her return. Chandler hated admitting he needed the original Winter with him. Was lost, no sense of direction without her.

Jamie's Delight. Yes, Mara would become Jamie's Delight. Her new name would be Delight. He would introduce her as Miss Delight. He'd been looking to have two new special nights a month. Jamie and Miss Delight would be the primary actors one week each month. He would need to think on the role he wished for them to play. Jimmy might have a few ideas about how he would like to present his special partner. Chandler thought his idea a dandy one…a delight to his senses.

"Take her to Jimmy. Tell him to teach her what she needs to know about my establishment. He mustn't take her though, not until I break through her maiden head." Again, he had different thoughts about this unfolding scenario. Why should he take her first if he no longer cared. Why, if Delight was for Jamie. "That pleasure was to be mine and mine alone for what her brothers did to me. Otherwise, he can do whatever he feels appropriate. Maybe he could find a means to abduct the older sister." Chandler paused. "No, I've changed my mind again. Want her to stay with me for the next few hours. Jimmy is too soft-hearted. He will coddle her. Would work to take away her fears."

Against Bertram's shoulders, Mara struggled. Through the tight gag made small noises of distress. She tried to wriggle from his shoulder. The sight amused Chandler. Delight could battle all she wanted. She wasn't going anywhere except to his suite of rooms.

"I'll take her to your rooms. Should I untie her?"

His smile of pleasure widened. "No. Miss Delight can stay the way she is for now. I'll do the honor when I feel the time is right. Leave her on the floor in front of the fire. Don't want her chilled."

Chandler watched Bertram with Mara slung over his shoulder, her breasts still exposed, walking up the long winding stairs to the second-floor room. She was struggling so hard Bertram hit her small butt then held her still with his hand on her rear. He was going to leave her to stew for the time it took him to speak with Jimmy, to set the wheels in motion for the new play he orchestrated in his head. He believed Jimmy would be pleased with the girl. Jimmy would control her. After he took her virginity, Mara would remain with Jimmy until she was ready for the shows she would act in with her new lover.

As anticipated, the other two carriages arrived. Jimmy walked through the door, looking pleased. Saw Mara struggling on Bertram's shoulder. Chandler heard the tiny gasp of air from the lad when she pushed off Bertram's back. At first sight, there was an unusual look on his face. Chandler felt a moment's unease. What the devil was happening?

"Jimmy, want to speak with you about the girl, Miss Delight is her given name. Can we go to your rooms?" Chandler was eager to put this next act into motion. Excitement for the new attraction heated his blood.

"About the girl?" Jimmy questioned, appearing intrigued by the words. "I'd be interested to learn your plans. She is a beauty. Young but she will ripen within the year. Heard she was seventeen. Though," he paused, tapped a finger on his chin. "I feel as if I've been looking for this adorable creature all my adult life. I saw her face before Bertram tossed her in the carriage. Just now observed the wiggling of her delicious butt. Found myself aroused both times. She means something to me I don't understand." He walked side by side with Chandler.

"Seventeen, yes. Miss Delight is her new name, supposed I'd reward your year and a half of loyalty to me. Thought after I take her first, I would give her to you. She would be your special plaything, a bauble to fondle whenever the mood struck. You can have a special night once a month with Miss Delight. Thought to call the night, Jamie's Delight. What do you think? Would you enjoy having Miss Delight all your own?" Chandler enjoyed the grin on Jimmy's handsome face. Realized Jamie was eager. The man was not hard to look at. Delight should appreciate his man's body once she understood the pleasure she could derive from the association.

"I'm honored," Jimmy said, his hand to his chest then a small bow of respect. "When can I meet Miss Delight? Would like to ease the way somewhat for her. She will have fears. Mean to help her through the difficult times. You do realize Delight won't sign the contracts if given a choice. What are your plans?"

"Laudanum."

"Dosed." Jamie focused on the stairs. Bertram and Delight were no longer in view. "Imagine medications will be the only way. Might have to keep her a bit medicated for the first few months during productions. She will know what is happening but will be unable to protest or fight what I do with her sweetness. In time she will come to accept her position as my sex slave."

"You can meet her this evening. Want her to feel real terror for a few hours. She needs to realize there are no options for her except to go along with your plans. Her brothers don't know where she is now. They won't come to her rescue. Whatever your strategies might be, she will need to comply. Complaisance will aid her. What do you say? Tonight, after the show?"

"Would love to meet her this evening. What script do you wish for our performance? I would like to meet her first. Might have a few ideas to share." Jamie beamed his pleasure. "I'm looking forward to meeting Miss Delight."

Jimmy's reaction to the new girl pleased Chandler. "We can hash over a few different scenarios. Reenacting her abduction is a possibility at least for the first show. If the performance is a hit, we can continue with the same script until you become bored. Since I wasn't inside while she was abducted, I would need all the particulars. Might turn into a lively show with lots of participation from the audience."

"What time tonight? There is the show. I've a small part. Tonight is Johnny's night. Since I'm his twin, I'm usually by his side." Seemed Jimmy, now to be known as James or Jamie, was very eager to begin his acquaintance with Delight. "You do understand Johnny also deserves a special lady unique to him. Perhaps we can discover another beautiful creature for his viewing pleasure. We could call her Miss Desire. Johnathan's Desire."

"Perfect." Chandler slapped Jimmy on the back. "Do love your idea. Johnathan's Desire. Couldn't have thought of anything better. Another special night of decadence. I'll spill the idea by Johnny. He can begin to look for the perfect lady. I'll explain to him, she should be young. Another seventeen-year-old or eighteen-year-old, no older. I would accept a girl who was only sixteen if she has the needed attributes.

"Ah, yes, I've been laid up for so long, I've almost forgotten about the performances. During the show, I'll take her to the viewing room. Show her, her new protector. Watching what goes on in the theatre should give Miss Delight some idea of what fun awaits her."

"She will be embarrassed?" Jimmy lifted a dark brow upward. "Are you certain Miss Delight is as innocent as she appears?"

"Can't be positive. Her brothers did defend her virtue brutally. Nonetheless…when I first had her in my arms, she seemed to have no idea about kissing. I would be shocked if she wasn't a maiden."

"If Miss Delight is mine, I've strong feelings about any other man being inside her. If you are indeed giving her to me, she is mine. I want her virginity. Can you deal with that?" James' harsh voice, brooked no argument.

For a few seconds Chandler was taken back by the intensity of Jimmy's words. Had not expected his friend to challenge him in such a manner. In this circle what he said was unheard of. Chandler supposed he had a point. Felt the same about his first, Winter. He shrugged his shoulders. "Why not? Her maidenhead is yours unless that thin piece of skin has been broken before now."

"Thank you, didn't expect my request to be honored with such ease on your part. Believed there would be an argument. I do understand how much you wish for revenge."

"This is better. The fact you receive her innocence will never quell the fact she is forever without her family or that she will belong to you for as long as you wish to own her."

"Thank you again. Need to prepare. Take her to the viewing room when the spectacle begins. Want her to see me. Will she be drugged?"

"Your choice since Delight is now yours."

"Not this time. Delight needs to be aware of me, my sex when I'm aroused, as well as what will happen when we make love. I do mean to make love to her. Do not intend to force her. What will go on between us will be more than just sex."

Chandler knew only of sex with a woman. Never believed he ever made love, not even with Winter. Perhaps there was a difference. Lust, sex, to make love...gave him something to think about. Thought of the more tender times with Winter when they were not part of the evening's entertainment forged through his mind. Strong memories of Winter moaning her pleasure while he was deep inside her heat. Lovemaking...had a nice ring to it. Hoped he might enjoy lovemaking with his Winter again.

Well, he needed to spend some time on the books. When he returned to his rooms, Delight would still be lying by the fire all trussed up with the gag in place. She would wonder what was going to happen next. He thought about her attire. Again, what she was allowed to put on her body was now up to Jamie. He no longer had a say in anything about Jamie's Delight. Again, to his confusion, he found he was alright with the prospect.

A few hours later, he walked into his suite of rooms. Delight was lying on her side facing the fireplace. Celine must have come in to add wood as the flames still danced within the grate. If no one tended the fire, it would have died down to mere embers. Mara would have been cold.

Beside her, he sat on his haunches. Trailed a fingertip across her bare shoulder. Watched the shudder of revulsion slide through her young body, coupled with the sway of her breasts. He caressed both nipples. Delight tried to squirm away from him. There was nowhere for her to go as she was pinned between him and the fireplace.

"Delight…Miss Delight is your name from this point forward. You will no longer be known as Mara."

She tossed her head around, tiny feminine noises filtered past the gag in her mouth. He let a slow even breath of air whisper from his mouth, keeping his hoot of laughter behind his teeth. "You should try to speak your words with more clarity. Can't understand anything you said, my dear."

She squirmed and mewled more. He moved forward. "Oh, you say for me to take the gag from your mouth. I can remove the restraint. You should have asked. However," Chandler stroked her cheek, placed a finger on the tip of one breast that was now Jamie's, twisted the crest. He wasn't aroused by the sight of her. "You didn't say please." This time he didn't keep his hoot of laughter muffled. Above the gag her eyes flared with her anger. She would be a handful for Jamie. A beautiful handful until he tamed her. Jamie could always keep her impaired with just enough laudanum to keep her placid. Keeping her drugged was what he would do until she understood how she should behave.

Ah, but Delight wasn't his to tame. Chandler found he didn't care. The revenge was just beginning. Now, he could sit back, enjoy the show. He didn't need to participate.

He untied the gag. She worked her jaw. Watched her swallow. Her mouth would be parched. So dry she wouldn't be able to speak very well. Chandler decided he would wait until she asked for something to drink. The moment came sooner than he expected. She did garble the single word.

"W—" swallowed. "wa…" swallowed again. "Water."

"Wine for you this time. Believe I will let you get away without a please and a thank you. Once you are in better shape, I will expect common civilities."

"Water…"

Ignoring Miss Delight, Chandler walked to the sideboard where he poured her a small glass of wine. Debated the laudanum. Decided against the drug. How much as well as when was now up to Jimmy. He did tell him, he didn't wish her dosed just yet.

Holding her head he tipped the glass so a few drops slipped between her lips. He stroked her neck hoping the liquid would go down her throat and not on him. She closed her eyes.

"You enjoy the taste of wine?"

She licked her lips. "Ah, that pretty pink tongue of yours beckons." Not for me, though he did enjoy her taste. Too bad those few moments had to end so wretchedly.

"Don't drink wine," she muttered but didn't complain.

"More? There will be no water for you. Must get use to the wine. This will be your drink of choice."

She nodded, agreeing with his proposal. "Please…" she sounded desperate.

"Ah." He tipped the glass again. This time she drank more of the liquid. "Didn't hear a thank you, though the word please was nice."

"Will you untie me?" she looked at him with those beguiling blue eyes, coupled with her thick light blond hair some of the blond strands were nearly white. The color of her hair drew her to him in the first place, that and the little dimple by her mouth. He touched the indentation. "Please."

"Yes, well that was my intention all along. You didn't need to ask. I'm going to take you where you can see tonight's show. I'm certain you will appreciate all the fine nuances of the spectacle. Keep in mind you will have an active part sometime in the next week or so. Whenever Jamie deems you are ready to be a participant rather than a spectator."

"I don't understand what you are talking about."

Delight shook out her hands in an attempt to get the blood flowing again. She would need to do the same with her feet. Tried to bring her gown to cover her. Chandler stopped her.

"You will, maybe not right away…but you will. Jamie will take very good care of you. He will become your master, you, his sex slave. What happens to you will depend on how well you please the audience as well as Jamie. You must please your master. You are now Jamie's plaything. His toy."

His hands under her arms, Chandler helped her to her feet. Carried her to a chair. He rubbed her ankles. Enjoyed her soft moan of relief. When he finished, he helped her adjust her bodice so the fabric covered her. Didn't think Jamie would like anyone to see what was his until he was ready.

"Can you walk or do I need to carry you?"

"Where?"

"Thought I told you. We are going where you can enjoy the spectacle. It's a viewing room. I will point out Jamie to you. Most of the time your new owner is referred to as Jimmy. You will know him as Jamie. Now, can you walk?"

"I think so."

"Don't try to run. There is nowhere for you to run to. Your brothers don't know where you are. So, there will be no rescue coming from your family."

On their way, Chandler kept her close. He opened the curtains that would look down on his little theatre. "There." He pointed, "See over there the man who is fondling Autumn Bounty's breasts, sucking those large globes deep into his mouth. That's Jamie. What do you think? He is splendid, isn't he?"

"He's..." Delight fainted at his feet.

"Bloody eyes, damn woman."

~ * ~

Georgia paced the small kitchen in her cottage. She heard every word Chandler thought during the abduction. He kidnapped Mara Chamberlin. Stole her right out of the tavern in broad daylight. She never thought he would succeed. Her heart lurched. She understood better than anyone what Mara would go through in the brothel.

"You can't do anything about Mara's kidnapping. Don't want the good people here to learn of your association with Chandler Wolcott. Of course, they don't know his name." Hollis held up his hands to stop her arguments. "You cannot go tell them what you know about the man. He is after all, your mate. In time, they will discover their daughter's whereabouts then they will rescue her. You must remain silent on the topic. If you choose not to follow my advice, you might find yourself run out of the village, tarred and feathered as an accomplice to this horrendous act."

She gasped in a frantic breath of air. No, they wouldn't accuse her of his crimes. Guilt by association was below the law. "By then Mara will be ruined. I know Chandler's mind. He will humiliate her, bend her to his every whim while seeking his vengeance. Even if they are able to rescue the girl, she won't wish to return home. He will let every man who wants to have sex with her, to have at her. He might even watch. Mara will become a broken shell of herself. I must do something. Can't just sit around and wait for her brothers to find her. Doing so will take too much time. Chandler may well be my mate, nonetheless, I do not owe him my loyalty. He is a despicable human being. In this life, he will never have my allegiance."

"The three will kill Chandler if they can," Bea joined in on the conversation. "By stealing Mara away from her home, Chandler has put his life at risk along with Georgia's. Still, you cannot think to do anything to change the facts other than warn your mate if you get wind of some facts, he might need to keep himself alive. That is the only thing you should allow yourself to do. Your heart is too tender for the likes of Chandler Wolcott."

Georgia turned on her two friends. Shook her fist at both of them, feeling as if she'd been chastised. She wasn't a little girl. Could make up her mind after sifting through all the information. "I know that's what you wish for…his death. I don't want him dead. I'm going to talk to him. If he won't come to me, I'll go to the damn whorehouse. He can't treat that young girl with impunity. I won't allow him to use her against her brother's. If he wants revenge, have at it with the boys." Minute by minute, she was growing angrier as well as more frustrated by the horrific turn of events. In order to distance herself from her anger, she withdrew into herself.

"No," Hollis said, his voice low, moderated but laced with steel behind the words. "You will not go into London with the intention of speaking with Chandler. If you do, you will never return here. The man will have you right where he wants you, in his domain. Once inside his brothel, you might not ever see the light of day again. He will keep you locked inside his rooms. Are you ready for him to imprison you? Is your intention to become his captive? Even if you don't take Maeve with you, he will have his son. When you left the first time, Chandler was confused. He didn't yet realize you meant to leave him forever. The man is no longer muddled about your intentions."

"You don't wish for your son to be born at that brothel as Maeve was. If you are there, he will impregnate you again as soon as possible. This time he will keep you locked in his suite of rooms even if there is no contract to fulfill. He might be able to find the means for you to sign another binding contract. Drug you so you won't realize what you are doing. Rest assured Chandler would try anything. He would keep you working for him as well as under his thumb for the entirety of your life."

She turned away from Hollis. Absorbed the words for the truth they were. A long deep breath of air didn't make her feel any better or cleaner. Georgia felt dirty. Ugly. Setting her hands on the windowsill overlooking the street in front of her home, she admitted the only possible answer. "I know. I'll have to speak with him in my head. Both of you are right. Seeing him in his domain would mean disaster for me. Talking in our heads is not good enough but it will have to do. A person needs to be able to read the eyes along with the expressions exhibited by a person. Chandler doesn't have the ability to hide his true feelings from me when we speak person to person."

When Georgia turned back to look at the two of them, both showed relief in their eyes. The tight lines around their eyes and mouth relaxed. Stress vanished with her words of conciliation. She wasn't stupid. The truth need only be pointed out once.

"Even if you went to his brothel to talk to him, you wouldn't change his mind. Talking to him through your head won't change his mind either. Once the man has decided on a course of action, nothing changes," Bea said with harsh clarity. Maeve's nanny pointed her finger at her. "I'm surprised he ever allowed you to leave him. Must have been a weak moment. Chandler will never make the same mistake again."

"Chandler is the man who is set on his course. His actions were despicable. Now he seeks revenge against this poor family who did naught but try to protect the youngest member. What man wouldn't do the same in a similar situation?" Hollis lifted his broad shoulders in a very masculine shrug. His question rang true. "Every male worthy of being called a man would do all in his power to protect their own."

Chandler started this ball rolling forward. As the game played out, the consequences gained momentum. If he'd not tried to seduce Mara, her brothers would not have beaten him to a pulp. What a domino effect. If the brothers had not beaten Chandler to a bloody pulp, he would not have sought revenge by using the little sister as his means of retaliation. He should have sought vengeance against the brothers. They at least would have had a fighting chance."

"If I went to the tavern to speak..." Georgia stopped midsentence, understanding she needed to think this over more thoroughly. If she went for a meal, she could determine the best course she should take as well as how she should confront Chandler. She might learn what the Chamberlins knew about the abduction.

"No, I say again, you must let Chandler's affair run its course by itself. You hear me. Don't interfere. You can't tell me you were surprised at what he did?" Hollis asked, sounding as if he too was frustrated beyond endurance.

"No..." She picked up a biscuit still warm from the oven. Spread a wealth of honey across the top. Before she answered she chewed then swallowed. "No, I'm not surprised. I'm hungry. Believe we should go to the tavern for a hot meal."

"We've an entire dinner waiting to be eaten right here in this cottage. Why would we go to the tavern to eat? It's a waste of good food as well as money," Bea said with more force than Georgia ever heard from her before.

"Oh...oh, my, Mara is watching the show in the upstairs room where Chandler likes to view the debauchery when he is not on stage. I can't believe...of course I believe he's taken her there. Wants to embarrass her as well as terrify her."

Chandler no! Mara...

Ah...you finally came to talk to me. So, now my Ice Queen will talk to me. I've been waiting for you to put in an appearance. How do you like my new star? She is beautiful, young, innocent... Her name is Miss Delight. She will be Jimmy's to have for as long as he wishes. We will call him Jamie from now on. The name Jamie has an older ring to it, sounds more mature. I've given Miss Delight to the young stallion. What do you think?

I believe Jimmy is a better choice than you.

Jamie

Nonetheless, Jamie is a better choice than you. At least he will be kind to her. The man doesn't have a cruel streak. Is soft hearted.

Now, you shouldn't be so harsh with my character. I did treat you well. Jamie will take her virtue. When is the only question. Ah, you are right about Jamie. I didn't want Delight because you will come back to me someday soon. By the time the first script is more than a thought in my imagination, Miss Delight will be ruined. Her brothers will arrive too late to save her. Jamie will protect her from the brother's wrath. For some reason I do believe Jamie might have found his mate in Delight. You did know he is a shifter. Ah, don't believe I ever told you that startling bit of news. His brother is also able to change form. I'm going to find a lass for Johnny. When we find the perfect girl, she will become Johnathan's Desire.

They will kill you.

Georgia heard Chandler's long sigh of displeasure. He did have a point. She was too melodramatic. The brothers would never get past the guards at the front door. If they managed that huge feat, there were still six guards within the viewing area. If anyone died, it would be one or all three of the brothers.

Doubt it. My bodyguards will be ready for their appearance. I'm guessing they will appear in two or three weeks, hope to have Miss Delight on stage before they discover where their baby sister went. Told Jamie he had one week to get her ready. If she balks, which she will, we decided to give her a small dose of laudanum to make her more biddable. She will do whatever Jamie asks of her. Miss Delight will have a dreamy expression on her face while Jamie is pleasuring her, plowing her small belly. Sounds like a titillating script. Believe my audience will enjoy the new girl. They do already love Jamie. She will be his virgin bride. Won't be long before she carries his child.

I don't like this. Don't like it at all. Mara is a beautiful young woman. She doesn't deserve the brutality waiting for her. Is she going to be auctioned every night to the highest bidder? She would never survive. She is a country lass.

Jamie will take good care of his Delight. Don't believe he will allow Miss Delight to be auctioned even for the extra money. He is quite wealthy as it stands. Even stood up to me. Told me if Delight was his, he would take her virginity not me. I respected him for the challenge then agreed with him. He was a bit stunned by my easy compliance. Find I want you not this innocent country maid. Her hair is too light. Her eyes too blue. Not like yours. Her breasts are too small. So, you don't need to worry about me abusing Miss Delight. I'm not going to touch the little whore.

If you don't let Mara...

Delight.

If you don't let Mara go this instant, I'll go to the tavern. Tell the brothers where you are holding their sister. Jamie won't have the needed time to deflower her. You won't be able to get your hands on her. I don't trust you Chandler. Jamie shouldn't either. You are bound to change your mind. This nonsense about altering your ways because you want me, is just that, nonsense. You never did understand shifters mate for life. Once you found me, you should have turned away from other women. Instead you had to have sex with every lady you ran across.

Jealous? Find I like that notion. As to your telling the family you know where I am. No, you won't. If you did something so foolish, you would need to move to some other remote place. Seems your little home in the village suits you just fine. Can't see you moving even to save the chit.

Georgia left him for a few seconds. Needed to clear her head of his stinging words. Through Chandler's eyes she'd seen what Mara was watching. Jimmy was naked, fondling Autumn Bounty's huge breasts just as he always did. Bertram was having sex with her. She was crying out her pleasure. Her head thrown back with the ecstasy. Autumn loved sex with most men. Enjoyed Bertram more than the others. That scene must have been overwhelming for an innocent young woman. What would they do to her next?

How fantastic, my little victim fainted at my feet. Poor Jamie, Delight seems to be a wilted flower at the moment. If I can't revive her with a few soft slaps to her cheeks, believe I'll take her to Jamie's room to wait for him. He'll be finished soon. Jamie won't want for me to harm his Delight. No, he will expect to teach her what she needs to learn in his way. He is a gentle man...more than most males of my acquaintance.

Georgia turned to her friends sitting in the kitchen waiting for her to explain. They would realize she was speaking with her mate. "Maybe Chandler's father will talk to him. What he's done is horrible. He can't think he will get away with kidnapping a young woman then converting her to a whore. She will have to sign the consent form. Would be shocked if Mara gives her agreement to continuous rape even though Jamie would give her as much pleasure as possible. Chandler told me they would drug her to get her to do things in their fashion. Jamie can't possibly be in agreement." Georgia assumed Jamie might if he believed she was his mate. He would need for her to remain with him. Would wish to have time to convince her to stay the course. Jamie would have to show her his cat.

"There are ways," Hollis tapped his fingers beneath his chin. "There are many different ways to coerce a person into signing something they have a perverse dislike for. Chandler would know more than one. Would stop at nothing to get his way in this matter. He does have reason though. It is the brothers who he should seek his revenge upon not the poor girl."

"You need to concentrate on the dinner party tomorrow night. Forget about what you cannot change," Bea was telling her. "We've a lot of work to do before we can be ready to feed all those people who will be at James' home. How many did you say? Twenty is what I'm remembering."

"We will shop in London. Smith-Jones will be our protector. Maeve's grandfather insists on Smith-Jones staying by my side while we are in the city. Perhaps Ash will talk to his brother," Georgia said, though she understood his speech would make little to no difference under the circumstances. "Believe I'm foolish to think along those lines. Chandler as much as told me he washed his hands of the girl. Mara now belongs to Jimmy whose new name for ensuing spectacles is Jamie. I much prefer the new name though it doesn't mean much. Jamie won't hurt her though he will still ruin her." She wondered if Jamie would marry her. Chandler did say he thought Mara was Jamie's mate.

"Since we are leaving in the morning and even though our dinner is prepared, we should go to the tavern. There is a small possibility we can learn something. Don't have to have anything to eat but a glass of ale to sip on would give us the opportunity to listen as well as ask questions. Can come back to the cottage to eat later."

Georgia was toying with ideas. She needed to see for herself what if anything was being done to seek out Mara's location.

"What are we waiting for?" Bea asked as she stood then marched to the front door to grab her cloak. "At least the rain has stopped for the time being. We won't find ourselves drenched to the bone from this short walk."

Georgia sent Hollis a look that asked if he believed what he was seeing. She didn't. Bea had been against going to the tavern from the first mention. This time, when the topic came up, it was to tell the family where their daughter had been taken. That wasn't part of the scenario any longer. They were going for information themselves, nothing more. Whether or not they heard anything useful would be left to chance. No one would give anything away.

Inside the Devil's Own Place, the air was somber, too quiet to be a tavern. Georgia felt as if everyone thought Mara had been killed. Georgia's guilt swamped her. She almost turned to leave. The pain of betrayal was so intense, too hard to bear without the threat of tears. Hollis appeared to understand her feelings. He held her arm with gentle ease ushering her to a table near the back as well as in a corner of the room. It was darker there than in the rest of the tavern. A single candle burned on top of the table.

Hollis seated her then Bea. A waitress approached the table...a sister...older...Georgia thought to herself only it wasn't to herself. Seemed Chandler was listening to her musings. She forgot to block him. Wasn't certain she wanted to do so. Perhaps she needed to learn his intentions.

Mackenzie's her name. She is older, a beauty too. Maybe I could grab her for Johnny. The two sisters could perform the same night with the twins. What exciting entertainment. Do you think Makenzie is also a virgin?

Don't you dare! You visited enough heartache on this family as it is. I won't need to think twice to turn you in if you try something so despicable.

Ah, yes, I thought to let Johnny find his playmate by himself. He said he also wishes to find a maiden. Decided to look in the country. Too big a risk for us to go back to the tavern. Someone would recognize us. People would begin to grumble. No, I love this business I built from the ground up with no help except for Bertram. Will never take the risk of losing my dream. However, if Johnny found her outside the tavern, some place private, he could nab her. Don't protest. It's only a thought.

"Chandler?" Bea whispered, slanting her a disapproving look. "You should push that man out of your thoughts. He should not have a place there."

Fear snaked down Georgia's spine. Gasping for a breath of air, she shook her head, hoping to distract the waitress. She didn't want anyone here to guess. Beneath her ribs her heart thundered. The woman might recognize his name. Prayed Mackenzie would not. She tapped the tablet of paper she held with her pencil as she waltzed toward them. Mackenzie's walk was graceful, seductive. If Mara was even close in form to her older sister, Georgia well understood what attracted Chandler to the young woman.

"What can I get you?" she asked as she stepped up to the table. "We've a daily special. Beef stew with lots of potatoes and carrots."

"Why is everything so somber?" Hollis asked as he searched the room, seeming to look everywhere. "Feels as if this is a wake. Did someone pass on? Should we be here? Feel a bit out of place."

"Oh…no…my little sister is gone. No one saw her leave. We don't know what happened to her. She vanished without a trace this morning. We're all frightened for her. Scared to death. She did have a few regular customers who always sat at her tables. We're all trying to look for clues that might lead us to her."

Bloody eyes, Georgia's heart went out to her family. Wished she could yell out all the information she had in her head. Acknowledged the fact she could not. She heaved a breath of air. "I'm sorry. Was she unhappy here? Did she have a beau she might have run off with to Gretna Green?"

"No, nothing like that. At least not anyone we know of."

"We'd each like a glass of your finest ale," Bea said as she took over where Georgia could not and Hollis seemed to be just as stunned as she was.

"A loaf of warm bread, too. Also, a tray of meat, beef, chicken, whatever you have," Hollis added to the order as he began to gather his wits about him.

She nodded, wrote down the order then said, "Be my pleasure. You folks from around here? Haven't seen you before," she said as she tilted her head a bit to the side while she studied their features. "My name is Mackenzie. I'll be your server."

"Yes, we are newcomers to the area. A few months ago, I bought Orange Blossom cottage. Didn't like the noise along with the stress of the city. Living here is much nicer, calmer…quieter too," Georgia said her voice soft. "My name is Georgia O'brien. I'm glad to make your acquaintance. We will come here more often now that we know this place is so friendly. This is my little girl. Maeve is her name."

"Ah, an Irish lass. What a wonderful name for a little Irish girl, Maeve O'brien. I'll have your drinks here in an instant. The food will take a mite longer. Enjoy yourselves. If there is anything I can do for you, just give me a wave. I'll be right over."

Georgia watched her walk away, regretting everything that happened here the last few weeks. This family didn't deserve the sorrow. "Mackenzie is very friendly. Imagine that was how Chandler got to Mara with no difficulty. The little sister would have been just as warm as well as welcoming to a stranger."

You're right. When I asked if the family rented rooms for the night, she volunteered to show me the best room. That was her first mistake. Seems at least for Delight, a fatal mistake. Ah, but if she falls in love…

Georgia's heart froze. *You took advantage of Mara. How can she fall in love in that horrible place where she is terrified.*

Delight is her name. She can fall for Jamie. You fell in love with me.

I won't call her by that horrible name you made up to suit your business. She is Mara Chamberlin to me. I'm not in love with you. I refused to marry you. If you ever ask again, I will refuse again and again then again.

Whatever you wish. Believe you are in love with me. Delight won't ever return to the life she once knew. As I said, she belongs to Jamie. He intimated she was his mate more than once. Delight will always be with Jamie, just as you will always belong to me. You cannot change those facts with wishes and dreams. I won't ever again ask you to marry me. One rejection was enough for me. Nonetheless, given time you will be back with me. Of that I promise you.

Georgia struggled for air. She needed this conversation to be done with. She was terrified he spoke the truth. Chandler would never give up his quest.

"Seems the family has set up the main part of the tavern as a place for the people of the village to gather with information," Hollis pointed to a large table where papers were strewn. "I'm going to walk over there to take a look."

She watched him stride around the table, stare at the papers scattered about. With a finger on his chin, he listened to a man speaking. Georgia wondered what was being said. She prayed they would discover who took her. Next, she was terrified. If they did, Chandler's head would be on the chopping block. If the brothers tried to take her at the brothel, they would suffer for the attempt, possibly die.

Their drinks then their food arrived. Hollis walked back to the table. He shook his head, an indication he learned nothing.

Relief or despair, Georgia didn't know which emotion she was feeling.

Mackenzie was there, "Can I get you anything else? Another glass of ale perhaps? More bread? I see that the four of you must be hungry." She bent over to smile at Maeve. Tussled her hair. Her little girl giggled. "She's a little beauty. Where's her daddy?"

Air fled in a woosh. "Dead," Georgia said, cleared her throat then decided to be a bit more diplomatic. "He passed on. A sickness no one understood. Shouldn't have died. His death was a shock to everyone.

Interesting reply, Winter. I'm dead, am I? Well, we shall see how that goes. Thought I would visit soon. What do you say? Tomorrow?

No. You're dead to me.

Whyever not? You've nothing better to do.

I'll be at your father's townhouse in London. I'm hosting a dinner party for his family. Ash and his wife will be there as will Harris' parents, brothers, cousins. About twenty in all will be in attendance. It's to be a reunion.

You're not to get any ideas. I know Ash offered to help you if necessary. You won't go with him to Dover. I won't have it.

You, Chandler, have no say in what I do.

~ * ~

Jamie was eager to meet his Delight in person. He loved the little dimple by her mouth. Throughout the show his mind was centered on her, on her little butt pointed in the air. He caught a quick glimpse of her face. That first sight stole his breath right out from under him. Without seeing her he knew she watched him from the viewing room. Could read her thoughts. She was petrified with terror. The only way to rid herself of the unwanted sights presented to her was to collapse. Realized when she fainted, she was more innocent than he believed at first. She had three older brothers. He would need to discover a way to make that incident up to her. He didn't expect the female to swoon at the sight of him or what they were doing. In his mind, he heard her small whimper of distress. The pain of loss was also heavy in her head. Delight understood she was going nowhere. Realized she would never return home. Wouldn't realize the exact nature of what was in store for her. Teaching her what her new life entailed, easing her way was up to him.

After exiting the stage, he donned his buckskins along with his boots. Pulled his shirt over his shoulders then left it unfastened. Eager to meet his Delight, Jamie two-stepped his way to his suite of rooms on the second floor. Told the guard Chandler left at the door he could leave. With baited breath, he unlocked the door leaving it to swing open. Half expected Delight to rush from his room. He would catch her in his arms. Savor her small form melded against his. Enjoy the rush of pleasure, holding her would gift him with.

All that met him was a whispering silence. A log in the fireplace sputtered before crashing into the grate. Stepping inside he closed then locked the door. Slipped the key into his pocket. Except for a lone candle burning along with the light from the small fire, the room was dark. With unease, he searched the main room, knowing she would not have been able to leave. As his eyes adjusted to the semi-darkness, he recognized more shapes.

Jamie first saw Delight sitting on a huge chair, her legs tucked in beneath her. She was fully clothed though her bodice had been ripped earlier. He saw the valley between her breasts. Chandler did tell him he wouldn't touch her in anyway except to keep her from running. Her head lolled to one side. Her long hair curled around her shoulders reaching well past her tiny waist. She appeared completely defeated. It was then she sensed another person in the room. Her head tilted up. She drew in a huge terrified breath of air. Tugged her gaping bodice together. Jamie didn't want her to be afraid of him. Hell, she saw him naked as well as fully aroused. A maiden might be terrified. For Jamie there had been no maidens in his life. The only women he had sex with were experienced. He wasn't certain what to do with an innocent.

Her glare was furious. With lips thinned and eyebrows drawn together, she stared at him. The girl didn't stand. Except for her change of expression, she seemed frozen in time. From what he could see of her eyes, she appeared exhausted as well as overwhelmed by the day's turn of events. Proceedings she didn't enjoy. She didn't understand all that would happen. Her life had taken a distinct and very sudden turn in an opposite direction.

"Delight," he spoke with a soft voice as he walked toward her. He meant to soothe some of her tattered nerves. Jamie held out his hands palms up, his heart in his throat. "I won't hurt you. Don't wish for you to fear me. However, you must come to realize you are mine. I won't take you back to the tavern where you once lived. Your home is now in this building, with me. I will honor as many of your wishes as possible. The sooner you come to accept all these facts, the sooner you will accustom yourself to our way of living. Life here is not bad. Just different from what you are used to."

While Delight stared straight ahead, she grew even more still. Her silence unnerved him. He wasn't certain how to proceed. This was not what he expected. He thought she would fight, battle him, kick and scream until her limbs couldn't move and her throat was raw. He realized she must be waiting for him to explain things. Maybe not.

Pulling up a chair beside her, he placed her hand in his. Saw the delicate blue veins along the underside of her wrist. Despite the heat of the fire her fingers felt as if they were encrusted with ice. When he focused on her, she continued to stare at him. Best to start at the beginning. Problem was, he didn't know where the beginning was.

"You fainted."

Delight gazed into his eyes, questioning. Didn't blink. Didn't say a single word. She appeared immobile in time. If he didn't witness the slow rise then fall of her breasts, there would be no movement to see. Even Winter was never so still and cold as this woman.

How do you know? You weren't in the room with me...only Chandler.

The question brought a smile to his lips. Ah, so he was right. Delight was his mate. He understood what she thought. That little piece of information would give him a distinct advantage in their future dealings together. While he understood the importance, she wouldn't. She wasn't a shifter. He knew the truth of that detail deep in his belly. She would never be able to be inside his mind except when she carried their shifter child. Didn't matter. He wasn't going to give her an explanation…not yet. Given time, he would need to show her his cat. Couldn't until he could trust her. Meant the claiming might be a while in coming. He could marry her first. Delight didn't know he could hear her thoughts. Jamie decided her ignorance of who he was, was a good way to proceed. It would also give him an edge while dealing with her.

He passed his thumb across her wrist, slow at first then again. Felt her pulse race. *Fear or arousal? Maybe a bit of both.* "You must wish for a bath as well as a change of clothes. What clothing you are wearing is filthy as well as torn. Not fit for a beautiful girl to wear. Have you eaten? No, Chandler said he wouldn't do anything with you except escort you to the viewing room. I will take care of all your needs."

She stared into his eyes. *I don't want anything from you except for you to take me home. I don't belong here. Don't wish to have anything to do with you. I hate you. There is nothing here for me. Chandler tricked me.*

Her thoughts about him rocked his confidence. She detested him. Jamie didn't appreciate the horrible sentiment from his mate. The knock on his door came before he decided whether or not to answer her silent statement. Perhaps it would be best for her if she was left in the dark. He rose to answer the door. That would be her bath water. He ordered the bath as he made his way to his rooms.

"Yes, in the bedroom. Take the water to the tub. Then you may leave. Tell the cook, we will require food in about a half hour."

Servants filed in with buckets of hot water. Jamie waited until everything was ready and all the servants vacated the room before he addressed Delight.

Looking down on her, he spoke, keeping his voice soft, modulated. Again, he hoped to pacify her nerves. "Your bath is ready. I will leave you alone to take a bath if you toss your clothing into this room. There is something else for you to wear on the bed. This gown needs to be washed as well as pressed and also needs to be repaired from the afternoon's events. As it is now, it's unwearable."

The gown would be burned. Delight would never wear this one again. Though he did intend to have a few things fashioned for her.

Not one muscle moved. No part of her even twitched. Her chin was tilted high and her back was stiff. Delight gave him no acknowledgement that she heard. Even in her mind, he heard nothing.

To proceed with caution would serve better than anger. "The water will get cold," Jamie warned, tamping down his frustration. "Do you need help? I'm more than willing to disrobe you. While you still can, I'm giving you the opportunity to undress yourself. The choice is yours to make."

Choice? That is no choice at all.

He smiled, a slow smile that she noticed but didn't comment about. "Delight? Which way will we proceed? The easy way for you or the hard way?"

Jamie didn't believe he needed to elaborate. Her expression changed back to the scowl he saw earlier.

Still, without speaking, she rose. Walked with regal splendor into the bedroom. Jamie didn't say anything. He remained where he stood, watching the closed door. A few minutes later her clothing lay in a pile outside his bedchamber. He heard the splash of water as she settled into the heat. Caught the scent of roses on the air. Someone must have put rose scented oil into the tub. Thought he might have heard a contented sigh.

Smiling, he picked up her clothing before placing them in the hall outside the main room. Her clothing as she once knew was gone. Had no intention of giving the gown back to her. He had one week to get her ready for their first show together. Becoming weak-willed or giving into her silent pleas for help would serve no purpose. She was going to fight him even if it meant she remained silent. He wished she was willing. She wasn't.

Knew when her bath was finished. Heard outrage when she saw herself in the gown and peignoir he left for her to wear. If or when she looked in the mirror, she would see herself, all of herself. While she wasn't naked, when he looked upon her, there would be nothing left to his imagination. He would view every luscious feminine part of her, all her female endowments.

He was eager to see her, all of her. "Come let me see you. Look at you." Jamie stood at the door. His hand outstretched hoping she would take his hand. He wanted to feel her small fingers inside his.

"No!"

Understood, Delight would play her cards this way. He had a great deal to teach her in a short amount of time. If he were to meet the deadline Chandler gave him, he could accept no disobedience. She needed to learn then to accept the reality he was her master. He would make certain she understood he would be the only man to have her. She was not going to become a whore. He would never allow his mate to become a prostitute. She would never understand the difference.

"…then…I will come to you." Jamie walked into the room, a glass of wine in his hand to give her. Hoped the wine would ease some of her fears. "A meal will be served in a few minutes."

Bloody hell, he hoped she didn't plan on starving herself. He handed her the glass of wine. She tossed the contents in his face. With slow precision, he wiped the liquid away with the tip of his shirt. Tossed the fabric to the floor. She gawked at him. Her small pink tongue roamed across her mouth. Damn, he wanted to taste. The dimple called to him. "If that's the way you want this to play out…"

The laudanum mixed into the wine would have relaxed her. Since she didn't want to drink the wine, he might have to pour the lovely burgundy down her throat. "Should we try this again?"

"Don't want anything from you."

"The lady does speak. That wasn't smart of you. Don't appreciate childish tantrums. I won't allow you to waste away. So, get that thought out of your lovely head. If you make it necessary, I will force food along with drink down your throat. The two of us, you and me, have a future together. A long and very intimate future. I won't be deprived."

Her chin tilted higher. She didn't answer. The look of defeat on her beautiful face gave him a moment to breathe. "Shall we start over? Wine. It's a very good burgundy. Your pallet will enjoy the flavor."

To his surprise she nodded. He turned back to the main room to prepare the second drink. When he handed the second glass of wine to her, she stood in the middle of the doorway, her small frame shaking. She was beautiful. Her long blond hair curled around her body, dipping to her tiny waist. While he could see all of her lovely curves, what he focused on were the beautiful tips of her breasts along with dark-golden hair of her mound.

Food arrived. She drank the glass of wine. With each sip he watched her relax. The trembling slowed. Without fighting him, she ate. Drank another prepared glass of wine. She was ready for the first stage of her learning experience.

Jamie stood in front of her. Was already naked from the waist up. Sat down to remove his shoes. His hands on the fasteners of his pants, he dropped them to the floor. Fully aroused, he stood so she could cast her gaze on whatever part of him she wished to examine. In the viewing room, she'd watched. She fainted. When Jamie undressed, her eyes were dazed from laudanum. He touched her. Wrapped his arms around her. With a futile effort she pushed on his hands. "I don't…"

"What?"

"Please?"

Jamie lifted one eyebrow with a lazy smile on his mouth. "Please take you to bed. That's what I intend. For now, though, I'm not going to join you. You are too sleepy for playtime. If I lay down beside you, one thing will lead to another. The time isn't yet right for the two of us to make love."

Make love? No…

Yes. He led her into the room. Stopped beside the bed. She didn't fight him. Instead, Delight withdrew further into herself. After undressing her, he placed her under the covers, drawing them to her chin. The drug seemed to make her more accepting of her plight.

"Go to sleep, Delight. I'll join you in another hour or two." He needed her to be asleep when he came to bed. Planned on holding her close. If she was awake, he would have a difficult time keeping his hands to himself.

When he woke the next morning, she lay sprawled on top of him. Her legs were entwined with his while her nose was buried in his chest. He enjoyed the way she felt all warm and soft against his hard body. She would complain. For the next few beats of his heart, he meant to enjoy the fragile contact. He cupped her breast in his hand. Touched the nipple with his thumb, hardened by the cool air. This needed to end before it went any farther.

"Delight."

"Hmm…"

His Delight wiggled against him. Ran her hand along his chest down to his belly.

He jumped to life. "It's time to wake up, sleepy head. We have a long day ahead of us. Lots of things to do before the show in six days."

Seemed she woke up all at once. Pushed against his chest. Her sweet breasts, swayed. He stared, looking his fill. Her eyes blazed fire. He wasn't certain if she felt fear or anger. From what he could read of her mind, the emotions were both there.

"You forced me!"

He found himself shaking his head and at the same time wanting to howl with laughter. "You are the one who was spreadeagled on top of me, my sweet." After removing her, he stood. His body primed as well as ready. "Come, it's time for breakfast. The meal will be here within a very few minutes."

Chapter Five

Chandler watched Jamie pace the room. He was amused with this turn of events. The girl befuddled the man. Tossed him in one direction then another. Did all women do the same to the men in their lives? Winter perplexed him. Sometimes he didn't know whether he was coming or going. While Jamie walked, he pushed hair through his fingers then cracked each and every one of his knuckles.

"Talk to me, Jamie. This pacing isn't getting you anywhere. Won't solve one problem. I do know this from experience. Delight is tucked safely away in your rooms I assume?"

Chandler didn't think howling with laughter would sit well with one of his favorite men.

"Yes, she is in my room. Yes, we did sleep together last night. Yes, I memorized all her sweet curves. Delight will not come around easily. While we didn't make love yet, we will soon. I promise she will be ready in six days."

"What do you want me to do?"

Chandler needed to get into his mate's head right now. Last night she kept things from him that he wished to learn. Winter would be in London soon. Wondered if he dared crash the family dinner party that no one invited him to attend. Wasn't he family too? Thought back to Jamie's problems.

"Two things." Jamie paused midstride, "Two very important items." He sat down, sipped the tea he'd been offered. "Would rather have a brandy. Strung up too tight to think straight. Know what I want to do though. It's what I need to do."

Chandler nodded. "The sideboard. Help yourself to anything you wish. Brandy, a croissant, bacon, eggs there is more than enough for both of us. Bertram will join me soon. Put our heads together to figure out the best course to take with Delight. Tell me what has your nerves about to snap."

"I wish to marry her…as soon as possible." Jamie held up his hands as if that would stop his questions. "Her family will discover where she is hopefully later than sooner. If we are a married couple, the brothers will have no say in what happens to her. They have no recourse left to them except leaving her with me. The marriage will have been consummated. There won't be a damn thing they can do. Want to do this today which might pose a problem or two. Maybe more than two difficulties."

Chandler drummed his fingers on the teacup while he thought. Set it down. Decided he needed brandy too. Poured two glasses. "A bit drastic don't you think? You can't wait to think about the repercussions."

"She is my mate. I can't claim her until she learns to trust me and I her. My only option is to marry her. Get her with child. Given enough time, she will come around. Maybe as the days pass, she will no longer despise me."

"Will she agree to a marriage? The little chit does need to say the proper words at the right time."

Inside Chandler was smiling. There were ways as they both realized to get a woman to say the correct words as well as act the way a man wanted.

Jamie was shaking his head, pacing. Brandy splashed from the glass then slid down to his fingers. He licked the amber liquid from his thumb then the glass. "If Delight agreed to my proposal the positive answer would shock me to the tips of my toes. Last night she was colder than I've ever seen your Ice Queen. Said only a few words. What I learned from her, I learned from her thoughts. She was not appreciative of me."

"If she won't say 'I do', what do you plan?"

Delight was Jamie's. Chandler meant to leave everything up to him.

"You do understand I used the laudanum to relax her last night. This morning wasn't much better. Don't know if she realizes what happened in the viewing room or the bed we shared. When she does comprehend why she is behaving so out of character, giving her the drug will be more difficult. Don't intend to give her too much. Don't want her to become dependent. We could try some cocaine." Jamie downed his brandy. Set the glass on the counter by the bottle.

"I'll send Bertram for a minister. You will need a special license. Go to the church. You can take care of that detail." Chandler was still amused.

"I will work on the arrangements from my end. You will have your wedding today."

He can't think to marry Mara. If...

I see you've been listening. Are you in London? I would like to see you. I would that you came here. You do know the way.

No, not unless you wish to come to your father's townhouse. James has agreed to let me see you at his place. Smith-Jones will be with me the entire time. I won't go to the brothel. I'm not the fool you seem to believe I am.

He brushed his nails on his sleeve. *Sounds boring, sweetheart. Come here, to my place, then we will talk about Delight. You could be a witness to the wedding of Jamie and Delight. They slept together last night. So, it is too late for her family to save her. Jamie wants to marry by the end of the day.*

You took advantage of a warm and welcoming young girl. Jamie...I can't believe he is so arrogant he would not give her the time she needs to adjust.

Chandler lifted his shoulders in an indifferent shrug. "Winter tuned me out. Nice that Delight doesn't realize you know everything she is thinking."

"She detests me. Can you believe it? Delight hates me, the man who is her mate. The man who will marry her as well as claim her so we can be together in future lives. She will carry my children. Hope they are all shifters."

Chandler did give into a soft chuckle. He waved his hand in the direction of the door. "Go on, go get that special license you will need. I will make arrangements on the home front. Johnny will want to be there as will Bertram and Celine. I invited Winter. She declined with adamant words to the contrary. Don't think she believes the two of you are mates. Told me it seemed like too big a coincidence. Summer will not want to have any part of the wedding. Autumn and Spring might." Chandler stopped talking for a few seconds. "On second thought, I don't intend to give anyone a choice. They will all attend yours and Delight's wedding. The entire cast will be there to celebrate a new cast member's initiation into the fold. Let's make the wedding for eight o'clock this evening. Do you think those few hours at your disposal will give you enough time to get the special license? We are creeping up on the noon hour. The two of you will be the show tonight. You will marry as well as take the sweet shield of innocence away from her in front of a huge audience of fans. Her family will have no recourse except to welcome you as one of them."

"It has to be," Jamie said, "I need to see Delight before I head to the church. Talk to her just to gauge her mood. The atmosphere is certain to be frigid. You take care of everything else. What will she wear? She has nothing but the filmy nightgown I gave her last night. Her gown from the day before was destroyed."

Chandler's mind spun in a multitude of directions. He looked to Jamie with a huge grin. "Nothing. She has nothing at all to put on her lovely white body. Why, Delight will be naked as will you. A perfect wedding, a lovely script for tonight's fun and entertainment. The show will begin at eight o'clock as usual. Both of you will take part. The star entertainers of the evening. I'll have cook prepare a cake that will feed the entire audience. This is perfect. A perfect beginning for the newlyweds."

Jamie frowned at him. "I don't know. She will have to be very drugged to stand in front of an audience wearing nothing. If not, she will never cooperate. I have too many misgivings in this scenario."

"Tonight, Delight will sign both the five-year contract that will keep her bound to the brothel along with the marriage documents. We will kill two problems in a matter of minutes. If I'd had the forethought to have Winter sign a contract of more than one year, she would still be with us. Must learn from my mistakes."

So, thrilled with his new plan, Chandler found himself rubbing his hands together with glee. All that would make this moment better was to bring Winter back to the brothel. He needed a perfect plan. The damn woman had too many bodyguards.

"I want her to wear something," Jamie challenged his dictates. "Something white, a long filmy gown perhaps. Don't care if it can be seen through. My Delight will feel somewhat protected if there is fabric surrounding her."

"Very well...this is your wedding. Run along now. Get that license. Believe I've got just the right clothing for both of you. You will wear the sheerest of pants. You can enter the theatre with capes around you so no parts of you can be viewed. The two of you won't be unveiled until you are both standing at the altar. Celine can be her bridesmaid and as the father of the blushing bride, I will give her away. Will enjoy the role. Good practice for my Maeve. Walk her between the rows of spectators to your waiting arms. Do get a ring for her too. Want every detail seen to before the show begins."

Chandler called for Bertram. He would need his best friend to help put this night's entertainment together. The new lady along with her lover would do their first show this evening, written to his script. Jamie would take her virginity in front of the live audience. She would comply because she was his mate. Mates never hated each other. Perhaps while she is drugged Delight will realize how much she loves and wants Jamie. The first kiss might change her perspective. Though…he didn't doubt for a moment, once the laudanum wore off she would despise Jamie again. Over the next months the two were in for an interesting ride.

"Chandler?" Bertram asked with curiosity in his voice as he entered. "You have that look on your face that means we'll be having more fun than planned. Tell me all about the notions that are on your mind."

"Sit down. Grab whatever you wish to drink. We've a special show tonight. The entertainment will be unlike anything we've presented before. Jamie and his Delight are to wed at eight o'clock sharp in our theater." Chandler sat back and watched the myriads of expressions cross Bertram's face.

Bertram poured a generous amount of brandy. "Jamie wishes to marry the little whore? Not what I would have expected. Are you quite certain you are not making this up? We could have the show even if the wedding is fake."

"Oh…the chit of his is no whore. Jamie won't allow another man to touch her. He appears very possessive." Chandler went on to explain the situation. "He's even thinking of her feelings. Always believed the twins were far too nice for this profession."

"So, Delight is his mate. If she detests the very ground he walks on, I believe we will have one hell of a show tonight. Do you think she will fight him? Protest the vows? What do you want me to do?"

"Make certain the proper clothing is in their room, the sheer white pants for Jamie and the filmy white gown for Delight. The clothes shifters wear to their claiming. They will need capes to wear over the gown and pants."

He had been and still was just as possessive of Winter. Chandler was reminded of the mating ceremony he had with Winter. The marks were on her shoulders proclaiming her as his very own. Winter never told him what she'd seen or experienced during the ceremony. She refused. Hell, she should have been grateful he allowed her that much. He could have refused to claim her. If so, would she have stayed with him? Too late for that question, to have meaning.

Chandler cleared his throat while he thought. "I'll see to the wedding cake. It will need to be large enough to feed one hundred people...maybe more. We can sell more tickets. Not everyone needs to have a chair to sit on. Tonight is not one of the special evenings that only fifty may attend. Too late to change the price of tickets or the number attending the performance. Too bad for the price. Perhaps if there were empty seats the price could be doubled for those buying at the door."

"Don't wish to start a riot," Bertram murmured with a sly grin on his face. He cleared his throat before he spoke his mind. "But...your contemplations are good, very good. If the tickets aren't presold then the price will double. We can do a bit of advertising. Jamie and Delight wed then consummate the vows in our theatre. Let it be known Miss Delight is a virgin."

"Got to put all this in motion with speed if anything is to come to fruition. I'll see you tonight. Go to the church down the block. Bring back the minister. Keep him here. Pay him double whatever the going rate is. Don't wish for him to balk at marrying these two. When he sees them naked, he might turn and run. A man of God would detest a ceremony of this sort. As soon as he pronounces them man and wife, have Johnny get him out the back door. Don't waste time. Don't wish to have him watch the consummation of their marriage."

Yes, everyone had to be willing, even the minister. He should have the man sign a contract saying he was enthusiastic to marry these two people. All the loose ends needed to be tied up before eight o'clock.

For the first time in a very long time, Chandler was excited at the prospect of this new show. This originality of it all would serve to stimulate business that seemed to be lagging. Even the Saturday Night Naked shows had dwindled in size. Yes, he would think on this matter. Wished to have such as this every week. The week could vary. Neither the ceremony or the minister needed to be real.

He would advertise this theatrical event. Chandler knew the exact right people to contact. He would send one of his other employees to the men he had in mind. Ah, and there was one lady who attended the shows on a regular basis. He would send a message to her also. She had matronly friends who would be interested. They loved the sex. Purchased some of the male players at auction at the end of the night. Chandler decided he served a higher purpose.

You are a despicable human being, Chandler Wolcott. Can't believe I once thought you would change. That won't ever happen. You can't possibly think of using that poor girl in such a way. Wedding vows are sacred. Just as sacred as the claiming ritual.

You love me anyway. You would enjoy the show. If all works out, Jamie will take Delight's virginity in front of the audience of one hundred starved for sex people. They will all fall in love with Miss Delight. Don't know why I didn't think of this sooner. We will look for more virgins. Perhaps one a week. Will charge more for those shows. Unlike Jamie's Delight, these virgins will be auctioned the week after their initiation. Do believe that's a grand idea.

Chandler knew the moment she tuned him out. He wouldn't be surprised if she stormed over here. Unfortunately for him, she wouldn't arrive alone. No, Ash along with Smith-Jones would be with her. There wasn't a bloody thing she could do to change what was orchestrated tonight. He wasn't certain if she was still listening to his plans. Maybe he should go into greater detail. What he did know was the reality he was no longer privy to her condemnations. Whistling a little ditty, he heard a few days ago, he left his rooms.

He was satisfied.

Yes, he was very happy.

The chef was eager to create a wedding cake for the soon to be newlyweds. The two decided the cake would be chocolate. Didn't everyone love chocolate? They would have a mint flavored icing to go along with the chocolate cake. Champagne, the best France had to offer would be served to his patrons to celebrate the joining of these two lovely individuals.

Delights champagne would be prepared special for her. Keeping her relaxed as well as easy going until the nuptials were finished seemed to be the way to proceed. His heart sped. All that would make this evening better was if Winter would show up then play an integral part in the script. He let out a slow breath of air.

Chandler was surprised but again not surprised when he received missives from the people he asked to advertise tonight's show. All the responses spoke of how unique this particular show would be. They would all attend as well as publicize the one-of-a-kind event. He anticipated a full house. Standing room only after the advertisement was completed. Delight might be pleased when she discovers how much money she would make with the one show. Until she came to trust Jamie, she would never have access to the groats. Chandler wondered how long it would take for the trust to grow. Jamie had a way with women. Understood just what the female needed.

In the theatre, Jamie gave orders. The chairs needed to be aligned so there would be an aisle where he could walk with Delight. The irony didn't escape him. He was more than pleased at the direction this took. When the morning began, he'd not expected Jamie to marry Delight this evening.

"What do you think?" Chandler asked Bertram who now stood next to him. "Are you as excited as I am about tonight's prospects? Thinking about this show steals my breath from my lungs. Wish I had a bigger part to play. Perhaps in future shows, I'll be the minister. We could take turns."

"Can't be the best man. That role must go to Johnny, his twin. If we had another maid of honor, you could be one of his best men." Chandler stroked his chin, hoping Winter would pop back into his thoughts.

"Celine the maid of honor?"

"Yes, she was pleased to gain the role. She was the woman who led Delight from the tavern with no one being any the wiser. Celine is crafty. It did not take her more than a few minutes to gain Delight's complete trust. I'll give her that. We got away with no suspicions. Wonder how long it will take the Chamberlin brothers to discover her whereabouts. I've still a mind to try for her sister Mackenzie. She would need to leave the tavern. We could set someone to watching. Maybe the older sister has somewhere to go on a regular basis."

Chandler had mused the thought since they drove away. He was hoping for weeks before the family discovered her location. If Winter had anything to do with this, they would be here tomorrow.

Tomorrow would be too late…way too late.

"Depends on Winter. Telling those boys is eating on her. She feels guilty to the tips of her delicious little toes. It's fortunate that after tonight, it won't make any difference. We have a new star on the horizon."

"Been looking for you," Jamie now stood with the two men. He pulled out the special license. "Do you have the contract made up? I wish for Delight to sign the agreement before I accompany her to the theatre for the wedding. It's six thirty now. Could you bring the document to my rooms in thirty minutes. I'll have her prepared. All afternoon, Celine has been keeping her in a stupor. She tells me all will be ready. I will help her put her name on the paper if she has any problems manipulating her fingers."

"Both names for the contract to be valid."

"Yes, Mara Chamberlin AKA Delight. Both names should also be on the certificate of marriage. That way there can be no contention," Jamie said as he stared up to the viewing room. Tonight no one would be there.

"Agreed. We've never had a wedding here. I've been informed there will be standing room only. Perhaps close to one hundred fifty eager viewers. We will have over one hundred in attendance. This will be a show worth remembering as well as talking about for the rest of the year. My chef has agreed to bake a second cake."

"You look nervous, Jamie," Bertram said with a bark of laughter.

"I am. Never done this before. Nervous as hell. If Delight figures out I've been drugging her, she's going to fight the laudanum. I might need to pour it down her throat. Not looking forward to an argument. Johnny has the ring I purchased. He's laughing his head off at the predicament I've gotten myself into. Can't say I regret anything." He pinched the bridge of his nose. "Need to see to my soon to be wife. Make certain all is ready."

"Good luck," Chandler chuckled as he watched Jamie leave through the back door. "Did you see him? Sweat was beading on his forehead."

"Glad I'm not in his shoes. Don't ever want to marry," Bertram said on a harsh note. "Wives, nothing but trouble."

"If you ever find your mate, you might change your mind," finding his mate did that exact thing. Problem was Winter told him no…a resounding no.

~ * ~

Mara was out of sorts. All afternoon she'd been so drowsy she had trouble keeping her eyes open. A pretty woman with the largest breasts she'd ever seen brought her tea every couple of hours. She'd been so thirsty, she welcomed the drink. Craved the liquid warmth. Soothed her throat. Once she received a plate of food. Wasn't hungry though she nibbled on a few pieces of cheese.

What is to happen to me? Jamie told me he owns me. I don't want the man to be my master. Told me I was his sex slave. How can that be? I'm Mara Chamberlin, a free woman. He tells me what she believed previously was no longer true.

She held her throbbing head in her hands. Seemed since she woke up this morning, she'd been dizzy. The room was hazy, spinning at times. When she heard the door opening, she looked up to see Jamie swagger into the room. He was so handsome. The stubborn chin of his was set in a no-nonsense way. His body was big and hard. His muscles bulged. When she woke up this morning spread across him, she wasn't upset, just surprised. He was everything she'd ever looked for in a man. His sex was so huge…the sight terrified the air from her lungs. Living in the country, she did have some idea as to what he planned. This notion of his wouldn't work. She would need to tell him the irreversible fact. He would need to set his sights on a different woman.

Why couldn't he have been smaller. He stole her away from her family and friends. Told her she belonged to him. She didn't. He would need to understand the truth. She would tell him what she thought if she could figure it out. Her mind was so hazy all the time she didn't know if she was coming or going. In some primitive way Mara didn't understand, she did wish to belong to him.

Not as his sex slave. Never that.

"Delight? How are you doing? Autumn told me you drank the tea she brought. She also said you didn't eat anything except a slice or two of cheese. Is that right? You must keep up your strength. Tonight will be a long one for you." He stepped up to her then ran his knuckles across her cheek. Smoothed her eyebrows with the tip of one finger.

She shivered with the sensual contact. Enjoyed the way that small caress made her feel. Heated her in places she'd never thought about before he touched her. The tender caresses ignited flames. When she woke up this morning and he was holding her breast, fondling the nipple, she thought she would expire from the intense heat. She enjoyed what he did. Didn't wish for him to stop. When he sipped on the crest, twirled his tongue in the same place, she thought she would jump out of her skin.

"I'm…"

She ran her tongue across her mouth. He was hazy. His smile endearing. She couldn't quite focus. In the chair where she sat, she swayed. Was content to be sitting rather than standing.

"I'm?" he asked while one finger skimmed along the column of her neck then across the tops of her breasts. With a light touch, he passed his palm across each veiled nipple. "What is it you are feeling, sweet? You're not wearing the peignoir. I am enjoying the delectable view of your delicious body. The fire has died down to almost nothing. The chill has raised goose bumps in delightful places. Would like to explore those same spots."

"Hot when you touch me…," she said, her voice questioning. "Hot and dizzy after the tea. I shouldn't. Your moving…you should stand still so I can get a good look at you. Jamie…I enjoy looking at you."

He chuckled at her comment. "We're celebrating tonight. You must let me help you get ready. We'll be married in," Jamie pulled out his pocket watch. "About one hour. We've a lot to do before then."

Mara shook her head. Uttered an unlady like snort. Her mother would reprimand her if she heard that noise. Whenever she disagreed with someone she snorted. Couldn't stop herself. Her mother would tell her she should think of some other way to express her opinions. A lady would never snort. "No, I'm not marrying you tonight or any other night. I don't even like you. Marriage is supposed to be about love. We don't love each other." She swayed, caught herself using the arms of the chair.

I do like him. He's beautiful. Can a man be beautiful? Her brothers would tell her no to that question. They would say men are big as well as hairy creatures. They weren't soft and sweet like a woman. They were wrong. Jamie was beautiful.

As if he heard what she thought, he smiled. His was a beautiful smile. "Celebrate with me?" With his back to her, he poured them both a glass of champagne. "You need to have a little bit more liquid courage. With this glass of champagne, you will be perfect. We'll begin with a celebratory glass of the bubbly stuff." He turned. He was dressed all in black, except for the snowy white cravat and shirt. His boots were polished to a glossy shine. She didn't think Jamie could be any more perfect than he already was.

"I'm not celebrating anything with you, least of all a marriage I don't want. Not marrying anyone." She tried to stand then sunk back to the chair with a tiny giggle. Put her hands on the arms. Tried to stand again. Failed. "Can't seem to get my feet beneath me. Don't understand why I want to stand when this chair is so comfortable."

"If need be, I'll hold you up," Jamie handed her the drink. Clicked his glass with hers.

Champagne spilled along the lip of the glass. She touched the small drop with the tip of her tongue. Stared at him beneath lowered lashes. Slipped her tongue across her mouth. "It's delicious. Can I have more than one?"

Jamie lifted his broad male shoulders. Shoulders she thought would be nice to caress. She didn't remember much from last night. She'd been asleep when he came to bed. When she woke, her naked self was sprawled across him. She recalled the way the hair on his chest felt on her breasts. She wanted to feel those same sensations again.

"It's your wedding day. You can have as many as you like. Here is to us as well as our happiness into eternity." His smile stole her breath. She gasped for air. When she inhaled again, she caught the scent of Jamie, spicy and all male.

Recovering from the sipped air, Mara held her glass up, tossing him what she thought might be a flirtatious smile, "Here's to us…" She drank the entire glass in one gulp, swallowed. "Another. Can't be muddled. I've only had one glass." Mara fell back on the chair, closing her eyes. Jamie took the glass from her. "Never had champagne before. It tastes so good, better than wine. What do you think? Do you like it as much as I do?"

She regarded him for several tender seconds. To her surprise, he did pour her another. Her brothers would have told her she drank too much along with the stern words that she would regret the second drink in the morning when her head pounded.

"You must be muzzled. You're adorable. Your cheeks are flushed a pretty shade of rose. Are the tops of your breasts the same color. Should like to keep you this way for our wedding night. What do you think? Would you enjoy being this way while I make love to you? A little bit fuzzy headed?" He sipped. That was his first glass. Mara took note of the fact.

"Needed to talk to you about that. About," she stopped to run her sweaty palms along her gown. "I'm not. Couldn't be. You're not going to make love to me tonight or any other night." She tried again to sit. Looked him over, up then down. Stopped at his groin. Was transfixed for several ticks of the clock on the shelf. Her gaze swept to his eyes. Shaking her head, feeling as if her eyes crossed. "No, we can't have sex or make love. Whatever you wish to call the act. You are too big…way too big. I saw you from the viewing room. Too big." Mara shook her head again, downed the champagne. Gulped air for courage. She blurted, "You won't fit."

Jamie barked his laughter. "Trust me, sweet. We will fit together. Might be snug for me inside you, a virgin. We will have sex. I know tricks that will ease your way. I'll have a slow hand. Won't do anything until you are ready."

"No, you're too big. Why argue? Soon enough you will know I'm right. You won't fit. You won't be able to stuff yourself inside me," Mara repeated, thinking he wasn't paying attention to her.

"Does this mean you're not averse to my attention? If so…" Jamie set his glass on the counter.

With the agility and speed of a cat, Mara found herself swept into his arms. "Shall we begin with a kiss? Do you like to be kissed? I want you to understand you should open your mouth," Jamie pointed out. "Need to feel the rub of your sweet pink tongue on mine. Should we try it now? Before…" He stopped talking to study her eyes.

She looked into the quicksilver of his eyes, alight with hints of amusement. Right before her eyes, his darkened turning a sultry pewter. What did that mean? "Don't know if I like kisses. Never been..."

"Why is that? I wonder? You must have had a few beaus in your life. Did one of them steal a kiss at the back door? Or inside the barn in the hayloft? Have you been in a hayloft with a boy?" he asked. "If not, we will need to remedy the fact. Know the perfect hayloft. Everyone should have sex in a hayloft at least once."

He didn't give her a chance to answer. His mouth molded over hers. The touch was warm, vibrant. The kiss was hot and hard. He tugged on her bottom lip. She found herself open to him. His tongue forged its way inside.

Mara gave a little squeak then a soft moan of ecstasy. His tongue explored inside her mouth. She pushed on him, touching as well as smoothing, loving the texture along with the taste. She moved. Her breasts floated across his chest. She thought she might have heard a groan. Was the sound pleasure or pain? The ecstasy of it all was undeniable. She molded herself against the hard planes of his body. Her hands moved up his arms to circle around his back then his neck. She slid her fingers through his hair that was thick softness. The glide of the strands between her fingers made her tremble. His hands smoothed down her back until they cupped her bottom. He hauled her close. She felt the male part of him that was too big for her pulse against the softness of her belly. James brought her higher. Her breasts pushed against his chest then his chin smoothed across the tops. The stubble of a day's growth scratched. She was on fire, a cinder that could not be doused.

He set his mouth on hers again. His tongue penetrated. She let him suck her tongue into his mouth. He tasted of the champagne they drank. They kissed forever, their mouths fused in a passionate embrace. Mara didn't want the delicious contact to ever end.

The knock at the door brought the kiss to an abrupt finish. He stared into her eyes. She found herself shaking her head. Mara didn't want this to stop. "No...why? Please, kiss me again," she murmured, her voice throaty and dark vibrated from her. The sound was so deep and raw she didn't recognize herself. "Don't stop."

"Need to end this...don't have time to bring the kissing to its proper conclusion. We have some business to attend to before the wedding. The knock must be Chandler here to take care of a few of the details. We don't wish to forget anything. The night is too important for us. I'll get the door." "Oh…"

Mara needed to explain to him there would be no ceremony today. She couldn't…wouldn't marry a man she didn't love. Love might be there if she gave him the chance. No, he was too big. She couldn't stop the giggle. Her hand covered her mouth. Lost in thoughts of how huge he was, she giggled again. Maybe she was a bit muzzled. A draft of cool air from the hallway sent a chill down her spine.

Realized Chandler was staring at her. She reached for her peignoir. Found air.

"Put this on." Jamie's voice was hard. "Don't wish for Chandler to see anymore of you than necessary. He helped her put her arms through the sleeves then fastened the peignoir. His knuckles brushed against her breasts.

This was heaven. Mara wished he would touch the hard tips again. Wished Chandler would go away. She didn't like that man. He was a horrid mean man. Chandler tried to force her. Would have if her brothers hadn't found her. Now, she didn't understand what Chandler wanted from her.

"I brought the contract. See that Delight is as ready as possible. She is still standing. That is good. We don't want her asleep. Another glass of the bubbly before you bring her downstairs will do the trick. Keep her mind hazy for the short wedding along with the consummation of the vows. The house will be full to the brim. People who have heard of the unique show have been arriving early to get a seat. The minister has arrived. Johnny is making certain he is content. He was served some champagne and some of cook's delicious lemon tarts. The man of God is treating the food and drink as if he has had nothing to eat for weeks."

"Come along, Delight. I'll help you."

Jamie held her steady while he guided her to the table. A piece of paper with a lot of writing was presented to her. He held a pen out for her use. "Sign your name. Your legal name as well as your new one. Once we are married, we'll make Delight your new legal name."

"My new legal name? Whatever for?" she questioned. "Mara Chamberlin works just fine for me."

"This document needs your signature. Before we can go on with the wedding, we need your consent," Jamie explained.

"The contract is for five years," Chandler told them. "Best you understand what you're putting your name to. When you sign this your signature will tell everyone you are eager to participate in the plans set forth for you. You will also be the recipient of a great deal of money. Jamie will help you with investments."

"Eager for what? Investments? How?" Mara couldn't think. Didn't understand what Chandler was telling her. "Willing to do what?" She did wish for Jamie to kiss her more. Was eager to taste him with her tongue again to catch his scent.

"To entertain the good God-fearing folks that come to enjoy our shows. To have sex with your master," Chandler told her. "With your signature on this paper you will be forever known as Delight...Jamie's Delight. You do want to belong to Jamie."

So confused, Mara didn't wish to disappoint Jamie. Deep down she was thinking she shouldn't put her name to this piece of paper. "Oh." She tried to take deep breaths. Nothing seemed to make it to her lungs. Her heart raced. She massaged her temples then looked to Jamie for support. He nodded. "Suppose I need a pen. Do you have one?" She was a muddled mess. Didn't comprehend half of what Chandler told her. She was eager to be Jamie's Delight. As long as he didn't try to have sex with her. He just wouldn't fit. Didn't know how to convince him of something that was so obvious to her.

Chandler handed her the pen he'd been holding in front of her face. Her hand shook. Standing was near to impossible. The pen slid through her fingers to land on the floor. It bounced. When she tried to pick it up, she would have toppled over if Jamie didn't have such a firm hold on her arm.

"Hush now, all is right." Jamie gave her back the pen. Smiled with what appeared to be encouragement.

Chandler looked at Jamie then said, "You've done well. This should go off without a hitch. I find I'm looking forward to this show very much. We will make more money tonight than we ever have."

With Jamie's urgings, she bent over staring at the paper as well as the blurred lines in front of her. Bending closer the nearness didn't help her see the words any better. She couldn't read them. Knew she should do that, read the words. When she looked at Jamie, she asked, "Where? Where do I sign."

"Do you need help? I would guide you." His voice was soft yet firm. "I can move your hand for you if that's what you want. It's a husband's job to monitor his wife in her endeavors, the important ones so she doesn't go astray."

His words sounded to be a bit of blather. She did need his help though. Needed him to show her where her signature should go. "I do. I can't see the lines. Father always told us to read everything we sign. It's imperative so we don't make a mistake that can't be rectified," Mara said while Jamie closed his big hand around her fingers.

"Chandler told you the gist of the agreement. You will be with me in the shows we put on for five years. Right here." He set the pen on the line. Helped direct her hand to write her name, Mara Chamberlin…then Delight.

She stood so fast she hit his chin with the back of her head. Furious, she yelled at him, "Delight isn't my name." She felt the first rise of anger since Jamie came into the room to speak with her. "It's not! I won't sign that detestable name."

Jamie was quick to explain. "No, you're right. It's your AKA. See before the name Delight the paper reads AKA. Your name is still Mara Chamberlin. In this house, you will be known as Delight or Jamie's Delight. Is the show name alright with you? Must obtain your approval. Don't wish to do anything that goes against your wishes."

"Oh…" Jamie guided her hand along the line. With Jamie's help, she wrote her AKA. "Can I sit down now?" Mara didn't think her knees would hold her another second.

Jamie scooped her into his arms. Mara liked the way that felt. Last night he held her this way too. Thought she was too heavy for anyone to carry. She wasn't a baby. He set her on the large wing chair. Tucked her robe around her making certain to cover her feet. She thought it strange he was taking care of her. He was solicitous to her every whim. Helped her sign the document. Both he and Chandler explained what she signed. Mara realized she might need to reevaluate her opinion of the man.

"Thank you," she told Jamie, closing her eyes then breathing as deep as possible while she tried to soak up energy. The room was still moving a little. When she closed her eyes, she no longer felt as dizzy.

After looking at her, his eyes darkening to that beautiful shade of pewter she so loved, he strode to Chandler. She didn't want him to go away. He couldn't continue watching her. He told her they had things to do, necessary things. Things to ensure her future as well as his. Now, Jamie was talking to Chandler. While their voices weren't hushed, she couldn't make out what they were saying. Found she wanted to go to sleep. She was so tired.

Mara couldn't hear the whispered words. She wanted to learn what they were saying. As the door was closing behind Chandler, Jamie handed her another glass of Champagne. She knew she'd had two too many. She was so thirsty. The liquid tasted so good. She drank. The liquid slid down her throat as if it was water. He smiled at her. Picked up her hand turned it over. He bent to kiss the heart of her palm. She felt the damp glide of his tongue touch her. A shiver of raw hunger sluiced through her.

"We need to dress for the ceremony. Our wedding is to begin in about fifteen minutes." Jamie stood over her now. "Would you like help? Dressing? I would be pleased if you allowed me the honor. We will, after all, soon be husband and wife."

Her limbs were floppy. Eyes glazed over, she nodded. Didn't think she could rise off the chair let alone dress herself. "Please. That would be wune...wunerful." She couldn't even talk.

He worked with speed. Without having time to blink, she was naked. Mara tried to cover herself with hands that didn't cooperate. Heard Jamie's soft chuckle of what must be amusement. Holding her hands away from her body, he stepped back. The slow glide of his hands traveled along her shaking form. She didn't see anything amusing here. Next, she knew she wore a thin white gown. Mara was certain he could see all of her. The fabric hid nothing of her. Jamie enclosed her with a light blue cape then fastened the front so she was shielded. She was barefoot. With wide fascinated eyes, she watched him disrobe then pull on a pair of pants made from the same gossamer material as her gown. She saw his male part, hard as well as long. Gulping air, she realized again with shocking clarity he was too big for her. What did her brothers tell her that thing was called? Her tongue slid across her mouth. She couldn't call it that thing. Jamie would laugh at her.

"Thirsty."

"Don't know if you will be able to stay awake for the ceremony if I give you another glass. We should wait. Just a few more minutes until we reach our destination. After we are married, you can have whatever suits you. You need to be able to tell the minister, 'I do.'"

"I do? I do…?" Mara felt as if her brain was made of straw. She was confused. What was she going to do. Didn't seem as if Jamie was going to answer her question.

One more time, she was in his arms cuddling into the solid wall of his broad chest. Soaking in the heat of his powerful male body. Would he always make her this hot? Mara enjoyed the spicy scent that filled her when she snuggled against the hard angles and planes she was coming to associate with Jamie. Unable to stop herself, she kissed his neck. Ran her tongue across his collarbone. Bit. He groaned again.

"If you keep this up, I might not wait until we're married," he groaned again when she bit then laved the same spot.

"You taste better than you smell. Though the scent of you is quite pleasing. I do enjoy the salty taste of you." Mara rubbed her face against this chest. The thick hair tickled her cheek. She giggled. "You please me."

His arms tightened around her. He kissed her hard. Sent his tongue between her lips. "You're going to be the death of me."

In the theatre he set her down. "Give Chandler your arm." He supported her then handed her to Chandler. She stood but she was wobbling, swaying against him. She didn't wish to be anywhere near that man. Remembered she'd thought to reevaluate her feelings toward Chandler. "Don't go…" She reached out to Jamie understanding he was leaving her where she didn't wish to be. The room was full of people, clapping as well as cheering. What were all these people doing here? There were so many.

"Be advised you might need to carry her down the aisle. She's as weak as a newborn kitten," Jamie told Chandler.

Before he strode away from her, he kissed her forehead. Smoothed her brows with the tip of his finger. "Behave yourself?"

When had she ever not behaved herself? Mara knew his strides were long as well as powerful. His back always straight, determined. She also knew her Jamie to be a stubborn man. How long had she known this man?

Had it been an entire day? She recalled some of the night. Remembered this morning waking up her legs spread across his. She'd been naked then. She was almost naked now. Naked in front of all these people seemed bizarre, embarrassing too.

"Whatever it takes," Chandler replied to Jamie. "I will get her to the altar all in one piece. Don't worry. Believe I want this marriage as much as you."

"Why are all these people here? They are applauding and yelling for something to go on. I don't understand."

"To watch the show," Chandler told her as he tried to keep her upright. "You and Jamie are the stars."

"What show?"

"They are impatient to watch you and Jamie tie the knot. They wish to see what is going to happen. All of these people came to watch you and Jamie marry then consummate the marriage. Money, a great deal of money was paid to watch you along with Jamie act out the script Jamie wrote. Some of those groats will be yours. The two of you are all the talk of the town. The buzz brought all of these wonderful people here to witness a beautiful wedding along with an even more lovely consummation."

She licked her lips. Shaking her head she spoke her thoughts out loud to the one man she disliked more than anyone else. "We can't consummate the marriage. He's too big. We won't fit."

Mara didn't understand why no one listened to her. All Chandler did was yowl with his laughter.

Mara didn't believe this to be amusing.

There was an aisle. When she looked down, she saw Celine standing on one side and Bertram on the other. Jamie and what seemed to be a minister who was holding a bible stood in the middle. It must be Celine getting married to Bertram. I'm the bridesmaid. That's what is happening. Never been a bridesmaid before. This is the wrong dress. Shouldn't be wearing something so see-through. Her mother would tell her this wasn't acceptable.

Chandler swept her into his arms before walking toward Jamie. Mara didn't like the way this man felt or the scent of him. If she didn't place her arms around his neck, she would fall. She wanted Jamie again. Needed one of his frenzied kisses. Wished to feel his tongue between her lips deep inside her. Loved the way he penetrated then withdrew to repeat the process again. "Behave yourself," Chandler whispered to her. "No, on second thought, behaving won't get the needed applause and the extra coin. Make this last as long as possible. Titillate the audience. Jamie will know how to deal with you. He's done a remarkable job to this point. Can't believe this day came so soon. It has been one hour more than twenty-four hours since the abduction."

He set her down in front of Jamie then spoke. "Don't believe your Delight can stand for the entire ceremony. You need to keep her upright. Hold onto her so she doesn't topple over. She might hurt herself. I'll be sitting nearby."

As soon as Chandler left her, her knees crumbled. Before she reached the ground, Jamie held her in his arms. That was fine by her. In his embrace, curled next to him was the exact spot where she wished to be. Felt her eyelashes flutter against his warm flesh. He untied her cloak, swept the fabric from her shoulders. Bertram untied Jamie's cape. Mara leaned against his hard frame again. This was right where she wished to be. On contact her nipples hardened…ached to feel his touch.

The man with the bible droned on and on. She closed her eyes, unable to concentrate on the words. Not that her attentiveness mattered. Celine and Bertram were tying the knot. They were the ones who needed to listen to the words of commitment.

Mara felt the soft, warm whisper against her cheek. Jamie was talking about something. There was amusement in the tone of his voice. "Say I do, sweet. The minister is waiting for you to speak."

"Oh, okay…I do. What am I doing?"

She was confused again. Wished she understood why her thoughts were in such disorder. When his mouth found hers, she was pleased. "I love your kisses," she murmured when the heat of his lips closed around hers. "Maybe I don't detest you."

"That's nice for a husband to learn on his wedding day. Put your sweet little tongue in my mouth, love. Show me what you can do…all I've taught you." His hands cupped her rear. He brought her close. She felt him hard against the softness of her belly.

She obeyed. Jamie kissed her and kissed her more. The gown she wore fell away from her. After what seemed like hours of kissing, he set her on the bed that had been placed on the Dias. His weight pressed into her. His length blanketed her. Her legs were spread wide alarming her until he kissed her again. Reached deep inside her with his tongue. With the contact she forgot everything.

"Easy sweet. I'll be careful with you."

She felt his hands fondling her, caressing her everywhere. Her breasts. Her belly. The juncture between her thighs. Heard herself whimper with the enjoyment of all he did, the ecstasy, all the quicksilver heat. This was amazing. Mercuric. She never wanted him to stop. One finger was inside her, moving in then out. Penetrate. Retreat. Next there was more of him inside. She didn't understand. Decided she didn't care. Her body pulsed to life. She arched against him, moaning. The wicked sound was coming from the back of her throat. The fire he orchestrated heated all of her. She pushed against him needing more. Begging.

"Please…"

"I need to kiss you more. Won't ever have enough of your mouth, your tongue, the deep raw heat inside you. Need to explore all your dark secret parts. Let me inside you. Let me see as well as feel all of you.

Next, he was inside her. She was stretching. She moaned her pleasure deep in the back of her throat. He moved with slow measured precision. In then out, seeming to take special care of her.

Braced on his forearms, he hovered above her. His lips drawn back as if he was in pain. "We fit very nicely, sweet. I am not too big as you can attest to now that I've shown you. So, as to the proof of your virginity. I'm about to remove the shield proclaiming your sweet innocence. This will sting for a moment. After the bite goes away you will know only pleasure. I do not want to hurt you, my Delight. Nonetheless, this must be done. Finished. The proof of my seed inside you for all to see. All these people are witnesses to our marriage along with the consummation. There can be no annulment."

Mara didn't understand why they needed witnesses as to this event or that he would show all these strangers' proof of her innocence. An annulment for what? Seemed she heard every word yet she didn't understand what it had to do with her. Uncomprehending, her mind seemed to work in slow motion.

All around her there was a huge roar of excitement. He filled her deep and hard. Her nails scraped into his flesh. She bit his shoulder trying to buck him off. Her movement sent him deeper. This pain was far more than a little sting or bite. Why did he hurt her? She didn't like what he was doing to her. Above her Jamie held still.

"Hush, I know I hurt you. It's almost over. There will be no more pain. Try to relax."

Relax, ha!

Just as he told her, the burn vanished. He kissed her again then more of the same. Kissed her breasts. Her mouth, even her ears. He found this place with his finger in the most intimate part of her that sent her into a frenzy of raw desire. Her body pulsed. Arched against his. Without warning, she cried out, her body splintering into millions of pieces of pleasure. Above her, she heard his loud growl. Felt warm fluid flow inside her.

Mara couldn't move. She was shaking from the top of her head to the tips of her toes. Wasn't able to think. Jamie was deep inside her. He withdrew. When she was able to open her eyes, she saw that someone brought a basin of rose scented water. Jamie was bathing her. Touching her where no one should touch. The crowd roared. Sent coins flying their way. He'd done more than touch. When she opened her eyes to the scene in front of her, everyone was watching them. She was naked in front of too many people to count. Her legs spread to their view. They saw all of her.

"It's alright, sweet. Nothing bad is going to happen to you. As soon as I'm done here, I'll give you another glass of champagne. We can eat a piece of our wedding cake. After we finish eating, we can retire to our bedchamber."

There was blood along with something else between her legs. She was embarrassed to the heated roots of her hair. When he finished washing her, he cleaned the blood from himself. From that male part of him, she didn't have a name for. She made a note to ask him what he called it.

The room spun but not as much as before. She felt as if she could breathe. Jamie dressed her in the white filmy gown before pulling on his pants. Pants she could see through. Saw the part of him that was no longer so big. He was beautiful both ways. Mara loved to look at him in his naked state.

What just happened?

Hand in hand, he led her to a table that had just been brought in. The cakes were huge. There were bottles upon bottles of champagne. Jamie turned her so she faced the large audience who were still hooting their pleasure, stomping their feet on the ground as well as clapping.

"More! More!" They yelled.

Jamie kissed her hard. His tongue delving inside her mouth. He turned to the crowd, speaking, "More another time. Now I have my wedding night in front of me." He held out his hands. "All of you witnessed the consummation of my marriage to Miss Delight. Now she is Jamie's Delight. You saw the virgin blood on her thighs as well as my sex. We are now going to sign the certificate of marriage. No one, no one can now contest this marriage, nor can it be annulled. Delight is mine. She belongs to me through eternity." Jamie held her hand in the air. Her nipples rubbed against the soft fabric of the gown that wasn't truly a gown.

Chandler placed the license on the table for their signature. Just as she signed the document in Jamie's room upstairs, she signed this one. He helped her form the letters. For a few seconds, she thought her mind was clearing. Was beginning to feel close to normal. No longer. When she finished with her signature she leaned back absorbed by Jamie's arms. She hoped he'd make love to her again. Except for the first sting, she liked what he did.

The applause was deafening. Chandler's cook brought them a piece of cake. They performed the usual ritual. Mara thought the cake tasted divine. Jamie kissed her again, deep. Intimate, licking sweet icing from her lips. She thought she might swoon from the gentleness.

"Drink your champagne." He told her. Smiled when she complied to his command. This was her second glass since they left his rooms.

After she drank, he swept her into his arms before striding through the back door on his way to their bedchamber.

~ * ~

Damn Chandler to hell and back. A breath of furious air shuddered into her lungs. "Chandler accomplished his plan. He had his revenge. Jamie and Mara are married. Consummated the marriage in front of a live audience. This is horrible. Mara was so drugged she didn't know what she was doing. Couldn't make a logical decision. Chandler has no shame. He plans on sending an announcement of their marriage to the Chamberlin family. Of course, he intends to wait a few weeks just to orchestrate more attention when the truth emerges."

Ash along with Harris, her parents and siblings, cousins also, were sitting in the drawing room of the Wolcott townhouse. She was drinking a cup of tea along with the ladies. Hollis and all the other men had snifters of brandy. Georgia was having a difficult time keeping Chandler from her head.

"There is nothing we can do now. Don't believe it would be wise to inform the family of her plight since it appears Chandler will do the honors. You won't be involved. Knowing Chandler's proclivities, I'm certain he will wait until Mara is with child. The pair need time to cool their heels. To figure out how to proceed during the next five years of Mara's commitment. Until her family finds her and they will, there is no doubt in my mind they will think the worst possible scenario. Believe the family will be relieved she is alive," James reinforced all the words Hollis along with Bea warned her about. Patience needed to be her mantra until Chandler showed his true colors. Then she would no longer feel the guilt embedded deep in her soul.

"Whatever happens, you will not confront that man. You don't know she didn't wish to be part of Chandler's or even Jamie's plans. From what you've told us, Mara has signed everything put in front of her. The young man is so devil-may-care handsome the sight of him makes a woman need to swoon. What if they truly are each other's mate? What then? The natural course would be for them to marry. Jamie would claim her in the ways of his clan. The pair have not done anything wrong. Jamie has done nothing wrong. Even Chandler should be guilt free since he brought the unlikely pair together," Ash said while he brought his wife's hand to his lips. Slow kissed the palm, until Harris got this dreamy look on her face.

Realizing all that was said tonight was true, Georgia felt both a small wave of despair as well as one of relief. The two did need to find each other. Chandler unwittingly accomplished the deed. Once she hoped for the kind of love these two had, the type of love all Harris' siblings and cousins enjoyed. Georgia tamped down the rise of moisture in her throat. Tears were unwelcome. When she met Chandler, this was not the end she hoped for. Would it be so bad to return to the brothel? She might be able to keep her children safe from the wickedness surrounding them. She would never sign an agreement to perform in his shows. For her, entertaining crowds of people would never happen again. Even though at first, the process was exciting. If honest with herself, she enjoyed the shows until Chandler brought Bertram into the mix involving the two of them.

"I was in Chandler's head when Mara signed the contract. A document I know to be binding. Chandler owns her for the next five years. I'm surprised the document didn't read for life," Georgia told the group that was gathered in the room. Her voice was as bitter as her thoughts.

The dinner party was a success. She thought it was nice James included her for the meal. At first, she refused. All in attendance, would spread the word about the menu that was a huge success. The food was delicious. Georgia hoped she would gain more customers. As time passed, she also hoped people would forget her performances in Chandler's establishment.

In the morning, her little family would return to Orange Blossom cottage. She missed her bed. Disliked sleeping in a strange room. Smith-Jones would accompany them in the Wolcott carriage. Everyone was still afraid Chandler would find a means to kidnap her. At this time, his mind was engaged with his new star. Once the excitement of Jamie's Delight wore off, Chandler would turn his attention back on her.

Until Chandler grew tired of pursuing her, he would hope for her to return to him on her own. Chandler's hope wasn't going to happen. She would rather leave the country than live with him again. For a change of scenery, she could always go to Carnoch, Scotland with the Frasier family. They invited her. Georgia wondered if Chandler would look for her there. This was a conundrum she didn't appreciate. Perhaps a change of scenery would give her a new outlook on life. She didn't know. Could guess at the possibilities.

"Are you speaking to that beast again," Bea asked. "You've that faraway look on your face that always accompanies his thoughts."

"No, not this time. Though my head was in the clouds. I was wondering if we should move to Carnoch. A variation of landscape would be nice." The distance would give her more time to figure out what she wanted. Deep in her soul, she realized sooner than later Chandler would own her with no restrictions.

"Moving close to us would be a splendid idea. You would be protected by our clan," Lainie, Cameron Frasier's wife, clapped her hands together.

Lainie was the woman Cameron searched for. She tumbled through time to appear to him. The order of events was strange. At times unaccountable. When all was finished, the two women, Dallas Shaw and Lanie ended up in the year they were meant to live. How the universe set things straight was unknown.

"We'd all like you to live close by. If moving would help to keep you safe, we would support all your plans. There could be a catering service in Carnoch for you. You wouldn't need to fear someone recognizing you. You've had one close call as it is," Hawk agreed.

Hawk was the oldest of the Frasiers, a doctor in Carnoch.

"I don't know. I'll need to think about this. Moving to Scotland would be a huge change for all of us. Though the switch in scenery would be helpful." Georgia turned to James. "If we decide on relocating, will you oversee the selling of my home?"

"Of course, my dear. Doing so would be my pleasure. Maybe your father would want to travel with you. He could share a home."

"No…" Georgia looked at her father. "Believe I'm too old to live with my father again. Need my privacy. What I don't know is if I can keep all my thoughts to myself. Chandler is better at getting into my head than he used to be. Someone, most likely Bertram, has been giving him pointers. Each day it grows harder for me to block him. Though," Georgia paused. "Father is always welcome to move. Don't wish to share a home. Doubt if he would enjoy sharing a residence either."

"You must stay strong." As if to lend support, Harris reached out to touch her hand.

She sent a little puff of air out of her lungs. "The only reason he hasn't made an appearance this evening is because he's in the middle of his show. After Jamie left with Mara, the four seasons all made an appearance. He's raking in money with this new theme. Virgins. Don't know how this idea will end up."

"The four seasons are the special acts, right?" Harris asked. "I was on stage once with Autumn Bounty when Chandler abducted me as was Lainie. I was so mortified. Don't understand how all those women..." her voice trailed off as if she was remembering the unpleasantness. "I think you should move if my opinion holds any merit. You could come to Dover with us. I told you, you would always be welcome."

"Your home is the first place Chandler would look for me. Doubt if yours is a good idea." Georgia knew the auctioning off of the girls for a night of pleasure was happening right now. As soon as the sale was finished, he would roam her mind. It would never do for her to think about the move to Carnoch. She had to keep her thoughts centered on Mara.

Georgia turned to the Frasier clan. "I will think on the move. I will discuss this with both Hollis as well as Bea. Must keep in mind that Chandler will be furious when he discovers me missing. As is always his won't, he will seek revenge. His fury will fall on me. If I thought he would blame the clan for moving me, I would take my chances and stay where I am."

"We are a strong clan. Stronger than Chandler. We can defend our own," Hawk said with fierce pride echoing in his voice.

She did have second along with third thoughts about who he would unleash his fury on. Georgia wasn't certain she could withstand what he would do. With every breath in her body, she missed Chandler. He never understood her departure from his brothel. She was never able to explain why she didn't wish to bring up her children in a whorehouse. Touching the marks that proclaimed her as his through eternity, she fought tears.

Why are you crying?

Startled Georgia let out a tiny cry of dismay. She brushed the moisture from her eyes. *Don't wish to speak with you. Go away. You're a horrible human being.*

Ah, you witnessed the fun entertainment. Delight has been introduced to the patrons of my shows. The lady is one of us now. She loved every moment just as you used to enjoy others seeing us make love. I want your lovely white body back, love. In time, my dear...in time, I will have you beneath me or on top of me, or in front of me, showing off all your sweetest secrets.

What we did together was not making love. It was sex. Lust. Call it what it is, pure lust. Nothing more.

Why are you crying?

I'm not.

Liar. I'm not an idiot. I heard the tiny sob you hid from everyone else. Why? Was it because Delight lost her innocence in front of more than one hundred men as well as women. That's the nature of things. A woman will lose her virginity. Best get over the small fact.

I would never give you my reason. Don't wish for you to have my confidence or know anything about my emotions.

You miss me. You miss the sex. The lust. The frenzy that becomes part of you when I fondle my favorite parts.

No!

Damn she could never hide her feelings from him. Nothing he could say would induce her to admit to the fact.

Chapter Six

The move to Carnoch took over a month to complete. Georgia and company were able to travel to Carnoch in the coaches provided by James Wolcott. The Frasiers brought some of her household needs in various carts as they returned earlier. When she was able to leave, she brought the remainder of the furnishings with her. Some of the less useful items were left in the attic at the Wolcott townhouse in London.

Smith-Jones provided more protection in case Chandler got wind of the change of address. Twice she visited the tavern to learn there was still no sign of Mara. Georgia managed to keep her mind blocked from Chandler's prying while she went about the business of selling the cottage. Chandler even visited her twice during the month when all the preparations were being made. Seemed he was so focused on her, he never noticed the missing furniture. All he cared about was the bed. Not that he made it to the bed. With Maeve in her arms along with the help from Bea and Hollis, she evaded his advances. Each time she succeeded, he cursed. Would leave her home in a blinding rage.

In avoiding his attentions, she couldn't believe her good luck. Part of her good fortune was due to the fact his mind was focused on Jamie and Delight, his new entertainers. Chandler lobbied for Delight to participate in other shows. Jamie refused. So possessive, he would never allow Delight to have another man inside her sweet body. If he had to leave her alone in his rooms, one of the girls would be called to sit with her. Jamie was protective.

With a slow hand, Jamie took her off the laudanum. Mara began to realize what transpired the second night she was at the brothel. Recalled her abduction. Demanded to no avail to see her parents. Accepted the fact she had been coerced into acting in a manner contrary to her nature. Acknowledged the notion she could change nothing. After a few days sober, she no longer asked to see her family. If they learned what she'd done, they would be horrified, might seek retribution. She didn't want anyone to be hurt. What Chandler along with Jamie did was legal. All was wrapped up tight with her signature on the legal documents binding her to both Jamie as well as Chandler's business. If she said they drugged her, all involved would deny doing so. Her family didn't know where she was.

The day before she left for Carnoch, Georgia visited the tavern for the third time since the kidnapping. Was not shocked by the somber air in the dining room. Mackenzie waited on her table. Told her how they would never give up the search for her little sister. She'd been so tempted to tell her what she knew. Seeming to understand the gigantic wave of guilt that possessed her, Hollis squeezed her hand hard, giving her warning of the dire nature of her thoughts.

Now, standing in front of the new home she purchased, Georgia was able to smile. For the time being she was well away from Chandler. The decision freed her from his looming presence. Over the month they did converse. She did tell him how she felt about Mara. Told him he needed to find some way to let the family know Mara was alive and healthy. He was a creative man. Could do so without implicating himself. Would never need to tell them where she was.

Mara was pregnant with a little male shifter. Jamie had not claimed her yet nor shown her his cat. He'd told Chandler she was too distraught about the nights she now entertained crowds to introduce her to something that would shock her. Those nights she was embarrassed. Mortified to the tips of her delicious toes. Chandler explained to her there was no way she could get out of the contract she signed. While telling her all the details, Chandler gloated. He was quite pleased with Delight.

At least the two were only on stage once a week, four times so far. Just as Chandler loved to be part of the decadence, so did Jamie. Jamie was so much like Chandler, Georgia cringed. She reminded herself for at least the thousandths time, there was nothing to be done about the situation.

"What do you think?" Bea interrupted her contemplations while she looked toward their new home. "Believe this house is just what we needed. It's a bit larger than Orange Blossom cottage. Should we christen it with a name? I'm eager to begin fixing this place up, making it our own. Even the nursery is larger."

"This home is beautiful. It will do until Chandler finds us. After he discovers our location, I don't know what will happen. We are so far away. He will not be able to visit often. I'll think of a name. The name must be perfect." Georgia was worried. Understood the fury in Chandler when he discovered how far he would need to travel to possess her again.

"Are you my new neighbor?"

Startled, her hand on her chest, she swiveled. "Oh my, you frightened me from my musings. If you are saying you live in the cottage just a half mile down the road well then yes. I suppose I am the neighbor." She paused, staring at the man. What she saw was uncanny. This man looked so much like Chandler he could be a brother. Georgia knew he wasn't. Chandler had only one brother, Ash.

His hand outstretched. Not giving her a chance to decline, he placed her hand in his then kissed the back. Looked up then smiled. "Pleased to meet you. My name is Hamilton Addair. Yes, I live just down the road. For the past month, I've been watching the proceedings. Where are you from?"

He was a handsome man. Tall, with a strong chin. His chestnut-colored hair was too long, curling around the collar of his white shirt that molded to a broad chest. Georgia felt a strange calling to run her fingers through his hair. The buckskins he wore shaped his hard thighs. The man stole her breath. Gave her pulse a leap.

After he let her go, Georgia placed her hand on her growing belly. Felt the babe kick. She would give birth soon. Hamilton would wonder about her husband. Georgia decided she would be a widow if he asked. No, she needed to stay as close to the truth as possible. Unable to stop herself from staring at him, she didn't understand the emotions blazing through her head. She held the uncanny notion, he knew what she was thinking. Well, he couldn't read her mind. That wasn't possible. Getting to know him better was first in her thoughts.

"I'm Georgia O'brien," Georgia said as she lowered her lashes in an attempt to hide her very real admiration of him. Her thoughts shocked her.

Could a person have more than one mate in her lifetime? She felt as if this man was made for her. Possessed her soul as well as her heart. Had she been wrong about Chandler? No, he claimed her. She saw their past lives together.

Chandler was her mate.

What was going on here?

"May I ask about your husband? I don't see anyone who might fill that role. Over the past month, I haven't seen anyone I don't know. The other man I saw you speak to earlier is old enough to be your father."

Georgia sipped air. Felt her eyes widen. She totally abandoned the thought she could pass herself off as a widow. Decided he was too polite to tell her she was so obviously with child. "I have no husband." The words sounded bitter to her ears, never having wished to be a single mother.

"Oh...can't say that I mind? You are very beautiful. I do enjoy looking at lovely women. Not that I ogle them, just appreciate rare beauty. You are rare. A gem."

As well as very pregnant. "It's almost as it seems. The man who..."

She waved her hand in the air. Didn't understand why she needed to explain. For some reason she believed she should. "He asked me to marry him. I refused."

"You don't love him?"

The question was meant to pilfer more information. The answer to his invasive question was not his business. She found herself more than willing to divulge her secrets. "He loves himself along with his profession too much. The little girl," she turned to Bea, "Is also his. I don't want my children to be influenced by the man. He is not a very nice person. His residence is..."

All she said was true. For some reason she wasn't going to tell Hamilton any lies. She didn't know how to tell Hamilton the man who fathered her children was the proud owner of a whorehouse located on one of the shadier streets in London.

"...but you love him. I can hear the truth in the tone of your voice. For you to leave him, he must have disappointed you very much." His voice sounded so patient and endearing. She wished she could snuggle into his warmth.

Her breath hitched. "You hear too much. Probably more than I'd like a man I've known less than ten minutes to learn. Yes, I do love the man. Don't intend to ever see him again. I'm better off without him. At least that is my wish to not see him. He might have something else to say about my wishes. He usually does. There is no doubt in my mind he will find me. Don't know what I'll do when that happens. The man is tenacious. Believes if he wants something or someone then it is his."

"You need protection. More than you can get from the older man. His name is…did you say? Sometimes I don't pay attention the way I should. My mind was focusing more concentration on you, as well as all you were not saying."

At his last words she swallowed air. Hamilton was turning out to be nosy. Funny thing was, she didn't mind. The silver-blue of his eyes twinkled when he looked at her. His smile charmed, his lips firm. He possessed a stubborn tilt to his chin she appreciated.

"Chandler won't hurt me. All he wants is to take me back to the whor… He believes I belong to him. I don't." She blinked. Stopped the words. "Never mind." That was more than she wished to tell this man who she just met.

One dark eyebrow arched skyward. Again, he heard more than she wished to tell him. "I'd like to talk to you more. Learn about this man you love. Would you come to dinner?" He rubbed the back of his neck, obvious he was a bit hesitant. "I'll understand if you decline. To you, I'm a stranger. Would love to change the fact. Want to come to mean something to you."

Georgia wondered what was behind the invitation. Did he believe she would be easy? While she once was, she never would be again. She wasn't going to give her body to just any man. For some reason, Georgia felt more for Hamilton than she should on such short notice.

"You come to my house for dinner. That way I won't worry about… Never mind again. Bea is a marvelous cook. I would feel more comfortable in my home." More comfortable with Hollis along with Bea as companions. Didn't need or want a chaperone just longed to have companionship in case anything got out of hand.

She was far too old and jaded to need or want a chaperone. After her sojourn at the brothel, she didn't believe she could ever be seduced except by Chandler. Hamilton seemed to be a gentleman. What she'd learned over the last two years was that even gentlemen felt lust. Men all looked for easy sex. Chandler provided that commodity for the right price. She watched so many men enjoy the charms of the women in the brothel.

"I would love to come to your home. I would bring wine? If you like that is."

Her frown would stop him. She was thinking about the wine Jamie drugged Mara with. She sipped a token of air. "I would love wine. Would be a nice addition to the meal."

"What time?"

"How about eight. That would give me time to arrange the kitchen into better order. Bea can begin the meal. Her homemade bread is to die for. The Frasiers provided me with fresh rainbow trout. They are relatives of a sort. Distant relatives. In truth the Frasiers are friends. Nothing more. Nonetheless they've taken a shine to me. The family has helped me when I needed aid the most. They gave me vegetables along with some other staples. We can have baby potatoes smothered in butter. Lainie sent over a lemon pie. She is a remarkable cook."

"Know the family well. I work with Hawk Frasier along with Houston Stuart. I'm the third doctor here in Carnoch. When it's your time, send for me. I'll be pleased to deliver your baby."

Bold as you please, Hamilton set his hand on her swollen belly. Found the happenstance strange that she didn't move away. Georgia normally didn't like people touching her in that way. He didn't even ask.

Georgia wasn't at all certain about having this man with her when the child was born. Until this moment she assumed Bea would help her. Celine was there for her when Maeve was born. She felt comfortable with a woman, not a man she was just beginning to know.

"I'll think about it. I'm not..."

If Hamilton heard the word whore when she was about to refer to the whorehouse, he would get the wrong impression. She wasn't a whore. Chandler was the only man who made love to her. Her mate was too possessive to allow another male to have sex with her. He did threaten her with Bertram every time she angered him.

"I understand. Perhaps you would rather Hawk or Houston see to you. Believe me when I say, you should consult a doctor. Have you seen one ever...about your pregnancy? There are things we can tell you that will help make the pregnancy as well as the birth easier." Hamilton appeared eager to set his opinions into action.

Unable to stop the smile at his concern, she went on to speak her mind. "Bea will do just fine. My nanny has delivered other babies. She is an experienced midwife. There will be no problems."

Georgia understood her stubborn nature was revealed. She had second along with third thoughts about a doctor, a man, seeing her that way...giving birth.

"Anything could go wrong. There is no way to anticipate a problem except to have the most experienced people with you on your delivery day. The three of us are all very good with deliveries. All of us have researched the safest ways to go about the delivery of the precious little bundles women carry for their men. What if the umbilical cord is wrapped around the baby's neck? What would you do? There are other difficulties that just occur unannounced. What would happen if your baby didn't turn? This is your second child." Hamilton stated as if that meant something else.

Hamilton was giving her more insecurities than she'd ever thought about. Georgia never heard of those things happening. Doubted if Bea would understand what to do. She tried to ignore his dire warnings. Needed to concentrate on anything else. "Yes...does that make a difference? She knew next to nothing about birthing except from her first experience.

"Should be much faster. Second babies tend to find themselves breathing fresh air then screaming at the top of their lungs much sooner than first ones. I do live very close to you. Bea can always help you until I arrive. When you go into labor, Hollis can fetch me here in a few minutes. I will come night or day, no matter the time. I'm used to being awakened in the middle of the night. Thrive on it." Hamilton didn't appear too worried about her indecision. "I will speak to Hollis myself."

"Well, where is this office of yours? Is it closer than your home? If you are at work, any doctor could be just as fast."

She wouldn't want either of the other two men to deliver her baby. She was just being obtuse. Unless something changed, she wasn't about to call a man, any man, to deliver Colin.

"All true. No, the office is farther than my home. It's in the village. Hollis can still come for me. Bea can still take care of you until I can get to you. I'd like you to come into the office the next day or two for an examination. Should check on the placement of the baby. Check internally.

Knowledge as to where the head is will give me an idea as to an approximate date of delivery. Do you know when the child was conceived?"

No, no…he wasn't going to feel inside her for any reason. Was that what he meant by checking her internally. "I feel fine. Maeve was seven days late. No, I don't know the day. Chandler would know…he's the baby's father." An examination by this man sounded frightening. Georgia didn't know what that would entail. Naked with this man…dear lord her mind was stumbling in all the wrong directions. She was getting ahead of herself. Found she was panting from the suggestion of nakedness.

"You won't be naked if my seeing you without clothing is what is stopping you…worrying you. In fact, I could give you a partial examination this evening after we eat. Would my doing so make you feel better?" He sounded solicitous.

"No!"

"I've frightened you. Don't wish to terrify. Just want to help out. The examination would take all of five minutes. In the drawing room if you like. Would not need to retire to your bedchamber. When you come to the office for a thorough exam, you can have a companion. Hawk's wife, Leah, can be in the room with us."

"Terrified me, yes. I'm treading on ground I don't understand. No one was with me except the father and one of the girls when Maeve was born." Again, she said too much. Bloody eyes, Maeve was born in a brothel. She could never tell him. Her mortification would know no end. She met Hawk and Leah at the dinner party in London.

"I am a doctor, a real doctor. If you asked either Hawk or Houston, they too would insist that you are examined. It's important for the health of the baby as well as the mother. I want you to have the best medical care possible. Don't you?"

He tossed the gist of the conversation onto her doorstep. Of course, she wanted the best. It's just…the best frightened her. Made her uncomfortable.

"Your question is unfair." Georgia stared into his eyes, honest eyes, silver blue eyes. Eyes that seemed to delve into her mind. "Alright, this evening. If you find any reason for a more thorough exam then I will come into the office. Feel fine though. Nothing to worry about. All that's wrong with me is the reality I have trouble getting up from a chair as well as walking. As you must have noticed, my walk is awkward."

"It's endearing. A very charming waddle if I do say so myself. I do adore pregnant ladies. They always have this glow about them. The anticipation of holding a newborn to one's breast makes them shine bright."

At his words, heat stained her cheeks then progressed all the way to her toes. Yes, she loved the sensations when Maeve suckled at her breast. For a few hot seconds, she looked away from the man.

"Sorry, didn't mean to embarrass you. What I said is the truth. You are a charming lady. For the moment, I'll take my leave and cease to embarrass you. Will be here at seven." He reached out then as if thinking better of the idea, he drew his hand back.

"Eight."

"Seven. The extra hour will give us time to chat more about the baby. Discuss your medical care. You did tell me you don't know when you conceived. Perhaps you could make a guess. Ah…such a difficult question. Would also like to learn more about your charming self."

One more time heat flooded her face. "No."

Her lips thinned. She frowned at him. This topic of childbirth was becoming more uncomfortable as the seconds ticked along. Telling him the father made love to her every day, every time the whim came upon him would continue her character decline in his eyes. Georgia wasn't sure why she cared.

"We will speak of this again." He placed a quick kiss on her cheek then grinned at her. When he strode to his horse, he was whistling.

With the quick kiss on her cheek, air caught in her throat. Hamilton had grinned at her. She swallowed hard. If she allowed it, this man would come to mean something to her. She knew he was important in her life. He was too handsome by far. He was a beautiful man. Strong. Stubborn. Arrogant.

I will be more important to you as the days pass. You are my mate. I ken you are a shifter, a beautiful white tiger. Cannot tell about the babe because the wee bairn is not mine. You and I, we will be together now as well as in the distant future. You can count on the fact. I will see you at seven.

What?

Georgia was baffled by his words. His mate? His statement couldn't be true. She was Chandler's mate. Oh, my, he would hear every befuddled word. Her brain must be made of sawdust.

You are my mate, love. I ken the fact just as I ken you will be my patient. Tonight, we can take the first few tentative steps toward trust. I realize you don't trust men, at least not many of us male creatures. By the way, my second shape is a black panther. Most shifters in the Highlands change to black panthers.

Can a person have two mates in one lifetime? Didn't know if that was possible. You can't be what you claim.

I'm hearing your thoughts. That fact should speak volumes in my favor.

Can a person have two mates at once? Georgia repeated the question.

Have no idea. Never heard of such a thing happening before. Suppose anything is possible. Is the father of your babe a shifter? Not that it's my business. I realize I've pushed you too far, way too soon. We need to learn about each other before you confide in me. Know that what has happened in your past makes no difference to this man. Also, you should learn I will never hurt you. Never expect something from you that you are not willing to give. Doesn't mean I won't try persuasion as a means to achieve my goal. Maybe even a little seduction if the opportunity arrives.

This is too much to absorb at this instant. I will see you at seven. You might wish to bring more than one bottle of wine.

Georgia heard his laughter.

They'd been talking to each other while he was riding away. She didn't have anyone to ask about this double entendre…two times the mates. Chandler would be furious if she ever gave herself to another man. At this juncture, Georgia didn't care how Chandler felt. She did wish for marriage someday. Hoped to have a father for her children. Never wished to be a single mother.

Hamilton appeared too good to be true. Georgia decided she must take care not to fall too fast or too hard. Dusting off her skirts, she realized she needed to hurry. Seven would be here far too soon. Hollis and Bea would prepare a splendid dinner. She wanted a bath. Would soak in lavender oil. Damn, but she felt like a débutante getting ready for her first ball. This situation seemed so unreal.

"Bea! Where are you?" Georgia's heart raced with anticipation of the night to come. She strode through the entryway. "I need you. Can't wait another moment. Also, can't tell you about my impatience. Not yet. I do have a few secrets. Time will tell how this will unfold. I'm too uncertain now."

"In the kitchen." Bea turned to look at her when she stepped into the warmth of the room. The counters sparkled. Sunlight slanted in through the window. This morning there had been fog along with ice. Now a brilliant sun bathed the highlands. Bea was drying her hands on a dishtowel, grinning at her. "That young man looks very nice. Not at all like the other one I don't wish to talk about. Do you like him? Do you think he might take the place of Chandler?"

"Yes, very much. You're right. Hamilton is very nice. He's coming to dinner tonight. He will be here at seven but dinner doesn't need to be ready until eight. Will you fix the rainbow trout along with the baby potatoes soaked in butter? Is there anything else we might have to fill out the meal. I'm going to have a bath."

Georgia put water on to boil. Sat down with a cup of tea to wait. Her mind wandered back to Hamilton along with all he said about the dangers of childbirth. Didn't elaborate too much. Imagined, he didn't wish to terrify her. She could ask Bea if she knew what to do if those horrible things happened.

"I'm happy you like this man. To me, Hamilton seems like a breath of fresh air. All sunlight where the days had been dark before. I know you didn't see a way out of the situation with Chandler," Bea said, leaving all kinds of innuendos behind her teeth. "You do need a change of scenery when it comes to males. Now, don't you be giving your favors away, at least not too soon. A man needs to work for that first kiss then everything after that."

This situation was more than just liking Hamilton. If lust was an emotion she was unfamiliar with, she wouldn't understand how much she wanted him to make love to her. Since she understood raw passion, she would have the devil's own time denying Hamilton anything he asked her for. Before Chandler ricocheted into her life, she never felt that way about anyone. Always believed Chandler would be the only man for her. Once she left, Chandler had no reason to think there would be another man.

Now…now she was contemplating lovemaking with Hamilton.

Georgia cleared her throat before she began to tell Bea what she learned about their neighbor. Some of what she learned, the part about him also being her mate, she would leave out for the time being. "Hamilton is one of the village doctors. Says I need to be examined."

Bea snorted then chuckled with what appeared to Georgia as amusement. "Is that another fancy way of telling you he wants you in his bed? You hold off on that bedding stuff. We both understand how that worked out the first time. Not that any of us regret meeting little Maeve. She is beautiful. This new lad you carry will be just as charming."

"Yes and no. He does want me in his bed. I can see into his mind just as I read Chandler's. He tells me we are mates." Good Lord she wasn't intending to mention that incredible fact. "Since we have the ability to talk to each other through our thoughts, I must believe him."

Until she revisited this communication of theirs, she was troubled by the double mate business. She didn't think she knew anyone who could answer her question.

"Do you wish to be there…in Hamilton's bed?" Bea was blunt with her query even though she was smiling. "I would that you find a way to protect yourself from Chandler. Hamilton does have much the same appearance as the other man who we don't like to talk about. Do you think he can provide the buffer you need?"

Georgia lifted her shoulders in a shrug that didn't feel at all nonchalant. "When Chandler claimed me, I saw several of our past lives. All the men had a similar appearance. Hamilton knew I was a white tiger in my second shape. Told me he was a black panther. Seems those in this area who are related to the McKennas are black panthers."

"I would never second guess this mate business then. Can two people have different shapes as shifters and be mates?" Bea set the bread that had been rising this afternoon into the oven to bake.

"Yes, Harris and Ash have different shapes. Walker and Crissie, another Mckenna, also changes to a different form. Their children, depending on the sex, shift to whatever form compliments the sex. Wait, I'm not certain if Crissie is a shifter. I don't believe she is."

"Is that a fancy was of saying the girls will become shifters similar to their mothers and boys similar to their fathers?" Bea chuckled at her look of dismay.

"I did garble the message. Didn't I?" The water for her bath was boiling. "Do you mind too much if I get ready for dinner? Leave you with the preparations?" She rose to find Hollis. Needed him to carry the water to the bathing room downstairs. "I'll need to hire a few more servants. Would just as soon take a bath in my room upstairs."

"Hollis saw to hiring servants while you were outside chatting with your new beau. I'll call the two lads to take care of the water…in your room."

"Thank you, glad Hollis is so efficient."

She talked to Bea for a few more minutes while her water was carried upstairs.

"What do you plan on wearing tonight? You will wish to look your best for the new man in your life." Bea stated as she started washing the small potatoes. "Do you think Hamilton will like turnips? Not everyone does. No! Wait. Lainie brought over some butternut squash. That will be delicious with butter along with brown sugar bubbling in the middle."

"You have any suggestion as to what I should wear? Must be something that has been unpacked." In her head, Georgia was going over all the gowns she had acquired since leaving the brothel months ago.

"Oh, Hollis saw to the unpacking also. All your clothes are in their proper places. He hired two ladies to keep the place clean as well as do odd jobs that we might need. You should wear the apricot gown. I've always loved that one on you. Compliments your coloring. Makes your skin glow."

Hamilton told her she glowed. "Ah but you've always told me the blue dress brings out the color of my eyes."

"They both will look beautiful on you. Now that your breasts are larger with the baby and all, you don't wish to show too much cleavage. The blue dress might be a better choice for your Mr. Hamilton. Don't want to over advertise your abundant charms too soon. Chandler always wanted to see you in the least possible."

Georgia couldn't help herself. Bea's words made her laugh. "Believe all or most men have the same desire. Chandler is just more open about what he likes. You do realize all of the time I lived at the brothel, I was either naked or wearing something so revealing the gown left nothing to the imagination."

Recalling the dress she wore the first night she was presented as Winter Snow, the Queen of the Ice, brought heat to her face. Now, when she thought back on those days, she didn't see how she ever went through with the act. The only reason was the fact she was enthralled with Chandler. At first, sex with people watching aroused, the nature of the idea exciting. Understood he was her mate. Never thought he would insist she act the last month and a half after she delivered Maeve. Chandler had ulterior motives. He meant to get her pregnant with another child.

"Go on now. Go take your bath. The water will be ready. Don't come down here until everything is perfect. I have the dinner menu in hand. If Maeve wakes up from her nap, I'll take care of her. She is nearing one year. I'll feed her some mashed bananas along with a small bowl of oatmeal. She loves the two foods."

"Where did we get bananas?" She felt a bit perplexed with all the food that was coming their way.

"One of the McKennas brought them over. Don't recall which one it was. Can't keep all those Stuart and Frasiers along with the McKennas straight. Seems someone is always showing up on the doorstep with a treat in hand. Don't know that I mind. In another week or two, we'll be all settled in. For now, the extra help is nice."

Georgia left the kitchen. Poked her head into Maeve's nursery next to her room. She was still sound asleep. Running her palm gently across her downy head was wonderful. She blew her daughter a kiss. Stepping inside her bedchamber she saw the steaming water. Caught the scent of lavender swirling in the room. A bath sheet had been hung near the fire to warm.

Humming she undressed then settled into the lavender scented water. This was heaven. Thinking of Hamilton, he must have sensed her thoughts.

What are you up to? Would love to be there with you.

Pure bliss. Sweet hot bliss.

I know. You're stark naked and you're in lavender scented water. You were thinking of me, weren't you? I like that. I was thinking of you also. Need to speak with you again. Can't seem to get you out of...thoughts...so many revolving around you. To think, a few hours ago I only dreamed of meeting you...my mate.

You shouldn't be in my head right now when I'm not wearing one stitch. It's not well done of you. Close your eyes.

Who are you talking to?

Oh, bloody eyes, it was Chandler's voice coming through to her when she least expected him. She couldn't deny speaking with Hamilton. He heard her. Georgia didn't know what to do. This was all too unexpected. All of it, finding a second mate, running from the first. Chandler would come here if he discovered anything. She didn't know what to do.

Tell him the truth, Georgia. You do understand he doesn't deserve you. The man is not good enough to shine your shoes. He never will be. Georgia, you are too good for the likes of him. I will protect you. You're mine now. What is mine I keep safe.

Answer me, damn you! There can't be another person you are talking to. I'm your mate. I own you. I'll drag you back to the brothel, screaming and kicking if need be! You'll perform every night. I'll give you to Bertram then auction you to entertain any man who can afford you in the third-floor rooms.

Georgia was terrified she would lose the little bit of food she'd eaten today. Dear God, both men thought she was theirs. Stark fear filled her. She felt frozen from the inside out. She didn't understand how to get Chandler out of her head. She forced herself to shut out his hatred. Wanted to yell back at him. Yell the fact he didn't own her. Would never possess her again. Realized Hamilton was blocking him now. Chandler wasn't getting through. Funny, Hamilton was singing to her with words she didn't understand. Believed they must be words from an ancient language. The words coupled with the tune soothed her cramped nerves.

Just as fast as Chandler entered her mind he was gone. At peace with herself, she slid deeper into the hot water, soaking up the heat. Set her head on the lip of the tub. When she closed her eyes, she saw Hamilton as clear as if he stood in front of her watching her take a bath. The thought startled. Sitting bolt upright, water sloshing across the floor, she looked around the room.

While I'd enjoy taking a bath with you, I'm in my own home thinking about you naked. Did you know I can see you? Promise to keep my eyes closed when you get out of the tub. As of right now, all I see is the back of your head. I did see your beautiful white shoulders. Promise, I won't invade your privacy again unless you ask.

You know too much. Can do too much. It's not right you can see me anytime you wish.

My mental skills are quite advanced. Much more advanced than some. While I do have the ability to not only talk with you, I can also see you if I wish. Rest assured I'll stop looking at you. I'm concentrating on keeping the other man out of your head. He surprised me or he would have never been able to speak with you.

You can do all that?

...and more.

Oh, my.

~ * ~

The discovery of his mate this afternoon pleased Hamilton. He was as baffled as Georgia about Chandler also being her mate. Shifters, to his knowledge, never had two mates in the same era. He was furious when he heard Chandler speaking to her, telling her he owned her. His anger erupted. Had never felt anything such as this unique possessiveness. Before now, never realized the intense feeling that accompanied the woman who was his forever person. The man was not very talented at reading his mates thoughts. It was easy enough to keep him from Georgia. This was something new he would need to attend to. Didn't want the man finding her until Georgia felt ready to meet him head on. There was certain to be a battle...a battle between good and evil.

When she was in the tub, he did see her lovely white shoulders. Her hair so black, he saw blue highlights. ...and her eyes...such a beautiful shade of blue. Compared side by side, her eyes put a clear summer sky to shame. When he looked at the clock, Hamilton knew he would be early. Didn't intend to stay away from her longer than necessary. Thought tomorrow night a trip to the bonfire would be nice. If she was up for a short walk, tonight would be better. There was much for him to learn about her.

In the privacy of the secluded bonfire, flames shooting to the sky, he could hold her next to him. He wanted to put his hands on her belly. Stroke her. Feel the babe inside. Assess his position within her womb. Hoped the lad would kick. Colin is the name she chose for her *bairn*. It was a nice name. With her approval, he intended to adopt both children. Hoped Chandler had overlooked doing so with Maeve. From the few thoughts he garnered from Chandler, he didn't care for girls…women…believed they had only one use. Sex. Chandler was also possessive of Georgia. There would be that contention between them. Hamilton felt certain, Chandler would never give her up.

What name did Chandler call her? Winter. Hamilton decided he would speak to Georgia about the name. Would like to understand why he called her by a name that wasn't her own. They did have a great deal to chat about. Introducing Georgia to the priest at the McKenna keep was high on his agenda. Father Damian might be able to shed light on the notion of two possible mates. She should meet Connal McKenna and his wife. He wished to be married at the keep with all the traditional ceremonies. Having his wedding night there was an important tradition among the clan. Pleasure Georgia during the feast. The sooner he could arrange a marriage, the better. Hoped to be wed before Colin's birth.

He understood he was getting ahead of himself. They'd known each other for too short of a time, less than five hours. The devil, he was planning their wedding. What he understood of her history, he couldn't rush her. Didn't wish to do anything in haste. Needed to savor all the small moments he would have with her. Convincing Chandler he could never have her again would be more difficult. Chandler was the sole reason; time was of the essence.

He decided on casual attire for this first meal. He picked out his favorite buckskins and knee-high moccasins then began to dress. Slipped on a white shirt that laced in front. Whistling, he strode down the steps. Picked out two bottles of wine, a red along with a white. Mounted his favorite stallion, Rex then set off for Georgia's cottage.

All this time he kept his mind guarding hers, blocking Chandler. When he was occupied at work, he wouldn't be able to protect her as he would like. Maybe he could teach her a few tricks. Hamilton knew Colin spoke with his father. As things were now, Colin didn't understand enough to know their location. The boy realized they moved. Understood enough to know his mother was talking with a different person than he was used to hearing.

Perhaps if he set his mind directed toward Colin, he would be able to speak, to give encouragement. Even help the lad to realize, he was the best mate for his mother. Help him understand he needed to cut Chandler from his thoughts.

I'm here. Taking Rex to the stable. I will be at your door in a few minutes. Brought two bottles of wine for everyone's enjoyment.

You're early.

Is that a problem? He understood the exact nature of the issue. *I would go to your room. Hold you in my arms. We both understand my doing so will happen in time. My hope is that I will be with you in an intimate way sooner than later.*

I'm not dressed.

Seeing you wearing nothing at all is not a problem for me. If you said yes, I would two-step the stairs to your bedchamber. You realize we will make love. As soon as you acknowledge our connection we can move forward with our relationship. Hamilton understood he rushed her. He was unable to help himself. Wanting her yesterday was difficult to deal with. Needing her this instant was harder than he would have imagined. He realized sex with Georgia would be better than anything he knew in his past.

Beast.

I'll wait for you in the drawing room. Hamilton let out a slow breath of air. Needing Georgia then not having her was going to be difficult. She burned a fire in his soul. Thinking of her made his heart race while his body hardened and he pulsed to life.

Should I pour you a glass of wine? He was thinking she shouldn't have more than one. They counseled all their pregnant ladies not to drink wine. Fool that he was he brought two bottles. Two bottles to share with both Bea and Hollis.

Yes, a glass of wine would be nice. A small one.

Do you drink wine often? The question popped out before he thought better of asking. At this point, he didn't have the right to question her. The child wasn't his. Since Georgia was his mate, he had every right to ask. Found his mind was at odds with his base desires. Drinking wine did pertain to the health of the child. There was no proof of his assumption.

No, she paused after the no as if thinking about why he asked. The realization she was thinking was good. *Let Bea know you are here. She will be in the kitchen putting finishing touches to our meal.*

Hamilton didn't answer again. He sensed Chandler banging his head on Georgia's locked mind. He had a good notion to tell the man what he thought of him. The verbal abuse Hamilton was thinking about inflicting Chandler's way, might be heard by Georgia. Didn't wish to risk that confrontation yet.

"Bea?" Hamilton was in the house striding through the entryway. "You in the kitchen?"

He chuckled when Bea came from one of doors that wasn't the right direction. He thought the kitchen was in a different place.

"Just setting the table for the two of you. Hollis and I decided to take a ride into the village. Check out one of the restaurants. Both of us decided..." She stopped as if she didn't wish to finish the sentence. "The two of you don't need chaperones."

"You're not staying?" he asked, pleased with the thought.

This was perfect for him. He needed to be alone with Georgia.

"Assumed the two of you would wish to eat alone. Get to know each other better." Bea shook her finger at him, her lips thinning into a tight line. Hamilton kept his chuckle to himself.

"Oh...?" Hamilton lifted his brows, speculating.

She snorted. "Not a lot better, mind you. Not in that sense, the biblical...you know what I'm saying. She's not ready. I can see the wheels in your head turning. If you hurt Georgia, you will have to deal with me, Hollis as well."

This time, unable to help himself, Hamilton gave a short bark of laughter. "Georgia is my mate. I won't ever hurt her. You're right about all you've told me. Georgia and I do need to learn more about each other before we become intimate. Thank you for giving us some time alone. Private time is always important. When we are alone, we can ask the more difficult questions."

"Chandler is also Georgia's mate. He hurts her all the time," Bea's voice was bitter. Shaking her finger at him, she continued, "That man is horrid. How she could love him is beyond me. You take care of her. You are the only person who can make her feel whole again. Since we know you are a shifter then be appraised also that both Hollis and I can shift. It's why Cormack, her father, hired me. Crazy thing is, Chandler hired Hollis. Hollis is only loyal to Georgia."

"I understand. Thank you for telling me though I'd guessed at the truth. Much better to be upfront from the start." Hamilton caught the scent of lavender then heard the soft tread of her slippers as she walked down the stairs.

As he turned, he saw her dressed in an apricot gown tied beneath her remarkable bosom. Caught the site of the tops of her breasts. Stopped himself from drooling. Hiding his emotions from her would be difficult. The devil take him, he wanted her now…this beat of his heart he wanted her. "You look beautiful. The color becomes you."

With his words a soft rose hue painted her cheeks as well the lovely tops of her breasts. Hamilton was pleased she chose this gown and not the one that covered her to her chin. He'd listened in on her conversation with Bea.

"Come let's go into the dining room." She stopped when she saw the table set for two. "Bea? What is this?"

"Don't fret. Hollis and I decided to check out a tavern in the village. Realized without much thought, you and Hamilton have a great deal to hash over. Don't wish to be an obstruction to your first evening together." Bea smoothed her gown then, "You two enjoy yourselves. Don't do anything foolish."

Hollis appeared with a knowing grin on his face. "We are off. Don't expect us back for quite some time."

With her hands clasped in front of her, Georgia watched them leave. A bit of trepidation unsettled her. "I didn't expect those two to leave. Thought the two of them would stay here with us."

He chuckled, watching the ever-changing emotions flash across her face. "Did you wish for a chaperone? I, for one, am quite happy the pair decided we needed to chat in private. I've questions for you as I'm positive you have questions for me. Am I right? None of those queries would feel comfortable in front of an audience."

"Yes...I want to know everything about you." Georgia flashed him a smile that ripped straight to his heart then centered in his groin.

As he brought her hand to his arm then placed her fingers in the crook, he felt the connection between them so deep and so hard the sensation jolted a gush of air from his lungs. A breath shuddered into him. This joining of their hearts had nothing to do with sex and everything to do with Georgia...all of her deep into her soul. They were meant to be together through eternity.

If he'd had any doubts about this woman as his mate, the impact of what just happened would have shaken those doubts away. At that same moment, he heard a tiny gasp from his mate. When she looked at him, there was wonder in those China blue eyes of hers. Georgia must have felt the recognition also.

"We will go far, you and I."

Hamilton couldn't think of anything else to say. Words would come later. Once he digested the wonderful emotions coursing through him. At the table he pulled out the chair next to him for her to sit. As if dazed she sat down. For a few beats of his heart, she stared at him, seeming mesmerized.

They passed the food to each other. Georgia put little on her plate. Hamilton added to the food already there. "While it's true, you are not eating for two, you do need adequate nourishment." He poured her a small glass of wine, half of what he gave himself. "Wine might not be good for the *bairn*. I'm not telling you what to do. Just informing you of my thoughts on the subject. Doubt if this one small glass will harm the baby."

Her eyes widened. She set the glass down. "I didn't know. Should I not...?"

"As I just said, doubt if that much will do harm. Go ahead. Does your compliance in this little matter mean you've accepted me as your doctor? The man who will deliver your child?"

He found he grinned like a besotted fool. Well, he was infatuated with this lovely woman sitting in front of him.

"Why did you become a doctor?" Georgia played with the food on her plate. "I wonder..."

"My calling...believe it's because I do like to help people. Make them well when they are sick. Heal them when they are hurt. Protect them from hurting themselves. When I was younger, I found animals to mend. Once there was a bird with a broken wing. Another time a dog's foot was caught in a hunting trap. I'm at my happiest when I'm healing a person or an animal. Leah is much the same. When she lived alone in the hills, she had a place where she kept her wounded animals. It's the same for me." He speared a small potato. Held the morsel in front of him as if studying, "We've begun the questioning about our lives. Suppose the next question is mine to ask."

"Whatever you ask, I'm certain the question will embarrass me. My immediate past is sordid. Something I'm not proud of. Most of my life with Chandler is embarrassing, mortifying. I will tell you everything you ask. More if I think of something pertinent. Promise I won't hold back."

"Understand telling your story will be painful. Believe I need to know if I'm going to protect you from this man who wishes to harm you." Hamilton felt as if he should know everything about her. Given enough time with this lovely woman he would learn all he needed.

"Yes…" She chewed the piece of trout she speared earlier. Swallowed while she waited for the first question. "It's painful to look back on the year I spent with Chandler. He is selfish as well as arrogant. What Chandler wants he makes certain he gets. He wanted me. At the time, I wanted him too. I won't deny that fact. Our wishes united for a short amount of time."

"Tell me about Winter. How she got her name. Why… anything else of importance." Hamilton felt as if learning the reason for her name would garner a wealth of intelligence.

For a few beats of his heart, Hamilton watched her close her eyes. Saw the frown crease her brow. Wished he dared smooth the lines from her forehead. Watched her bosom heave with a steady inhale of air.

"My full name was Winter Snow, the Ice Queen or Queen of the Ice depending on how Chandler wanted to present me to his audience." Hamilton thought the moniker might have fit her character during the time she spent with Chandler. Now, Georgia was warm as well as giving.

"Chandler wanted one woman for every season of the year. We performed once a month. In the end I was thankful for the reprieve none of the other ladies received. He also named a woman Spring Mist the Princess of Rain, Summer Passion the Innocent Virgin the last one being Autumn

Bounty the Countess of Harvest." All the ladies except me were auctioned to the patron willing to pay the most, male or female, the night of their performance. The woman was then expected to entertain the person who bought them in one of the rooms on the third floor. Chandler was possessive of me. I was never auctioned. For that small fact, I'm grateful."

Hamilton sat back, the base of his glass resting on his belly. He mulled over what Georgia revealed as well as what she did not. In time he would learn everything about the year in question. She was embarrassed about her actions. There was no need. Not in front of him. He would never judge his mate.

"Are you telling me the sex was in front of an audience?"

From the hesitant jumble of her thoughts. Hamilton understood her statement to be true. Georgia didn't want to reinforce the question with an affirmative answer.

While the clock ticked away the seconds, she focused on her plate of food. "Yes. I signed a contract for a year stating I was a willing participant in whatever play he chose for me to perform as did everyone else who took part in the entertainment."

"You acted even when your pregnancy showed."

Hamilton supposed the sight might be titillating for some. If Georgia was swelling with his child, he would be aroused to a raging fever even in her ninth month.

"Yes, even the week of Maeve's birth. The evening was the ninth time I was Winter Snow. During the show I was having contractions. Chandler still calls me by the name he created for me. At the brothel no one knew any of the women's given names. I gave birth the morning after what I thought would be my final performance."

Listening to her words his guts cramped. Turned sour with the knowledge of all she endured. He sucked in a deep breath of air. "That night wasn't your finale. Was it?"

"No, I signed a contract giving Chandler the use of my body for one year. Now, all the contracts are for five years. He just signed a young innocent for five long years. While I was willing, she isn't. Chandler kidnapped then drugged Mara so she wouldn't understand what she put her name to. Her first show was the afternoon after she arrived at the brothel with Jamie, one of his male entertainers. Mara was dressed in a gown of see through material. A minister married them in front of a live audience. She was still drugged when the two were married. Held no idea what happened. The certificate that proclaimed them husband and wife was signed by Mara. Again, she didn't understand what she was signing. Jamie made love to her, took her innocence even before the document became official. Consummated the marriage in front of the people who paid to see them wed as well as take his virgin wife. This was a standing room only crowd. Her virgin's blood proof of her innocence. Jamie knew Mara was his mate. Thought everything was fine. Chandler renamed her. She is now known as Delight, Jamie's Delight. The pair must perform once a week," Georgia choked on the statement.

To Hamilton it was clear, she was mortified at what was happening to the girl. "Mara isn't willing?"

"No. Not to the decadence. She might, in time, be willing to be with Jamie." Her breath seemed to shudder deep inside. "It's your turn to answer questions. This was a lot to tell."

"You are exhausted. Perhaps this was too much for you to go through in such a short amount of time."

While he didn't wish to cause her pain, the information was important. She didn't need to recall all of the year she spent with Chandler tonight.

"No, I'm relieved part of my life is out for you to understand. Now that you understand what I've done, you might not wish to have anything more to do with me. The part I left out was the fact that once I was healed from the birth of Maeve. He made me go back to the shows. I despised him for making me perform. When I balked, he threatened me with Bertram. Told me he would tie my arms to the headboard of a bed and allow Bertram to plow my white belly. His words not mine. I performed in two more shows before the year-long contract ended."

"You left him. How?"

"Put on the gown I arrived in. Packed my two other gowns along with underwear and some personal items then walked out the back door. He was gone at the time. I had money. Hired a cab to take me to my father's townhouse."

"Your father came here to Carnoch with you? Where is he living?" Her father was one more person who could help keep her away from Chandler.

"In the village. I'll show you where he lives some time. Didn't wish to have him live with me even though there are enough rooms.

"Bought Orange Blossom cottage in a small country village outside London. Chandler wanted me to beg him to come home with him. Realized in time, he would lose patience then force me back. That's why I moved here with help from the Wolcott's."

"I've always lived here. The head of the McKenna's, Connal McKenna is married to Wynnie Adair. Wynnie is a distant relative of mine. I know the McKenna's well. Are you going to eat anything more?" Hamilton asked, pointing to her half-eaten plate of food.

"The truth upset my stomach. No, I've eaten enough."

"I'll take you to the place where we can make a bonfire then watch the stars. We can relax as well as put the past into the back of your head. I will hold you. Touch your sweetly rounded belly. By doing so I can both get to know you better as well as learn about the placement of your *wee bairn*. Learning those things will help me predict a due date. Believe the day of your wee lad's birth is not too far away. What do you think?"

Don't know if I want you to touch me. You holding my belly seems strange to me. Too intimate for the short number of hours I've known you. Don't understand how you would know all what you say by feeling there.

Today, I'm a doctor not a lover. Though, I do plan to become your lover at some later date. This a tiny examination. One that will take less than five minutes.

He wanted to hold her longer than five minutes. If she protested, he would comply with her wishes. Hoped to feel little Colin kick and move around in the warm womb sheltering him.

I do understand. Asked Bea about the problems at birth you told me about. She did tell me she didn't know how to attend to those difficulties. I'm beginning to come around to your way of thinking. Would like to have a doctor, someone who understands what should be done in an emergency.

Appreciate that. "Now, do you wish to walk to the bonfire or ride. When I stabled Rex, I noticed a hack in your carriage house."

"The days have been busy. Would love to go with you to the bonfire. Maybe another time we can walk. Tonight, let's ride. I do feel a bit on the weary side."

It didn't take long to travel to the campsite. "One of the McKenna servants keeps wood here. This is a place anyone in the vicinity is welcome though most times immediate family are the ones who come here. Most of the village people feel as if the place is off limits. They don't wish to intrude on what might be a lover's tryst."

Hamilton led her to a large flat rock. "Sit here until I get this fire blazing. Brought some herbal tea for you. Might ease some of your nerves. I understand the stress of telling your story. The year you revealed to me is no longer part of your life. Together we will put the past behind you. We will forge a new life together."

In a matter of minutes, the kindling then the larger pieces of wood caught fire. Hamilton stood back to watch the blaze, sparks shooting into the sky. Smiling, he turned to Georgia. "What do you think? Is this romantic?"

Georgia giggled. He liked the soft trill of laughter. Hoped to hear more merriment. Wasn't certain Georgia was ready for romance of any sort.

"Yes, I suppose so. Have never been romanced. Did you wish this to become a romantic tryst for us." With her hand she covered the yawn she must have thought to hide.

"You're too tired for romance. Should have waited to do this for another night. Do need to…"

"Examine me. How?" From the soft light cast off by the fire, he read a myriad of emotions Her brows were drawn together as if in concentration. "I…maybe second thoughts…"

"With tender care," he told her with grave sincerity. Hamilton spread a blanket on the ground. He sat moving his legs to make a V. "Sit here." He patted the ground in front of him. Smiled to give encouragement.

"I don't know. This is all so new… this feels like courting. Never been courted. Never been with a man bent on romance." The hesitation along with a moment of fear showed on her face.

"I won't hurt you." Again, he patted the ground. "I'll even wrap a blanket around us to keep us warm as well as cozy." Georgia was thinking of Chandler. Didn't wish for thoughts of this other man to surface while he smoothed her belly with his tender hand. Wanted her to dream only of him.

"Alright. Promise?" She didn't wait for his answer. Moved to the place he showed her. Georgia sat, crossing her legs. Hamilton wrapped the big blanket around his shoulders before pulling the covering around her shoulders.

For a few seconds, he didn't move. Georgia, sitting here next to him, felt right, perfect. Her back pressed against his chest. The deep hard connection he felt earlier in the day swept his emotions again. His breath staggered into his lungs.

"May I set my hands on your belly?"

Holding his breath he waited for the answer. Understood she would agree. Felt her small body mold against his, soaking in his heat. Her little bottom pushed against his groin. Unlike an innocent, she would understand the hard part of him as well as what he was feeling for her.

"Yes," the one word tumbled from her lips. Her roughly spoken answer was enough.

Hamilton set his hands on top of her swollen stomach. "Put your hands on top of mine." She did. He didn't move them at first. Felt Colin kick against his hand as if the lad wanted him to leave.

I'm not leaving your mother when she needs me. I'm the man in your future. You need to get your birth father out of your head. I'll talk with you every day. You will realize I love both you and your mother.

"Where did you go?" In his arms she turned to study his face. Georgia brought her hand up to touch his cheek. She ran a fingertip along his jaw. "I would know some of your thoughts. You left me."

For a few seconds, he let her explore. "I was speaking with Colin, telling him I will always be here for both of you. Did you feel him kick me? The force I felt was hard as well as strong. The lad is healthy as a stoat. You've taken good care of the *bairn*. May I feel you, all of your belly. Need to figure out where his head is."

"Yes." This time she didn't hesitate.

Do you enjoy the feel of my hands on you?

I can say that I do.

He smoothed his hand along her stomach. Stopped various places to ascertain an elbow or a foot. Found a hand then his head. This was as he suspected from her size as well as the shape of her. The boy was turned, readying himself for his birth. The baby was large. Georgia was small. Moving lower, he spread his hand to measure her hips. They were very feminine. He needed to be at the birth for her.

"I want to see you tomorrow in my office. If you wish, Leah will chaperone the examination. Georgia, this is necessary. Within this week or the next, you should give birth. I'm going to be with you every step of the way unless you would rather have Houston or Hawk. Every woman should have a doctor or a qualified midwife. As far as I can tell you have neither."

She was shaking her head. The fine hair on the top of her head tickled his nose. "Don't want anyone but you." Georgia's statement pleased him. "How do you know he will be born within two weeks?"

Hamilton was pleased she questioned. This was good. "The babe's head is down. Do you feel him pressing against your pelvic bones?"

"There is pressure there. Is that what you mean? I recall with Maeve, that was how I felt before giving birth."

"Have you noticed any contractions? Sometimes, a woman has what we call fake contractions. Ones that start then stop with no apparent reason."

"No, nothing. What will you do differently at your office? I don't want a chaperone. This will be embarrassing as it is with someone I don't know watching."

"If I tell you, promise you will still come tomorrow. Come at noon. Twelve o'clock would be a good time. Don't believe I've anything scheduled for that part of the day. After we are finished, I'll take you to lunch. Does the time work for you?"

"Promise. However, you are frightening me. Is what you plan to do so terrible?" Georgia asked a slight quaver in her voice.

After what he learned tonight about her past, this shouldn't frighten her. He would give her a bit of knowledge. Hamilton let out a long sigh, disturbed now that she would not like what he was going to tell her. Acknowledged the fact she wasn't prepared for a man to touch her intimately. For him this wasn't sex. This was an integral part of his profession.

"I will feel inside you. Need to see if your cervix is softening for the birth as well as dilating. This knowledge will help tell me when you will go into labor. With the position of the head, you might even have Colin by tomorrow. If you wish, I could do this after I take you home."

Her skin grew cold. He set a finger on her chin to turn her. Needed to see her eyes as well as her face. What he saw frightened him. She was pale. "Don't faint on me. Doubt if the babe will come tomorrow before your appointment. I'm looking forward to taking you to lunch." The small encouragement didn't seem to help put color on her face.

"I survived one child. I will survive this one. To keep us both safe, I'll do what you suggest. If you believe it is necessary to see to me tonight, so be it. I won't protest."

Georgia was trying to be brave. As a male, he could never understand the fear that accompanied childbirth. "Did you have any fears with Maeve? Tell me something about the birth. Was it easy or hard? How long were you in labor? Anything you can think of."

"I was having contractions while Chandler was putting on his show. He knew. Could tell by the whimpers of pain with the cramps circling my stomach. I think some of the members of the audience guessed. The dollar signs in front of his eyes meant more to him than me. I wasn't surprised. Understood from the beginning that was how he felt. Hoped I could change him." She was hanging on to her wits by a slender thread. "At one point the pain made me cry out for him to stop. He wouldn't, not until he was finished with the script he envisioned. I bit my lip. It bled. By then the crowd of spectators knew I was in labor. They loved the show. The floor was packed with people standing, cheering for Chandler to keep me there. More money than ever before was tossed to the stage."

Hamilton felt a wave of tenderness wash through him, the deep sensation remained inside. He hugged her close, said sweet nothings into her ear. Soothed her with soft caresses on her belly. Even then, with the touch, he felt the hardening of her muscles. The contractions were beginning. If she didn't understand this moment, she would soon. This might be a fake one he spoke to her about. He wasn't about to guess.

"Come, I must get you home."

He was glad they didn't walk. While walking was good during the contractions, Georgia needed to be in a safe place when the babe was pushing his head out her vagina.

Helping her up, he pulled her into his arms. Kissed the top of her head. He knew his face was set with grim lines. She would see the concern in his eyes. In such a short time, Georgia had come to mean everything to him.

"I felt a contraction. Does that mean?" she asked, her eyes bright, hands on the swell of her womb.

Pleased she was curious. She didn't sound frightened. "Maybe…maybe not, the birth might be starting. Sometimes contractions stop for no reason we can understand." He helped her into the hack then collected the blankets. Ten minutes later they were at his place. During the ride, he explained why he was taking her to his home. Tools of his trade were in his home. He had everything he needed for the birth of Colin. Those things would not be at her cottage. Sometimes in the middle of the night, husbands would bring their wives to the closest place.

In a small room near the rear of the house, he set her on a bed. The tarp was laid out in case of the unexpected. "What are you doing?"

"I'll be back in a few seconds. I'm sending for Bea and Hollis. Hollis will need to stay with Maeve or bring her here. They don't need to come. However, believe both of your friends will wish to be nearby during the birth. The pair can bring you a gown to wear as well as whatever clothing you've put together for the baby. Don't go anywhere."

She scowled at him. He smiled; his heart filled with tenderness.

~ * ~

Chandler sat back in the viewing room, watching Jamie and Delight play on stage. By the look on her face, she detested what she was doing. He needed to tell her to be enthusiastic, cry out her pleasure. If the audience adored her, she would make more money. This wasn't the way she would increase her coffers. Several times in the last month she begged him to forego the contract. He howled his laughter.

The strange thing was while he watched his audience, they seemed to appreciate her pain. Pain was something he did understand when it concerned sex. Realized a woman's agony, emotional or physical, was something he could capitalize on. Tonight, they were reenacting the wedding script along with the consummation. The minister was fake. Last week, Jamie pretended to attack her. He came up behind her then grabbed her. She fought. Kicked at him hard while he subdued her. Chandler did understand why some men loved the violence toward women. He provided the scripts for the money. As Winter reminded him, he would do anything to increase his wealth.

His spectators appreciated the fighting along with the woman's struggles, her cries of helplessness. Jamie tossed Delight on the bed. Came down hard on her. She kicked him. Jamie would rear back then laugh. He held her arms over head. Kissed her hard. Delight told him what she thought. He told her she had no choice. With cloth provided for Jamie, he tied her hands to the backboard of the bed. He ran his hands along her body, fondling in intimate places, sipping on her breasts while she bucked and tugged on her restraints. This time was different. Instead of laudanum, Jamie gave her a small dose of cocaine. Now she was on fire for him, writhing with her need. Her body would be in flames from the aphrodisiac. Delight was begging him for more.

Harems always intrigued Chandler. He would make Jamie a sultan. Having many women at his disposal was what he had here. Delight could crawl to Jamie on her hands and knees. Jamie told him he needed to take care with Delight. She was nearing a point where she might refuse. If she did, he would never force her. So far, all she did, she did while needing him. She loved him. Told him so. Delight meant too much to him. Some of the scripts Chandler wrote hurt her. Jamie refused. Chandler wasn't beyond drugging her again. The cocaine made her giddy. His crowds both loved to hear her cry out with pain or pleasure as well as the sound of her giggles. Jamie refused the drugs whenever he could. Jamie would need to come to terms with what was necessary to keep his wife in line. She now had four years and ten months left to serve. If she acted in a drugged haze, so be it. If she became a little wanton, all the better. Both scenarios pleased his audience. She could choose to play her parts with willing enthusiasm or dosed with cocaine. Neither Jamie or Delight had a choice. The show was everything to Chandler. He would always dictate the terms.

Startled, Chandler bolted to stand. Bloody hell, Winter was having contractions. His boy, his son would be here soon. Despite all the feelers he put out, he wasn't able to find her. That man who was in her head blocked him each time he attempted to reach out to her. Was it too soon for her to birth the babe, unless she conceived that first time they performed six weeks after the birth? Of course, he had his way with her when they were in their rooms. Still...

Chandler needed to be with her so he could claim the boy as his, the moment the lad popped out. Needed to have his son with him, here in the brothel where he could supervise his tender formative years. He paced the confines of the room, trying with desperation to reach into her head.

He heard nothing. Only silence greeted his attempts to penetrate her mind. Damn shifter. He had no business interfering. Curse his hide. He wanted to kill the man. Would, if he could find him.

Where the bloody hell was Winter? Below the viewing room, Delight cried out. Screamed. Pleaded for her release. The spectators roared their approval. He moved to the window. Watched Delight shove Jamie off her. Jamie laughed. Kissed her hard again, swept his hands along her body. After that he pulled her to stand. Held her hand in the air.

"Delight is mine," Jamie cried out. He pulled her close for a hard embrace. His hand cupped around her little rump.

Delight appeared frozen in time. The coke must be wearing off. Tears slid down her cheeks. Jamie walked with her around the room, showing her off. This was incredible. The spectators thundered their applause. Coins along with bills showing their appreciation cluttered the stage. A few of the extras in the show collected the money which showed the appreciation of the audience. All the coin that was tossed their way would go to the couple. His audiences adored Delight. He needed to find Johnny's desire. Mackenzie was his chosen lady for the job. Soon he would have Delight's big sister under his thumb. He'd been tracking her movements. She was a creature of habit. Soon, soon both sisters would be ensconced in his establishment.

Chandler didn't know what to do about Winter. Until he discovered where she was, he couldn't do anything. Once he found the location, he would retrieve her. Keep her under lock and key. Create a new script for them. She would refuse to perform. He would take a page out of Jamie's book. If Winter was drugged, all her choices would be taken away. He would force her to sign a contract that would last into forever, endure until she was old and gray. They would marry on stage just as Jamie and delight had. He would give her no choices.

Feeling satisfied, Chandler rubbed his hands together. The plotting as to what he would do when Winter was found was easier than finding her. The damn shifter kept him blocked from her head. Who the devil was that man?

You will never have Georgia back. She is too good for you, for the perpetuation of your evil. She is sweet as well as gentle. She no longer loves you. Georgia is with me now. She loves me.

Winter is my mate.

Damn! This man drove him to fury he never felt before. Even when his father disowned him then gave the title along with his families' holdings, his rightful inheritance, to his little brother, he'd not been angry. After he thought about the disloyalty by his father, he'd been relieved. No longer had to do anything he didn't wish to do. When he came up with this plan for the bordello, he and Bertram could have all the women they wanted in any way they wished, at any time they needed sex. Damn, he had to have someone now…this instant. Decided he would go see Summer Passion. After he finished with Summer, he would look in on her younger sister who just arrived into his keeping.

No longer. Georgia doesn't want you. I'll never allow her to return. Her children will all be safe from you.

Where are you?

Some place you will never be able to touch Georgia.

You filthy bastard! I'll make you regret this. I'll see you dead before I allow you to have my mate.

My mate.

Chandler waited to hear from him again. Wished he could rip him apart with both his teeth as well as his claws. Sent more hated words his way. Nothing. There was nothing else. What the hell was he supposed to do now?

Chapter Seven

Georgia decided she wasn't going to be uncomfortable when he examined her, put his fingers there where Chandler had been too many times to count. Hamilton was a professional, a doctor. She would forget her embarrassment. Accepted the upcoming invasion of her body as something responsible. She was seeing to the needs of her baby. The baby came first.

Georgia was holding her belly, wondering what was happening. Trying to understand how he would learn so much by touching inside her. He did explain a few things. Though nothing he said made sense. She felt no tightening of her muscles. Since the first then the second hardening of her belly, she felt nothing. After those first two, Hamilton rushed her from the bonfire to his home. He sent for Hollis along with Bea and Maeve. More than an hour passed since she felt the first two as well as the only contractions.

His whistling in the other room came through loud and clear. Hamilton sounded pleased. He told her how much he liked babies along with pregnant ladies. Over the last few hours, she wondered if he was attracted to her because her belly was swollen with child. Had to dismiss that notion when he found his way into her head. The man was considerate of her, nice to her so unlike Chandler who thought only of himself.

"What are you doing?" Georgia called out, tired of walking around the small room. Hamilton told her walking would increase the contractions or help the baby come sooner. Ha! They stopped. An hour ago, she'd been eager to finally hold Colin in her arms. Now it seemed she would need to wait longer. Waiting was hard. She was exhausted from waddling. Hamilton chuckled when he watched her walk. Told her that particular swagger from a pregnant woman was one of his favorite sights. Said to her how much he enjoyed helping her stand. She had the urge to punch him in his flat belly.

Hamilton told her several times in the last hour it was good for the birthing if she walked. She was tired. Exhausted from the day's work. Needed to sit on her fanny, not walk. Every time he found her sitting, he would pull her to her feet then tell her to walk. She felt as if she walked to China then back.

"Washing my hands, and anything I might use to help you with the birth. It's very important to be clean, not just clean, sterile."

He chuckled; his laughter soft. He would be thinking about her waddling. What else would Hamilton be thinking now?

"Why? You must have washed those hands of yours for thirty minutes straight. There couldn't be a speck of dirt on them." Georgia found she was curious. Hamilton seemed to know so much about childbirth. Clean hands? Cleanliness did make an inordinate amount of sense to her. Dirt always disgusted. She liked clean.

"Don't know why." Hamilton looked into the room to grin at her. "No proof that it's the best for the mother and babe. Don't like dirt when I work. Seems to me the cleaner the environment the better. I've seen babies as well as mothers die of infection when the environment wasn't clean. When the doctor or midwife didn't bother to wash their hands." He stepped back into the side room. Shrugging, he acknowledged another possible fact. "Doesn't mean that's the reason for the deaths." He stepped from the back room drying his hands. "This towel was boiled in water then steam pressed and folded so it would remain free of anything that might harm you."

"Oh…" Well, about that information, she didn't know what to say. "I'm tired. May I sit for a breather. Don't think this walking is making for more contractions."

"What else are you feeling? The contractions should be getting closer to each other. Have they?"

He looked at the door when Hollis, Bea, as well as Maeve, made an appearance. They huddled around Georgia.

Bea handed her the baby. "She's been fed. Gave the *wee* one a bottle, she didn't much like it. Appears she likes to suck on her mother."

Hamilton grinned. *I'd enjoy sucking on her mother's breast, other places too. Will you allow me the privilege…sometime?*

Hamilton!

"Take the baby, Bea. Get the little one adjusted to her new room for the night. Need to speak in private with Georgia. Give us some time. I'll let you know when you may come in to see Georgia."

"I certainly hope it's not about what you just told me," Georgia said, thinking about Hamilton's mouth on her nipples, sucking.

Her body heated. Knew her face reddened. She understood arousal came from his ungentlemanly comment. By the look on his face, she felt a twinge of something she couldn't identify. There was more to his expression than his thoughts about sucking on the tips of her breasts. The feeling was deep and real, traveled to every part of her. "What is it?"

"Have you had any more contractions?" Hamilton asked, seeming aware that perhaps she hadn't. He told her about fake contractions.

"No, what do you mean by fake contractions?" Despite the possible objection then the ensuing lecture from Hamilton, she sat down. She felt tired as well as confused. Disoriented from all that was happening to her.

"I'm thinking perhaps this was a false alarm. You might not hold Colin in your arms in the next hours. I spoke with Chandler for a few seconds while I was washing. He believes you're having the baby now. I didn't say anything different. Didn't know at the time the cramps ceased. The man is more determined than ever to find you." He set the towel he'd been using in a hamper. "We both need to take abundant caution. I will continue to keep him from entering your mind."

"Should you let him into your head? Isn't that asking for trouble also?"

When Hamilton mentioned Chandler, her heart jumped a beat. She'd not heard from him for quite some time. Thought it odd. Now that Hamilton told her he was blocking the man from her head, everything made more sense.

"The man is always talking, trying to reach you. Except…when he's not watching the evening's entertainment. Caught him off guard tonight. His attention on something else was the only reason I spoke to him. If he gets you back, which he won't, he plans to keep you drugged just as Jamie did with Delight. Will force you to sign a contract not for one or even five years but for the extent of your life. I won't allow Chandler to get to you. Will protect you along with the children, with my life."

She clutched her belly. Hamilton was beside her, his hand pressing.

"No contraction? What is it that has turned you white as new fallen snow?"

"No…I…what now? I need to sleep. Can't sleep here. This is a bachelor household. Not that it should make a difference to me. I've done worse."

She wondered if she possessed the energy to make it home.

"Why not? This is the safest place for you. The most convenient if you go into labor before morning. Though I would doubt that circumstance for the night. Your extended family is here. Maeve is just down the hall. This room is ready for you. What more could you ask for?"

"What about tomorrow? The office visit? Lunch?"

She understood he would want to look at her now. Her mind felt ready to think about tomorrow afternoon, not this moment. In the muddled abyss of her mind, tonight was too soon.

"Nothing has changed except I wish to take a more in depth look at you right now." His mouth was set, his jaw firm. "Doing so is necessary. I would want both of us to understand what the state of your pregnancy is."

With the hard set of his mouth, Georgia understood what that look meant. Hamilton was going to have his way despite any objections she might voice. She imagined she'd like to know more about the baby's soon to be appearance in the world. Tonight, or tomorrow what difference did it make.

"Alright. What do you want me to do?" She had no arguments or protestations. "I would get this over with."

"Thank you for coming to terms and agreeing with me so soon. Believed you would have more arguments. I will go in the other room while you remove your gown along with your underthings. Keep your chemise on. He pointed to a folded sheet. "Put the sheet over your lap. The second one over your shoulders if you wish. I'll knock on the door before I enter. If you're not covered, tell me. I'll wait until you say it's okay for me to come into the room."

She brought in a deep breath of air then nodded her understanding. "Alright." Hamilton was keeping her covered, keeping her modesty intact. She was surprised then not surprised. It was the kind of man he was. Didn't know what she did expect. This was professional nothing else. The exam was not about sex or distressing her. Hamilton was a doctor. In this, he would remain detached.

Removing her clothing seemed surreal. She'd had sex, naked, in front of thousands of viewers. She folded everything then set the items on a chair. Except for her chemise she was naked. How many times had she been naked for Chandler? She didn't know. This was so different. While she wasn't yet in love with Hamilton, she was falling for the handsome man. He was beautiful in so many different ways.

A little giggle escaped her when she thought of someone boiling everything that was used then pressing the fabric so every side was sterile. After picking up the sheets, she sat down on the bed where he instructed her. Covered herself. Georgia looked around at all the walls. Saw framed pictures of pregnant ladies. Witnessed a certificate of some sort he exhibited. A few minutes later, she heard the knock.

Breath rushed into her lungs when she gulped the air. "I'm ready." Her heart was in her throat. Felt as if the blasted thing raced with a frenzied beat. She would never be ready for this.

When Hamilton walked in, he smiled at her. The smile was different from his usual greeting. Must be his doctor's smile. "I do like the picture you make."

Georgia wanted to tell him she also enjoyed the picture he made. Tall as well as broad of shoulder. He wore a white jacket that reached to his knees covering his clothing. She pointed. "Was the white coat boiled too?"

"Yes, everything you see has been sterilized with heat. As I said before, this is for yours as well as the baby's health. Let me give you a quick breakdown of what I'm going to do." He paused for a few beats of her heart. Seemed he was going over in his mind everything that must be said. "If you have questions, please ask." Again, Hamilton paused.

"At this moment, I don't have questions." Her breath shook as she spoke.

"You should attempt to relax. This won't hurt. First, I'm going to run my hands along the swell of your stomach. Even though we say belly or stomach, what I'm feeling is the babe inside your womb. A very comfortable placc for the little tyke."

She was nodding her head as if she were an idiot. "It's what you did at the bonfire. That was fine. What's second?" Georgia didn't think she'd appreciate the second part.

"I must put two fingers inside you in order to feel your cervix. This won't hurt. I will put a cream on my fingers so they will slip inside without causing pain."

He cleared his throat waiting as if expecting a question.

"Why? What will you learn?" She was curious. Nothing like that was done at the first birth. Of course, one of the ladies who lived at the whorehouse helped her birth Maeve. Her only qualification was the fact she was the oldest of seven children.

"I will see if your cervix has softened as well as if it is dilated. Both will tell me more about the time of Colin's birth. If the cervix is neither, you might have a couple more weeks to wait. If there is any dilation, you are in labor. Your contractions will begin again."

"I think I understand what you are saying."

"Are you ready?" Hamilton asked.

He was being so patient with her. "Yes."

Then, Hamilton stepped up to the edge of the bed where she sat. He pulled out a padded board. "I want you to set your feet, here and here."

Her eyes widened. Her legs would be bent at the knee and spread wide for him. She did what he told her, keeping the sheet covering her. He would look at her. Maybe not. She shouldn't care. He was doing his job, nothing more. Hamilton was a doctor. This was clinical not personal.

Beneath the sheet he lifted her chemise so he touched the flesh of her distended belly. His hands were rough with a few callouses. He stopped in places then continued. She lay on the bed on her back, with her head propped up by a pillow.

"You feel much the same as you did the first time. The lad's head is down. Let me see how far along you are, if at all. He dipped two fingers into a jar of cream. "This won't hurt," he reminded her.

Georgia closed her eyes. Felt his fingers travel inside her. Stopped when they were deep inside. Felt him touch her womb. Stayed there for a few seconds. Tense concentration shown on his face. Hamilton was worried about hurting her. Of course, he didn't.

Strange that she felt the loss when he removed himself. Disappearing for a few minutes, he washed his hands. When he returned, he had that doctor smile on his face.

"There is no dilation or softening. I would say the contraction you felt was false. You should have two to three weeks before Colin makes his debut into this world. You can put your legs down." After she did, he pushed in the board. "I would like you to dress yourself. Open the door when you have your clothing on. We need to speak of a few practical matters."

"Oh…"

She watched Hamilton discard his coat into the hamper as he strode from the room. For a few ticks of the clock on the nearby shelf, she stared at the closed door. Before he left, he set a cloth next to her. Didn't tell her what it was for. Georgia guessed. She scrambled from the bed as if he might walk in on her. He wouldn't. Wiped away the excess cream then scurried into her clothing before she tossed the cloth along with her sheets into the hamper.

When she finished, she opened the door for him. He was across the hall, leaning on the wall with both his arms and legs crossed. His smile was not one of a doctor. His grin reached from ear to ear. She realized he was no longer the professional but a man who was interested in her as a man is interested in a woman.

"Let's go into the drawing room to talk. I've told Hollis as well as Bea what I've told you about the baby's arrival. They've both retired for the night. Maeve is asleep though she will most likely be wanting her mother soon since she hasn't nursed. Bea prepared a nice herbal tea for you. The drink will help you sleep."

Georgia didn't know what to say. Chandler had never been so nice to her. Hamilton set her arm in the crook of his elbow, just as he'd done hours earlier. She felt a deep rush of emotions. What she experienced was hard and raw with bits of passion thrown into the mix. Realized again this man was meant for her, unlike Chandler. Perhaps a second mate was sent to her so she would be happy in this life.

"Sit." He told her with what appeared to be a wicked grin. "No more walking this evening. You do appear exhausted. In the next few weeks, you must rest. You will need to be strong for your baby. As soon as we talk, I'll bring you to your room. It's across the hall from mine in case I'm wrong about the babe."

"What more do we have to talk about? I understand what you did. Appreciate the doctoring. Imagine you must be thinking about what I owe you."

"You don't owe me a thing. Believe we should speak of our upcoming wedding." Hamilton held up his hands to stop her from declining the invitation. "You have less than three weeks before the birth of Colin. We must tie the knot before he arrives. We've been granted the time. Thank God, he is not coming tonight."

"That is what you've told me. What does the time of Colin's birth have to do with marriage?" In time, she did think marriage to this man would happen. "Don't you think it's too soon. I haven't known you for one day."

"No. We are mates. If you marry me, I can claim Colin as mine. I'll adopt Maeve." He poured them both a cup of tea. Sat beside her on the sofa. "Chandler will have no claim to either child."

"Can you do that? Claim him? Just because we are married at the time of his birth?"

She didn't understand law or how it worked in these cases. Only knew she would do anything possible to keep Colin out of Chandler's hands.

"Yes, and I'll officially adopt the lad just to make certain there are no loop holes. What do you say? Should we just get married for the hell of it?" Hamilton asked, a wicked grin on his handsome face.

While she was moved by his words, she was also uncertain. Her cup shook so hard, drops of tea slid down the edge. She placed it on the saucer then picked up a napkin to wipe the liquid from her fingers.

You didn't need the cream. You were quite ready without it. A precaution I won't need to take in our future.

Oh! Again Georgia didn't know what to think of this man's audacity. She should retaliate with some bravado of her own. Couldn't think of words that might embarrass him. Hamilton was like most men, difficult to disconcert.

Marry me. I will ask you until you give the proper answer. You know, the one I'm in search of. Marry me. I promise, you won't regret doing so. I will make you happy.

Well…yes…maybe…could you give me a better proposal. Even Chandler hit the floor with his knee. I would like to remember all the pertinent traditions.

Didn't wish for you to refuse me. Was afraid you might laugh. After all, how long have we known each other?

"If you do ask the question in the right manner, I won't refuse." She wouldn't. All he said made sense.

In front of her Hamilton was on bended knee. The moment lasted a minute or two. He cleared his throat. "I don't have a ring as yet. Tomorrow, after we go to lunch, you can pick one out at the jewelers. I'd like to see Father Damian. We can speak to him about a person having two different mates in one lifetime. Say yes."

"You don't need to examine me again."

Georgia didn't phrase her words as a question. While she didn't look with disfavor on the procedure, she wasn't ready to have any part of him inside her again until she came to terms with their relationship.

"No, not for another week unless you begin contractions. Need the marriage to take place as soon as possible. After we see Father Damian, we can speak to Connal along with Wynnie about the soonest possible wedding date. Would like to have everything finalized before Colin makes an appearance into this world."

Hamilton still held her hand. Touched the light blue veins on the inside of her wrist. Brought her fingers to his lips. Pressed a quick kiss on her palm before he let her go, then stood.

She shuddered from the tender touch. Flames ignited. Georgia ran her hands along her gown unsure once more. Her palms were sweaty. She felt both frightened as well as pleased. "You've overwhelmed me. I just agreed to marry a man I've known for less than a day. Never thought that would happen. When I refused Chandler, never believed I would marry anyone. Thought I would remain a spinster for the rest of my life."

"You've made me happier than I've ever thought to be. Shall we enjoy a little prewedding fondling, a kiss here, maybe one there? I've a need to taste you. Would this be acceptable, a few kisses this evening? Tomorrow we could explore a little more of each other. I do intend to carry through with all the Clan Chattan traditions. Would you like to learn about some?" He swept her into his arms then onto his lap. "To begin..."

Unable to stop the laughter, she indulged herself then wrapped her arms around him hugging him close. Pulled back to focus on his eyes then his mouth. Bit his chin then laughed again.

"Ah, I see you don't play fair."

"Tell me about these traditions. Don't know much about the clans at all. Chandler did the least possible when he claimed me. Can I see your cat?" She was curious. Had seen Chandler in his tiger form. He was impressive. Realized, Hamilton would be more extraordinary. He would need to take all his clothes off to change. The idea held merit. She did wish to see him in all his glory.

"Are you saying you wish to see me naked?" Hamilton sipped on the lobe of her ear, touched inside with his tongue. One hand ran along her arm to stop at her shoulder to finally wrap around her neck.

Georgia gasped at the intensity of the small nip to her ear. With Chandler she hated it when he sipped on her ear. The smoothing of her hand along her arm caused another high intensity jolt. She needed more. Her body reverberated with passion. Raw desire burst into secret intimate areas. No, she wasn't at all surprised he didn't need the cream. Her arousal beginning at the campfire was penetrating, powerful in the extreme. At the campfire, when he ran his hands along her swollen belly, she felt the first stirrings of desire. They increased as the moments passed.

"Naked would be nice."

She moistened her lips. He watched the slow glide of her tongue. Imagined how his would feel on her mouth. Needed the kiss he intimated they would share. For a moment, she closed her eyes. This was all happening so fast.

"Not going to be naked with you unless you are in the same state of dishabille as me. I would also enjoy witnessing your cat. We could play together as cats. After the babe is born, we can go deep into the highlands. I know of a sweet place we could be alone. We could swim in the nearby lock. Do you like water?"

Unable to withstand the silver-blue blaze of his eyes she looked away. With the tip of his finger, he turned her face to him. Again, she stared into silver-blue eyes that were darkening with raw desire. In anticipation of the kiss she yearned for, her tongue swept across her lips. His thumb followed the same path.

"I might want more tonight than a few kisses."

Georgia understood she was too bold, too brazen. She would shock the poor man. No, she didn't believe he would be surprised. She did wish for him to make love to her.

"Well, as much as I would love the pleasure of your body cradling mine, not tonight. You are too tired. We are too new to each other. Tomorrow, we can reconsider the possibilities of further explorations." He tasted her lips with his mouth and tongue. Touched with gentle, tender caresses that left her panting with unbridled need.

Even though she felt disappointment to the tips of her toes, Georgia knew he was right. "If you insist. Is this the doctor's orders?"

"Yes. I do expect you to obey me when I'm your physician. Other than that, you may do what you will, when you will. When we wed, we will take the obey out of the vows. It's not the first time Father Damian has done so."

"Are you giving me *carte blanche* with your body?" She giggled, thinking of him spread out in front of her. Her imagination vivid. The picture in her mind pleased her. "You do understand I'm not innocent. I've too much experience. That year of my life changed me. Not in a good way."

The sudden words she spoke left her feeling disappointed. Georgia wished she could have come to this man a virgin. Instead, Chandler ripped her innocence away from her, thinking he was her mate, well he was, she gave all of herself to the man. For reasons she didn't understand, her world was knocked topsy-turvy when she met Hamilton. He was her mate now. For the rest of her life.

Do not fret about what you cannot change. You are perfect for me. Kiss me now as if you mean all those feelings swirling around in your mind. I'm certain you know how. Need to taste you as well as catch the beautiful scent of you.

I intend everything we do together to be beautiful. In such a short time, you've come to mean everything to me.

As his mouth captured hers, explored amid the deep heat that filled her with exquisite pleasure, she gave of herself. Wanted him to learn everything there was to know about her. She sensed he wanted the same. Magic exploded in those moments where he tasted her and she tasted him as well. Her body pulsed, leaping to life, needing all the enchantment he could give her. This was mercuric pleasure as old as time primitive in the exquisite sensations. His tenderness unnerved her. Beneath his gentle assault Chandler's presence dimmed. Was becoming a distant memory.

Hamilton cupped her breast. Swept the palm of his hand across the hardened tip. Georgia wished for more. Needed to feel him pulse to life inside her. For now, the penetration of his tongue was all there would be of pleasure.

"I want you in my bed. I've tried to be noble, Georgia. Don't wish to rush you. Understand you are puzzled with the way these strange events are unfolding," he told her, the timber of his voice so low and deep she felt the strain of his physical emotions wash over her. Understood all that kept him from tossing her skirts was iron control. "Wish to hold you through the night. What do you say? We won't do anything. You can wear the nightgown Bea brought."

"Yes. Can you do that? Hold me and not have sex?"

"Make love." Hamilton corrected, "Imagine we will see. Won't do anything you don't wish for. Realize, there will be more between us than mere sex. I will make love to you. Given time you will discern the difference."

"I want to feel all of you. Need to know you intimately, feel you deep inside me. I sound crazy to myself. We don't know each other."

"We've known each other throughout the generations. Time and again we've come together to be as one. There is nothing different now."

~ * ~

He was a fool to believe he could do what he told her. Doing so would take all the willpower he possessed, the iron command of his body. He meant to hold true to his intentions. The plans he made in these few short hours would not deviate. He was a man of his word. Georgia's small body against his would remind him of what he wasn't going to take this evening.

As a man of his word, the night seemed to be the longest of his life. In the morning, he woke up with Georgia within the shelter of his arms. Her little butt was snuggled against his sex. One hand cupped a soft breast. Tested the hard tip. Heard a soft feminine sound of pleasure. For a few beats of his heart, he thought he must have died then gone to heaven. He sipped in the scent of her, all-lavender coupled with winter snowflakes. She told him Chandler gave her the name of Winter Snow. In many ways the moniker fit.

Pushing her hair aside, he nuzzled the soft down on the back of her neck. Kissed with tender finesse, once then twice. She was exquisite. Knew he needed to remove himself. Drawing in another deep breath of Georgia scented air, he held still to soak up the warmth of the woman he held within his arms, his mate.

At all costs, he must protect her from Chandler Wolcott. In order to do so, he had some major decisions to clarify in his mind. If necessary, he would bring the fight to Chandler. Would never allow the man to come to Georgia along with the children. If that wasn't going to happen, he needed to go on the defensive. If or when necessary he would make a trip to London, to the infamous bordello. He intended to make his feelings clear.

With another soft caress to her neck, she sighed a whisper of a sound. The day was beginning. He needed to get up. She should sleep as long as necessary. Yesterday exhausted her. Rising naked from the bed, he padded to the window, staring out on the yard below then closed the curtains blocking the sunlight.

Hamilton wrote her a quick note telling her his plans for the day as well as directions to his place of work. She should meet him at his office at noon. After he bathed then dressed, he found Bea and Hollis in the kitchen debating with his cook as to the best breakfast for Georgia. Maeve sat on her highchair banging a spoon on the wood. A bowl of porridge sat in front of her along with some apple sauce. When Maeve saw him, she dropped the spoon, sticking her arms out in an invitation for Hamilton to pick her up. He ruffed her hair then gave her a quick kiss to her cheek. Picking up the spoon, he set the utensil on her high chair. With a slight lift of an eyebrow, he silently asked Bea about the appearance of Maeve's chair.

Bea continued cooking while she spoke. "I sent Hollis for Maeve's highchair." Bea answered his question before he could ask.

"Good, good," his mind was scrambling with all he needed to do. "Do whatever you think is best for Georgia. You know her well. I'll take the food that is ready now." He eyed the fried eggs and potatoes. There was crisp bacon that smelled heavenly along with fresh baked bread. His mouth watered with the promise of food. He could get used to this pampering. His residence had been a bachelor's pad for too many years.

"Georgia is still sleeping. She was when I left the room. Doubt if she will rise for another hour." Hamilton held up his hands. "She needs my protection. Nothing happened between us last night except I held her. Won't make any promises for the future or even tonight. How are relationship proceeds is our business."

"You're right," Bea said with a tiny snort that surprised Hamilton. "Hollis and I talked about this for some time yesterday. We don't disapprove of anything that might happen between the two of you. Chandler will make an appearance. There is no doubt in either of our minds. When he does, you will need to be there for her."

"After the *bairn* is born, I intend to confront him in London. Don't want the battle between us to take place anywhere near those I love." The word love stopped him for a few seconds. He rolled the sound of it around in his head. Of course, he loved her as well as her children. Georgia was his mate. There was no question in his mind. When he would tell her, he wasn't positive. Should explain his feelings before the ceremony that would bind them together.

"You love Georgia?" Hollis asked with a broad grin on his face. "Have you told her your feelings? She needs to know."

All Hollis said was true. Why did it seem so hard to do? "No, I haven't. Just now said the word I've been feeling since I first saw her. The fact is out in the open." He ate for a few minutes expecting those two to say more. There was nothing from either person. Hamilton realized he needed to speak of his future plans, the ones in the immediate future. "Don't want either of you telling her before I can find the best opportunity."

"Won't say a word," the pair told him in unison.

Maeve's porridge found the floor, the bowl on top of the mess. She screamed with delight. Clapped her hands as if she'd done something to be proud about. "I'll clean it up," Bea said as she eyed the gooey mess. "You two finish your breakfast. I'm going to make something for Georgia. She never sleeps late. I'll wager she'll be down before the hour is up."

"I'll be gone when she comes down." Hamilton didn't think Georgia was awake yet, let alone bathed as well as dressed. "I'm taking her to lunch at noon. After that we will visit with Father Damian at the McKenna keep then Winnie and Connal. We've a wedding to arrange. The sooner the ceremony takes place the better for her well-being." He continued to make lists in his mind. There was so much to accomplish.

"Georgia agreed?" Bea's mouth gaped open after she asked the question. Hollis shut it with the tip of his finger.

"This is for the best. He loves her. She loves him. I doubt it not. The wedding will give the pair an advantage. Since they are mates for life, the ceremony will take place. Why not as soon as possible?" Hollis clapped his hands together. "This is a magnificent idea. I applaud you for acting so fast. The two of you will begin your new lives together. For Georgia, I never thought anything this good would come her way. I will visit Cormack today to give him the good news. He will want to be there for his daughter."

"No, I need to see him first to ask permission. He is the father of the bride. Maybe we will see her father before we visit the keep later this afternoon." That added one more item to his list of things he needed to accomplish today. With the palm of his hand, he hit his forehead. He'd been so busy with other ideas, he never once thought of Georgia's father.

"Just magnificent..." Bea mumbled. "She will need a gown. That will take time. Flowers, cake, the list will go on. Where will we have this affair? Suppose you have a wealth of family and friends who will need invitations. All that takes time."

"At the keep, McKennas are proficient with weddings. One look at my blushing bride and all hands will be on deck. Certain the gown will be fashioned in record time." Inside Hamilton laughed. They didn't know how well the Clan Chattan worked together. Nothing was impossible. If they asked to marry tomorrow, Wynnie would clap her hands together then make it happen. "She will wear a sash of Clan Adair's dress tartan. I, my kilt. Georgia can plan the menu with Wynnie. Everything will be completed by the date we choose. Tomorrow would be wonderful. Not certain Georgia will agree to something so soon. We will see."

"Thought the wearing of kilts was against the law," Hollis said.

"It is. Nonetheless the gates of the keep will be locked for the event. No one who might protest will be allowed inside."

"What you've told us is a lot to take in Hamilton Adair. You've got everything under control." Bea was shaking her finger at him. "No matter how proficient these Scottish folk are, this cannot be done in twenty-four hours. I would maybe think two days would be possible if they are so talented."

Hamilton hooted a laugh that startled Maeve. Her clear blue eyes were focused on him. In her little mind she was asking him what was so funny. The thought surprised him. He'd spoken with Colin. Nonetheless, this was the first time with Maeve.

The devil, this tiny shifter heard his thoughts. In the way of the shifters, she was becoming his. This was odd though nice. Perhaps the event had something to do with his being Georgia's mate. Something else he would speak to Father Damian about.

You will treat my mama nice. Not like the man who thinks he's my father. He isn't, you understand. You are.

I will love you with all my heart, Colin.

All the other man wanted was to use me as he did mother. She hated what he made her do that last month and a half. I was conceived in the first show he made her act in.

What would Father Damian have to say about this continuous turning of events? This boggled his mind, which now seemed to be filled with sawdust. Hamilton finished his meal. Said his goodbyes then, whistling, left the house. Georgia would be at his office at noon. Looking at his watch, he had a couple hours of work ahead of him.

He rode Rex to the office. Waved at the people of the village while he passed them. When he walked into the office, Hamilton was all smiles.

"Hawk, Houston, you won't believe what has happened."

He wanted to shout to the world he found his mate. They would never believe the circumstance. He couldn't believe the facts though he had to.

Hawk walked out; his hands stuck in his coat pocket. Leah appeared with a cup of coffee. "Houston is out on an emergency. He's delivering a child. Won't be back until who knows when?" Leah lifted her shoulders in a delicate feminine shrug. "I'll be pleased to pass on whatever news you have. What's so important?" She handed the fresh brewed coffee to him. "Know you've only had tea at your place. Too bad you won't admit to loving coffee like the rest of us."

He sipped. "Ouch!" The brew was hot. Rubbed his tongue along the roof of his mouth. "First, I found my mate. Second, we will be wed as soon as Wynnie can put together a wedding. Going to talk with my fiancée to Father Damian along with Wynnie and Connal this afternoon."

Leah sat down, a stunned expression on her beautiful face. "You are certain about this? Who is she?"

"The new lady who has been moving in for the last two weeks? My parents brought several carts with them when they returned from London after visiting Harris. Found the cottage for her before she arrived. Georgia is beautiful as well as delightful. Met her at a dinner party in London. She has a daughter as well as one on the way," Hawk said.

"I know. I'm not hearing misgivings, am I? Georgia is my mate. Know the reality just as the two of you realized the moment you met. There is no question in my mind. You can meet her again at noon. She will be here. I'm taking her to lunch then the McKenna Keep. We've things to discuss with important people." Thinking about this afternoon's discussions brightened his day. He hoped Father Damian would help unriddle some of their confusion.

"A ready-made family is a lot to deal with. How far along is she?" Hawk asked. "Will you be her doctor? Perhaps one of us should take on the physician role. We all understand one should never doctor people they care about, least of all love."

There was that word again, love. He needed to tell her. Hoped she would reciprocate the sentiment. "Georgia could give birth anytime. Though from what I learned last night, I believe she has two to three weeks before the blessed date. There is no dilation of the cervix though the lad's head is down." Hamilton was thinking about how she felt in his arms last night. How he would feel when he made love to her. "Despite what both of you will say about my delivering the baby, it's what I intend to do. Will only call on one of you if there appears to be complications."

Hawk sent out a huff of air. "Felt the same about Maisie. Seems we all tend to think alike when it comes to our women. I do understand. You need to be at her side. Most deliveries are easy. Don't see any reason for you to decline."

"The pregnancy as well as the delivery of her first child were normal. So far all appears fine. Don't see why there should be any problems. Since this is her second child, this one should make his appearance sooner."

The threesome chatted for a while. Saw a few patients. Time continued to pass with slowness. Hamilton's list grew longer. He would speak with her about her father. Her father was one factor they had yet to discuss. Since her father accompanied her to Coronach, he assumed they got along.

The bell on the outer door chimed. When he saw her, Hamilton pulled out his watch. Georgia was early. Hoped she was as eager as he was. Georgia stood in the waiting room, shifting from one foot to the other. Her reticule dangled from hands that were clutched in front of her. Hamilton's face lit up with welcome. He was pleased to see her.

"Welcome to my place of work."

Hamilton held out his hand to her. Swept his arm around her to hold her close. Seemed to have been a deucedly long time since he held her. He soaked in the scent of her.

"That's not your doctor smile," she told him her, voice on a wobble. "I'm…early. I know. I'll just take a seat in the corner then wait until you are ready. Don't wish to get in your way."

"Ready now. Let me introduce you to one of my partners. Wait, you met Hawk in London. Houston is delivering a baby but his wife Leah is in the office."

She looked so damn beautiful, insecure too. He needed to change the self-doubt to confidence. Supposed after the year she spent with Chandler the uncertainty could be expected.

Hamilton called out. Both stepped into the waiting area. "Hello," Leah walked up to her then gave her a hug as if she'd known her forever. "I'm so pleased to meet you. Ham, here, has been singing your praises. Has told us what a lovely person you are. Told us the two of you plan to marry as soon as possible. We will all be at your wedding. In this clan, everyone looks forward to the festivities."

Hawk picked up her hand, kissed the back. Smiled at her. "This is wonderful. Ham seems to be head-over-heels in love with you. Do you feel the same?" Hawk asked while he grinned at his cousin.

Her mouth gaped open. Hamilton barked a laugh. Hugged her tighter. Saw the surprise in her eyes.

"He is?"

She looked more astonished than he felt when Hawk made the announcement. Wondered again if she returned the feelings. Hoped she did. Maybe when he confessed his love she would also.

Still wondering about love. Hamilton closed her mouth with the tip of his finger. "Are you hungry?"

"I was. Now I'm just anxious. What did you tell your friends?" Georgia was gnawing on her bottom lip. Seemed to be a nervous habit of hers.

"That you are near family. Told them the tenuous connection. Hawk is a Frasier. One of Harris' brothers, the oldest. You remember. Right? From meeting you in London learned what a lovely person you are. Understood you made the move up here, because his family insisted you needed friends you could count on. A place to live where you weren't looking over your shoulder, expecting trouble."

"Oh…"

From the coat stand, he grabbed his coat then held out his arm. She wrapped her fingers around the crook of his elbow. Every time she touched him her emotions grew more intense, deeper, bottomless. He felt each of her heartbeats meld with his. The sensation was profound. With speed that surprised him, she delved into his mind. Became closer to him than he could ever have imagined. No one had affected him like this. Understood all she meant to him from the first moment he saw her.

Hamilton helped her into the carriage, he arranged for their visits. "We are off to lunch at my favorite tavern in the village. I will point out some of the places where you might wish to shop. The dressmaker here seems to be liked by the women of the village. You will want a wedding dress." He thought he might be moving too fast again. Couldn't help himself. He was so very eager to call Georgia his wife. Enthusiastic to start their life together as a couple. Impatient to claim her as his very own. "After we eat, we will visit your father. I do have an important question to ask." He chuckled at her look of curiosity.

"You do?" Georgia blinked once then a second time as she seemed to be mulling over his words. "What are you going to ask?"

He tapped her nose, smiling with excitement. "His permission for your hand in marriage. What else? Explain a few details of our meeting to him. Your father will want to understand how this happened so fast."

Georgia's hands were clasped tight in her lap. Her face was pale. She was silent for the longest time, too calm for his way of thinking. Before she spoke, she sipped a breath of air. "You have this all figured out. Don't you? Where do my wishes come into play? I did agree to the marriage. Didn't understand how fast you move when you have a target in mind. Believed I would be able to adjust to the new idea."

"Target? No," he said, thinking he should be more cautious. Shouldn't spew all his thoughts at one time. "No, nothing is set in stone. I've had one patient all morning so I continued making lists in my head. A list I began at breakfast, mind you. You…us were at the top of that list. Your thoughts are most important. Expect input from you about everything. If I'm moving too fast, tell me." He paused for breath. Believed a change of subject might further the conversation. "Did you know both your children spoke to me this morning. Warned me against hurting you. I was amazed as well as pleased about their input. I assured both I would never harm you."

"They didn't…? You won't hurt me. I know the truth soul deep. You are nothing like Chandler. In the depth of his soul, he is dark as well as mean spirited. Selfish in the extreme."

Hamilton regretted the fact he didn't meet her before Chandler became part of her life. Chandler's connection to Georgia was something he needed to deal with. "The pair of them, Maeve along with Colin, most certainly did say a great deal. I was quite pleased with their reaction to me. Both feel as if I'm the father they want. Funny, I haven't had the need to block Chandler from you since you rose this morning. Perhaps he is getting on with his life. Maybe the children are blocking him. That's an interesting thought."

She was shaking her head, not seeming to understand the scope of his words then… He helped her into the carriage. "My children should prefer you to Chandler. I do. However, I doubt if he will ever give up until he is defeated. Until there is no recourse except to leave us alone. Marriage will help in that aspect. If Colin stops talking to him, he will be devastated then more determined to get his way. You said you haven't been blocking his thoughts from Colin? Don't think he's ever spoken to Maeve that way."

"Yes, to taking the situation over with Colin. The infant is too young to understand he has the power to block Chandler's thoughts. If he does, the deed will be done without him knowing. What I've garnered from Chandler is the reality he is preoccupied with building his show so the acts will include more virgins. He along with Bertram have been roaming the rural areas seeking families in need of funds. Enough so they are willing to sell their innocent daughters to these men. Johnny, as well as Bertram, are taking their innocence in front of the audience. Johnny is searching for his mate. Not that it is likely he will find his mate in this manner."

"I…"

Hamilton placed his hand on hers. Squeezed. Pointed to a building. "There is the print shop where Cameron Frasier works. You met him along with Lainie at the Wolcott townhouse in London. He owns the place. If you like, he will print invitations for our wedding." Hamilton witnessed the stunned look on her face.

"I don't have anyone to invite."

"Yes, you do. You've met Leah as well as Houston. You met Cam along with Hawk in London. That's what I've been told anyway. We can send invitations to the entire clan. Think about it. Your hand will go numb from addressing all the invitations."

He leaned over her, pointing to a building on the opposite side of the street. "There is the dressmakers. I will give the modiste enough good Scottish coin so she can hire as many seamstresses as needed to finish your gown in record time. I do think however, Wynnie should accompany you when you go to purchase a gown. I've heard tell it's bad look for the groom to see the bride in her wedding dress before the ceremony begins."

Georgia sipped air. "You're overwhelming me again. I am just beginning to adjust to the notion I'll be married very soon. All these details depress me. If we had more time, I could wrap my head around all I've got to do. As it is now…" she puffed out a tiny whisper of air. "As it is now, how am I going to get it all done in a couple of days?"

"You do want a grand wedding. Don't you? I *ken* I do. Want the best for you. It's a day I hope to remember for the rest of my life. As to getting everything completed in a couple of days, we will look to the ladies of the clan for help. They all are talented women. All you will need do is sit down with them to say yes or no to the plans. You can offer advice. Choose colors as well as plan the menu for the feast. You along with Bea can even cater the feast if that is what you would like? Whatever you wish for is yours. This is going to be your special day."

He pulled up in front of the little tavern on the green. "Here it is, The Tavern on the Green. In the summer they put tables outside beneath the trees. Has the ambiance of a picnic…very idyllic. We will come here when the weather warms. Sit outside. Sip from the best wines."

Inside, the atmosphere was cozy. Every table held a candle. Warm scents of baking filled the room. Several serving girls were busy bringing food as well as drinks to the patrons. They found a table overlooking the street.

She ordered tea. Hamilton ordered a glass of ale. They both asked for Shepard's Pie. For a few minutes nothing was said. Hamilton was so eager. He was overdoing his elation. He knew that for a fact. Needed to temper his enthusiasm. Didn't know how to do so.

"Hawk called you Ham?"

Found he was surprised by her statement. He wasn't positive where she was going with the question. "My friends do shorten my name. Hamilton tends to be a mouthful, too many syllables. Is there something wrong?"

Georgia stirred sugar into her tea. Kept stirring. When she didn't look up, he reached out to stop the movement. Her nervous energy unnerved him. Needed to discover why. "What is it? Talk to me." Hamilton didn't understand. She needed to say something.

"Am I a friend?" Georgia asked with too much hesitation for his state of mind. "We are getting married. Nonetheless, don't know if we are friends. Could we be? Shouldn't we be friends before we are lovers?"

He cursed thinking this was the biggest part of their problems. Despite all the facts, they knew little of each other. "You are more than a friend."

He loved her. She was his mate. What more is there? She could call him by any name she liked.

"Does that mean I can call you by the shortened version? You did say your name was a mouthful."

"Except when I give you pleasure. Don't want you yelling Ham when you shatter into thousands of heated shards in my arms. My entire name would be nice. Yes, I would be a pleased man if you cried out Hamilton in the throes of your ecstasy."

With those words, she paled. "I'm sorry... I don't understand. Shouldn't have asked."

Hamilton didn't know what to think of her apology. Georgia had nothing to apologize for. "I'm teasing. It's obvious this isn't a joke to you." Hamilton picked up her hands. Touched each knuckle with his lips. A tender kiss to each one. "You are my mate. Nod your head if you understand." He rubbed the inside of her wrists. Watched the tiny shudder of desire rush through her. Felt her pulse leap to life.

When she faced him, looked at him, the China blue of her eyes darkened. She nodded telling him she understood.

"You will be my wife soon. You are the most important person in my life," he told her, slipping his fingers between hers, sliding them against the silk of her flesh. "Your happiness pleases me."

The next nod brought a tiny smile on her lips. She pursed her lips together when he reciprocated.

"I love you."

Her eyes widened in both disbelief as well as something else; he wasn't certain. Wished she would return the words. For the longest time, he was met with silence. Wanted to remind her to nod so he would know she understood the message.

"You love me? I find the sentiment hard to believe. When did you decide you loved me?" China blue eyes questioned then implored him to answer. "Chandler never told me he loved me. The man could never love anyone but himself."

To yell his frustration was something he needed to do. She should believe his words of love. "I decided," he spoke from deep in his heart. "Last night when I was holding you when you were sleeping next to me. To tell the truth, I didn't make a conscious decision. The feelings within me were profound, deep with their power. Intense in the extreme. I just knew there was a lot between us, bringing us together. For hours after the feelings came to me, I mulled the thought around in my head. My reaction was much the same as yours. Confused as to how I reached the amazing conclusion so soon after knowing you. Imagine that's the way of it for most shifters if not all. The children speaking to me cemented my thoughts. At that moment, I became an integral part of your life. The emotion of love rocked me hard."

"You'll forgive me if I think about this for a while. Your words took me by surprise. I'm not certain what to think or feel. What I do know is that my feelings for you are deep in my heart. The warmth I feel for you radiates within. As you mentioned, cemented. Not positive what that means. Never had feelings such as these. I haven't had the same revelation. If I had, I'm not at all certain I could share something so intimate with you so soon. When I fell in love with Chandler, I told him. Often, he taunted me with the sentiment. I'm afraid to say the words again. He never loved me. Don't know if I'll ever be able to make myself so vulnerable another time."

To say he wasn't disappointed would be a lie. Hamilton acknowledged the fact he would need to wait until she felt more secure within herself. During that one year of her life, she'd been abused as well as used by a hateful man. "I sent a message to your father. Told him we would be at his home around one o'clock."

~ * ~

Cormack O'brien opened the door of his home at one o'clock sharp. Georgia along with Hamilton Adair stood on the front porch. The man was a handsome devil, a fine figure of a man. He hoped this relationship would be different for his daughter. This one had much the same look as Chandler Wolcott. A wave of fear swamped him. Felt as if another grave was being dug for his beautiful, loving daughter who wore her heart on her sleeve. Understood, his daughter wouldn't survive another cruel relationship. He held onto the door so the emotion wouldn't send him to his knees. Fought to remain standing. He tried to keep the dread from showing on his face. This was not the same man. He didn't have the same proclivities. Georgia wouldn't fall under the spell of another evil man.

The message didn't tell him as to why the visit. Cormack had one guess. Hoped he was wrong. This was too soon to be thinking about a marriage to a man she just met. *Unless he was a shifter.* "Come in, welcome to my new home. There is still some clutter to put away. Don't trip over the boxes in the hall." He stood aside so the couple could pass. Georgia stopped to give him a hug. "Would you like tea? Brandy?"

"Not for me," Hamilton told him. "We just ate lunch. Would you?" He turned to Georgia, a smile on his face.

"No, Father, we came from the Tavern on The Green. I don't wish for anything more to go into my stomach. I ate too much as it is. Will more than likely give me indigestion. With my pregnancy there is not much room for food in my stomach." Her sigh of contentment was soft, wistful sounding. "Your grandchild grows bigger each day."

Cormack led the way into the drawing room. Offered them both a seat. "Tell me then, why are the two of you here? Must say the visit is nice. However, it is a surprise. Didn't expect to see you for a few more days. You must be as busy as myself with the unpacking."

"I have Hollis and Bea to help me. Would you like me to send Bea to help you?"

Hamilton didn't sit. He stood near the fireplace, his hands locked behind his back, feet braced apart. "Suppose you have a lot of questions. Imagine I should begin when I met your daughter. Yesterday…" When he looked at Georgia, Cormack realized the strength of his feelings.

"When you met, might be a good beginning," Cormack agreed with a voice harsher than what he wished for.

He poured himself a brandy. Held it up to the light. "You sure you don't want something. By the grim look on your face, you've information that might…" Cormack left off there. He wasn't at all certain what was going on with his daughter and this man. He hoped she wouldn't be hurt again. Chandler left her with too many self-doubts.

"Nothing for me." Hamilton cleared his throat. "Let me tell the story in its entirety. I met your daughter yesterday afternoon while she was moving into her new home. She caught my eye, blinded me with her smile. Knew when our gazes met, she would be mine. We've known each other before." He continued with the story. "This morning, we decided we should marry to protect her from Chandler who is no longer her mate. I am."

The intensity in Hamilton's voice didn't surprise Cormack. If what he said was true, which he had no reason to believe otherwise, Cormack would be surprised if he wasn't a formidable opponent to Chandler Wolcott.

At this juncture, Cormack wasn't certain how to proceed. He rubbed the back of his neck while he thought of possibilities "You're asking my permission to wed my daughter. I gather though, you'll marry Georgia with or without my consent. Is that true?" When Hamilton started to speak, he held up his hand to stop him. "How do I know you won't hurt Georgia? My daughter is in a vulnerable state of mind. She is not ready for marriage. You might be just as mean spirited as Chandler Wolcott."

"He isn't, Papa." Georgia was shaking her head. "Even when I first met Chandler, he held evil within him. I understood he was my mate. Had to stay with him until I no longer could. He claimed me." She turned to Hamilton, an interesting expression on her lovely face. "I noticed this morning the marks are fading. Isn't that strange? Both my children speak to Hamilton as if he is their true father. He will claim them as his, adopt both if need be. Hamilton will also protect my children."

"Our children," Hamilton corrected her with a boyish smile. "We wish to be married in the way of the Clan Chattan as soon as possible. I would like your approval. Would welcome you at both ceremonies as well as the feast after." Hamilton looked and sounded nervous. The very fact he was anxious about his answer, told Cormack as much as he needed to learn about the young man.

Cormack liked the detail he wished to carry through with all the clan traditions. "How do you explain the fading marks? Never known anything you are describing to happen?"

This was all passing strange. People didn't have two life-mates in one lifetime. Marks from claiming never faded. What was happening to his daughter?

"I can't explain anything," Georgia said, sounding as perplexed as he felt. "Seems Chandler's power over me is also vanishing. Can say it's a relief if true. He hasn't spoken to me in hours. Hope it will turn out to be days then weeks. Don't ever wish to hear from him again." With wide hope-filled eyes she turned to Hamilton.

"I didn't know," Hamilton said, a look of astonishment on his face. "When did you...you should have told me." He stepped to her, held her hand within his.

Cormack saw the love in his eyes. Also saw love in his daughters' eyes. Moisture clogged his throat. He couldn't be happier for her. Finally, she was getting what she deserved, a true life mate. A man who would treat her in the manner she deserved.

Georgia bowed her head before she turned her attention on Hamilton. To Cormack's thoughts the love was obvious. "I didn't think about the fading marks at lunch. As you know you were gone when I rose this morning. I couldn't tell you then."

Her face heated with thoughts he shouldn't know about. He would know what she was thinking.

Hamilton beamed. "Well…"

Cormack didn't intend to let the suspense about his answer continue another moment. "Yes, the two of you have my permission to wed as soon as possible. Though there might not be the rush we thought would be needed. I will attend all the proceedings you described. Will enjoy the time spent with your clan. Since there is attendance at the ritual, I believe this ceremony, of the Clan Chattan, must be a bit different than my clan. When is the wedding to take place?"

His old heart raced with excitement for his daughter. Somehow, he understood this relationship would be different than the first. This man was confident as well as self-assured in a good way. Hamilton appeared fully capable of protecting Georgia with his life if necessary.

"Now, with your approval we are off to talk to Father Damian at the McKenna keep. After our visit with the father, we will speak to Connal along with Wynnie to set the date and begin making arrangements. I will let you know all the details as soon as we know them."

"Good, good," Cormack saluted the two with what was left in his glass of brandy. "I wish you all good luck. He drank the last of the potent liquid. Set the glass on the table then kissed Georgia's cheek. He followed them to the door. "I love you. All I want is your happiness. If this man can give you a lifetime of contentment, I will embrace Hamilton too."

Chapter Eight

"That went well. Don't you think?"

Hamilton squeezed Georgia's hand as they walked toward Father Damian's office. He stopped walking near the top of the stairs. Turned her. Brushed soft tender kisses across her mouth.

She sighed, a whispered sound on the stairway. She stood one step higher. He didn't need to bend down to kiss her. They were eye level. Georgia liked being of the same height. She touched his mouth with her tongue, inviting more adventurous play. His hands on her shoulders, he pulled away. She made an expression before she spoke.

"Better than I expected. Father seemed taken with you." Georgia let loose a tiny puff of air while Hamilton ran his thumb across her damp lip. "I don't know what I expected from my father. Perhaps we should be glad he gave his approval then leave the topic alone. Don't wish to speculate further about anything. He was afraid you'd be too much like Chandler. We had sex the day I met him. He took my innocence then used that valued commodity to make money. Don't truly understand why I went along with his plans. Why I signed the contract."

"Agreed, the meeting went well. Come, we need to stop kissing before I do something that would embarrass us both right here in front of a priest's office. Your father wouldn't give his permission lightly. He must believe I will make you happy. What do you think about asking Father Damian about the marks fading? On the way here, I've been thinking about little else. Wish to take a look myself. With the vanishing of his claim on you, does this mean you will no longer be his mate?"

His hand on the small of her back, Hamilton guided her up the steps toward the office. Truth was a lot of her memories about Chandler were fading. If she had not been reminded of her mate, she would have a difficult time with his name.

"I hope to know what is happening to me...to us." Georgia stopped speaking to look at him to search his face as if he would have answers. "Do we need this man's approval to marry?" With the question her heart lodged in her throat. Nervous energy ricocheted around in her head. "What if he doesn't like me? Do we need tell him about the things I've done?" Found she was terrified.

"Yes and no. Father Damian can withhold his consent to wed us as well as the claiming ceremony. He can refuse to perform either of the services. We could marry somewhere else. However, I don't know of another priest who knows the chants for the claiming ritual. I should explain more about the ceremony. This evening, I'll tell you what we do. Is it alright to wait?"

The direction of her thoughts didn't travel in a good course. Nudity had been part of the ceremony she went through with Chandler. Had to assume there would be similarities. Didn't wish an audience having been through the ritual once before. "So, then, we would have the opposite circumstance that I had with Chandler. The claiming is the most important tradition for our future lives. Oh, what if we meet Chandler in another life? Would we go through this all over again? Would he also be a horrible man?"

"We are here. As you well know, I don't have any more answers than you do. I would pray you never again meet with anyone at all like Chandler Wolcott. For the most part, shifters are good people." Hamilton knocked.

Her palms were sweaty. She wiped them on her skirts. Her nerves felt as if they snapped one at a time until she was a mess of nervous energy. A breath of air hitched in her throat while her heart beat with frenzied speed.

"Come in." The door opened. Father Damian stood on the other side, his eyes smiling at her, at them. "You are right on time. Like it when the young folk respect time. So many nowadays are late. I received your message, Hamilton. The communiqué was quite involved. Since I've read the missive, I've been going over some old journals, which speak of the history of the clans. I'm very curious. Might have a few answers for the two of you. Might just be deductions. Can't tell. Never been witness to this circumstance before." He offered them chairs in front of his huge desk. "Sit down please. Make yourselves comfortable. Tea?"

They both shook their heads no. Her stomach was doing somersaults.

If she swallowed anything she would never be able to keep the food or the liquid down. Didn't wish to throw up on his beautiful blue and yellow carpet.

"Father, this is my fiancée, Georgia O'brien. She is also my mate as I wrote in the message. Less than a day ago, Georgia thought she was another man's mate. She was claimed by Chandler Wolcott. She is not a black panther but a white tiger as is Chandler. I understand since other shifters have mated with a different cat; our union is possible. I'm supposing this is not a factor that will serve to keep us apart. All our hopes can still continue as planned. I wish to marry Georgia as well as declare her as my own."

"That's what you wrote. I understand some of your fears." Father Damian addressed his attention to her. Tapped the tip of his finger on the letter Hamilton wrote. "You have two mates in this era. This particular happenstance is rare but not unheard of according to the pages of past history I've been reading. You can only entertain one mate per lifetime." He sat back watching them setting his clasped hands on his belly.

"No…" she whispered in a thin wail of pain. She retrieved her mind from the pain she felt at his words. "Does that mean I can choose?"

"I don't know. I believe your destiny will choose for you. There is one true person out there who is meant only for you. From what you've told me so far, believe that person is Hamilton."

Father Damian's hair was graying around the edges. His smile was filled with hope, his eyes kind. As time passed and the two men talked, some of her anxious energy left her. Hamilton told him the most important parts of her story. Father Damian knew Hamilton's story.

"Before we take this conversation any further, will you marry us as well as perform the claiming ceremony before the feast?" Hamilton asked, worrying about Father Damian's response. "If not, we are wasting both our time as well as yours. I'll have to make other arrangements, though doing so would not please me."

"Yes, of course I'll perform both ceremonies. Now…" He leaned forward, his forearms on the desk. The expression on his face intense. "There is still more I need to understand. Learning this will never change my mind about the two of you. I've a sixth sense where shifters are concerned. The two of you belong together. Tell me all about this man who you say was once your mate. Why didn't you wish to stay with him?"

She was startled by the intimidating question. Explaining her relationship to Hamilton was one thing, to this priest something else entirely. With Hamilton she could keep no secrets from him. With ease he delved into her mind. With Father Damian she was mortified. The things she did for her mate... She even taught him how to shift. Tears pricked the inside of her throat. Georgia didn't wish to cry. A lone tear slipped from her eyes. She wiped the drop away, hoping the priest wouldn't see.

Setting her hands in her lap, she struggled for the courage needed. "The story is not meant for a priest's ears. I'm embarrassed to say anything more about the year of my life I would rather forget."

"There is nothing you can say that would make me judge you in a negative light. Nothing you can tell me would surprise me. I've heard most everything. Women survive by their wits along with immense courage. They have little power over men. Men who would abuse them. If you believed this man to be your mate, you would do everything necessary to secure your future with him. The fact you refused to wed him, tells a tale all its own. Even if what he did was horrible. Am I close to the truth?"

"That's just the thing. When I was first with him at the brothel, I didn't mind what we did. It wasn't until Maeve was born that I balked at what he wanted from me. He refused to let me go. Made me fulfill the contract I signed."

With great pain, as well as trepidation, Georgia went on to tell the story of the year of her life she'd rather forget then the subsequent months that followed. She was both ashamed of what she did as well as embarrassed. Still furious at the man she believed was her mate for making her stay then perform in his shows.

What was his name?

Hamilton looked at her with a stunned expression. "What just happened?" Hamilton asked.

"I forgot his name." Georgia looked to the priest who was smiling. No one volunteered to refresh her memory. Was the year of her life she'd rather forget dimming too?

"I understand a bit more of the tale. You left the man as soon as you could. After meeting you at the Wolcott residence, the Frasiers brought you here. Thought this might be far enough away from the man to keep you safe.

Am I right in this assumption?"

"Yes, that was the idea. The moment I saw Hamilton I adored him. He asked me to his place for dinner. I decided it would be more appropriate for him to come to my home since my nanny as well as my bodyguard would be chaperones. I was wrong. Not that Hamilton did anything untoward..." she cleared her throat, uncertain what to say next, pausing for time. "He was a perfect gentleman."

Almost perfect. She thought of sleeping with him last night. The warmth that radiated from his huge body filled her with soul deep peace. She could never remember feeling so serene before.

"The unlikely pair of chaperones went to dinner in the village leaving us alone," Hamilton added to Georgia's story. "We had excellent food along with good conversation. After our lovely dinner we decided a nice ride to the bonfire would be enjoyable. I learned more about Georgia than she most likely wished to divulge."

Hamilton told him about the trip to the bonfire as well as the false contractions then what came after. Left out the part of sleeping together. The information was not something Father Damian needed to learn. Father Damian possessed a welcoming nature. He seemed at ease with the discussion despite her pain of embarrassment.

"The two of you have been intimate?" Father Damian questioned with the hint of a smile on his face. Explained, "Most shifters are before they are wed. Seems to be the way they do things in the highlands. As I told the two of you before, I don't judge. We are all who we are meant to be. Nothing more, nothing less."

"No, not yet. Won't make promises to stay celibate before the wedding. Will do whatever is right for the two of us," Hamilton told him as he squeezed her hand. Slipping his fingers between hers. "As you say, we will do what is right for both of us. Believe intimacy is important if the partners are willing. If Georgia wishes to wait until we are married, I won't have a problem with her decision."

Heat rushed to her face with his words, coupled with the hungry way he looked at her when he spoke the words. She wished she was a virgin. Wouldn't be able to gift him with her innocence. The mistake she made with Chandler would haunt her for the rest of her life. Without the mistake she would have never ended up in Coronach.

"You told me the marks were vanishing. Have you looked at them since this morning?" Hamilton asked, a pensive expression on his face. He looked to Father Damian. "What does it mean? Didn't think those marks could vanish."

"Sometimes they fade with the death of one or the other shifter," Father Damian said. "If Georgia's marks are dimming perhaps her association with the other shifter is doing the same. Doesn't mean the man has died. Means their relationship is dying."

She was shaking her head, looking with a puzzled expression at Hamilton. Thought his question was strange. "No, haven't had the chance. We've been busy. Saw my father who gave his blessings to us." After we left his home, she stared at the priest. "You say my relationship with this other shifter is dead?"

"That's the only rational explanation I can see. Some of the histories of past shifters speak to the phenomenon," Father Damian said.

"Since you agreed to perform the ritual, we are going to speak with the McKenna along with his wife," Hamilton answered. "I will let you know the date of the wedding. Will be the soonest possible date we can put this together. Need to be wed before our child is born."

Seemed he had every intention of looking at her shoulders. She didn't mind if he did. Perhaps they could stop in the rose garden. He could push the fabric of her gown aside. She was sitting in a priest's office in a church. Shouldn't be having such thoughts.

Father Damian was rising, the interview appearing to come to an end. He cleared his throat. "I believe that soon, you will have one mate not two. That man will be Hamilton. Everything you've known about your past mate including his name is dimming in your mind. Hamilton said he no longer needs to block the man from your mind. Your children are speaking to Hamilton about you as well as to you. This will be your new home. No more degradation. Your mate will take care of you, protect you."

"Will he forget me? That man who was her mate?"

His name still eluded her. Neither Hamilton or the father spoke his name. Was there a reason the two remained silent?

"Not any time soon. Just as Hamilton wouldn't forget you. Believe he will have lapses where he will become busy with his life and forget you exist. Then…there will be other times when you are a fever in his blood. Take care to guard your thoughts from this man until he is no longer part of you. That time will come. How long it will take, I've no idea. He is still capable of hurting you. Hamilton, you will need to always be aware. Believe your powers are stronger than your first mate. A weak evil man always has feeble powers."

Hamilton nodded then looked at his watch. "Believe it's time to see the McKennas. Don't wish to be tardy for this upcoming meeting either." He stood. Shook Father Damian's hand before escorting her from the room. Once down the long stairs, Georgia leaned into him, needing the reassurance only he could give.

In the middle of the rose garden, they stopped. Kissed again. "I do feel better now," Georgia told him when the play of their tongues ended. "Though," she hesitated. "I'm still edgy. The McKennas could refuse to help us. They might take exception to my past." Even the things she did were leaving her mind. This scenario was so very strange. She wasn't certain about her past. Remembered bits and pieces.

With the tip of his finger, he tapped the end of her nose. "Hush, with those thoughts. You are a beautiful person inside as well as out. If it's the last thing…no, it will be the first thing I do. I will help you to feel good about yourself. We will build your self-confidence until you have no more doubts about who you truly are. I can tell you have forgotten some of the year of your life you lived with Chandler. Soon it will be as if the year never existed."

"You are succeeding already. You have this way of giving me confidence, more than I've had in a long time. You make me feel beautiful when I've felt used and dirty, cheap. While I've been determined to live my life to the best of my abilities, I've not been able to feel good about myself." Those words were a huge truth she couldn't deny.

They started walking again, along the path winding through the rose garden. There were no blossoms this time of year. Georgia thought it would be nice to stroll through the garden in the summer, smell the soft rose scent, touch the velvet petals to her cheek. She felt at home here, at the McKenna keep. Seemed as though the place provided an extension of herself. She brought a huge dose of the fresh winter air into her lungs.

I will bring you here when the roses are in bloom. After Colin is born, we will bring the children here to play. The keep remains open to members of the clan. What do you think? Would you like to visit?

You know I'd like coming here. You listened to me. There was no reason to ask the question. I adore flowers. We will plant all kinds of them around your home. What do you like best? Roses? Lilacs? Perhaps hydrangea?

Whatever is your favorite will also be mine. Don't possess a great deal of knowledge about types of flowers. Perhaps you can teach me. The only plant I know that you mentioned was the rose. I do love the roses here.

He tugged her close. Her breast pushed against his arm. She was so aware of Hamilton physically as well as mentally. She could keep no secrets from him. Thought to have him make love to her. Wondered what it would be like to be made love to by this man. Would it be more than just sex? What she recalled of sex was debasing. With a flash into her mind, she saw herself naked in front of an audience. She shuddered with the horrible thought then the scene vanished from her head. Vanished into oblivion. Georgia didn't understand what she was doing there or why?

Yes, love, making love is more than just sex. Lovemaking involves the heart as well as the soul coupled with deep intense feelings. Soon, we will be together in the way you've dreamed. Have you had any more contractions? If you have any pain, tell me.

No.

Seemed he changed the subject rather abruptly. "There have been none since last night. I'm glad. Though I am ready to hold Colin in my arms. Would like to have the wedding night you are hoping for. You must tell me all about these important traditions you wish to experience. Don't wish to be shocked if you do something outrageous."

"Good. I too want to have the wedding before the babe is born. Will Bea be able to take care of Maeve if we are away from her for an entire night? One of the things we will do..." he paused, seeming uncertain. "I don't know what the ladies talk about when they take the bride to the bridal chamber. They will take you there after the feast. Prepare you for the night in whatever ways you need to be prepared. After they finish or deem the right amount of time has passed, Wynnie will come for me. If my mother was still living, she would come down the stairs to invite me to the bridal chamber."

When he spoke of his mother, she felt the wave of sadness that swept through him. "Maeve is almost a year old. While she doesn't like taking the bottle, she will if she is hungry. The little one is enjoying the mashed food Bea has been preparing for her. She adores both Hollis as well as Bea. Maeve will be fine with those two. She's known them both almost the entirety of her life."

"Look, we are here at the huge front door. Take a deep breath. I know you're nervous. Wynnie is one of the nicest women I know. She will make you feel at home as will Connal."

Hamilton offered her his arm. They stepped inside. The main room was huge. A fireplace to the right kept the hall warm.

Her stomach twisted. The baby kicked. She gulped air that had the hint of fresh baked bread to it. Striding to meet them was a large man with dark hair. The dark brown of his eyes was nothing like the silver-blue of Hamilton's eyes. Believed most shifters' eyes were the silver blue similar to Hamilton's. His age escaped her. Strands of grey were intermeshed with the black of his hair, most of the grey was around his hairline. Thin laugh lines radiated out from his eyes as well as his mouth. Wynnie's arm was locked in his. Her red hair was coiled around her head. Little strands of curling hair framed her face. She was beautiful.

"You are here right on time," Connal said, extending his hand along with a broad smile of greeting to Hamilton. "This is your fiancée you wrote about. You're a very lucky man. She is lovely. Georgia…" Connal smiled at her. With a nod, encouraged her to feel at ease with the look on his face.

Georgia felt the heat of her blood rise to her face. Tried to recall what Hamilton might have told him about her. "Yes, I'm Georgia O'brien. You know that."

She sucked in a deep breath of air. Felt the gentle squeeze of Hamilton's fingers. Georgia didn't know why she was so tense as well as insecure. Yes, she did. Making a good impression for Hamilton was very important to her. These people meant the world to her fiancé.

"Yes," Wynnie said, looking pleased. "Come along. We'll go up to our suite of rooms. You will be more comfortable there. We can discuss what, as well as when, all this is going to happen. If there is to be a wedding as Hamilton said he wishes, we must make haste. Want the wedding to take place before the sweet *bairn* arrives. Seems he is due at any time now."

While they walked the long staircase leading to the upstairs rooms, little was said. Georgia was immersed in her thoughts as well as all the portraits on the wall. All along the winding stairs to the second floor there were portraits of the McKenna clan. Women sitting with their husbands standing behind them. She was fascinated.

"Those are not all McKenna's," Connal informed her with a wry smile. He pointed to the wall. "They are also Stuarts along with Frasiers. The paintings date back hundreds of years. If you are an historian, you can tell the era by the clothing they are wearing. To me the portraits are fascinating." He pointed to one near the top of the stairs. "There is Wynnie and myself."

So many thoughts splintered in her head, spreading in an arc around her. Georgia hoped these people wouldn't expect her to tell them about the other man in her life. She no longer remembered very much of him. When she tried to recall, she would see flashes of naked women and men. She saw herself wearing nothing, sitting on a man. She didn't know who he was. Thought she should. No, as nice as Hamilton said the McKenna's were, her past was not something she could explain. Her life before Hamilton wasn't something she wanted to remember.

Inside, the room was cheery. A thick blue carpet was on the floor. The drapes were a darker blue. On a small table, small cakes were set out. There was a pot of tea. A fire burned in the hearth. Her stomach rolled then somersaulted. Colin's knee, or elbow, she didn't know which, pushed against her. With the palm of her hand, she pressed them back. Hamilton sensed her distress, tightening his hold upon her.

Wynnie poured tea for everyone. Offered the cakes. Hamilton snagged one of the cakes. A couple of hours passed since they ate. She still didn't wish for anything in her stomach. Didn't wish to lose what she ate on the beautiful carpet. Georgia sipped the tea. The sweet brew soothed her stomach.

"So, the two of you wish to wed. I can hardly wait. I do love planning weddings," Wynnie began with a dazzling smile. She clapped her hands together, the tips of her fingers settling beneath her chin. "Yes. Do so love to plan weddings. Hamilton wrote that he wanted everything for you. Everything you might wish for. It's going to be a fantastic day. All the traditions to be fulfilled. We will invite everyone."

"Everyone? As in all in Carnoch? I don't think so. Maybe just those who are close to Hamilton's family." She fought the bile rising in her throat. Nervous energy controlling her.

"You will be so busy with everything else we are doing, you won't notice all the people," Hamilton chuckled.

"Have you explained these traditions to your blushing bride?" Connal asked. He too was grinning as if he knew something very funny. "The lady needs to know all you've planned; the good along with the embarrassing."

Embarrassing! What are you planning, Hamilton Adair? I don't wish to find myself embarrassed in front of all your friends. You do realize I will have only three people there for me.

Nothing you need to worry over. You will love what I do, every single moment. Will give you pleasure though… maybe under the circumstances we'll forego this one tradition. Depends on what you remember. I do want everything traditions demand.

Don't you dare leave anything out. This is our day, not just mine. Want you to recall everything with pleasure. Can't forget or forego anything. I also want you to have everything you've ever wished for.

As you wish.

She had the distinct feeling she should not have sounded so adamant about that particular tradition. Nonetheless, if that was something he wanted, she would grant whatever it was to him no matter how mortifying. Georgia knew he wouldn't hurt her.

"Not yet," Hamilton picked up her hands, wound his fingers between hers before bringing them to his lips for a swift kiss. "I will explain some, maybe not all. Did tell her about the wives taking her upstairs to prepare for the groom. Couldn't tell her anything else since I've never heard what goes on upstairs. Believe tonight's privacy once Maeve is put to bed will be an excellent time to speak with Georgia."

She heated more. Her cheeks were on fire. Felt her body stir to life just as the recent kisses in the flower garden as well as on the stairs leading to Father Damian's office did. Thought of Hamilton holding her while they slept. Wondered how making love with him would feel. She didn't think she'd ever done that before...make love. Why did she see herself naked sitting on a man she couldn't recall? The image was disconcerting.

"Don't explain all of them. There is one that should be a surprise otherwise she might run from the feast before you can finish with the particular tradition at the head table. To my knowledge all the brides enjoy the experience. They all have laughed about the time after the fact. Sometimes I've heard tell, the bride also gives a great deal of pleasure to the groom. Believe Harris did surprise her husband beneath the table. Ash was forced to tell her father he should not look for her when he started to bend down then lift the tablecloth."

When he first began, Georgia thought he might be speaking about the claiming. She paused and tilted her head to the side. Wondered if what happened at the head table would hurt. His claws would go into her shoulders...all ten claws. Inadvertently, she touched her shoulder. There was something she should remember. Didn't know what it was. How did she know about the claws? Imagined claiming was something her father might have told her. She wished her mind was not such a muddled mess. Hamilton hadn't mentioned it yet.

Claiming? I don't know what that entails though the word came into my head. What are you going to do at the head table? What are the women going to talk to me about? All these secrets are making me panicky. If you don't want me to be a mess of stretched nerves for the next few days, you must tell me everything. Don't leave anything out.

If I spoke of it now, then there would be no surprise. ...and brides are always tense. It's supposed to be that way. I will tell you most of what is going to happen. While I understand the nerves, there is no reason to be frightened. I will be with you the entire time...except when the wives have your ear.

What if I don't want a surprise? Dislike surprises.

"*You will love what I do. I guarantee, you will...no you can't howl with your pleasure in front of the clan. You will have to keep the sound of your ecstasy behind your small, white teeth. Perhaps I can absorb your yell*

224

of delight into my mouth when I'm kissing you.

That wicked grin on your face is speaking of other things. I'm not liking the look on your face. You tell me as soon as we are alone. I won't mind the kissing. If that is the pleasure you speak of, yes, I will enjoy kissing.

You don't recall claiming?

No. would you tell me?

Not right now.

"Where have the two of you been? You certainly haven't been part of this conversation. As if I couldn't guess, the two of you have been speaking privately. For the sake of the short time we have together, the two of you must remain attentive here," Wynnie said while she appeared to be in Connal's head. They too were having a private conversation.

Hamilton brought her fingers to his mouth, touched each one with the tip of his tongue then stared into her eyes while he spoke. "We'd like the wedding to take place as soon as possible. I'm certain you've figured all that out. How soon…?" He lifted his shoulders while focusing on Wynnie. "I would know how long it will take for the wives to put together this affair. Need to make plans."

"We can all put our heads together. Three days should be enough time to plan an exceptional affair. You my dear, Georgia, will need to visit with me tomorrow first thing in the morning. I'll send messages out to Brenna Stuart and Heather Frasier. They will love to be part of the planning. First thing though, I'll escort you to the modiste in the village. We will get your wedding gown started. Do you have any ideas of what you might like?" Wynnie looked to Hamilton. "You will give permission to hire as many seamstresses as needed to finish the dress in three days?" She continued without giving him a chance to answer.

"Well, yes…" Hamilton beamed, looking pleased. "That was what I planned. I'm also grateful you will take her to the seamstress. Don't wish to see the gown until the day of the wedding. Don't wish to risk bad luck."

Bad luck? All his plans were coming together. Three days and she'd be married to Hamilton Adair. She wondered at her good fortune. At the fact she met Hamilton quite by chance. What the devil was claiming? Georgia believed she should recall what it was. She didn't. Who was the man she saw herself with? He looked so much like Hamilton. He wasn't. This was unnerving as well as confusing. Part of her past seemed to be vanishing more rapidly with each passing second. She wondered at the relief she felt.

"Georgia?"

"What…oh…!"

"Where were you? Speaking to your soon to be husband again, I gather," Wynnie said with a soft lilt to her voice. "The two of you are so much in love. Brings me back to our hasty wedding. Wasn't at all what I would have thought my wedding would be like. Though at one time, I never believed I would find a man who could love me."

"No, I was wondering about claiming. Imagine I should know what that entails. I don't. Is the tradition something a person would forget?" Georgia asked, looking more to Hamilton for an answer than Wynnie or Connal.

"We can talk about this forgetfulness of yours in the privacy of our home. Seems as if Wynnie has some questions for you about the wedding." Hamilton brought her fingers to his lips for another soft kiss.

For the next hour, they put their heads together and spoke of flowers, and cakes, of menus for the feast. By the time they said their goodbyes then reached his home, she felt weary to the tips of her toes. All she wished for was sleep. The day had been so busy. Sweet slumber wasn't to be. She needed to see to Maeve. Nurse her. It had been an entire day. The little girl would not be at all pleased. She would let her mama know her displeasure before she snuggled into her breast. Now, she nursed more for comfort than for nourishment.

"I'm staying here tonight?" she asked, feeling blindsided while he ushered her into the entry of his home. "You didn't ask my opinion. You just brought me here." Georgia wasn't certain whether to be angry or go along with his decision. She needed him close. Didn't want to go to her cottage along with an empty bed.

"For the last hour, Chandler's voice has been hammering in my head. He wants you. Still doesn't know where you are. I can't trust the man. For all we know he could be here in Carnoch. He's not above lying to get what he wants. You need my protection as does Maeve. Don't appreciate his thoughts about my daughter."

"Chandler? Who?" Her head was a blank slate. She was so confused.

"Should I know this name? I don't recall it. Why do I need protection? What does he want with our daughter?" Her questions were all relevant. At least, she thought so.

"I don't know what to tell you. Appears as if all traces of this man are vanishing from your head if they are not already gone. Do you recall nothing of Chandler Wolcott? If you don't remember, I'm pleased. Do you remember the year you spent with him?"

"I don't recall the name. Don't know anything about claiming. I'm supposed to understand the ritual, aren't I? I don't. During the last hours I've had some flashes of insight. Saw myself naked in front of people I didn't know. Now even those images are fading. It's as if my body turns into a grey mist then such a clear white, I can barely see shapes. After that nothing..."

"This evening, as soon as you are comfortable, I have every intention of looking at your shoulders. Maybe look at more of you. We will see," Hamilton winked at her then tapped her on the nose. "Bea and Hollis will stay here tonight again. Bea told me this morning; she would make a wonderful dinner for all of us. We will sleep together as we did last night. Do you remember sleeping with me?"

"Oh, yes...you were so warm. I felt relaxed as if I'd come home. We shouldn't be sleeping together anymore. We aren't married. I'm supposed to be innocent. I've the strange feeling that I'm not. Hamilton, who am I now? Who was I? I'm not a virgin. I've a little girl along with a boy on the way. I don't understand."

"In three days, we will be wed. Shouldn't make a difference if I make love to you for the first time this evening or on our wedding night. What would you like? Do you wish to sleep with me, maybe more? Father Damian told us most shifters sleep with their mates before the ceremony to link them together as husband and wife. I want to ease some of the unknown for you. Hope for you to be at ease with me. Take this one slow step at a time. I won't rush you. Last night you wished for more than I gave you."

"You didn't...we didn't...last night you didn't make love to me. I'm still a virgin? That's a stupid question. I have a baby. I'm pregnant, almost due to give birth. Forget I said the stupidity."

Georgia waved her hand in the air. She felt both hesitant as well as curious. She didn't think they did anything except sleep together. Her hand settled on her swelled stomach. She didn't recall making love to anyone. The proof was here with her unborn child.

"I do hope you will remember the event when we make love. Can hurt a man's pride if the woman he loves doesn't recall making love to her husband. Or tonight, in this instance her fiancé. What do you think? Will you remember?"

She fluffed up her skirts. Stuck her chin in the air. "I was just checking. I agree making love to you is something I should recall. Didn't wish to make a mistake. When we are together in that way, I'll remember everything. I promise." Under these strange set of circumstances, Georgia understood she shouldn't promise anything of the sort.

~ * ~

Hamilton was sitting in the drawing room, sipping a brandy when Georgia joined him. He felt relaxed as well as pleased with the outcome of today's visits. As far as he was concerned the day could not have gone any better. Father Damian provided some information as to Georgia having two mates. She was forgetting Chandler which pleased him. Soon, if not already, she wouldn't remember anything about the horrible man. The McKenna's were wonderful. Tomorrow morning, they would continue planning the wedding. Her wedding gown would be designed. He wondered what she liked.

"Is Maeve taken care of? All bundled up tight in her crib?" He hoped she would sleep through the night as she did last night. Georgia appeared exhausted. "We have time for ourselves now. Though you do look tired."

"Ah, she is asleep, her little thumb tucked tight between her lips. Maeve wore me out. She wanted to play. Imagine she missed me. I've never left her this long." Georgia sat in the chair next to him.

Hamilton set his glass down. Patted his thighs. He wanted to hold Georgia. Feel her warmth close to him. Needed those soul deep feelings that swept into him when they touched. "Come here," his voice was too husky. The sound was deep and raw from wanting her. He was hard with his need. Had been that way for most of the day. The few kisses they shared today were not enough. All they did was put him in a state of semi-arousal; one that only Georgia could quench. If she didn't protest, he meant to make love to his soon to be wife. They would sleep together from now on. There would be no distance between them ever again.

With what appeared to be hesitant steps, Georgia walked to him. Taking her hand in his, he brought her down on his lap. Slid his hand along her hip. Squeezed, felt the softness of her body. She adjusted her position. Her delicious little butt rubbed against his sex. Somehow, Hamilton managed to keep his groan behind his teeth. He wondered how much of her memory was gone. With every passing second, she was acting more the innocent. When he met her, she knew things she didn't recall now.

"Are you going to tell me about the traditions you wish to experience?" Her small voice trembled when she spoke to him. "More than any of the others I want you to tell me about the surprise pleasure. Would like to give you pleasure too."

"Yes, you've no reason to be nervous. I promise to answer all your questions to the best of my ability." That was the clincher. He could cry off at any time by telling her he knew nothing else. "Where do you wish to begin?" She wouldn't know. He would need to start with what would happen first. "Feel free to stop me anytime if you have a question. I'll start with the wedding ceremony. Which will be typical for the highlands. Nothing different there for shifter or non-shifter alike. We'll be married in front of the big door to the church. Anyone who wishes can be there to witness the joining of our lives. After that, we'll go inside the church where the ceremony will be a typical Catholic wedding." He paused, stroking her hip then higher up the ladder of her ribs to just beneath her breast. Rubbed the underside with his thumb. As if wishing for more contact she leaned into him. His searching hands would travel higher soon. "Are you catholic?"

"No, very protestant. Does it matter?"

Georgia turned to face him. Her breasts pushed against his chest. They were very large, tipped with hard nipples. She'd not donned her corset after feeding Maeve. Even through all the cloth between them he felt the hard crests, just as she would feel his sex.

"No, I'm surprised Father Damian didn't ask you that question himself. Imagine there were many more pertinent subjects to be considered. So much we don't understand is happening." He paused to search her face.

Touched his mouth on hers. Tasted her lips with a lazy motion. "Any questions yet?"

Georgia shook her head. Placed one hand on his shoulder before moving her fingers to wind around his neck. Ran her thumb along his chin. "Nothing to ask. Go on. I'm interested." She slipped her fingers into his hair.

"After the second ceremony, we will walk into a small room behind the sanctuary. There will be places for the audience to sit. We will stand in the middle of the room. Father Damian will be nearby. In this service there will be no bible. This one is not religious. It is pagan in nature."

"Audience? There will be people watching us? What could possibly happen that would be different from the other two rites." Georgia was playing with his hair. He found concentrating to be difficult.

He willed his thoughts back to the details he needed to speak of. "This is very different."

The devil, he didn't wish to tell her she would be naked. Those words might bring memories back. He didn't want her to have memories of the year of her life she was forgetting. "Your father will be there as well as all the Frasiers. They feel as if they've a vested interest in you since Harris is wed to Ash Wolcott. There is a small connection. Nonetheless, the association does exist. I don't suppose you remember? Nevertheless, I gave them permission on your behalf. As head of the Clan Chattan the McKennas will also watch. They all come to lend support along with encouragement. If you wish, you can refuse anyone the right to see this pagan ritual. Who attends is up to the bride and groom."

Georgia shook her head. "I don't recall why or how we are connected. Do recall Harris along with her husband, Ash. Know the Frasiers helped me move here. Would like them at the ceremony if they wish to be there. The McKenna's were sweet today. I've no problem with their attendance. Why do you say pagan?"

"Pagan because that is what it is. The process dates back hundreds or more generations. The priest always chants words few know. They are old Scottish Gaelic words. Most highlanders who have lived here from birth understand some of the words if not all. Few others do."

"I won't understand the words."

Georgia found his ear. Slid a fingertip around the outside, traveled down his neck.

"You won't. So, I'm pleased you wish to have the Frasiers along with the McKennas in attendance. They will also be delighted to receive the invitation. The Frasier's hope you will think of them as family as do the McKennas. Wynnie is bringing two white capes for the ceremony. One is for you to wear; the other is for me. With the capes on, we will disrobe beneath the shelter of the fabric. During the chanting, I will hold you. Keep you from falling." He brushed his mouth on hers for a gentle reassuring caress. Touched his tongue with gentle finesse on her mouth. Bit then tugged on her lip.

"Falling? Why would I fall?" Her breath whispered across the skin she bared when she unfastened the ties on his shirt. Touched his chest. Ran her hand along the width of his chest, explored.

"Yes, the bride is weak after the ritual. You will have a difficult time standing. She goes through a lot during this period. Father Damian will chant. You will experience things I've no idea about. I've heard the bride will encounter the elements of the earth, fire, wind and water. Don't know in what order they appear. Afterward you will tell me what happened. All you witnessed as well as felt. The bride is supposed to see some of the couple's past lives. It's important to share the experience."

"I can do that, share. I would see what you looked like long ago. Will you look the same as you do now? Will you be in your cat? I do wish to see your cat."

Georgia set her hands on his chest. Ran the palm across the width. Wound her fingers in the hair on his chest. She explored. Tempted. Deep inside he groaned. Tried to concentrate. "What happens next? Is that when we eat? Is that when you surprise me?"

"Once all is finished, the people viewing the ritual will leave us alone to recuperate. I don't know how long it will take you to gain your strength. Most brides are very weak, drained of all energy when it's all finished. Once you're feeling better, we will dress in our wedding finery then walk to the feast. I will walk and carry you."

His hand cupped her breast, moved with languid strokes his thumb across the hardening crest. He wanted her so much his hand was shaking. Didn't know if he could control himself if he touched her intimately. Georgia whimpered into his neck. Touched her tongue at the place where his blood thundered. Bit.

He wanted to taste her. Suck the round globes into his mouth. She would taste like winter snowflakes and warm woman. The scent of lavender always surrounded her. He slipped a hand through her hair. Enjoyed the silken glide of the strands between his fingers. There was still more to talk about. Trying to command his body to behave, he drew in a strong breath of air. Attempted to forget her questing fingers.

"What will happen at the feast? What kind of surprise do you have for me? The McKenna had a wicked gleam in his eye when he spoke of this time. I will be at the banquet table. What could you do? You told me I would howl with the ecstasy you gave me. What are you talking about? What does that mean howl with ecstasy? I would know all your plans. You taste salty and warm. Like your flavor."

Georgia was blunt. He didn't know if he would survive. "I'm going to make you wait for that explanation. Maybe after tonight you will have a better idea about yelling when you receive your pleasure. When you reach that pinnacle of delight, I can send you to. There needs to be one astonishment at a wedding. He found her ankle, brought her dress higher while he caressed the softness of her legs. "After we eat, we'll dance then cut the cake. The women will whisk you away to the bridal chamber then do what they do. Whatever that is. You will have to tell me that part. Again, I've no idea what they say to the bride."

"When will you claim me? You spoke of the ritual. That isn't when you will set your claws into my shoulder. What will you do?" Georgia pulled his shirt from his pants. Ran her hands along his belly. "Your stomach is hard, not like mine. All of you is hard. Can I feel lower?" She ran a fingertip along the top of his waistband.

Hamilton just barely stifled the groan. His body clenched with raw desire. "You are going to be the death of me yet."

"How?"

Georgia continued her explorations along his chest and belly. The palms of her hands pressed across his nipples. She bent to kiss each tiny bud. Swirled her tongue. Tugged on his chest hair.

He raised his arms. "Take it off." The devil, he wanted to feel her naked flesh pressed against his. Needed to finish this telling of events before he made love to his soon to be wife. She might not have her maidenhead but she was innocent. Needed to move with a slow hand. Wanted her to reach that pinnacle of delight before he came inside her.

With a shy smile on her face Georgia brought his shirt over his head. "I like the way you look. So different from me." Her hands traveled across his shoulders then down his arms. Stopped to fiddle with the fasteners of his breeches. Set her hand on the hard line of his sex. Her gaze shot to meet his. Her eyes were wide. "What is this?"

The change of subject was necessary. He held onto her wrists, lifting them away before he erupted. "It seems we are distracted. Now listen, when we are in bed together on our wedding night. When you are ready for me to see you, Wynnie will let all downstairs know it is time. She will wait at the bottom of the steps. The men will lift me on top of their shoulders then carry me to your room. They will remove all my clothing except my kilt."

With her hands sightseeing, he needed to command the rest of the discussion. Unable to stop himself, he fiddled with the buttons on her gown. A line of small buttons marched up the front. He needed both hands to unfasten them. Impatient to see her, frustrated with the damn little fasteners, he almost tore one from its holder. Tearing her gown wouldn't do. He wasn't going to rip her bodice. He huffed in a huge mouthful of air. When his fingers shook so hard he couldn't finish, Georgia did the deed for him. She seemed to understand what he wanted. Either that or she wanted the same. She smiled at him as she took over with her buttons.

She finished. The front of her gown gaped open. The chemise was still laced. The sheer fabric did nothing to hide her breasts, the darkness of the hard tips. Her face was a beautiful shade of rose. He wanted to rip off her clothing. Pull her beneath him then thrust into her until she screamed her pleasure.

He tipped back more air, forcing the thought of her naked body joined with his from his head. "I'm going to look at your shoulders now. It's been all day since you told me the marks were fading. Do you think they've vanished?"

"What is vanishing?" She asked, a puzzled look in her eyes. "I don't understand what you are speaking of. If your question has something to do with you claiming me then there will be no marks. Why are you curious about this? You're not making sense, Ham."

"Never mind. I just want to look at you. Need to see all of you, including your cat. Is that alright with you? Do you want to show me what you look like wearing nothing at all? I will help now that those tiny buttons are out of the way."

He found his hands weren't shaking as bad. Hamilton didn't wish to make a fool of himself.

"Alright. I want to see you also. Know your cat will be magnificent. Just as stunning as you are." Her gaze roamed the length of his chest then back to reach his eyes. Hers were sparkling with blue fire. He wanted to feel the depth of her passion, feel the enchantment that would meet him when he entered into her.

Hamilton was startled by her words. Never thought of himself as magnificent or stunning. Hesitant as well as afraid, he smoothed the fabric of her gown from her shoulders then down her arms. His breath hitched when he looked at all her beautiful white skin. Her beauty stunned. Shook him to the core.

All he saw was her soft white skin. So white he knew he'd never seen anything lovelier. There were no claw marks in front by her collarbone. Turning her so he could look at her back, the flesh was smooth and white. Just as he hoped her skin would be. There was nothing to see except the length of her back, the line of small bones marching down the middle. He groaned his need. Traced each bone with the tips of his fingers. She shivered.

"What do you see?" She fiddled with the ribbons of her chemise as if she wished to finish unlacing the ties. "I think I should see more of you. Will you…" Once again, she seemed hesitant. Unable to put the words together she wanted to say.

"I see, just your lovely female flesh. You've never been…"

He stopped, realizing he should say no more. Georgia didn't recall intimacy with Chandler or the claiming. Her memory loss was the way this should be. She would be all his. No one claimed her before him. In a couple of nights, he would put the marks on her that would make her his through the entirety of their lives then on into eternity. Relief washed through him. While nothing in her past made a difference in his feelings toward her, he adored the notion he would be the only shifter to claim her. He didn't appreciate the idea she might have had another man's marks on her shoulders.

"Been what?"

Her chemise fell apart showing the deep cleavage between those two beautiful globes of female flesh. Silken fabric caught on hard tipped nipples. Clung with love to each one. He bent to taste. Twirled his tongue around first one then the other. The wetted fabric remained.

"Nothing. What I was going to say is not important in our lives. We have everything to look forward to." The only thing that would make this better would be if she was a virgin. Her virgin status was impossible. In a matter of days or weeks, she would have two children. The membrane claiming her innocence would not be there for him to break through. He should be pleased he wasn't going to hurt her.

"When will you claim me?" Georgia ran her hands along his shoulders. "Could you do so tonight. I would like to get this pain thing over with. On the wedding night there would be no fears." Georgia's movement was restless.

"No."

He could tell her yes. Give in to her wishes. As he told her before he wanted the traditions to remain. Claiming the mate on the wedding night was custom even when breaching the maidenhead was not.

"Alright. When?" She was playing with the hair on his chest, sliding her hands to the top of his breeches. Fiddled with the laces, tugging then...

He held her hands, stopping her. She was far too curious. Needed to take a moment to pause. "When we make love in the bridal chamber the night of our wedding, I will claim you. The all-important moment will hurt but just for a moment. My cat's claws will come out. If you close your eyes, you won't see them. They will score your shoulders. There will be a tiny amount of blood. I will clean off your shoulders. Kiss each mark. You will have those ten marks there for the rest of your life."

"Oh... I think I like what you're telling me." She pulled the ties through more openings. He felt the heat of her body against him. Needed to resist a few more seconds.

Control of the lovemaking was what he wished for. If she continued in this vein, he would lose command of his body. Hamilton lifted her, brought Georgia to straddle his hips. Her thighs were on either side of his. He pushed his thighs against hers, parting her. The gown she wore hiked high on her legs. He saw more white skin. Her legs were long, well formed. She wore white stockings tied with blue garters the same color as her eyes. His mouth watered. Ran his finger along bare flesh just above the stockings. The best was the sight of her beautiful breasts swaying so close to his mouth he imagined the taste of them.

Needing her more than he'd ever wanted another woman, he pushed the opened fabric of her chemise to the side, slid the silken straps down her arms until there was nothing covering her. He saw her white belly. Kissed. Wished to see more of her. He covered those lovely nipples of hers with the palms of his hands. Pressed with a light touch. A feminine sigh floated from her lips. He felt the tips harden more with each caress. His mouth watered to savor the exquisite ripeness. He tugged on each pinnacle. Twisted them between his fingers. His love for this woman was deep, reaching into his soul.

Georgia whimpered, let her head fall back, arching her body, long black hair tumbling down her back. Her breasts more exposed than ever. Hamilton didn't believe she had any idea what pushing her chest forward did to those large globes he needed to suckle. With a light touch he tapped his tongue on one hard bud then blew. Watched the nipple grow. He bent close, sipped on the crest. Drew it further into his mouth, sucked. Savored the sweetness. Drew hard on the bud. Wanted to see the tip elongated as well as wet. He gave his attention to that perfect spot for long drawn-out seconds. When he drew back to look his fill, he was delighted with the perfection in front of him.

Hamilton wanted her to see. "Look…they are perfection. Flawless in every way."

Stunned, her eyes a bit dazed, she did look at her nipples then him. Her eyes widened, shimmered with intensity. "They are different. I've never seen them…like this. What did you do?"

"Gave you pleasure. Just a little taste of more to come. Your nipples respond to my lovemaking. Does the rest of you answer in such a delightful way? Hmm…would love to discover the truth. Should I suck on the other nipple? See if the tip tastes the same or maybe better."

"Please…"

Favoring the other hard pinnacle he kissed then sucked.

Her fingers wove into his hair. Pushed him against her. Arched her back. "That's what Maeve does. Oh… She sucks on them. They don't look like that when she's finished." Her words were a whisper thin wobble.

"I hope not."

He almost hooted with laughter. Her expression was so deliciously innocent. He needed to see if her sweet, pink petals at the apex of her thighs were swollen with her hunger. With his ardent attention and maneuvering, her skirt rose so high he could almost see the object of his thoughts.

"Hamilton…"

"Yes?"

He enjoyed the throaty purr emanating from her. Understood she needed him maybe as much as he wanted her. Georgia was giving him all he could hope for. Everything he longed to have with her. Her passion was raw, plentiful. She responded with sweet sincerity to every caress.

"I feel so…I ache in places I've never thought about before. Is that the way it's supposed to be? Am I…"

"You're perfect, love." He needed to kiss her mouth. He'd not done that enough. Had to touch her everywhere. His mouth found hers. Swept his tongue across the bottom then the top. "Open those sweet lips of yours so I can taste you. Give me your tongue so we can play together." His tongue probed her mouth. Rubbed then just as he did with her lovely, white breasts, he sucked. Pulled her lip into his mouth. He would like her inside him.

She did…opened even wider. Hamilton groaned, kissed the pureness of her then kissed her some more. He was inside her. She tasted of the tea with honey she must have been drinking earlier while he was sipping his brandy. Her scent was lavender coupled with snowflakes. He held one breast in his hand while the other pushed unwanted fabric up her legs.

Seeming to have a will all its own, his hand slid along the inside of her leg until he reached her mound. Placed his hand over her then higher to her belly. She was right. Her stomach wasn't hard as his was. Still she was huge with a child waiting to leave the womb behind. He wanted her now! Heaving in air, he demanded his body to control itself.

"What are you doing?" Her words were a breathy whisper as she arched, pressing herself against him. "I don't know if you should touch me like that. Oh…what you are doing feels so good. Ham…!" Georgia jerked then arched. "You're scorching me."

"Giving you pleasure." He changed his position. "Does this feel just as good? Do you like my hand here? Or there?" He pressed on the swell of her belly. Slid one finger between her legs feeling the soft dampness of her petals. Georgia was spilling nectar onto his fingers. He felt Colin's elbow against the hand resting on her belly. Didn't want to know what his son was thinking at a time such as this one. The lad was too young to know anything about what he was doing with his mother.

He resumed his attention to the perfection between her legs. Massaging, fondling, helping her reach the depth of her passion. With another touch of his hand in the most intimate feminine part of her, the caress caused her to jerk against him. He found the sensitive little nub. Fondled the tiny pearl. She cried out, yelled. Bit his shoulder as he continued to massage the sensitized spot. The lush roundness of her breasts moved along his chest tantalizing all his male endowments. They were soft as well as warm.

"Please…there has to be more. I… oh! Oh…! Ham…Hamilton!"

"That's it, love. Relax, let it happen. I'm going to see to your satisfaction then I'm going to carry you upstairs to the bedroom. We have the entire night to learn about each other if that's what you would like."

Maybe not the whole night. She was supposed to meet Wynnie early in the morning. Wynnie might have to wait for Georgia's arrival. She would understand.

One finger then two entered her. She was small, tight. Too small to have given birth. She would have stretched to accommodate Maeve. He pushed higher. Stopped. No…it couldn't be? Butted his finger against the thin membrane proclaiming her a maiden. Hamilton acknowledged the notion that he must be imagining or hallucinating. The membrane wasn't there when he examined her the other night. Since he learned of her history, he'd wished she would know only him. When they first decided on marriage, he understood there had been another man in her life. To be certain, he touched again. Wasn't imagining.

She wasn't innocent. His brain was muddled…filled with straw. No,

Georgia has a little girl, was about to give birth to a boy. What was going on here? This was an illusion…perhaps a miracle.

If he made love to her tonight, he would hurt her. Hamilton tested the thin layer of skin again, then another time, still puzzled by this change of events. The membrane was very real but very thin. Maybe her maidenhead was growing back. He'd never heard of something so strange. If he waited until the wedding night, he might hurt her more.

His big body shuddered with the realization she was changing with each second ticking by on the clock. He needed to look at Maeve. Would she look more like him in the morning than she does now? There were some similar characteristics between Chandler and himself. In an instant, Hamilton realized Maeve was his…truly his. Colin was his also. It was as if…

Hamilton didn't want to figure this all out. Understanding would be impossible. What he needed to do was come to terms with the ever-changing facts. Even Father Damian wouldn't be able to explain what was happening. The claiming marks he could understand. The membrane he could not. Neither could he figure out how the children could be his. They were though. He knew for a fact.

"Hamilton…what's wrong?" Georgia set her hand on his face. The look of concern immobilized him for a few seconds. He needed to think of something to tell her she would believe.

He'd left her crazy with her rising passion. Abandoned her when she was almost reaching for the stars. Left her wild with raw desire. He needed to make up for the lapse in concentration. "Hmm…" he couldn't give her an answer.

Kissing her, then stroking her deep inside with his fingers, Hamilton brought her higher then higher still. He needed to watch her eyes glaze over with her climax. She was his. Would always belong to him.

"Nothing is wrong. Open your eyes. Let me look at you," Hamilton told her between sweet, tender kisses.

With his thumb along with fingers, he continued the sexual assault on her moist dark secrets. She cried out his name. Arched. Her head moved with excited abandon. Nearly bucked his finger out of her when she yelled her pleasure. When her head fell against his shoulder, her beautiful white flesh was damp. A fine sheen of sweat covered her. He smoothed a finger across her eyebrows.

"I can't breathe…I'm shaking so hard…" She whispered, her teeth grazing the skin on his shoulder.

"That's the way making love is supposed to be. We are going to bed now. I'm going to come inside you. After that we will sleep. We both have big days tomorrow." Hamilton thought the plan was delicious. Needed her. His sex so hard against his breeches, there wasn't enough room for him. Needed all the ties unfastened. He'd never wanted a woman with this intensity. Never knew his mate.

"You're going to do this to me again? I can't move. I've no strength." She held up her shaking hand. "I can't walk up those stairs. Not yet." He ran his fingers down the long column of her back. Stopped to cup her delicious bottom, his fingers fondling. With a gentle hand, he squeezed. Her hair spilled over her back. He twirled a strand around his finger, tugging her head back. Placing a light kiss on her lips then each breast, he smiled down at her.

"Your scream pleased me. Hope you didn't wake Hollis or Bea. Appreciated the fact you yowled out Hamilton and not Ham. Though it was a close call. No, Bea accompanied by Hollis would be here if the yowl of pleasure woke either one." He tapped her nose. "Now, you will recover soon enough. Tomorrow night we can show each other our cats. Tonight, I'm going to make love to you until we both can't move."

"I think I'll like that." She licked his shoulder where she bit him.

"Me too. Raise your hips." After removing the gown, he left it on the chair.

In the bedchamber he laid her on the bed. Spread her hair out on the pillow. It was so black, a deep rich color catching all the light from the candles, glistening with highlights. Her skin was so white. The contrast pleasant to his eyes. He didn't want to think about hurting her. There would be nothing to do about it. Though, he was pleased she was his in every way possible.

A virgin…

An innocent with two children. They were his children. He acknowledged the fact. They were his. Georgia was his. It was too much. Hamilton started to shake again.

You know you are a virgin. A virgin with two children. I touched your membrane with the tip of my finger. It's there. Don't expect me to explain how that could be. I've no idea how this came about. This fact puzzles my mind. The first time I come inside you will cause pain. Not too much though. The membrane is thin.

A virgin? I thought that earlier, then knew it to be a stupid idea. Can't be a virgin. I've a child and one on the way. Almost two children. To create our children, you were inside me before. Don't remember. I did promise you I wouldn't forget making love with you.

You are a virgin. Perhaps Father Damian will be able to shed some light on this crazy fact. While you are doing all your wedding planning tomorrow, I'll pay the priest a visit. He should write down in that journal what has happened to us. If he searches for more information, he might find another clue or another couple who experienced something similar.

You are the father of my children. I don't understand anything. Why don't I remember? I don't like this, not remembering.

Neither do I. Nonetheless, I'm pleased. It's the universe righting itself. At least that is the only way I can explain what is happening here. This is fate at its best. We might never understand the secrets that have unraveled here. Nonetheless, our lives have been set right.

I'm going to undress now. Would you enjoy watching me? Do you remember seeing me naked before? No, you don't. Just a few minutes ago, I had never seen you naked. I'm not going to puzzle over this any longer. Going to enjoy you the way a man should enjoy his fiancée. Will see to our pleasure.

He didn't take long to disrobe. For quite a few ticks of his heart, he stood in front of her, letting Georgia look her fill. As she stared at him, his sex grew harder, larger. Hamilton didn't believe that could happen. He ached with desire to know his woman the way a man knows his mate.

Georgia moistened her lips with that precious little tongue of hers he so adored. *You are very large. Do you think...*

Yes. All will be fine. My size won't hurt you.

Will you fit inside me? I...you must since we have children. Wish I could remember even half of what I don't.

Now that she forgot, he didn't wish for her to remember her past with

Chandler. She reached out as if she wished to touch him. With the near contact, he pulsed to life with eager anticipation. If she touched him now, he would burst into flames. Would lose his seed. Shame himself. He needed to be inside her when he exploded.

Coming down on top of her and supporting himself above her with his forearms, he spread her legs. Looked at her intimately. She was a beautiful shade of pink as well as damp, dripping with her cream. He wanted to touch her. Slide his fingers along her softness, revel in her moist heat. Held her hands by the sides of her head. At this instant, he couldn't risk her touching him. Maybe next time he would have greater command of his body.

"No don't touch me yet. Don't want this to be over with so fast you won't feel pleasure. Later, maybe next year some time, you can touch me all you like, fondle my male parts to your heart's content. Just not right now."

"Alright. I'd like that…to touch you. You looked all hard and smooth. You will feel like satin to my fingers. I know. Would like to taste you."

Taste me? Oh, God…

He kissed her forehead, the tip of her nose then either side of her mouth. His hands were shaking again. He wanted to make this right for her. Was afraid he wouldn't last.

~ * ~

Winter was forgetting him. Damn her icy hide. He was almost gone from her mind. Reaching out to her was impossible. Chandler didn't like the fact he couldn't get into her head. He needed to talk to her. Wanted to tell her what he meant to do with her after he caught up to her. Didn't wish to be forgotten by Winter Snow, his Ice Queen. Bloody eyes, how could what they did together disappear from her mind? She shouldn't ever forget him. Why? He needed to find her. Bring her back to the fold.

Winter didn't want to return to him, fled as soon as he thought to trust her. Didn't take her long to burrow into another man's soul. She found another man, a bloody shifter. A man who could challenge him. Bringing her back would give him more delight. If necessary, wouldn't mind using force to put her on stage with him again. Needed their act to continue. His audience loved her. Devoured her with their eyes. She had the loveliest breasts he'd ever seen in a woman, all white and rose-tipped...and huge. Winter deserved to be treated the way she treated him.

She left him! Bloody hell!

He needed revenge, wanted to see her grovel at his feet, beg for him. Wanted her mouth on his sex again. Needed to feel the sweet suck of her mouth, fill her with his seed. Once she gave birth to Colin, he would get her pregnant again. Would keep her with child.

He could hold the children over her head to get all he wanted. Threaten Maeve's life, her very existence. If Winter didn't do what he wanted, he would make certain Bertram took Maeve on stage as a virgin bride. Fifteen might be a good age, maybe younger if Winter made his life too difficult. Both Winter along with her daughter would find themselves auctioned to the highest bidder to entertain in the upstairs rooms. They would have to service any man who could pay the most for their feminine ornaments. Could put them in a threesome for even more pounds...mother and daughter had a nice ring. With glee, Chandler rubbed his hands together.

Chandler groaned when his new virgin cried out with the pain of his entry. Pain was normal. Thought to give her a moment's reprieve before he gave her his seed. She might get with child tonight. The first night with each virgin, no precautions were taken. Wishing this was Winter he shook, losing control. Before this new virgin came on stage he gave her cocaine. He thrust inside her not caring about this child-woman. All he could think about was hurting Winter. He married this new virgin of his in front of an audience of over one hundred men along with a few women. The minister, of course, was fake as was the certificate of marriage. Chandler wanted to marry Winter. She refused his proposal. Now, he no longer wished to have a wife. What he wished for was to have Winter Snow under his thumb to manage until he tired of her. He didn't know if he would ever tire of his Ice Queen. She was beautiful. Everything he ever wished for in a woman. Damn her beautiful white hide.

She didn't remember him or her past. Didn't recall the titillating shows they put on for their voracious crowds. Winter would sit on him, facing the crowds. The way her breast perked out when he put her arms behind his head pleased his audience. Winter enjoyed those moments as much as he did…except when he made her take him inside his mouth. He hooted with laughter. She didn't like that part of the show. Too bad for Winter. She would obey him in every way. Would learn what he could do if she thought to disobey. He knew all she detested. If she fought him too hard, he would allow Bertram to come inside her.

His spectators loved watching sexual encounters of others. Voyeurism was just the thing in London nowadays. Chandler had been amazed at how his success grew so rapidly in this stuffy town. He discovered London wasn't reserved at all. Men and women of all kinds loved their sordid little secrets.

Her loss of memory mattered little to him. When he found her, Chandler meant to give Winter new memories to build upon. Memories she would hold for the rest of her life because once he had her under his thumb, he would never allow her to leave the brothel. Her room would be bolted from the outside. His would be the only key. She would only leave the room at his command.

He didn't have a doubt in his mind. Winter would fight. A woman who struggled was even more enjoyable to his audiences, more charming to the gatherings of the lecherous. Before he became enamored with Winter, a struggling female was most enjoyable. Pain was always something he could hold over the woman's head, Maeve's pain. Chandler recalled the time he almost took Harris, his brother's wife, against the wall in the Wolcott townhouse. Ah…that had been a pleasant experience. He did regret that he was stopped, jerked away from her before he could feel her close around him, milk his sex with her pleasure. Revenge against his brother with his female was wonderful.

Males loved to subdue women, to have them on their knees doing whatever they asked, whatever pleased them. Subjugation of a woman was their right. His spectators would go wild with this new script. Just as they were crazy about watching the virgins lose their innocence. His imagination was playing havoc with reality.

His attention returned to the girl on the mattress. Her legs were spread just as he taught her. She whimpered with her need. Raised her arms to him. The girl wanted him, still did. He could sense the desire for him raging. Her sweet body was writhing. Hot. His seed coupled with her virgin's blood was smeared on her open legs. He stepped back to give the spectators a good view of untried flesh no longer. Her virgin's blood would be on him on her white thighs. Chandler was pleased with the view. He did like how long and white her legs were. Her beautiful long legs were one of the reasons he chose her from all her sisters. The other motive was her supple body. Was satisfied with her soft white belly. Her white rounded globes tipped with exquisite pink nipples shuddered with each moan of pleasure tearing through her. Deidra was her name a few days ago. Now she would be known as Noel. Christmas was almost upon them. Noel was a fitting name for his new whore. The girl would bring top dollar on the auction block.

Bertram would have her next. After she signed the fake wedding certificate, she would be granted more pleasure. Naked in front of his roaring spectators, Noel drank champagne with him to celebrate the marriage. Later Johnny would parade her around the room then down the aisles to allow the men and women who wanted to kiss and fondle the woman a chance to do so. Noel was still spread out on the mattress. He taught her not to move until he gave her permission. Chandler loved the power, the control he had over these possessions of his. She was obedient because she understood her family needed the money she would earn. Over the last month, he discovered the coke made the women eager for the culmination. If she disobeyed, he would hold back the necessary funds her family was desperate to receive.

He no longer wrote the contracts for one or even five years. With his wishes, he would have the youngest women for the next ten years of their lives. By then they would have served their purpose. He would keep them on as whores for the upstairs rooms, auctioned of course to the highest bidders. If they failed to command a sufficient price, he would relegate them to housekeeping duties. Housework would be better than work on the streets. He congratulated himself for not sending the ladies to the streets of London. Life out there was dangerous. He kept these women safe as well as well fed. The women would no longer make the money they were used to earning. Chandler was generous with the tips they earned. Would not be without his servants. Those women would work for their room and board.

This place was too small, Chandler realized one evening when he noticed the standing room only crowd growing in size. Didn't want to send any man or woman away. Loved counting the groats at the end of each evening. He started putting on two shows a night. His business was expanding at a rapid pace. He sent Jamie out to find a bigger house. Perhaps two would serve his purpose better. He could buy the place next to this one. The large townhouse had been for sale since his brothel became the talk of the town. The best women would work at this place of residence. They would continue to earn exorbitant amounts of cash. The women who did not garner the most money could ply their wares in the second house. He could give each lady the choice between whoring and housekeeping.

Noel was sold to him by her doting father for some of the big bucks she would bring to the household. Her father received one thousand pounds with the purchase. After that he would receive fifty percent of her earnings for the remainder of her contract. The father didn't appear to have a single misgiving with the sale. Offered a second daughter to him. He refused the oldest girl. She wasn't a virgin. Some randy boy had taken her virtue behind the stable one day. She was huge with child. After he bought the second house, he might go back for the oldest daughter.

Decided the audience would love to see him make love to his virgin bride one more time. As a group they were applauding them, cheering them on with chants. Standing over her, Chandler looked down. Her eyes were closed. Her breathing was shallow and ragged. He lay down between her legs. Bit the side of each breast leaving slight red marks, soothed with his tongue. Held her hands over her head then thrust inside. She cried out, surprised by the unexpected contact. Her eyelids flew open. The audience cheered their approval. Chandler moved inside her. Thrust hard then faster until he howled with the pleasure of it all. Noel stopped moaning with the unexpected pleasure. When he looked down at her face, she was sliding her tongue along her lip. There was hot moisture on her mouth. Chandler didn't understand why he paused before taking her a second time. Hesitating wasn't like him. He was getting weak. Needed to work harder to live up to his standards.

Winter made him weak. He would find her. When he found her, he would be strong again. Would control his empire.

One more time, he thrust hard. Spilled his seed then withdrew from her. Without another moment of thought, brought the lady to stand beside him. She was shaking, her knees weak from the ecstasy he granted her. Noel wasn't hurt. If he guessed right, in a few more minutes when the aphrodisiac kicked in, she would want him again. This was all part of the script he wrote. He held up her hand in celebration. Jamie brought them a glass of champagne which they both drank down. He washed himself of her virgin's blood.

"This woman is no longer a virgin. She won't be available tonight. Next week you all will be able to bid on her. She is lovely. Used by me only twice." He looked at her, running his gaze down the length of her beautiful white body. She needed to be taught what was expected. Nonetheless, he needed to take care of his property. "As I said, this evening, Noel cannot be used by my players, any of them. Since I always share with Bertram," He handed her over to his best friend. "One more time of pleasure will not hurt Noel. When I made love to her, she whispered how pleased she was to have me. Bertram will make love to her tonight. My friend will make her scream with frenzy. In another week, she'll be back for a second appearance. This evening, she will not be auctioned. Noel is a valuable commodity for this place of business. This was her first experience with men." Chandler understood he needed to repeat himself. The men in his audience all wanted her. They roared their disapproval. Desired this young woman. They would need to wait.

"Noel," Bertram said when he placed her little hand in his. "You will enjoy my attention. Everything I do is planned to give you pleasure. Now…"

He watched as Bertram set her on her hands and knees. He was through with her in seconds. After that Celine brought her around the room. Showed her off. Allowed his patrons to fondle and kiss with tender care. He wouldn't allow anything rough. Next week would be different.

Chandler understood he had a great deal to think about. While he watched the scenes unfolding, he tried to get into Winter's head. The bloody shifter blocked him at every turn. Who the devil was that man? He didn't even have a name for him.

With the screams of beautiful pleasure coming from Noel echoing in his head, he walked from the theatre then into his chambers. A hot bath was ready for him. He slid into the heated liquid then set his head on the lip of the tub.

Closing his eyes, he dreamed of Winter. What disturbed him was that her image seemed to be fading from his mind to be replaced with the other women in the brothel. He had to find her soon or he wouldn't know who she was to him. He would never be able to pursue his vengeance.

Chapter Nine

Georgia wanted Hamilton more than she could ever imagine. He stormed into her life expecting her to be one with him. From the moment they first spoke, she was aware of the deep connection between them. She was puzzled by all the new information inundating her brain. Confused with what he told her.

Frustrated by the truth she had no memory of part of her life. She recalled her life in Ireland with her father along with her mother. The life was idyllic. She was given everything she ever needed. Recalled the day she left for London. She explained to her father that she saw her mate in her dreams. Her mate was in London.

Cormack understood her need to seek the man she was meant to spend her life with. Her father also insisted on accompanying her. He was there for her until she left him. After that she held no recollections of what happened to her until she found herself in her father's townhouse in London.

She didn't wish to remain in the city. Georgia didn't know why. Insisting that she find a small cottage in the country, her father helped her. While he didn't hire Hollis, he was pleased with the man. Along with Bea to help her out, he knew this would be better than if she was alone. Hollis was to be her bodyguard, Bea her nanny. She loved both of them. They were kind to her despite the child she birthed without being wed.

"What has you so distant?" Hamilton asked while he stood in front of her naked, his sex jutting from him. She shivered with the pleasure of the sight.

"I was thinking of the parts of my life I remember."

"That's all fine. Right now, let's just think about the here and now. Hmm… Don't wish to have your head somewhere else when I make love to you."

"Alright. I want what you want."

Hamilton smiled at her then settled on top of her, covering her, giving her the warmth of his body. Found she was still shaking from the pleasure he gave her earlier. Just like he told her she would do, she screamed when she reached that startling place where she thought she shattered into thousands of tiny shards. Believed she could reach out and touch the sun. He braced himself on his forearms, looking into her eyes.

"Ham…what now?" This was something she wanted with all her heart. She needed to experience the pleasure of holding him inside her body.

"We are going to make love. Instead of my fingers inside you, that part of me you wanted to touch will be inside your wonderous body. The first thrust will sting a bit. I hope not much. Your membrane is thin. Don't understand." He smoothed his thumbs across her eyebrows. His knuckles along her cheek. "Will you be brave?"

Easy for you to say. You're not the one who is going to feel this tiny sting. Men have it all their way.

I know. Didn't know what else to tell you. Don't want to hurt you. Promise… No, I was going to say I will never hurt you again. When I claim you… After that, I can give you my promise. Imagine I'm the one who needs to be brave at the moment.

A man should have to feel the same pain as the woman. It's not fair. All the pleasure for the male, none of the… Men should have to give birth.

That's not possible. The human race would die out. Men are not strong enough to withstand the traumas of child birth. Should we get on with the pleasure? He was grinning down at her.

She steadied herself with a deep breath. "Alright." Georgia liked the sound of his idea. "More pleasure would please me. When will I be able to touch you? Want to feel you with the tips of my fingers."

"Maybe after a year," he repeated his earlier statement.

"So long?" She was surprised by his answer. Didn't understand why. "What about now?" Georgia asked one more time.

"The devil, I hope not that long. Not right now either." Hamilton barked a laugh then seemed to grow serious. Kisses on her nose then her mouth heated her, inflamed all the shadowy secret parts of her. His fingers threaded into her hair.

His mouth captured hers, his tongue exploring inside deep then deeper still. With hesitation, she touched the tip of his tongue with her own. She'd opened for him understanding he wanted her to part her lips for his gentle invasion. Hamilton wanted to come inside her. His hands were exploring along the length of her body creating an inferno of need. He knew where to touch as well as how to enflame. For the moment, his caresses were light, meant to entice a slow measured response. Georgia didn't want slow. Hard and chaotic was what she wanted. She arched trying to get closer to his heat to the feel of the length of his sex against her. Beneath him she felt small, fragile. Enjoyed the feeling of his strength atop her along with his warmth.

She ran her hands down his back. Stopped at his buttocks which were firm, muscled. A low rumble from the back of his throat enticed her to explore more. Smoothed her hands along his body sleek with his muscles. When she first saw him with nothing on, she wanted to touch the male part of him that was so different from her. Hamilton told her, no. Georgia meant to find a way to savor all of him.

The time is too soon, he told her.

I don't want to burst, Hamilton explained.

Understanding was impossible. She loved the way his body felt all sleek with power, the hard angles and plains that were so different from her softness. seemed as if that was the way they were supposed to fit together. Her breasts pushed against his hard chest. She felt each breath along with the beating of his heart.

His mouth moved against hers. Again, he slipped his tongue deep inside. His lips moved on hers. The velvet smoothness rubbed across her tongue. She touched him back. Played with him as he brought her inside the heat of his mouth. His large hands explored, touched upon her breasts, the curve of her hips. He pulled her legs up, opening herself to him more than before. Made her vulnerable.

"Wrap your legs around me. Need you soon," he murmured next to her ear. Touched the lobe with his tongue. Swirled then nipped. At the sweet, hot caresses she bucked. Her body ached for more. She moaned, arching against him, seeking.

He lowered himself to kiss her breasts. Bit with gentle precision the tips that were long and hard from his explorations. She moaned then curved against him. Rubbed her belly against his. Felt his sex touch upon her intimately. Shuddering, she leaned into him. Raked her teeth along his shoulder. His arms were thick with muscle. Trying to find some part of him to hold onto, she wrapped her fingers around the tops of his arms.

He helped her bring her legs around his flanks. Moving between them he kissed her belly. Slid his tongue into her belly button. Traveled lower. Pressed kisses on the insides of her thighs, alternating from one to the other. He cupped her bottom in his hands bringing her higher. She felt his breath whisper across her most intimate places. She was stunned. What was he going to do? He couldn't mean to...

"I'm going to taste you here. Savor, learn all that excites you." The touch of his tongue shocked her. Hamilton licked her tender flesh. Blew there where he shouldn't be. Sipped on her most sensitive flesh.

Again, she felt the warmth of his breath whisper over her. When his tongue touched her, entered her, she gasped. Bucked with the shock of it. "Hamilton... No! You cannot mean to..." She closed her eyes. Her body moved wildly with the intense pleasure he orchestrated. The sound startled her. Georgia realized the whimper was hers. She clung to his shoulders. Her nails scored his vibrant muscles.

"Hush, enjoy this. I *ken* I will. Need to taste every part of you. Want to watch you reach that edge where there is no return. Open your eyes." He continued, lashing her with his lips, teeth and tongue. Her body was in a turmoil of need. She was almost at that pinnacle where her body would react with more and more uncontrolled pleasure. Georgia felt as if she would touch the sun.

When his tongue parted tender flesh, she jerked up. Her body bowed with the sweetest pleasure. He nipped on more sensitive places. Slid his tongue inside her, penetrated then retreated. She yelled when he sent two fingers into her. Georgia knew she would shatter soon. She was so close to the point where her world would explode.

Hamilton rose above her again. He kissed her hard. Sent his tongue deep inside her mouth. She tasted herself. Kissed then kissed her more. Entered into her then withdrew, continued the slow, wicked assault. The incredible whimper she heard was hers. The groan was his. His fingers played with her nipples, plucking them, enticing the magic of the joining. He created mercuric enchantment.

"Please…" she moaned, understanding what she wanted. "Please Hamilton…now…" She twisted within his arms, arched, her body pleading for more. She bit his shoulder then licked where the small marks of pleasure were.

"Not yet…" he murmured once more, exploring the length of her. Continuing to touch sensitive places. Spots that aroused. He brought her higher then backed away. Seemed to want to prolong this mating. "Haven't tasted your delicate, little toes yet. Told you I'm going to savor every part of you. Not going to leave one place untouched or uncared for."

She didn't care if he tasted her toes. Wanted what he gave her when they were downstairs. Needed him inside her now, not later. He brought her legs down between his body. With his broad shoulders he pushed them to widen. Slid his mouth along the insides of her legs. Nipped tender flesh. Licked to sooth the tiny bites. Went lower until he tasted each of her toes. Just as he said he would. When he moved higher, following a sensitive path, her heels dug into the covers on the bed. Her body curved reaching for him, begging.

Again, he brought her legs around his hips. "Keep your long, white legs around me. She didn't understand why he prolonged this journey to pleasure. Her body was on the precipice. On purpose, he kept the waves of pleasure from exploding. "I want this to last as long as possible. You may not have your pleasure too soon. If that were to happen, we'd have to start all over. Though beginning again might be just as pleasant."

Slipped his fingers into her again. Withdrew then thrust. Repeated. Found the sensitive spot, he told her about. "You're hot and wet. You're ready for me. Tell me you want me."

"I want you. Please…" seemed she'd been begging him forever.

Hamilton set his damp fingers on her cheek. "This is you…" He sounded pleased with himself. Wanted her to understand something. She wasn't certain what it was he wanted her to comprehend. "Means you are ready to take me into your sultry hot sheath. Am I right?"

"Yes… I want you. Don't make me wait any longer."

Georgia moaned as he continued the gentle assault on her person. Felt the tip of his sex rest against her intimately. Knew he was ready to come inside. She didn't wish to be a virgin any longer. "Hamilton!" Felt him ease into her. Realized he stopped because he touched the barrier inside her. She didn't understand nor did she care at this moment.

"This will cause some pain. I hope not much. Try to relax." Above her, Hamilton's lips were pulled back from his teeth. He strained with his effort to hold back. "Now!"

When he thrust inside her she cried out. He held still, very still. She gulped air. The pain was less than what she would have imagined. With a blink of time, the small hurt vanished. She was no longer a virgin. Not that she should have been innocent, given the reality she'd given birth to a child and was pregnant. She didn't want to think about all those other things. Needed to enjoy his possession of her.

"Are you alright?" Hamilton asked, as he moved damp strands of hair from her face. Above her, he was bracing himself on his forearms, staring down. He smiled. Touched the tip of her nose with his. "This lovemaking between us won't hurt any longer." He kissed her eyelids closed. Touched the tip of her nose with his teeth. Across her lips he brushed soft kisses. He stopped to look down again.

Hamilton's eyes were dark pewter. She wondered if they would always be that color when they made love. "Yes, I'm fine except for the fact you are not kissing me the way I would like. Want you to finish this lovemaking. Want to feel your sex move inside me. You were right, Hamilton."

"Right?" Hamilton appeared puzzled. "About what?"

"You are not too big," she told him with a smile. Around him she clenched her muscles. Tightened. Heard him groan again.

"Thank God," he murmured. "The pain was not too much?"

"Not much at all."

He began to move with slow languid strokes inside her, pushing deeper then deeper still until she thought he must be so deep inside her he touched her womb. He found the small nub that sent her into a frenzy of need. His mouth closed over hers. She arched, bucking against him. He was thrusting harder and faster.

After she screamed his name, she watched him pull his lips back from his teeth again. He roared with what must be the pleasure for him. She felt the warmth of his seed fill her. He collapsed on her. She was filled with gentle heat. He covered all of her. Her body was exhausted from the lovemaking. Replete with satisfaction, Hamilton slipped from inside her. Brought her to snuggle against him, placing her head in the hollow of his shoulder.

"That was amazing," she told him, her voice soft. "You didn't hurt me very much. Just a tiny sting of pain as you said it would be. Will we do this every night? I would like to. Maybe more than once?"

"Yes, you are insatiable. I've created a wanton woman. A lady who needs her pleasure. I'm quite pleased with my efforts as well as the result." Hamilton trailed a finger along her arm, up then down. "I don't wish for you to go anywhere alone tomorrow. I understand most of the day will be with Wynnie and maybe the other wives. If I'm not with you, make certain Connal gives you a guard to escort you. Hollis will need to stay with Maeve." He pulled away so he could look at her. His gaze bore into hers.

The warning sent a shiver of dread coursing through her. The expression on his face was dead serious. For seconds she trembled, mulled over his warnings. "Why? Why do I need a person to protect me? What aren't you telling me? What about Maeve?"

Georgia understood deep in her heart. She didn't want to hear the reason. If he spoke, the threat would be far too genuine to ignore. She realized she needed to understand everything he wasn't telling her about her past. With the missing year of her life, all was so different. She understood she was a different person now. Different from before that misplaced year as well as altered since she met Hamilton and fell in love.

"Just heed my warning. If I tell you more…"

Hamilton rolled onto his back. She put her head on his chest. Placed her hand where she could play with the hair on his chest. Twirled the soft strands around her fingers. Felt the beat of his heart beneath her palm. With the tip of her finger, followed the path of his hair to his belly. She flattened her hand. His muscles contracted with the contact. "You're playing with fire."

"I hope so." She sucked on each of his nipples.

Hamilton groaned then set his hand on her belly. "Any contractions?" Smoothed along the contours of her stomach.

Georgia sat up, braced herself with her arms. The tips of her breast pressed against his chest. "Don't change the subject to the baby. I need to know…to understand what is expected of me. I realize I've forgotten important elements in my life. How can I protect myself if you keep secrets from me? What happened in that year I've forgotten?"

Hamilton grimaced with her words. She touched the edges of his beautiful mouth with the tip of her finger. Placed a brief kiss on either side then lay back to stare at the ceiling. Pulled the covers up to her chin. He pushed them down to her waist so her breasts were in his sight.

"Don't want you worried, thinking about problems. Tomorrow should be special for you with Wynnie. A special day where you'll fashion your wedding gown. The only thing you need to do for me is wear my dress tartan around your waist. The modiste will help fashion the sash. Wynnie will give you her advice."

She bit his chin. "I'm worried now. You shouldn't keep secrets from your soon to be wife. I won't stand for secrets between us. As to your tartan, I will be pleased to wear the dress plaid. Now, tell me what I need to know. If it's something terrible, I can handle the news. After all, I have you to protect me. You are strong." One more time she sent her hand lower, intent on touching his sex. Wished to learn how it felt in her hands.

He barked a laugh. Kept her questing hand on his belly. She snorted her displeasure.

"You won't stand for it? Will you?" Hamilton turned her onto her back. Kissed each breast then her belly. She felt her belly tighten from the sweet contact. "You were trying to take me by surprise. Thought if you were subtle, I wouldn't notice your destination. There was nothing understated about what you were doing. Felt every delicate move your fingers danced."

Her giggle brought his head up to look at her. With his knuckles, Hamilton caressed the side of her face. "I need for you to tell me everything I've forgotten."

"You insist?" The question told her she might have made inroads.

"Yes. Need to know everything there is to know about the time period I'm forgetting. Though I do understand I might not appreciate what I will learn."

"After we make love again." He was inside her. Rocking her. "Can't seem to get enough of you. Need you."

She moaned and heaved against him, pulling him deeper then deeper still. Found the pleasure more intense this time than before. When they were done, he cradled her in his arms. Ran the tip of his finger along her arm.

"I will give you a brief accounting of those days you lost. Keep in mind, I don't know everything that transpired. Only *ken* what you told me. Before you lost the year of your life, you were straightforward with me. Didn't hold back information. Though I'm certain I don't understand it all. Positive there are details you might not have wished to explain to me. If you didn't recount something, I won't be able to tell you."

"You're frightening me again. Can't seem…I wasn't a nice person back then. Was I?" She was very afraid of what she assumed was true. "Did I hurt people? Can't abide that thought. Wouldn't hurt anyone now."

"No and no. A person's basic nature doesn't change. At least I believe it wouldn't. Don't imagine you were anyone except the sweet woman I know and love today. I do love you. You are mine. Don't ever forget that little piece of information." Hamilton let out a long breath of air as if wondering about what to tell her.

"Please…I can…need to learn what I did. What my life was like. There had to have been another man since I've two children. Are there people who will want to…" She lifted her shoulders. Felt her breasts brush against him. At the contact she shivered. Would be easy to let this conversation go unanswered. She wanted him again. Tried to bring herself to the present. "You said I didn't hurt anyone."

"True. To my knowledge, you hurt no one except yourself. Believe in the missing year you were just as sweet as you are now. Someone hurt you."

"Tell me. It was a man. Wasn't it?" Hamilton held her hand in his. Stroked the underside of her wrist.

He let out a long slow breath of air. "Wish this wasn't a necessity. The problem I'm having is that I do agree with you. The need to know is foremost in your thoughts. Believe you are correct, knowing will help you comprehend the possible dangers waiting out there for you. When I ask you to always be with someone, you think I'm full of nonsense."

"You are talking in circles. I'm not easily frightened." Her words were a lie though. In this situation, something deep as well as evil lurked hidden in her thoughts, wrestling to get out in the open. "Is this something I will wish you didn't tell me after the fact?" She felt herself shaking. Didn't want to be terrified of words, words that were true.

"Could be." He kissed the tips of her fingers. "You might not enjoy hearing of this person who is not a nice man. For a year, he controlled you. Told you how to act along with what you were to do. When you tried to tell him no, he held your daughter's well-being over your head. No mother would allow a man to control her every move if she could stop him."

Georgia shuddered with the light contact. It took very little provocation for her to want him again. "Could be?" she questioned, struggling over the rest of what he told her. "How could someone hold the life of a baby over her mother's head? I don't understand. He must be a monster."

"Imagine that's a good description of the man." Hamilton continued brushing kisses on the palm of her hand.

"At the time you searched for your mate as all shifters do. You saw this man. Understood from the sight of him, he was your mate. His name is Chandler Wolcott. His younger brother is wed to Harris. You met her after you escaped from Chandler."

Hamilton explained how she followed him to his place of business. Entered into the brothel. "You signed a contract to entertain in said brothel, knowing you had no choice except to be with your mate. Chandler was disinherited. He was an evil man. Tried to kill his father so he would inherit. He was in debt because of his gambling habit along with his women. The gambling along with the women was before he was set aside as the heir to the title along with the family's wealth."

"What did he do? Chandler was…I don't have the word. He gambled away his money?" Georgia asked with wonder. "The man you described was my mate? I'm very glad I found you. Don't believe I could have lived the rest of my life with another man. Imagine what you've told me is the reason why I ran."

"Yes, at the time he was your mate. He is no longer anything to you. The word you were searching for is reprobate? Yes, a degenerate is what he is. What he will always be. The man loved sex. Most always found a willing woman to dally with. Sometimes he was cruel to the lady. Liked many different varieties of sex. Found women wherever it was convenient. Never cared if the lady was agreeable." He lifted her chin to look at him. "What are you thinking?" Hamilton brushed away a tear sliding down her cheek. "Don't cry over that man."

"Was Chandler cruel to me? Is it the reason why I can't remember anything about that time in my life? People say a person's mind sometimes shuts off when they don't wish to recall something that hurt them. Is that what is happening?"

"As to what you've told me, he was never physically cruel to you. In the last months after you gave birth to Maeve, he threatened you with the baby. He made you work for him even though you didn't want to perform any longer. You had a month and a half left on your contract. He made you fulfill those last weeks. During those last weeks you spent with him, Chandler got you pregnant again. He meant to use you as his plaything, a toy for his amusement."

"Perform? What do you mean by perform? What did I do?" Hamilton had her curiosity piqued. Seemed Georgia needed to learn everything.

"This is the hard part. Chandler found a means to make all the money he ever wanted doing exactly what he loved best, exploiting sex. He found women who liked to have sex with a multitude of men. Later, he found women he could buy from fathers who believed women were useless creatures. Good for one thing."

"How? I don't understand half of what you are telling me."

"He sold sex to the men and women of London as well as the surrounding villages. Found women who were down on their luck. Some sold themselves on the street. The ones who showed promise were brought to his establishment. Some were already in the trade. Some of the ladies were not. Everything was above board. Everyone, male as well as female employees, signed contracts stating they were willing to have sex with anyone of his choosing or theirs."

"People do that? Did I? What you said doesn't sound like something I would do. I wasn't down on my luck. Father would never have sold me to the horrible man you described." Georgia gasped the questions, incredulous that she might have been a willing participant.

"Yes, you believed with all your heart Chandler was your mate. In the beginning you went along with his wishes because he must have meant everything to you. You were presented once a month as Winter Snow, Queen of the Ice."

Georgia felt her eyes widening with shock. She couldn't imagine agreeing to this. "Winter Snow...? Once a month I performed for people...in front...was I naked? I cannot believe I would parade around nude in front of men as well as women. Have sex with any man in front of people."

"Who paid exorbitant amounts to watch you have sex with Chandler. From what you've told me, you were always naked. You would appear in a sheer gown that left nothing to be imagined. When he commanded you to take your gown off, you did. Then you would sit on him facing the audience while he as well as other men caressed and fondled your female endowments. Brought you to full arousal. You would climax with people ogling you and wishing you were having sex with them. All types of people came to his shows, titled...wealthy business men...women who wanted sex."

She buried her nose in his chest, closing her eyes as if the tiny act would rid her of the horrible images he conjured. "I did this until I gave birth to Maeve? After her birth he gave me six weeks off. That was kind of the man. From what you've told me, I'm surprised he didn't make me go back the day after." Her words sounded bitter. She should feel the bitterness of betrayal.

"Yes, you did. From what you told me six weeks after Maeve was born, he made you perform again just as you did before. You signed a yearlong contract. Chandler intended to make certain you put in all your time. You left after the allotted year. The thing was, you were pregnant again, this time with a boy."

"I fled. How did he know the children were his?"

"The children are mine," Hamilton corrected her. "The past has been rewritten. Once we are wed all Chandler's claims will be invalid. When I go see Father Damian, I will sign the papers needed to adopt them officially."

"Couldn't the children have been another man's?"

Hamilton cleared his throat, understanding what he was about to tell her was also true for him. "Chandler was possessive. He never shared you.

Now, however, if he finds you alone, vulnerable, he might not be so magnanimous. If he catches you, he might not be so possessive. Might enjoy sharing you with anyone who will pay the going price. I believe he is seeking revenge for what he considers your betrayal of him."

Georgia seemed to be having a difficult time processing the new information. "He threatened me with Maeve. I would never have wished for her to grow up in a whorehouse. Would not have wished it for Colin either. That's why I left. How did I get away?"

"Don't believe Chandler thought you would flee. In his arrogance, the man assumed he had an iron hold over your feelings. You did tell him you loved him. You allowed him to claim you in the way of your clan."

"Chandler did claim me? The marks vanished."

"Yes, and yes. You are no longer his mate. You are mine."

Possessiveness filled him to overflowing. He would never allow Chandler Wolcott to touch her again. He would die to protect her.

"You think he will come here to find me? If he caught me, he would drag me back to London to work for him. Is that what you are telling me?"

"Yes."

"I promise not to go anywhere alone. Images of some of what you are telling me terrify me. I didn't want that for my life then and don't want it now. Didn't wish to have this man use me. You must protect the children."

"That's my intention."

"Now, it's getting late. Should we make love again or sleep?"

Hamilton gave a short bark of laughter when he realized she was sound asleep.

~ * ~

At least an hour passed before Hamilton fell asleep. He'd not wished to tell Georgia what she did during the year she couldn't recall. Had to because he was afraid for her life. If Chandler found her then took her from him, he would enlist the aid of the Clan Chattan. They would come to her rescue. Chandler would never survive a battle with this clan. He would know where she was. If necessary, would storm the brothel, break down doors to get to Georgia.

As the night progressed, nightmares plagued his sleep. When he woke, there was no sunlight coming through the window. The day was dreary. Outside was clouded with fog, deep unforgiving fog. He felt as if he couldn't claw his way out. Depression pressed down on him.

When he felt her hand exploring his torso, moving downward, he grinned. The day brightened. For the moment, his fears vanished. Pleased she was bold this morning. Jerked when her small fingers closed around his fully aroused member. When she first touched his sex, he'd not been as hard as the fireplace poker sitting at the hearth. With the gentle pressure she applied, he grew, lengthened. Now he was as hard as that poker. The little witch. She could fondle him as much as she wanted.

When he smiled at her, she was leaning over him. A wealth of long black hair cascaded around him, touching, tickling. Setting fire in his blood. His fingers wound into her hair. The strands enticing sensitive flesh. He allowed her exploration. She kissed his belly. Moved lower, her intentions seemed obvious. He hoped she'd take him into her mouth.

His lady didn't know what to do with his rod. She squeezed. That was nice. Thought for a moment, he might spill his seed. Trembling from head to toe, Hamilton gritted his teeth in an attempt to command his body to be still. To a degree his efforts worked. He needed to be inside her hot tempting body so bad, he shook with the mere thought of how he would feel encircled by her.

She set the tip of her tongue on the top of his sex. Looked at him as if for approval then licked. Nipped. *The devil!* He bucked hard. Groaned aloud. Thought he'd explode from the contact. He clenched his teeth. His fingers fisted in the sheets. When she returned her gaze to him, she smiled as if she was a little girl with her first sucker. My God, he shouldn't have thought that word. She could suck on him all she wanted. No, maybe not. He was so damn close to bursting that a tiny bit of suction might send him over the edge. Given much more of her delicate investigations, he might shame himself any second.

He wanted to pull her up so she sat on him. Didn't wish to stir up a hornet's nest of memories. Georgia didn't recall anything from that year of her life, even after he told her what she did with the man in front of an audience, she didn't remember anything. He explained all she recounted to him before her memory of the year vanished. He was positive all of the sordidness was left out.

Hamilton decided then and there he wasn't going to allow his life to be ruled by memories of a distant past. Discovering if she recalled those times, would come soon enough. He didn't believe she would ever remember the year in question. What he told her last night evoked no memories. He was thankful for the small reprieve.

His hands around her waist, he brought her up his legs. Kissed her soundly on the mouth. Maneuvered her so her long white legs straddled him. He felt the heat from her core along with the damp petals touch his sex. The devil, he needed her now. This instant. Didn't wish to wait another moment. More than anything, wanted to bring himself inside her. Thrust until she cried out her pleasure.

"Sit on me." His voice was low with a dark whiskey tone to the timbre. "Put me inside you. All you need to do is lower yourself on my sex. You will like the sensations. I promise." Inside he was laughing. Her changing expressions were endearing. She was thinking his proposition over. He wanted to howl his pleasure. She was enchanting in her innocence. He never expected to see her hesitate.

She twisted her head to the side, still mulling over his words. "Alright. I think this will be interesting. You say I'd like to sit on you? What if I don't?" Georgia leaned on his chest, her palms flat against his nipples. The tips of her breasts sashaying across him. He was on tenterhooks waiting for her to decide. "What if there is nothing about this random thought of yours, I'll enjoy?"

"You will. Didn't I promise?" With his help, she lowered herself onto his shaft. He set his hands to fondling her breasts. "There. Do whatever you wish." This was so damn wonderful. Bless her softness…the sultry heat of her. He felt her muscles clench around him. The impish smile on her face delighted his senses.

One more time her expression changed. Now, it seemed to him she understood exactly what she was about. This new grin, this wicked smile of hers left him shaking, panting with anticipation for what was to come. He wouldn't be able to hold back much longer. Georgia was looking down. Her back was straight, very nearly rigid. As she resumed eye contact with him, her China blue eyes were darkening with the hunger she must be feeling. She looked down to where they were joined, then to him. At the wonder in her eyes, he almost yowled his laughter. Kept the sound behind his teeth. Wondered what she was thinking.

"You are inside me. I see…" Her words whispered with hesitation. She stared at him again. "I never thought…didn't…I…"

He brought his fingers to caress her with tender meticulousness. Massaged the little pearl between the fascinating pink petals that were sultry with her passion. "Yes, I'm so deep I'm touching your womb. Our little shifter might feel me. What do you think?" he asked, humor tinging his voice. He couldn't help teasing her.

"Oh, my! Don't think his knowing what we are doing would be right. Is this such a good idea for him to know where his father has put himself?" she asked.

She was panting for air. Her head was tossed back. Glossy black hair tumbled down her back while her rose tipped nipples danced in front of him. He brought her down so his lips touched the hard buds. He gave each one his tender consideration. Felt her core milk his sex. He pushed up then withdrew. Repeated the process while he suckled each nipple. She was so damn beautiful he couldn't breathe.

"Perhaps it is the way this is supposed to be. We aren't the first shifters to make love in this condition. Many before us have had pregnant wives. Had little bairns nestled in their mate's womb." He was still laughing at the amazement in her eyes. Ran his hand along her swollen belly. Didn't know what exactly she was amazed about. "Maybe that's how we learn our technique. The finesse is passed down from one generation to the next."

"You're teasing me." She swept her tongue along her mouth. Hamilton was certain the sensual gesture was a calculated move. She could flirt anytime she was in the mood. "What do I do now?" Georgia asked even while she rose on him then settled back down. Repeated the process. Seemed to be intuitive about the next steps. He caressed the tiny jewel that would send her higher. "I…oh!" She whimpered with her pleasure. Tiny feminine sounds of ecstasy floated from between her lips.

"Just what you are doing." Hamilton groaned with the hungry urgency she brought him. He would forever be delighted with this woman, his mate. "Perhaps, though, in lieu of all we need to do today, you should speed this up a *wee* bit. Wynnie will be waiting for you. Unless, of course, Connal along with Wynnie were involved with the same type of play in their bed." He didn't care what anyone else was managing at this hour.

The lovemaking was over sooner than he wished. They both reached their releases in a crescendo of pleasure. She cried out his full name. He growled with his release. Pulled her against him to cuddle for a few seconds before the reality of the day would set in. They both had so much to accomplish.

"Cover up, I'm going to order a bath. You may have the first one unless you wish to share." Damn, if they shared, they would never be on their way. They would make love again. "Never mind. What I asked was not the best of ideas. We can share some day when we have nothing but time to fill." Hamilton didn't know if a day such as he suggested would ever come to pass.

More than an hour ticked by before Hamilton along with Georgia entered into the McKenna keep. Wynnie was waiting for her in the main room while nursing a cup of tea. A fire blazed in the large fireplace, heating the room. She smiled at them. What seemed to be an all-knowing smile on her lips. Wynnie was an intuitive lady. She would comprehend why they were a bit late to the appointment.

"Welcome. Connal has assigned one of his men to tag along with us today. My husband thought an additional person would be for the best under the circumstances. To have a bodyguard was a suggestion of his I agreed with." Wynnie set her cup on the saucer then stood. She smoothed out her skirts. "I'm ready. Let's not waste time. Do you have anything in mind for a gown? If you do, the information will speed the process. Not that I'm in a hurry. We've got all day if we need the extra time to get the gown perfect."

"Would like the fabric to be silver with threads of white running through the gown. If that is possible. Matching white stockings with silver garters would be nice too." Georgia looked to him as if for approval.

"Must have two blue ones too," Wynnie told her, a smile of amusement on her face. "The groomsmen will remove the blue ones before we bring you upstairs to get you ready for the wedding night. Believe you stated a preference for a sash. The Adair dress tartan you mentioned."

Wynnie was watching Hamilton, staring actually. He grinned at her. "The groomsmen will wear the garters on their head and look ridiculous."

"Yes, if that's possible." Hamilton said. "The seamstress in the village has the fabric. Georgia has agreed to humor me with this request. The sash will match my kilt. Believe I would like to be united in this manner."

"Yes, I would like it very much," Georgia said, her voice soft, looking at him with those huge luminous blue eyes of hers. "Will enjoy seeing you wearing your kilt. Your knees, well…they are quite *bonny.*"

Hamilton couldn't stop the bark of laughter. "You think I've bonny knees?" he asked, incredulous at the idea.

"Changing the subject of Hamilton's knees. You have ideas for flowers?" Wynnie questioned, a crimson blush on her face. "This time of year, we might need to be selective. I'll send a message to the florist."

"As many as possible. I love flowers. Do we need to rob a greenhouse? Is there one in Carnoch?" Georgia asked with a huge smile on her beautiful mouth. "I am partial to roses. Too bad there are none in the keep's rose garden."

Hamilton kissed her hard, bringing her into his arms. He needed to get going. "Pick out everything you like. I've more than enough groats to cover what you choose. I'm certain there is at least one hothouse in Carnoch. I will be back after lunch to pick you up. Have a few things to attend to myself."

"Are you seeing Father Damian?"

Frown lines marred her face. Hamilton understood she was worried. "Will you see to the adoption of the children? That's important. I would be there with you."

"Adopting our children is not something I can do without your approval." Smoothing those creases on her forehead that told him she was worried was something he would have appreciated doing. "Right now." He paused, thinking of keeping a few secrets from Wynnie. "I'll let you know what he says about our…your…conversion… I can also arrange for the papers to be signed for the adoption. We can sign them after I pick you up this afternoon."

Hamilton grasped for words. Blurting anything about Georgia's transformation in front of Wynnie McKenna was not a good plan. Though he felt certain she would give nothing away except to her husband. This was between the two of them. He considered the circumstance to be private.

One of Wynnie's sunset-colored eyebrows lifted before she grinned at him. She understood they kept secrets. It was their prerogative. The more people who knew about Georgia, the better the possibility became that Chandler would find her.

I will stay in your mind today. If there is any trouble, call out to me. I'll be there for you. I'm certain Wynnie will be doing the same with Connal. We must take care all of the time. No risk taking. Understood?

There won't be trouble. You told me Chandler didn't know where I am. He's in London. Wouldn't it take him a few days to get here once he figures this out?

No, he knew nothing the last time I entered his head. I'll continue to check. If he thinks hard, he will figure out where you might have run off too. Bertram should also be able to figure this out. It is obvious if he kens the little village where Harris lived. If not, he will never think of this place. Right now, I believe his mind is centered on obtaining virgins to dally with on his stage. He found his second one right after the debut of Delight.

I don't know. Maybe you shouldn't delve into his head again. I am frightened he will show up unannounced. He terrifies me. Though as we just speculated, it will take a couple of days to reach here from London.

Can't just ask him. That would be detrimental to ourselves. We need to be married before he realizes where you are living. I need to claim you. Must adopt the children. This is the only possible way to go about dealing with Chandler. My biggest question is whether or not he will care enough to come after you. Believe he will choose to get you back. From what you've told me about Chandler, he never allows what he considers his to leave his domain. If nothing else, he will seek revenge on the wrongs he thinks you did unto him.

From all you explained last night, he's got everything he's ever wanted in his little whorehouse. Why would he seek me out even if all you say is true? Doesn't make sense. He's got almost all he's ever wanted. Don't think he cares about the title anymore. He just wants enough wealth to play his games with the lives of unfortunate women. Chandler can have any of the women in the brothel by crooking his little finger. Women, money then power, all three things are what Chandler is all about.

Revenge is why he will seek to find you. If he forgets, don't put it past Bertram to remind him. Chandler is filled with thoughts of vengeance. He doesn't care about you any longer. What he wants is to control you. To keep you from your happiness. He would like to make your life a living hell.

I don't understand anything about Chandler.

Keep your mind open. I'll do what you ask. I'll check into his head.

Don't take any chances.

I won't. I'll be subtle.

Pleased with the turn of events, Hamilton whistled on his way to Father Damian's office. He knew at this moment; Chandler didn't realize where Georgia was living. He felt relief to the tips of his toes. Walking through the rose garden, he wondered if there was anywhere in the village she could find roses for her bouquet. Wished to see those pretty white flowers he didn't have a name for in her bouquet as well. Maybe a garland to go around her head could be fashioned from some exotic orchids. He did have a preference for blue flowers. Would have a better chance of finding roses here than orchids.

Decided he would tell her some of his ideas before they began more planning. He wished to see flowers everywhere in the church as well as in the banquet hall where they would celebrate the union. Liked the idea of her silver garters coupled with the blue ones he would get to take off. Imagined his fingers sliding along the length of her beautifully shaped white legs. Thought the idea a splendid one.

Ah, the cake would be marvelous. Multiple layers interspersed with icing. He thought of breaking a small piece of the confection over her head. He could pick the pieces out of her hair. Should not like a chocolate cake. The dark brown color would blend into her hair. No, a white cake was what they would need.

Traditions…he told her he held all the traditions sacred. Thought of the feast where he would bring his bride to a startling climax right in front of the assemblage. Unlike the shows Chandler put on, no one would know yet everyone would guess. They would guess because this was what traditions were all about. He would need to make certain she screamed her pleasure into his chest or his mouth. He didn't wish for too much embarrassment. A slight shade of pink on her cheeks would be enough as well as fetching.

"Father Damian?" Hamilton was outside the open door looking inside. The good father sat at his desk leafing through papers. After he looked up, he smiled. "I've some interesting news to tell you."

Father Damian stood. Motioned for him to come inside the room. "Come in son, take a seat…your missive said you've something important to speak with me about. I take it this has something to do with Georgia as well as the children. Make yourself comfortable. What have you discovered? Fascinating news?" One snowy white eyebrow lifted in speculation. "Tell me all about it."

Father Damian poured rich black coffee for both of them. "Hope you like this bitter brew. Ever since Roby and his cousin returned from the colonies, coffee has become a favorite of mine. Enjoy the drink rich and black. Nothing in the coffee for me. Would you like cream or sugar…maybe both? Help yourself. Now…" Father Damian handed the cup to him then sat down behind his chair.

"Thought you might wish to write down some of what has happened to Georgia…to us, in one of those journals you've been reading."

Hamilton sipped the coffee, eyeing the priest from over the rim. The brew was strong as well as bitter. He was right about the taste. Didn't know if he would like this better than tea. He wasn't too fond of tea. If something else was being offered, he would pick the other choice. Unless the choice was lemonade. Didn't much care for that drink either. Lemonade was a child's drink.

"What do you think of the coffee? Picks up the spirits, don't you agree? Gives an aging man more energy to use during the day. I've cream," he repeated, "Sugar, if you would like to try some. Makes the coffee not quite so bitter."

"No," Hamilton sipped again, savoring the strong taste. "Could put more hair on a man's chest. Seems to be growing on me. Can say I do like coffee better than tea." Needed to get down to the business he came to discuss.

"Now, what do you have to tell me?" Father Damian shuffled through the journals on his desk, picking up one in particular. He handed the pages to him. "Take a look at this one. The specific article is noticeable. Been doing more reading. Have found another similar case to yours. At least, this one seems much the same."

"Georgia," Hamilton paused, thinking about what he needed to say along with the information he wished to leave out. While he didn't wish to tell him about her maidenhead, he acknowledged the fact he should. The knowledge might help piece together their everchanging relationship. In a little over twenty-four hours, she'd become a different person. "The claiming marks put on her shoulders by the other shifter have disappeared. As we speak now, there is no trace of them. The marks no longer exist. We did expect them to vanish when Georgia told me they were fading. There is something else." Hamilton drummed his fingers on the article he was supposed to read. Stared for a few beats of his heart at the first paragraph. "Can I take this with me? I'll bring the document back first thing tomorrow morning. Wish to sit down and read the words from front to back, perhaps more than once."

"Yes," Father Damian's hands were steepled beneath his chin, his fingers tapping while he appeared to be thinking. "You're right of course. We expected the marks to dissolve into nothingness. As with the other cases, the previous marks all disappeared. There was never a question as to the mate of the lady involved. You are here, meeting with me. You've come to tell me something else has happened?"

"Yes, this is more puzzling than the vanishing marks. To some degree the issue with the marks makes sense. You do know my Georgia is quite heavy with child. She is due soon within a week or two. In fact, the birth could be any day now. We both hope for the wedding to take place prior to the birthing. Don't know if we mentioned the other day she has a daughter who is closing in on a year."

"Two children, that's very interesting. No, don't recall the two of you handing over those facts. Though it was obvious she was with child. Seems we were concerned with more prevalent information." Father Damian was still tapping his fingers together. Still had an intense look of concentration on his face. His brows were drawn together, coupled with deep lines on his forehead. "The information you pointed out is thought-provoking. Yes, I knew she was with child. A person couldn't miss her condition unless they were blind. Understood you are not the father. Don't recall anyone mentioning the second child."

Hamilton growled out the words. "They are both mine. Don't know how the two can be. Deep in my soul, I understand they are mine. Nonetheless, must go about seeing to a legal adoption for both children. Doing this is imperative. You will draw up the legal papers so we can sign them this afternoon?" he asked as a question. Didn't mean it to be one.

"Yes," Father Damian tapped his fingers again. "You wish for them to be yours. You will take care of them as if they came from your seed. That's the kind of man you are…a good man. I will draw up the proper paperwork. The documents will be ready when you return with Georgia. Understand she is shopping with Wynnie for the wedding gown."

Hamilton found himself shaking his head at the father's conclusions about the children. "That's not what I mean. Those two children came from my seed. I've the shifter's intuition about this fact. The children are blood of my blood. Colin speaks with me. He's determined his mother is not harmed. I've made promises to the lad I mean to keep. There is no doubt in my mind the children are mine."

Father Damian's hands came down on his desk. The expression on his face was one of shock. He leaned forward, staring at him as if he could read his mind. "You believe this fact with all your heart? How? I'm not positive I heard you right."

"Yes. Furthermore, this is more puzzling than all the rest. I did make love to Georgia last evening not that I would shout out the news. You need to know this. Georgia possessed her maidenhead. Don't understand how this could be possible. I concluded that just as the marks vanished on her shoulders the tiny piece of flesh proclaiming her innocence grew back. Georgia was meant for me. Somehow, she found herself sidetracked with Chandler." Hamilton found he was watching Father Damian's facial expressions with an intensity he didn't understand. He needed the priest to believe him.

"There is no doubt in your mind? You are a doctor. Would know female anatomy."

Father Damian sipped his coffee. Sat back as if to consider the myriads of possibilities.

"Not one doubt in my mind. I hurt her when I broke through. Not a great deal. For that I'm relieved. Also pleased she is all mine." Hamilton smiled when he recalled the precious moment between them. Never thought the special moment would be his.

"In the other cases I read, there was only one where the mention of the maidenhead was written about. Believe what you told me is correct. How the children can be yours is beyond my rational abilities to explain."

"Neither Georgia nor I could figure out the facts. Yet it's true. I know, beyond any doubt others might have, Colin and Maeve are mine. As I said earlier, blood of my blood. They came from my seed." He let out a long slow breath of air, pleased with the circumstances so far.

"The other person involved with a maidenhead that had grown back didn't have a child. Everything else you spoke of is logical. As you were about to make love to Georgia then call her yours, the world fell into order. It is much the same as when Cameron and Lainie wed. She'd not been claimed by a man nor had she made love with anyone. Nonetheless, another woman traveled through time twice to set things right that had gone astray. I've often wondered what has become of the first Lainie."

"I'm beginning to think, we will have to accept this without an explanation. What has happened here does strain the rational mind. There is no logic, only faith. Suppose that is how many religious beliefs are founded. So far, you, Georgia and myself are the only ones who know. Don't wish for anyone else to get wind of this situation. What has happened is private between the two of us."

"What about the other shifter? You might not be able to keep him silent." Father Damian asked, his silver blue eyes shimmering "He knows about the children. Understands he claimed Georgia once. Was he the first to break through her maidenhead? He will consider the children to be his."

Hamilton shook his head while he considered the possibilities. "I cannot say what he knows. Should do some listening in on his thoughts. I cannot let him realize I'm with him. He might be able to figure out where we are. Though I need to confront the man. Hope the confrontation will be on my terms, not his. Will speak with the McKenna. Would hope he will lend support if Chandler arrives on our doorstep."

"As you just mentioned, the two of you are bound to confront each other at some time unless his recollection of Georgia vanishes altogether. I agree the battle between the two of you should be of your making."

"Yes, I once thought to take the fight to him rather than letting the battle come to me here in Carnoch. Didn't wish for Georgia to be put in danger. Now, however," Hamilton was drumming his fingers on his coffee cup. "Now, knowing I've the power of the Clan Chattan behind me, supporting me, it might be better to have him come here. Once we are wed and Colin is born, believe I'll let him know where we are. Will welcome the end of the situation. Tired of Georgia living in fear."

"The clan will circle Georgia to protect her. If you go to London, this man might have his clan behind him. The fight would be lopsided in the wrong direction."

"He does have a friend who he relies on to have his back. I've learned there are other shifters who work at the whorehouse, who participate in the showings," Hamilton mused as he rolled all the information around in his head. "I would not like to be alone with numerous shifters ready to claw me to shreds."

"My advice. Don't take the battle to him. The odds in this situation are that this man will forget Georgia. Will not be willing to fight for a woman he cannot recall. His memory might take longer to fade. He doesn't have another shifter to occupy his mind. As you explained earlier, he does have a friend who might keep his thoughts pointed in Georgia's direction."

Hamilton found himself nodding his head in agreement with the good father. He planned on a few minutes with Connal now that he spoke with the priest. Connal would need to know the details if the clan were to lend their support. He would need to explain to him most of the specifics.

The rest of the day passed in a blur. By two o'clock the sun came out, sitting low on the horizon. The brilliance was blinding yet beautiful. He visited with Connal. Told him about his fears. The head of the clan promised protection. Hoped this would end without a battle.

He visited the office where he informed both Houston along with Hawk the progress for the wedding. Asked his fellow doctors as well as their wives to be part of the wedding party. His best friends from his youth had all moved on to distant cities. He didn't have the time to visit them in order to ask them to be part of his wedding. They didn't have much time for all the plans to come together. He couldn't leave Georgia by herself even if she had Hollis along with Bea for companions.

Hamilton found a flower store. The owner was pleased to provide all the arrangements needed for the bouquet as well as the decorations for the church along with the banquet hall. He thought Georgia would be pleased with the endeavor. The florist had roses. She would appreciate his efforts on her behalf. All she would need to do would be to visit with the man then pick out the flowers she wanted. He decided he would take her to the little shop tomorrow morning then bring her to the keep to plan menus with Wynnie and the other matrons. Tomorrow he would also visit a jeweler with her so she could choose rings.

By the time he returned to the keep for his wife, the afternoon was beginning to darken, the sun sitting low on the horizon ready to dip behind the craigs. It had taken him most of the day to arrange all that was needed for the ceremony as well as the adoption. Now, what he wanted was to hold her in his arms then make love to her. They still had another visit. The last step in making certain the children could never be removed from his care.

At the keep, he was pleased to see her sipping tea and chatting with the wives. Perhaps they made inroads with the menu. He felt certain she might wish for some Irish food at their celebration. He speculated on her favorite food. Dismissed the thought, thinking he would learn more about her as the days passed. When she ran to him her arms outstretched, he pulled her close then kissed her hard. His tongue swept between her parted lips for a quick taste of her.

When he finally let her down, they were both breathing hard, panting with the quicksilver urgency this brief kiss created. He was too easily aroused. The love shining in her eyes gave his heart a jolt of happiness. Pure and simple, he was blessed to be part of her life.

"Wynnie…thank you for accompanying my fiancée to the dressmakers. I hope she found all she wanted. Tomorrow, I'll take her to the florist then the jewelers. We should be back to the keep by noon. Understand the menus will need to be planned. Today is Tuesday. If the wedding is to take place on Thursday does this give you enough time?"

Wynnie smiled then nodded. "Time is not a problem. If the florist can get everything she wants done by Thursday afternoon, all else will be finished. Her wedding gown will be done by then also."

"Good, then we will set Thursday the nineteenth as our wedding day. We must go see Father Damian to let him know. He will be ready for our signatures on the adoption papers." Hamilton was pleased by the excited expression on Georgia's face.

"The adoption papers?" Georgia asked wide eyed with surprise. "So soon? I thought we might need to wait a day or two."

"Yes, he will have everything in order tonight. The wedding in two days will cement all our wishes into place. The good father will keep the legal documents tucked away in his safe. Maeve and Colin will officially be mine...ours. There will be no need to worry about Chandler taking them from us." With the adoption accomplished, his heart felt lighter...much lighter.

He watched the deep breath of air she wrapped into her lungs. It was obvious she was also relieved by the knowledge. Georgia stood on the tips of her toes. Set a hand on his cheek then kissed him. He was surprised. Pleased by the contact. This was the first time she initiated a kiss.

Hand in hand, they walked to Father Damian's office. Together they met with the priest. Told him when the wedding would take place. Signed the papers then turned toward home to his cottage. Maeve was shrieking when they entered through the front door.

Bea held her out for Georgia, looking flustered and ready to hand the wailing baby to her mother. "Believe the *wee lassie* has had enough of me. She wants her mama along with the snuggle you two always have this time of evening."

"Ah...she just doesn't want another bottle. I see," Georgia murmured.

"Neither would I be happy if I knew what I was missing." Hamilton laughed while he ran his knuckles along her cheek. "What's for dinner? I'm famished."

~ * ~

Bertram sat in a large chair near the fire in Chandler's suite of rooms. He was leaning over, his forearms on his thighs, with his glass of brandy tucked between his hands. "I know where Winter Snow has fled. At least, I believe I've figured out the location. Now, it's up to you to retrieve her. Must decide if you still want her with us. Is there a reason you would have her back? Revenge? To claim your unborn son? Bring your small daughter into the business when she comes of age? You've a million motivations. Will it be worth the danger to have Winter under your thumb again? You must decide. I'll be good with whatever you choose…stand by your side in this endeavor."

"Who?" Chandler asked, a vague recollection of the lady Bertram spoke about dancing around in the back of his head. "Who am I trying to decide to find? My children? You must keep reminding me about this lady along with what I've forgotten. Is this other Winter Snow someone I don't wish to forget? There is the Winter Snow who works for me." Chandler didn't like the idea he was overlooking something important. Chandler didn't recall children with this woman or children at all. Didn't appreciate this feeling of not knowing. What he did understand was the reality his business came first in the scope of his desires. "We need to find some new virgins for the entertainment. What do you think? Noel was a hit, yes. The audience loves her as they do Jamie's Delight. We should present a new virgin once a month. More if we can locate these ladies. They will need to be young. Will need to be initiated into the ways of men. Need to teach them sex is all a woman needs to be content. If she pleases the man, she has performed well."

"Yes, that too. All you are saying is true. Should we see if we can locate Winter? We can search on our way to Carnoch for the perfect virgins. Carnoch is where she is living. Talked to a few people who knew her in the little village where her cottage was located. You are going to find Winter then return her here. On our way, we are certain to find some fathers who will be willing to sell their daughters for a few pounds. Daughters are worthless except for sex or an heir if either is something you would wish for."

"True, we've had abundant luck with virgins. They make fine sexual sacrifices. Our audiences love them. We do need to make certain our virgins are not abused. Must treat them with care. Allow them to struggle if they wish. Fight brings on lust. Some, I will allow to write their script if they are innovative." Chandler sat back in his chair, staring at the flames leaping in the fireplace. Sipped his brandy as he tapped his fingers together. "You believe Winter is in Carnoch? How so? What made you think of that little village in the northern highlands?" Chandler was thinking about virgins, concentrating on how to present them in the best light. New women for their shows, a fine idea. They would have to woo them with gentle ease. He grinned, gaining a wink in return from Bertram. In the past, they'd shared so many women. "I never shared Winter with you. Did I? When I get her back…well…I will enjoy sharing her with you as well as on the auction block. The woman means nothing to me now except more pounds into my bank account."

"Never shared," Bertram said as he rose to walk to the sideboard to fill his glass. "Would you if you got her back? Would you recall how possessive you were? Not certain, even for revenge, a man can change so much."

"Yes. There is no question in mind. I no longer feel the possessiveness I must have felt before. There are times I don't recall the woman. What you've told me is she would hate for me to share her with you. If I recall correctly, she doesn't like you."

"Winter loathed me though I've no idea what I did to bring those emotions about. I was always my charming self to her."

Chandler hooted. "Back to our new virgins. There is no doubt in my mind that if we enlarge our circle where we are searching, we will find more. We must make these new women love sex. They must be hungry to feel a man driving into their bodies. Teaching them to feed on the pleasures of the flesh will be more than enjoyable."

"Feed on the pleasures of the flesh," Bertram seemed to be mulling the thought over in his head. "I like the sound of those words. Strung together they hold the right sexual tones to inflame our audiences. We should have a night dedicated to the theme," he mused. "Feed on the pleasures of the flesh. Brilliant! If we give our virgins a tiny bit of cocaine, they will beg for sex. They will be hot, their bodies inflamed with need. Cocaine is the perfect aphrodisiac."

"Just as I gave Noel a few sniffs of the white powder. She was insatiable."

"When do you want to leave on this quest to bring Winter home to the man who will control her, to manage her every breath?"

Chandler surprised himself. He found he was eager to be on his way.

"Is tomorrow too soon to begin our quest?" Bertram asked as he splashed more brandy into his glass.

"I'll get Celine to pack what we need."

"On our way I will remind you of Winter Snow, our first Queen of the Ice. Tell you of the shows you created just for her. Every month when she performed, her body was more swollen with child. You had her the evening of the birth of her daughter. Winter is yours. We will get her back. Even if you've forgotten the past, you will create new memories with the lady. I won't ever allow you to forget what this whore owes you because of her betrayal."

It was the first overnight stop on the way to Carnoch where they found their first virgins. Chandler, along with Bertram, was eating at an inn about seventy miles from London. Pretty girls were serving them drinks. Their features were so similar, they had to be sisters. Chandler was reminded of Delight. He'd wanted her the moment he saw her. Knew she was a virgin ripe for plucking. She refused him. Women didn't get away with rejecting him. Her brothers beat him to a bloody pulp. He got even. Still had designs on Mackenzie, her sister. Somehow, sometime he would bring the big sister into his fold. Now, as to the serving ladies, he believed perhaps they might not have to kidnap any of these young women. There were two who might be good for their show, possibly three. The third was very young. The next two a bit younger. They all had varying shades of blond hair coupled with deep brown eyes. It was a rare pairing, brown eyes coupled with blond hair. The eldest's eyes were more golden than brown, a golden girl.

"I'll approach the father," Bertram told him. "Will nod if there is a possibility of purchase. We will have quite a bit of time to train the ladies in the ways of amour before we put them on stage. Yes, we must move with slow precision. As you said, we want the ladies to be hungry to experience men or women or both first hand. We want to pleasure them so much they will beg for more. They must be willing to have sex with other females."

Chandler sat back to sip his drink, watching Bertram as he sauntered up to the innkeeper. Not more than ten minutes passed before Bertram nodded for him to meet them. They walked into a back room of the inn. Five girls were lined up against the wall. Two were too young. The next in line was on the edge. She might work out.

"You can have the two or the three oldest if you've a mind. Bertram tells me you will pay five hundred pounds apiece. Is that right?" The man looked over his daughters with a lewd smile. "They cost money. Don't work upstairs for me. They've all refused to be more useful than serving the food. You want any of them. You can have whoever suits your fancy. I'm fed up with all the little sluts their mother birthed. Needed more sons."

Chandler walked down the line. Touched each girl on the cheek. Lowered his hand to brush across a shoulder then a breast. Watched as the first one flinched as did the next two. He stayed away from the girls who were obviously under fifteen even though he knew there was a market for girls of that tender age, even younger. While he always wanted to capitalize on sex, he drew the line with babies. The girls would not be so young in a few years. He should see what transpires.

"How old are these two? Are they virgins? If not virgins, they are not worth five hundred pounds. I'll still give you a small fee if you wish to sell them." He lifted the oldest one's hair. Ran the strands through his fingers. With his hand cradling her chin, he swept his thumb across her mouth. Her lips were soft, very kissable. He did like the way she looked, the way her breasts rose faster as he fondled her. She was golden. He could market her as the Golden Girl.

"These two are virgins. Lilidh, Opal, step forward. Give the men a curtsy. Show them you know how to be polite. The oldest, Màiri, no longer has her maidenhead. She was caught behind the stable with her lover. I beat her for her digression. The little tart couldn't sit for a week."

"How old," Chandler repeated his question, continuing to appraise the girls. He saw money. Lots of pounds from the scripts he could write to the auctioning of their lovely bodies.

"Lilidh is eighteen and Opal here is seventeen. Màiri is nineteen. I would make them all available for your viewing pleasures."

"That won't be necessary. If we decide to buy one or all three, we will do what is necessary to see their sweet, seductive charms. Rest assured we will view them in privacy. You will no longer be part of their lives."

He was walking, studying the girls. He wanted all three. Màiri was by far the most beautiful of all of them. Her breasts fuller, hips more curvaceous. She would be exquisite in harem pants coupled with a bolero. Maybe she could be taught to dance for his audience. His mouth watered to taste her breasts, pink nipples pushing against the fabric of her threadbare gown. He could wait until she was cleaned up.

Though, all three girls were not hard to look at. Since Màiri was no longer chaste, he and Bertram could use Màiri as they pleased. The other girls would be taught just how nice good sex could be. With a few sniffs of cocaine, he would bind them to him in their need for sexual pleasures. Treat them right as long as they participated with enthusiastic abandon. They were young. Malleable. They wouldn't know anything different than what he meant to teach them. He was too hard on Summer Passion. He learned his lesson with Summer's virgin status. The woman despised him. Still, Summer was one of his favorites, also a favorite at his auctions. She always brought top dollar after the show when the men bid to taste her charms.

"A pleasure…all three of your oldest girls. Perhaps in a few years, we'll return for the two youngest. Keep them virgins. I'll give you eleven hundred pounds for the three oldest. That is a fair price since the firstborn has experience. Because of that failing, she is not worth five hundred pounds." He turned to the innkeeper. "What do you say? Do we have a deal?"

"I don't want to leave, Papa. *Chan eil.*" Silver tears ran down Opal's cheeks while she clung to Lilidh. "What do these men want with us? I will be good. Promise. Don't want to leave with them."

The innkeeper slapped her hard. Opal's head jerked back then hit the wall. "How would I know what they want with the likes of you three? They didn't say. I didn't ask. Don't care. I would sell the other two if this man would take them."

With a tiny bit of kindness these girls would fall into his plans. This man beat his oldest. He just witnessed more abuse. His hands behind his back, Chandler rocked on the balls of his feet. Their clothing was ragged and worn. The girls were filthy. He would clothe them in gowns appropriate for whores. Nonetheless, they would own better than what they wore now. Ah…this was heaven. Before anything else happened, the girls needed baths.

Chandler turned to the Innkeeper, "Send up enough hot water for three separate baths. I want a lady who will bathe as well as wash their hair. Do you have someone you can send?"

"Yes," the man appeared surprised by the order. "What would they be needing a bath for?"

"These girls are no longer your concern," Chandler reminded him. He was harsh.

Chandler spoke to the girls. "Go pack a valise. Bertram will be with you. You won't return here…ever." Chandler didn't want to think either of the girls would run. He wasn't going to take the chance after paying the innkeeper. "Bring them to our rooms. We will begin their instructions tonight after the baths."

Turning to the inn keeper, he pulled out his money clip then handed over the allotted amount. "If you hear any crying or yelling tonight, I would advise you not to knock on our doors. Nothing bad will happen to your girls. Keep the two younger ones chaste. I will return for them." Not that the man would care.

"Wouldn't dream of it. Girls are a worthless lot," He mumbled while he walked away counting his money. "Good to poke, nothing more."

Upstairs in their suite of rooms, the girls sat by the fire. They each brought with them a small bag of clothing. Chandler looked them over. The knock caught his attention. Bertram opened the door to a stout lady with graying hair. She smiled.

"I've the bath water. More will come. Believe the girls will not be able to use the same water. When we're finished? What then?" she asked.

"Bring them into the adjoining room." Chandler motioned for the tub to be filled in one the bedrooms. "Bathe them in there. Make certain their hair is also clean." Chandler could never abide dirt.

An hour later, the girls were marched into the main living space. "Hope the gals meet with your approval. Will there be anything else?"

"No, this is nice, very nice." Bertram paid her. "You may go."

"Who should we begin with?" Chandler asked Bertram, knowing the answer. He was enjoying watching the girls. The woman made certain they were dressed. He was pleased. Something his virgins needed to learn was how to please a man. Undressing in front of them was one of the ways.

"The oldest," Bertram replied with a grin. "She's experienced. She's known a man once, maybe more than one time. We can ease ourselves with Màiri. That would be nice before we begin the initiation of the other two. We can use her to fondle her sisters. Teach them what will make them feel pleasure so great they will never want to refuse a man's hand...or a woman's."

"Màiri..." Chandler turned his attention to her. "How many times?"

"Times?" she questioned, her eyes wide, "Oh...only the one time when I was caught. I didn't like what happened. Was forced. Pa didn't believe me. Called me names. It's true though. The man forced me. I told him, no. Fought him. He never listened. He was stronger."

"This time no one will force you. Bertram and I will give you so much pleasure you will beg for more. Keep in mind we own you now. Your father sold you so you could be our plaything. You must do what we say. Obedience is something we insist upon. Do you understand?"

She nodded. Chandler saw the fear in her eyes. He didn't like the look. Might take a great deal of gentle persuasion for her to feel pleasure. They would work on relaxing her so she could enjoy the sex. Nothing tonight would be hard and fast. Slow seduction was the method he had in his mind. He looked at Bertram who seemed to have the same understanding of the situation.

"You want a slow hand with Màiri? May I?" He flexed his fingers then motioned for the girl to come to him.

"I'll watch. First..." Chandler poured a few grains of cocaine in his hand. Walked to Màiri. "Sniff this." She looked at him with wide eyes then did his bidding. Chandler sat back, ready to enjoy the show. Saw the moment the drug took effect.

By the time the two finished with Màiri, the sister's eyes were wide pools of dark brown. Chandler wasn't certain if the expression was fear or fascination. Màiri did moan, did cry out her pleasure when Bertram brought her to climax.

"Lilidh come here." Bertram ordered with a soft voice.

She didn't move. Had the look of a frightened animal in her eyes. Chandler thought he would need to soften the approach even more. An easy-going style was not something either of them was used to. They would need to be indulgent of the fear until they understood there was nothing to be frightened of.

"Come here, sweetheart. I'm not going to hurt you. Just make you feel pleasure so great you won't be able to refuse. You'll be surprised at the sensations you're going to have when I touch you in ways you've never dreamt about. If we do something that scares you, tell me." One more time he held out his hand. "Sniff the drug. It will ease your way."

Lilidh looked to her sister then back to him. She forced her gaze to return to Bertram. He saw her swallow hard. Appeared she was going to do as he asked. On wobbling legs, Lilidh stepped forward. Breathed in the white powder. Stood in front of Bertram. He placed his hands on her shoulders then turned her to face the oldest of the three.

"Good girl," he told before turning to Màiri, "unfasten Lilidh's gown. Let the dress fall to the floor. She won't need clothing tonight. Your sisters need to get used to being naked in front of an audience. Just as you are growing used to us seeing you in your…natural state."

Màiri nodded. Frown lines marred her forehead. Her naked breasts swayed when she walked to her sister. The girl was beautiful. Her legs were long and white, well-shaped. The color of her woman's mound was a bit darker than her wheat-colored hair. When Bertram made love to her, she cried out when she reached that special pinnacle of ecstasy, her hips bucking with the pleasure he gifted her with.

"There you go. That's right," Bertram said, keeping his voice gentle. His grin was one of satisfaction when the gown pooled to the floor around Lilidh's feet. "The rest of her clothing must come off."

Lilidh's breasts were not as large as Màiri's. She was still young, only eighteen. They would grow to be as sweet as her sister's. Her father signed the contract that gave these females to him for the next ten years. By then they would have nowhere to go. So far, Chandler was pleased with his purchases. Perhaps he should have made the contract for twenty years. The oldest would only be thirty-nine then.

"Now the chemise."

Màiri followed the order. Lilidh stood in front of them shaking, naked except for her slippers and stockings. The girl didn't refuse. Seemed to understand he owned her. She was coltish. Slim. Would fill out as the years passed. "Take everything else off." He waited. She stood, shivering trying to cover herself with her hands. "Suck on her breasts, Màiri. Make her feel the same ecstasy Bertram gave you."

"Oh!" Màiri looked stunned. "Me?"

"Now," Chandler tried for a gentle tone despite the impatience plaguing him. He was so hard he thought he would burst before he could ease himself with Màiri. Sex with the oldest would come later tonight. If Màiri told the truth and she had only been with one man, she might be sore. He didn't care. His needs came first.

Watching the older sister suck on her sibling's breast was titillating in the extreme. Where he was sitting, Chandler crossed his arms and watched fascinated by the unfolding scene. He felt himself growing harder with each passing second. This was what dreams were made of. Lilidh wasn't going to be able to stand much longer. He was going to have to remember this scenario for future shows.

"Take her to the bed. Lie down with her. Keep sucking on her breasts. I want to hear her moan with the good feelings you are giving her. Pleasure her with your mouth. Yes, that's the way to go forward."

From her chair near the fire, Opal whimpered. The littlest one would be more difficult to train. He might consider waiting until the other two could explain to her how wonderful the lovemaking was. No, he shouldn't put anything off for another day. Tonight, would be the time for Opal's introduction to sensual pleasures. The cocaine would ease the girl over the threshold.

There needed to be more pleasure. "Lilidh needs to feel a man's tongue inside her mouth. Want her aroused until she begs for more ecstasy. Need to view her body writhing with need. When that happens, we can move on to the little one here." Chandler was focused on Bertram. He would do what was asked with pleasure.

The girls were lying side by side. Màiri sucking on Lilidh's breasts while Bertram captured her mouth with his. Kissed her in slow increments. Touched his tongue across her mouth. Kissed her forehead then the tip of her nose. Returned to her mouth. Chandler found himself fascinated with the arching of her hips along with the restless moving of her legs. Lilidh was aroused. He was pleased with the outcome. Small feminine noises added to the enchantment. Opal's eyes were wide with wonder.

Chandler imagined the penetration, then the retreat of Bertram's tongue. Heard the next whimpers of pleasure being fulfilled from Lilidh. She arched again seeking more. Her heels dug into the bed as she arched. Lilidh wouldn't know what the feeling was. She would learn. Bertram's lips roved down her neck. Placed light kisses along her collarbone before returning to her mouth. He was gentle. Tender.

"Put Lilidh on her back. Spread her legs, Màiri. I think it's about my turn to become part of this play."

On her back, legs spread to accommodate him, Lilidh made a wanton picture. Màiri continued her focus on Lilidh's breasts while Bertram worked her mouth that was now swollen from the sweet attention.

"Change positions," Chandler ordered, knowing the hot suck of Bertram's mouth on Lilidh's breasts would make her buck with her pleasure. Bertram would know how to bring this seduction to the next level.

It was just as he thought. Lilidh cried out with the first hard suck on her breast. Chandler came between her legs. His hands beneath her rump, he lifted her. Lilidh was making tiny mewling noises in the back of her throat, hips arching. He nipped on the insides of her thighs then moved to her most intimate place.

He licked her sweetness. Tongued her damp folds. Lilidh was hot with the sultry drippings from her core. He nuzzled, shot his tongue inside her. Bit the tiny jewel of pleasure between her legs. Lilidh jerked then moaned deep in the back of her throat. Her raw desire obvious.

"Please…" Her head thrashed back and forth on the pillow. "Please…please…do something."

Chandler sent his finger inside her. Felt the evidence of her innocence. Lilidh was a gold mine for them. He hoped Opal would be innocent too. The girl was only seventeen. Thought of Maeve when she came of age.

Who the devil was Maeve?

Chapter Ten

Georgia stood by Hamilton, his arm lending support. The wedding ceremony in front of the doors of the church had been attended by at least one hundred smiling people from the village. Some of them were Hamilton's patients', others were friends of his from his earlier days along with family. Hollis and Bea were there. Bea held Maeve in her arms.

Inside the church the ceremony was more serious. Father Damian spoke in Latin. At least that was what she thought. She didn't understand any of the words. He pronounced them husband and wife. By the time they entered the small room where they would be naked, her knees were shaking.

Just as Hamilton told her he would do, he undressed her beneath the white cape Wynnie brought for her to wear. After he finished and she was naked, she undressed him. She was happy they made love before this. Now she only had one thing to fear. Standing against him if they'd not been intimate, their skin touching, would have been disconcerting.

His hands were around her waist. A few seconds later, he held her rump with both hands, pulling her close. She felt the rigid length of him against her. Knew his arousal was real. Within his strong arms, she shivered. Felt her breasts push against the hardness of his chest.

"This will be over soon. Promise. Don't worry. I know you are frightened. Can feel your fear. It's tangible." Hamilton kissed the top of her head. Held her close. "Not going anywhere. I'll be here for you."

Georgia heard the chanting. Father Damian was beside them. Again, the words were undiscernible. Leaning against Hamilton, her head began to spin along with the walls in the room. She felt as if she was swept off her feet looking down upon the two of them. They were different from before. The ceremony continued. Felt the hot wind blow against her. Water dashed around her. The earth tumbled. To steady herself, she closed her eyes.

During this time while they were beneath the cloaks and the good father chanted, she saw his cat. Hamilton was beautiful, sleek and black. Strong as well as powerful. In real life, he hadn't yet shown her his cat nor she hers. They would show each other their other forms soon, possibly tonight.

Always, as the scenes in front of her changed, there was a male tiger lurking close by. The second cat made her nervous. She didn't wish to see him any longer. Four different scenes were shown to her. Each one was different from the last. Every scenario seemed to come closer to this time. The white tiger leapt at them. Could never reach her. The black panther always stepped in front of her. Protected her.

Her nails bit into his arms. Silence filled her head before she heard the rustle of feet passing by them. The pagan ritual was finished. She was on the floor in Hamilton's arms. The ground was cold. He ran his hand along her back in an attempt to soothe the trembling of her body. She shook with exhaustion.

"Hamilton…" Georgia tried to say his name.

The sound was a whisper in the cold room. The floor where they were sitting was freezing. She heard her moan of pain. The feeling she would never be the same again intensified. The ceremony changed her. Made her different in many different ways.

"Hush, sweet…you don't need to say anything. Rest. I'll be right here with you. When you feel stronger, I can get you dressed. Are you dizzy?"

He pulled the cape tight to her. Tucked the edges around her body as he pulled her to sit on his lap. "I'm c-cold. The walls were spinning earlier." She opened one eye then the other. "No, not any longer, the walls are just fine now."

"I assumed as much. Snuggle in against me. I'll warm you." His small chuckle of amusement didn't sit well with her. He seemed to sense the annoyance. "Sorry," he mumbled. "Realize this wasn't easy for you. Just so pleased for the ceremony to be done. Soon you will have no more fears."

Against the heat of his chest, Georgia closed her eyes again. Felt her lashes sweep across his warm flesh. Hamilton would want to know what she saw. She couldn't speak now. Her throat was raw.

She didn't know how much time passed. Her shivers were harder now than before. Shaking from head to toe, she couldn't seem to relax. Didn't know if she was cold, nervous or both. Unable to do anything else, Georgia clung to him, her nails biting into his shoulders. She fought for warmth.

"Georgia," Hamilton sounded concerned. "I've got to get you dressed. We need to leave this room. Must get you warm. Don't want you to freeze to death on your wedding night."

With a free hand Hamilton ran his hand the length of her unbound hair. Tonight, their wedding night, she let her hair fall down her back. Hamilton liked the long black strands loose.

Her teeth were shattering so hard she couldn't talk. Her nose pressed against his shoulder. Caught his scent. Loved the way he smelled, powerful as well as confident, all male.

Hamilton seemed to understand some of her issues. "Nod your head if you know what I'm saying."

She could do what he asked. Nod.

"I'm going to dress you. Got to get you warmed up." He stroked her, brought the cloak around them. "Realize you are too fragile to do this by yourself."

Her nod was weak, her teeth chattering louder. Picking her up, he set her on top of his cape. Naked, she tried to wrap her arms around herself trying to warm her body. Seemed her arms were having trouble moving. Even though she'd been forewarned, she didn't understand the horrible weakness assailing her.

With quick deft movements he rid her of the cape then slipped her chemise over her head. Decided to leave the corset behind. He could send Bea to gather the garment after he entered the hall to celebrate the nuptials. Had trouble with her stockings. Once the wedding gown was on her, the sash didn't want to cooperate. She knew he wanted her to wear the sash.

With each second that passed by, Georgia grew stronger. She was warmer now. Her flesh no longer felt like ice. The thought she was queen of the ice flashed in her mind. No! No longer. She concentrated. Georgia was able to help him tie the sash. If not, she was certain Wynnie would assist. Keeping the cape around her, she sat in a chair while he dressed. When she felt the tightening constriction of her stomach, she chose to ignore the minor pain. Didn't want to tell Hamilton. The contraction was more than likely a false one. Wanted her wedding night to proceed as planned. All the traditions being met were important. Hamilton needed to claim her before the birth.

"Hamilton," that was the first word she'd been able to say without her teeth chattering so hard, his name came out in a strange way.

"Georgia?" He grinned at her. "Like it when you say my name. While you do look better, doubt if you are up to walking through the rose garden. Ah...another time we'll walk with a slow measured pace through the gardens. This summer we will enjoy all the roses. You can touch the soft petals to your cheeks. By the way, your bouquet was beautiful. The main hall will be filled with flowers. I'm eager to see your selections."

"You're teasing me about your name. This is the first time my teeth weren't chattering so bad you could understand me."

"Can you tell? Believe we are ready to leave here. Say good bye. We won't be back unless someone we are close to is in need of the ritual. You say Bea and Hollis are shifters? Has either one found their mate? They aren't getting any younger." Hamilton scooped her up into his arms. Striding from the church, he walked with her.

"We are done with the ceremony. Now all we have to do..." Georgia mulled over his words. She'd thought at one time, her father put the pair together for a reason. Neither one mentioned anything. "I don't know about Hollis and Bea. Do you think...?"

"As you just admitted, I have no idea. Perhaps they were waiting until our lives were fulfilled. Now, as to the ceremony, you must tell me what you saw. Not now though. Tonight, when we are alone in the privacy of our wedding suite."

He kissed her lips. The contact was light, airy.

She shuddered against him, thinking of the wedding night to come...the claiming. She wished for the remaining ritual to take place as soon as possible.

"I will tell you everything. Need to rest though. Still do not have my strength back. What will happen next? You will carry me into the hall. I comprehend I am still having trouble putting one foot in front of the other."

She was curious. Recalled him speaking of a tradition he meant to engage in while they sat at the table set aside for them.

Georgia's Rebellious Heart

"We will drink champagne when the clans toast to our marriage. After we sip, we will eat what we can. There will be more food in the bridal suite. When we cut the cake, I'll drop some of the pieces on your head."

She stiffened. Cake in her hair was not something she thought to enjoy. "I would rather you didn't partake of that custom. Don't want icing in my hair." She was not liking that particular practice at all. "If you do..."

"You can't reach the top of my head." He laughed then pulled her close. "Don't intend to bend over so you can."

She nipped his chin. "I would find a means to do so even if I have to stand on a chair," she retorted, all bravado. To stand on a chair she would need help. "If it's good for me then the same should be good for you."

"Can't argue with your statement. Maybe we'll forget that custom...the cake in the hair." Hamilton juggled her in his arms. Found a way beneath her skirt so he could caress tender flesh. She sipped air at the contact.

"I can walk," she told him, though she wasn't truthful. Since the first contraction she'd not had another. A sigh of relief swept through her. Tomorrow or the next day would be soon enough to have the baby. She yearned for the fulfillment of their wedding night.

"Not on your life." He kissed her, captured her mouth with his. "Are you getting warmer, lass? Don't like this chill I'm still feeling."

"Yes, I'm warmer. If you keep kissing me, I'm bound to heat all the way through, even to my ears." Georgia rubbed her cheek on his chest. Longed for a kiss. Understood she might need to wait until he was no longer carrying her.

"Can't kiss you if you don't look up." He read her mind.

She did. Hamilton stopped. Smiled at her parted lips. She swept her tongue across them, knowing he would understand her need. The kiss was longer, more potent than she expected. She opened wider for him, letting him pull her tongue inside his mouth. They played for a few beats. When she shivered again, he stopped the kiss to look at her. Touched the tip of her nose with his lips. "There will be more kisses later. Count on the fact."

She nodded as she felt the heat travel through her. "I'm warming up. Maybe one more." She told him, not wishing for him to end the intimacy. She shuddered, "what you must have felt was not from the cold."

Looking down on her, he grinned. "Good. We are almost there. I'll continue to warm you up until you are as hot as the sun," he warned as he barked a laugh. "I will give you pleasure soon. You will be hotter, panting with your need. I will see to the heating of your beautiful person."

"How? There are too many people in the main hall. Don't like what you are telling me." When she saw his features highlighted by moonlight she hit his chest. Georgia understood he would do as he pleased. Wasn't certain she cared. Maybe she wished for this tradition to take place as much as he did. "You are wicked. You would not..." She found her voice trailing as she began to realize this was the tradition Hamilton spoke of. The one he was not about to disregard.

"Pleased with my bride. You will be splendid beneath the table. All hot and wet, ready for my undivided attention. Should I check before we enter the main hall to see if you are ready for me now, this instant. My fingers are so close. I won't come inside you except with my fingers...my naughty fingers. What do you think of my plan? You will reach that splendid pinnacle with no one the wiser for my efforts."

Georgia snorted, thinking this plan of his was more than one sided. "What about you? I should see that you howl your pleasure in front of all those assembled tonight."

"Ah...you can try. I might not object if you closed your small fingers around my sex. Believe I would enjoy the wicked sensations too. Are you brave enough to try? I would howl with my delight. All eyes would be turned our way. All assembled to celebrate with us would understand what you did to your trusting groom."

The heat of her blush would be staining her cheeks right now. She still thought to reach beneath his kilt. Wanted to show Ham she could be both bold as well as audacious. Regaining her strength, she felt as if she should surprise him. Maybe she could find a way to disconcert him as well. Was struck with the thought he would be bloody hard to embarrass.

"We shall see," Georgia told him, smiling at him. Tapped her lashes down for a moment's blink. "We shall see," she repeated.

Finding a way to shock him, seemed to be taking the forefront of her thoughts.

"I'll wager you will not try," he whispered close to her ear, touching the outside then finishing with a startling nip. "You are not courageous enough to put yourself out on a limb so perilous. Are you sweet? Are you so bold you would give me my male pleasure in front of our friends?"

She squeaked. Thought doing so would be more than pleasant. She wished to surprise him. "I will do more than try. I can be daring."

He didn't know how bold she could be. Her hand smoothed across his chest while she wished she could move her fingers lower, touch him. She toyed with the fasteners on his shirt. Opened several then swept her hand along his hard male flesh. Her palm found the small, hard tip of his breast. The small pleasure also ignited her.

Georgia was pleased beyond measure when he groaned, low as well as husky in the back of his throat. The foreplay began. He laved kisses down the column of her throat. Set his mouth on the place that seemed to throb out of control. Sipped on the tender flesh he found at the frenzied spot.

Flicking open more buttons, she touched her tongue to his collarbone. Licked. Took a small bite of his shoulder. Smoothed with her cheek. Georgia loved the way his skin was smooth there. Toyed with the soft hair on his chest. Enticed, she hoped.

"Little witch, I can beat you at this game you are playing. Have had much more experience than you," he told her before setting his hand on her breast. Ran his thumb across the tip, once then twice. "You will be the death of me yet," he murmured, returning to her ear to the sensitive places behind, then following a path along her jaw until he reached her mouth. "Do you want a kiss or to keep playing?"

He stayed there for a few beats of her heart, seeming to wait for an answer. Continued to play with the hard tip of her breast. She whimpered with the heated attention. Her tiny mewl drifted from the back of her throat, hovering for a moment in the air. With his teeth, he tugged on her bottom lip. Without hesitating, she opened for him. Sent her tongue inside his parted lips. Rubbed hers across the velvet softness that was his. Heard Ham's growl of raw pleasure as she seemed to also find sensitive spots to excite.

"Devil…" she retorted when his lips left hers to explore more sensitive territory. "Don't go away."

He continued caressing her breast. Seemed he didn't plan on stopping. By the second, Georgia found she was growing stronger. Thought she might be able to walk. Didn't wish to lose the wonderful contact or the heat of his large body. She no longer felt the debilitating weakness that enclosed her. He slid his hand along her legs, reached higher to discover more tender areas.

She ached for him. Didn't know how she was going to survive the night with his ever-questing fingers touching in profound places. He understood what would excite her the most. When she brought her fingers up to caress his cheek, her hand shook with the pleasure he created. Hamilton was always generous in his lovemaking. Never held anything back.

"We are here. Will you fasten my shirt?" He chuckled at the face she made for him. Fastening the shirt was not something she wished to do. She liked the openness, his chest revealed to her. Enjoyed the scene just the way he appeared now.

All her handiwork would be undone. She would need to do everything a second time. Well, she did have a proposition for him, "If you will remove your fingers from beneath my gown, I would consider your request."

She didn't want his hand to leave her rump where he'd just been caressing, squeezing as if to make his point. She would reach her pleasure while they were feasting. At one point, he would slip his fingers between her legs. She wasn't going to argue. Acknowledged she would bury her face against his chest when she shattered with ecstasy. In some way she looked forward to the event.

"Must I?" He squeezed one side then sighed as if he too didn't want to change the position of his hands. With slow intimacy, moved his fingers down her thigh to her ankle before slipping his hand around her waist. Set her dress to cover her ankles. "Don't want to stop. Need my fingers to be where they were a moment ago."

She whimpered when he fondled her intimately then left her needing more of his attention. "You must," she told him as she fastened the last button on his shirt then closed the velvet jacket he wore. She was thinking along the same lines as he was. Wished they could go straight to the rooms where they would finish the lovemaking. Acknowledged the traditions needed to be seen to. Traditions…all the customs were what Ham told her he wished for. She wished for them too.

Another contraction tightened across her stomach. She didn't know how many minutes passed since the first one. He told her this second child of hers would arrive sooner than her first. Didn't know what to do. Needed to keep this from him as long as she could. Must make it through the feast. At least until the women came for her. She would tell Wynnie as soon as they reached the bridal suite. Wynnie would retrieve Hamilton with no fuss. All would be well. No, Ham must claim her before the birth. The doctor in him might not understand the necessity. The shifter would.

"You are hot and slick. Our wedding night cannot come soon enough." He touched her mouth with his.

As long as Ham didn't touch her stomach when a contraction hit, she would be able to keep the news of the impending birth a secret. The pain was barely there. If she had not had a child before this one, she might not have noticed what was happening to her body.

They entered the main hall to a roar of cheering. Everyone was glad to see them. The McKenna stood on the dais that would be their place to eat with his hand in the air. Connal held a glass of champagne in his hand.

"Let the traditions begin. Fond memories will be made this evening. To the newlyweds," he called out, his voice ringing over the cheers of the clan, "And to those all-important customs that must be seen to. Where would we be without the essential decisions?" Connal winked at them.

One more time, Georgia felt the heated rise of the blush she realized would be obvious for all to see. She found herself burying her face against Ham's chest. Wished to get through all this fanfare as soon as possible. She shuffled in a reluctant piece of air, wishing her breaths would be easier.

"Look up sweetheart. All wish to see that you've recovered sufficiently to celebrate. The sweet rosy bloom on your cheeks will please all who are looking at you. We will eat then dance. After we share dances the cake will be cut. Look, there are flowers everywhere. The scent of fresh cut roses permeates the air. Is all this to your liking?" Ham moved his hand through the air indicating the entire room was bathed in flowers.

Georgia smiled then waved at those assembled to rejoice their union. Hamilton set her down on the dais next to Connal. They were handed glasses of champagne. They drank to another round of applause. After setting her glass on the table, Hamilton swept her into his arms then pleased his welcoming audience with a hard, swift kiss.

"Thank you, all of you." Hamilton held up her hand with his. "This evening, we plan to honor all traditions of the Clan Chattan."

There was another roar of applause then the chant, "Kiss her...kiss your bride. Kiss her."

"Don't mind if I do," he roared over the noise of the crowd then lifted her chin. She watched the silver shimmer of his eyes darken. "Kissing you is never a problem," he told her his voice a soft whisper in the noisy hall.

He did kiss her. This time the contact was not hard and fast. Hamilton investigated with easy touches, the relaxed brushing of his mouth on hers. He explored then nibbled tender territory. Searched with loving finesse more sensitive evocative spots. Sent his tongue deep inside her parted lips. Penetrated then retreated with such slow precision Georgia melted into him, her hands clinging to his shoulders. She heard the tiny feminine mewls that floated in ribbons from the back of her throat, seeming to enclose the two of them with their warmth. When he pulled away from her, a hair's breadth away, the smile on his face was gentle as well as tender. He kissed her one more time to satisfy their audience. Settled his lips on hers. She responded in depth while his kiss continued to scorch her soul.

His touch never failed to mesmerize every part of her. Touched her soul deep. Their meeting was profound. Didn't wish to think about the future of her life without this caring man. She was his in every way as well as any way he wanted her. She would see to him the best she could for the rest of their lives.

Hamilton pulled away. She sent her tongue across her swollen mouth. With temperate concern, he followed the path with his thumb. The tenderness of his gaze spoke of his love for her. Even the way he looked at her now, as if he wished to devour her, set her heart to pound harder.

"Let's eat. Need to move on to the most enjoyable parts of the evening. If I don't stop now, we will need to run up those steps without the parting customs of the evening. I want to see you wearing nothing at all. Want it now. This instant. Despite the need, don't wish to be patient. We must."

Hamilton pulled out the chair for her. Stunned from the emotions of the evening boiling around her, simmering deep inside, she sipped in a deep breath of air. Her lungs filled with the scent of Hamilton. The wonderful man filled her senses. This was an evening she never intended to forget. The night was theirs to cherish.

Georgia found she was hungry, yet her stomach rolled in undulating waves. Her energy returned in small increments. Ham's fingers found hers beneath the table, winding together, his with hers. Caressed the tender flesh between them. More heat rushed within to pool in the most intimate parts. She felt as if she was going up in flames. The magic was mercurial pleasure intensifying with each quicksilver breath of air.

"If you don't wish to eat, we can move on to something else." He waggled his eyebrows at her, smiling.

She knew what he meant. What he was thinking. Setting her hand beneath his kilt, she moved fingers higher on his leg. Found his eyes narrowed as she approached his most sensitive territory. He stopped her. Brought her hand back to rest on top of the table. Wasn't going to allow her fingers to sightsee his manly endowments. Perhaps later, she would try again.

"That was quite far enough for now, my sweet highland *lassie*. Later, after we are upstairs in the bridal suite, you may discover whatever you would like. Touch as well as fondle me anywhere that pleases you." He placed a piece of bread with cheese atop on her lips. "Bite. You need sustenance for the evening adventures into our carnal pleasure."

Chewing then swallowing, she followed his orders. All types of dishes were brought to the table. Scottish as well as traditional Irish food arrived. She found herself wondering who was going to eat all this on the table. There was too much food for two people. Too much for one because she found she wasn't hungry for food. She was ravenous for Hamilton.

"Take a sip of the champagne, sweet," he told her as he did the same. She was thinking about the drink. Recalled his words about alcohol. He must have realized what she was thinking. "We won't drink very much, just a few tiny sips. This is the wedding feast. How are you feeling? Any cramping? No?"

As the doctor he was, he set his hand on her swollen belly. She felt nothing since that last tightening about two hours ago. The sensation wasn't a contraction, just a tightening of her muscles. The babe would not come tonight. Several days had passed since she arrived here in Carnoch, since the first sensation. This must be nothing to worry over. He told her the birth could be two more weeks away, even three. Beneath his broad hand, Ham would feel Colin move. Now that they were wed and after tonight when he set his marks on her, she wished for her son's birth. Didn't want to wait a week or even a day. Tomorrow would be a wonderful day for Colin to be born.

"What are you thinking?" Hamilton asked after he sipped some champagne.

He didn't pause for her to answer. Wouldn't have told him no, no matter what she knew or thought about the babe. "I'm thinking you would look lovely wearing the bubbly."

She stared at him with wide eyes. Tilted her head a little to the side, wondering what he meant. "Wearing Champagne? What do you mean?" She asked, thinking she might have an idea as to his thoughts. Discounted the notion as being absurd.

Oh, I do believe you might have an idea or two. Would enjoy your thoughts on the subject. Tell me…no…wait a moment, I'll explain to you my exact contemplations. Something we can do once we are alone. When we do not have an audience. That won't be soon enough by my way of thinking. Hope to have you wearing the champagne sooner than will be possible. Unfortunately for us, we have traditions to manage our way through.

You would pour the champagne on me then sip it off? No… Georgia found herself shaking her head, then her body quivered at his cheeky words, yet appreciating the idea. After a moment's thought, she realized he would pour the drink on her then sip the bubbly, her body flamed to life again.

Yes, you are thinking in the right way. You've got the idea and I didn't need to prompt you. Your lips would be a wonderful place to begin with the drops. Then each nipple, one at a time of course. I would move lower. Pour a drop or two on your belly. Lower still. Might put some between your legs in the sweet place we already know is enticed by my tongue along with my teeth when I fondle.

Georgia gasped air. More heat rushed to her cheeks. Set her hand there hoping to cool the rush of blood, felt her breath strain in her lungs. Saw him between her legs lifting her so he could watch her while he suckled. She had ideas of her own.

I would do the same to you. Would start with your mouth. Just as you mentioned, then move on to your collarbone, lower to attend to each hard little male nipple. Your navel would be next. She went on to say more intoxicating words. *Then...the tip of your sex. I would suckle there until you moaned with all the pleasure I would give.*

"Enough, you've made your point. Are you finished eating? I find I need to move on to more explorations beneath the table."

"If you discover sensitive territory then so will I. Not going to allow you to go away unscathed. A woman has rights too."

She smiled sweetly. Dropped her napkin. As gracefully as she could with her swollen belly, she dipped beneath the table. Came between his legs, pressing them to separate.

Hamilton set his hand on her head as if he didn't wish for her to pull away. She felt the tension created by her provocative move.

I needed my napkin. Next you will be glad I retrieved the little scrap of fabric. She placed a kiss on his knee, each one. *Believe I told you about your bonny knees.* Traveled higher with her caresses, along the inside of his thighs. He lurched then shuddered from the contact. *These are places, I could dribble champagne. Are you excited with desire? Hungry for me to taste you? Here? Or here?*

Her hands ran along his hard thighs until she reached the apex where she paused, her fingers barely touching. For a few beats of her heart, she cupped him. Fondled the spheres. Heard his masculine groan of pleasure rumble from deep in his chest. Realized he tried to keep the sound behind his teeth. She'd never stroked him there, in this sensitive spot. Understood he appreciated her endeavors to tantalize.

His fingers wound through her hair, tension building. Hamilton made no move to pull her away from his sex. She heard the stifled sounds of pleasure when she took him into her mouth. Knew when he'd reached his limit. His fingers tightened on her scalp, nails scraping. Pulled her from beneath the table. Buried his face between her breasts when she felt the rush of warm air across the valley between her breasts. With her hand she continued her explorations of his member. He exploded. Jerked. His seed would cover his belly

Where is that napkin?
Do you wish for me to clean you?
No! Little sorceress. I will do the job. After I finish, it's your turn.
Alright.

She felt humbled by the intensity of his pleasure. Georgia discovered she was looking forward to the seduction beneath the table. Pleased she satisfied Ham. She also wanted to feel the shattering of all her nerves into billions of fragments. She loved him so much. Would do anything for her new husband. He could request anything from her. She would give him her all.

"Now…" he said after a few seconds to get his breath. "Where should I begin? You are quite a tempting lady."

"Suppose anywhere you would like to start. I'm ready for so much more." *Need to feel you deep inside me. Wish to be alone with you. Don't much like waiting.*

His hand rested on her thigh. His fingers inched her gown higher. Cool air caressed her legs as he unveiled them. She separated her thighs for him, eager for the finishing touch on this tradition of his. Impatient to move on with the night.

She gasped when he touched her intimately. At the same time, he captured her lips with his. Her hand rested on his chest, kneading the material of his shirt. He sent two fingers inside her while his thumb enticed the hidden pearl.

~ * ~

When she whimpered into his chest, Hamilton grinned with the success of his activities. Her quick response always pleased him. He caressed her softness with broad strokes then tender ones. Felt her hips move to take more of his fingers inside her delicious core. She would shatter soon. Reach the sun with the heat of her release. He wished to send her to the sun then back.

Hamilton wanted to be alone with her. Needed to sip champagne from her nipples, the sensitive petals between her long, white legs. Understood he would need to wait for those moments. When he felt her reaching that desired high, he held her head against him while she buried her nose against his chest.

She was breathing hard now. With his hand along her back, he soothed her. Felt her shudders begin to relax.

Are you alright?

I will be, given enough time. I'm still shaking. My God, even my ears are hot.

You realize one custom has been finished. As soon as you feel fit enough to dance, we will begin the festivities. The Frasiers will expect a dance. You will need to oblige Connal as well. Houston too, as one of my partners, will wish to have his turn on the dance floor.

All those people?

Yes, it won't be so bad. As soon as those obligations have been seen to, we will cut the cake. Wynnie, along with the other married ladies, will take you upstairs to the bridal suite. Don't know what goes on there but as soon as the ladies deem you ready for me, Wynnie will return to retrieve me, the handsome groom.

Georgia giggled. He enjoyed the sound of her laughter. Still holding her close, he reveled in the amazing feelings she ignited within. Never expected this wonderful woman to come into his life. Had all but given up finding his mate. Did not know how he could live without her. She brightened every one of his days since they met.

"Tell me when you are revived." He ate some of the Shepperd's pie that was set in front of him. Put a fork full next to her mouth. She moaned but ate. "Need your energy. We've a full night ahead of us. Don't want you fainting in the middle of…" he left off staring at the commotion at the front door of the keep.

When he set the next bite in front of her lips, Georgia shook her head. "Can't," she told him. "My stomach."

"That's understandable. Are you nervous?"

Hamilton tried not to focus on the two men sauntering toward them. How the devil did these two manage to intrude on this celebration. Even though he'd only seen the men in his mind, he knew who they were. How did they finagle their way through the locked gate. He didn't know how to tell Georgia she needed to take care. Looked for someone who could escort her to the upstairs room where she would be safer.

"Very," she told him, her voice soft. "Must I dance with all those people? I don't think I have the energy. Maybe just you and Connal? The two of you should be enough to satisfy everyone as well as all the customs. No one would be too disappointed, would they?"

"Imagine if that's what you want, the others will need to understand your wishes."

The men of the clan surrounded the two intruders. Walked with them toward the dais. What on earth did this pair have in mind? If they thought to do anything untoward, they would die this night. The two were outnumbered by more than hundreds.

"Thank you." When she started to stand, he put his hand on her shoulder.

"Not yet. Seems we have unwanted company. Stay here. Don't say a word. I will do all the talking. There is no need for you to be part of this confrontation." He hoped she wouldn't recognize the pair.

"What?" She gulped when she saw Chandler along with Bertram standing in front of them. "No…" her whispered words died on her lips.

Hamilton regretted that both men found their way to Carnoch. Regretted a lot of things at this moment. Thought security at the keep was better. These two should not have been able to enter. The gates should have been closed to the two men. Sassenach, except for the related ones, were not welcome. He stood, the flat of his hands resting on the table.

"What do you want?" Hamilton thought to get straight to the point. "You're not welcome here. As you can tell I can command that you be thrown from the keep."

"At first, I thought to come for my daughter," Chandler told him. "She's still a baby. Believe I'll wait until she is thirteen. Maeve will fit right into my stable of women. If she's as passionate as her mother, she will command the best prices at the auctions. I will sell her body to the highest bidder every night. Of course, her name will be changed. I have several years to think of the perfect moniker for her."

"No…" Georgia's weak protest left the hair on the back of his neck standing on end.

"If you take my daughter, you'll die a slow horrible death." Hamilton was surprised when Chandler didn't correct him.

"I see my boy has yet to be born. Will come after him when he's old enough to teach him my ways," Chandler smiled around the room, seeming content to antagonize one and all. "Perhaps the best show would be one of him having sex with his sister."

"I like your idea. The thought tantalizes all my male parts. Makes me stand up then pay attention," Bertram added as he rubbed his hands together. "Colin could take his sister's virginity. At twelve I'm certain he will be old enough. That would make Maeve thirteen. Perfect."

"Come with me now, Winter." He held out his hand. "If you come with me willing and eager to be my bedmate, I might not introduce Maeve to the pleasures of the flesh at thirteen with Colin. Come!"

Hamilton strove for the calm demeanor he was known for. "By being here in Carnoch you put your life at risk. These men could rip you apart then leave you on the craigs for the vultures to devour your carcasses. Want you to leave while you can still walk from here. As I told you, you're not welcome. Your sordid plans will never come to fruition."

"I'm not stupid. Understand here in this small village you hold the power. Do love my business, the whores, the wealth they bring me along with the decadent sex, all the debauchery. Don't plan on giving all up for this brazen harlot. You know I have had her many times. Was always willing to display herself in front of a multitude of audiences. She will betray you just as she betrayed me. Winter? Come along now." Chandler held out his hand again as if he expected her to take it.

"No," Georgia mouthed the word.

"Out!" Hamilton pointed to the door. "Hawk! Houston! Connal!" he roared.

"Time for the two of you to leave if you want to remain alive."

Connal along with Houston flanked the two men. Hawk arrived behind them, seeming to prod them back to the door. Others, Roby, Kit, even more men strode behind. The escort was powerful. As Chandler said, he wasn't stupid. Hamilton had to wonder about the reasons for them to show up here. Maybe at some point in the future, he would need to worry more over Maeve's and Colin's safety. For now, Chandler didn't wish the burden of caring for babies. That was all well and good. He must have women in the brothel who would like to play mother to his children. A strangled breath of air filled his lungs with fear for the people he loved. The huge double doors banged shut behind the men. He imagined once the pair left, the gates would be barred against them.

With a new intake of air, Hamilton found he'd been holding his breath. He was both furious as well as terrified for Georgia. She was still weak from the pagan ritual. He further used up her energy by seducing her. She wasn't eating. This all seemed so wrong. He had the urgent feeling; she was holding something close to her heart, keeping something important from him. Georgia was hiding a secret. Soon enough, he would discover her secret.

Georgia was hearing Chandler's plans for their daughter on the night of her wedding. He hoped he could turn the ensuing hours around to something more pleasant. Much of their evening was still ahead of them. Once the clan escort returned, his breaths came with more ease. His nerves no longer felt as if they were about to snap. She would be able to relax now that the immediate threat passed.

"Can you dance?"

"Yes," she told him with little conviction in her voice.

Hamilton helped her stand. He noticed she was a *wee* bit wobbly on her legs. Acknowledged he might have to hold her up while they moved around the floor. She would not be able to do anything lively. "We will dance then I'll make my apologies to Connal. After what just happened, no one will expect you to remain here longer than necessary."

With a start of fear, he was worried about her. Set his hand on her belly. Felt nothing unusual. Colin was restless that was all. This day was wearing her to a thin frazzle. Too much happened to drain her reserves. Georgia was nine months pregnant. The need to finish the traditions then move on resurfaced. She would need to rest tonight. Even with no discernible evidence, he felt certain the *bairn* would be born within the next twenty-four hours.

Standing, he held out a hand for her. They walked to the men playing the bagpipes. Asked for something slow for their dance. The musicians complied. He did hold her close. Kept her from stumbling. Held her so the length of her body pressed against him. When the dance was over, he walked her to Connal.

"Looks as if your lovely bride is exhausted. I will explain to the rest of the clan. Everyone will understand your need to retire to the privacy of the bridal suite comes a *wee* bit earlier than the norm," he said. Connal motioned for Wynnie.

She led the way to the cake. Proceeded with the cutting. Hamilton gave her a sample of the sweet confection. Georgia fed him a piece. With the feeding accomplished the wives departed with Georgia, chattering nonstop.

The men slapped him on the back telling him he would have a momentous wait before Wynnie would appear at the foot of the stairs to give the signal he could proceed to the most pleasant part of the evening.

As it turned out, about five minutes later, he was summoned. Hamilton set his nearly full glass of ale on a table then hustled to Wynnie. Connal stopped him before he could reach her. For some reason his cat instincts kicked into overdrive. He was certain something was wrong. Wynnie would not have arrived so soon if something wasn't happening upstairs that he was needed for. Despite his struggles to race up the stairs, the men managed by brute force to heave him onto their shoulders.

Closing his eyes then crossing his arms over his chest, he tried to relax. So many thoughts raced through his head, his mind was inundated with fear. Georgia had been acting different since the ending of the last ceremony. He made excuses for the fact she was tired. Credited most of the upheaval to Chandler's unexpected appearance. The last three days had been hectic. In truth, since he met her, their lives had been in a frenzied rush of emotions to this moment. They'd had little time to relax. She was a very pregnant lady who was drained of energy. As she should be, considering the last few days.

Time and again his mind returned to Colin. If he didn't miss his guess, she would have the boy before dawn. She showed no visible signs of contractions. Could she have hidden her cramps from him? Perhaps he would have time to claim as well as make love to her before preparations for the birth would take place. With the sudden appearance of Chandler, he realized he did need to claim his woman tonight. Would doing so be possible?

Maybe his mind was dredging up trouble where there was nothing to worry over. This was all due to fatigue. She was nine months pregnant. A woman would be tired. Wynnie opened the door to the bridal suite. Georgia stood by the bed clothed in a very see-through gown. All the beauty of her body revealed. He sucked in a deep breath of air.

You are beautiful.

Her hands were pressed against her belly. Beyond any measure of a doubt, Hamilton knew he was right about the birth. She'd begun her contractions. The birth was imminent. They would not be able to proceed with the claiming. Doing so would need to wait.

I'm going to have the baby soon. We need to finish with the necessities of the evening so you can see to my needs. After seeing Chandler this evening, we cannot leave any loose ends. All must be done. I can manage. My pains are not so close together you need to worry.

We can't possibly. I won't hurt you tonight. This is too much for you.

Must finish so Chandler has no right to our son. For you to claim me is the reason why Wynnie retrieved you so soon. They understand the necessities. My contractions are barely there. The women will have everything waiting outside the door. Wynnie sent for Houston along with Leah. You will have the necessary help after you have finished all the required traditions.

No. Hamilton heard the desperation in her voice. The very raw panic he felt when she first recognized Chandler. This was not the right time. If not now, when? If not now, they would need to wait the mandatory six weeks. That was too long. So much could happen between then and now. Chandler would jump on any opportunity he could seize.

Yes, Hamilton, we must see this through. For us there are no more options. My contractions are not yet close. They are at least thirty minutes apart. Can we do this in ten minutes? Maybe? We should be finished before the next cramp.

We can try.

He'd given up convincing himself or Georgia they could wait. There was too much on the line, too much to risk. They could not fail the children. Good God, he heard Chandler's plans for Maeve along with Collin. They were untenable.

The men had all but his kilt folded. They set everything on a chair. He sat so they could remove his socks along with his shoes. His hands were shaking. How would he be able to make love to his wife? He was so worried. He didn't know how to proceed. Couldn't fathom the task. Understood he would need to set his claws into her at her climax. This was not his vision of the evening. There would be no gentle teasing, no showing her his cat. Everything he imagined for this night…nothing. His child would be born within the next few hours. The truth would more than suffice any regrets. He needed to hold his baby. This would all turn out the right way. Nothing bad would come of Chandler's visit. The men of the Clan Chattan would keep any trouble at bay.

The men along with the wives left in silence. There was no lewd jesting on their part. Nothing but eerie quiet coupled with what he imagined was grim determination.

For the first few breaths of air he inhaled, Hamilton studied her. He saw no pain on her features. The smile she sent him was hesitant but encouraging. She held her hands out to him, imploring him to meet her.

With a swift rush, he came to her. Swept her into his arms. Kissed her as if she was a fragile piece of porcelain. Touched gently on her neck, swept his mouth along her lips. His hands shook. He was afraid he would fail to give her pleasure. He was in such a hurry.

"I won't break," she told him as he lifted his mouth from her lips. "We do need to take care though. I am terrified of what is to come, the birthing. Let's do this now. Claim me as yours. If there is time, I'll tell you all I've experienced. If not, the tale will wait until another day."

"Yes…" he murmured as he undid the bows on her gown then watched as the fabric slid over her breasts, then lingered on the swell of her belly before dropping to the floor. For several seconds he gazed at her. Searched all of her for any signs of trauma. Didn't notice indications of pain.

With gentleness he'd not imagined for this evening, Hamilton lowered her onto the bed. He came down over her, making certain not to press too much of his weight on her swollen belly. They made love. When she screamed his name at the pinnacle of her release, he sent his claws into her shoulders. She stiffened at the impact. A lone tear slid down her cheek. This was the second time she experienced the claiming. Now, she was his through all eternity. Chandler no longer held any rights to her or their children.

Hamilton rolled to his side. Pulled her into his arms. Held her for as long as he dared. Felt the moisture from her tears slide across him. Hated the fact he hurt her. With the back of his hand, he touched her cheek. He pulled away from her to study her features. She seemed to understand his thoughts.

"I'm fine," Georgia murmured. "Shall we point ourselves in another direction. Speak of something else. I've not had any birthing pain for the last twenty minutes or so. The reality is good. We've accomplished all we hoped for tonight. We're also married. What more could we want? Nothing is going to go wrong."

After a low groan, he answered. "Don't have another choice but to proceed in another direction. You will have the baby soon." He set his hand on her belly. Waited a few seconds. "Houston and Leah will arrive with what I will need. Leah will stay here with us. Houston will wait downstairs in case he is needed."

A bowl of warm water was within easy reaching distance. Hamilton cleaned the blood from her shoulders before wiping his seed from her. He bathed himself then donned his kilt. He would have preferred something else to wear during the birth. Hoped either Hawk or Houston would think of his needs then bring him his buckskins.

"Wynnie said they would have birthing tools ready when we finished here. I'm going to examine you. See how far along you are. This will only take a few moments. Need to see how close you are to giving birth. This is your second child. Shouldn't take as long as the first one." He hoped she was dilating.

Georgia didn't say anything but she nodded. Her face paled at his words. He didn't understand why at this juncture she would be mortified by the exam. The first time, yes. Now, he silently shook his head. He'd touched her as well as tasted every beautiful part of her woman's form.

"First, I will take a look outside. See if my things have been brought. I'm certain Wynnie sent either Hawk or Houston to retrieve all that will be needed. For now, I wish for you to lie on the bed. Rest. Cover yourself with the sheet. Maybe someone will have thought of a better dressing gown for you to wear than the one I tossed to the floor." He picked up the sheer confection then set the gown over the chair.

"I'm certain Wynnie will have all under control. She is very efficient," Georgia told him, her voice weak. "This isn't the first time she has assisted with a birth. There were many before the town had doctors to do the work."

With the kilt covering him, Hamilton opened the door. Sure enough, Wynnie along with Hawk stood outside, a cart of supplies waiting for his use.

Hawk spoke first. "I've brought clothing for you. Something more practical than what you have on now. There is a dressing gown for Georgia." He pointed to the rest of the cart. "Brought all from the birthing room in your home. I would send Wynnie into help with the gown for Georgia…"

"I'll do it," he growled, startled by the sound of irritation in his voice. "Thank you for thinking of everything."

"Suppose you will oversee the birth. You should reconsider. I'll be back to help as soon as she is ready. Wynnie has a tarp for the bed. She is prepared to walk her around on this floor while we make up the bed. How long do you think?"

"Don't know yet. As soon as the door closes, I'll assess her progress. After my exam is finished, we will have a better idea as to when Colin will be born." Hamilton was gruff.

Couldn't help himself. Discovered he was nervous. Terrified of all the possible traumatic events that could go wrong.

Hawk cleared his throat before speaking. "We've important news to discuss. While Wynnie is walking with Georgia, I've more information about Chandler along with Bertram. The pair are up to no good. You would realize this. Certain a lot of what I'm going to tell you will not come as a surprise."

"Chandler?"

They put in an appearance at the celebration for a reason. Now he imagined he would learn their purpose.

"Yes. Don't appreciate what I've heard. The two are taunting us with the young women of the village. Plan on buying as many as possible for their entertainment. Heard rumors of a special night they've labeled Friday Night Virgins."

"The men of the clan have drawn straws as to the hours they will guard the keep as well as this door. We are not taking chances with the two of you. As long as those two reprobates are close, neither of you are safe. Don't understand how they managed to get into the main hall. Nonetheless, trying again would be a death wish for them. Even though we've learned they are both shifters, we will rip their throats out."

"The man would be a fool to show up at the keep again after what they spoke of the first time. What does Chandler hope to gain? Georgia is no longer connected to him in any way. The children are mine. He must realize he is a dead man if harm comes to any person I care about. Maeve is sleeping here, in the keep?" He assumed she would be close to her mother. Needed confirmation.

"Yes, Maeve is here, Bea and Hollis too. No one knows why the two reprobates showed up at the celebration feast. Maybe Chandler just wished to congratulate you on your marriage," Hawk said with a half-amused smirk on his face before he closed the room to the bridal suite.

When Hamilton turned his attention onto Georgia, he was surprised by the tension in her features. There were lines of pain radiating outward from her eyes and mouth. Her small fingers were splayed across her belly. She looked as if her knees were about to crumble. To him it was obvious she neared her time. This entire night, she'd been able to deceive him. He didn't like the notion, yet he understood.

He was suddenly angry with her. "How long has this been going on? The contractions?" He sat down beside her, waiting for a reasonable answer. Picking up her hand, he stroked the smooth skin. Didn't want to frighten her with his angry voice. Damn, he needed to learn how long she'd been having pains.

His other hand rested on her belly. He felt the contraction seize her. While he saw she tried not to make a sound, she cried out this time in a whisper thin voice. The feeling of panic rushing through him vivid and real would have sent him to his knees if he'd been standing. Things seemed to be gaining speed. He still hadn't examined her. Needed to do so.

She moistened her lips. "This is the first contraction that hurt...the rest have just been a tightening around my middle. I wasn't trying to hide it all from you. Well, maybe I was. Won't admit to anything."

"How long…?" He needed to persist in this questioning while he helped her into the gown Wynnie laid out for her. It was a white affair that buttoned to her neck.

"Since," she stopped again as another one hit her hard.

They were much closer together. Seemed, now that the festivities were finished, Colin wanted out. He was worried. With patience Hamilton didn't feel, he waited. "Since," he prompted her to finish with the information.

"The end of the ceremony was the first I felt. While we were lying on the floor and you were trying to warm me. Didn't truly think anything of it. I was too exhausted to tell you. He couldn't be born there. We needed to finish all the traditions that were so important."

If that was true, it had been several hours she had been in labor. The silly girl said nothing. He wanted to shake her until her eyes crossed. Of course, she might have given birth on the cold, stone floor. The birth of their child was more important than traditions.

"You would never have finished with the rituals that were so essential in our marriage. I couldn't let that happen. Fulfilling all the customs of the clan meant a great deal to you. What meant everything to you also meant everything to me."

"That was fantasy grounded in nothing. What is happening to you is reality. I should have noticed. Fulfilling a tradition is not worth a woman's life or a child's life. That's absurd if you think I would have put rituals over yours along with Colin's well-being."

"Maybe. Still…we accomplished all we waited for. Everything is done the right way. Colin will be born here in the bridal suite. We are wed. I am claimed as your woman. You can now protect me as well as our children from Chandler."

This was not the time to argue about something that could not be changed. He plumped the pillows for her. "Sit back. Try to relax. I'm going to feel you…see how much if at all you are dilated. When I discover the truth, we will have some idea as to how long before the *wee bairn* hurries out into this world. Cat instinct tells me our boy is in a rush to see the light of day."

After all was said and done, the birthing was going faster than planned. He never thought the birth of his child would have him shaking so hard he didn't believe he would be any good to Georgia. He wasn't certain he could make rational decisions if there were complications. Hawk was waiting for permission to see to the birth. He should give the job over to a doctor with a steady hand.

"I'm going to call Hawk in here. Leah will come also. I will stay with you. Nonetheless, I believe someone beside me should deliver this baby. I'm not in any condition to make decisions."

His hands were shaking. He never thought this would happen. Never realized how attached he'd become to this woman…to this child of his.

"No." Georgia reached out. Set her hand on his wrist. "No, I want you, only you. No other man…"

"In this I'm going to have to override your wishes. I will stay with you, right here. Hold your hand through the birth. I'm not going anywhere. Need to watch the birth of my child." Hamilton was hard pressed to deny Georgia anything. This was an issue he could not relent on. He was in no condition to deliver this baby. "Yes, but Hawk must be in the room with us. I don't trust myself with you. It's a strange thing, this bringing one's own baby into the world. Can't remain detached. Will you agree to have Hawk with us?"

She was shaking her head telling him no with her eyes yet saying the words he wished to hear. "If that's what you believe to be the best."

Hamilton did examine her. She would have the boy soon. Hamilton felt both fierce pride along with sheer terror for her. She was doing an excellent job. He told her it was fine for her to scream. She could yell as much as she wanted. Could curse him for putting this baby in her womb. Once the contractions began in earnest, they seemed to pick up speed, sending her crying out with each tightening.

Upon his request, Hawk entered the room. Smiled at her. Touched her forehead then helped her rise. He washed his hands three times before he was satisfied, they were clean enough.

"For now, I would like you to walk with Wynnie. Walking will speed the birth. Now that you're feeling contractions so close together, the time won't be long. Soon you will hold that adorable baby in your arms."

With the ladies out of the room, Hawk began to speak. Hamilton wasn't certain he wanted to hear the bad news. Understood this information had something to do with Chandler. While their appearance here did not surprise him, he wondered what the real motivation was. At this juncture it couldn't have anything to do with Georgia.

"Chandler along with a man named Bertram are in Coronach. We knew that. They did appear at the feast. We don't know yet what their main purpose here is. Have a feeling the motivation goes beyond Georgia. He didn't seem to have that great of an interest in her. Seemed he just wished to taunt her with her children. As you are aware, news travels with the speed of lightning in the highlands. We've set guards around the perimeter of the keep. However, I'm not certain the guards shouldn't be around all the young virgins as well as the surrounding homesteads. Seems to be what they are after. Virgins."

Hamilton stashed his hands through his hair. The news didn't surprise him. Earlier someone else said something similar. He did much the same in London. "This is making more sense. He wants to toss this in our face. Steal young women from beneath our noses. This is revenge of sorts." He understood more than he wished to admit. Chandler looked for women. He kidnapped a young lady, a virgin, from the tavern close to where Georgia's cottage was outside London. Held her in the brothel. By giving her drugs, he married her to one of the male employees. In the same manner as Georgia, this new lady signed a binding contract to work for him.

"Everyone who has unmarried daughters between the ages of ten and twenty are being informed of the dangers. Apparently, they are buying the virgins from parents who have no use for girls. They probably headed here with the intention of taking Georgia. Now their purpose seems to have changed. We cannot know the extent of all they are capable of doing."

"This situation might well be out of our control. How can we stop a father from selling an unwanted daughter? We can't." Hamilton paced the room. His thoughts wandering between Georgia and the issue at hand. "I've got to let Connal handle these concerns with Chandler. Connal is the head of the clan."

"You're right on that count. Connal will send word out to the families. All we can do is inform the villagers what Chandler has in store for their women folk if they sell. Their fate is not pretty," Hawk said as he washed his hands one more time in the soapy water that was provided for them.

The knock on the door told him the women were back. They stepped inside. Georgia's face was pale. Her gown was soaked through.

"Her water broke. I'm going to get her another gown. I will be right back," Wynnie said the obvious as she disappeared.

A few seconds later she returned with a fresh gown. From there on out the birth sped by. Not too much time passed before Colin's crying was loud. His lungs were so good, Hamilton felt certain they would hear him downstairs.

The birthing took only a few hours. Now, Hamilton sat on the edge of the bed watching, fascinated with the tiny boy as he nursed. He felt a surge of fatherhood, potent and strong. Looked at the following years as something important. He had a great deal to learn about rearing children. Believed with all his heart, he would be a good father. In the span of a few days, he had two children to take care of. Didn't expect to have children for many years to come. Wondered if Georgia would like to try this again in another couple of years.

Wynnie, along with her husband, brought a crib into the bridal suite both smiling at the tiny child. "First time this has happened in the bridal chamber. A birth during the bedding," Connal said with a soft chuckle. "Though it's rare for..." he stopped speaking. "Perhaps I'm saying more than necessary."

"Maybe you are. We all realize there were extenuating circumstances surrounding these two special children. Tell us more about Chandler. I discussed this with Georgia. Believe we are in agreement. We will remain here with the children until Chandler along with Bertram have left the area."

"With some of our daughters, no doubt," Connal spoke out, disgust in his tone. "I've heard they offer five hundred pounds for a virgin. One hundred for a girl who is not. To some of the poor crofters, this is an amount they won't be able to turn down."

"We both know the families who will profit from this. Know the families who don't care about their girls. See them only as additional mouths to feed. Money for females will put smiles on their faces," Hawk said as he put things away preparing to leave the new parents alone with the child.

"There is nothing we can do to prevent this from happening. Rumor has it he has already sent a carriage filled with five girls back to London. All from one family. He bought the eight-year-old as well the little girl who was ten," Connal added to the news.

"Dear, God, he wouldn't put children…" Georgia stopped speaking, seeming appalled at what the man did. "I never thought he was that despicable. Never believed he would stoop so low as to use children in his shows. Chandler will do anything for money. But this…" She waved her hand in the air. "This is horrific. Isn't there anything you can do to stop him?"

Hamilton apprised her of all she told him about the brothel before she lost the memory. Even with his recounting of events, thoughts of the whorehouse diminished in her mind. He understood she wished she could forget those times, all that happened to her. She couldn't forget. He was never going to allow that to happen. If she forgot, she would become more vulnerable than she was now. Their children would become targets. They needed to recall all this man has done and said to them.

"The question is whether or not he will show up at the keep again. If he does, would you wish to speak with him?"

He saw her shaking her head no. That was enough information for him. If possible, tomorrow he would seek out the man with the intention of making all clear to him. Georgia along with the children were his, adopted legally. If he made any move to abscond with either child, he would never live to see another day.

She was pale. Colin was now sleeping in the crib that Connal brought to the room. The wedding night was not one made from his dreams. However, he could recount parts of the moments with fondness.

Epilogue

Georgia was pregnant again. This would be her third child. Two years had passed since giving birth to Colin. Maeve was a precocious three-year-old who loved to shift into her kitten. Like her mother, she was a white tiger. Turned out Colin was a black panther as was his father. The pair were allowed to shift at bath time. The two loved to wrestle in their cat. Hamilton would shift to join in the game. She didn't participate as often. Decided she was too self-conscious around her babies.

She only just discovered her pregnancy. Hamilton knew before her which she didn't appreciate. This child was also male. Would most likely be able to change to a black panther. At the moment, the day was sunny, unseasonably warm. They left the children in the care of Bea along with Hollis so they could experience some alone time. Moments to themselves were precious. The two doted on the young ones. Spoiled them without a blink of an eye.

They tried not to think about Chandler along with the young women he purchased that day from their homes. Nonetheless, there were precautions laid in place in case of a surprise visit. Hamilton would never become complaisant. Chandler still might wish to take Maeve along with Colin back to the whorehouse.

At the bonfire, the brilliant sun hung low on the horizon. Soon it would dip down below the craigs. Georgia sat with her back pressed against Hamilton's chest. His hands rested on her still flat belly. She would have a tiny bump there soon. Felt thrilled to be having another child. Thought maybe she would like a fourth. They would see how everything went this time around.

"You are eager for this *bairn*? I can feel your emotions shining through." Hamilton asked, while his fingers pressed against her. "The lad is restless. It has been two months. Already he is eager to be out in the world experiencing life. The boy speaks with me daily." His soft chuckle told her he was thinking about something else.

She gasped with unspoken outrage. "You cannot know that. Making things up about our children is not right."

"You do know he talks to me. He wishes to meet his brother and sister. Says they have too much fun at bath time. He wants to join us, shifting as well as wrestling on the floor. Do you have a name picked out for the lad? I would like something very Scottish in nature. The other names are more Irish."

"You are incorrigible. I would not have you putting thoughts into my son's head," Georgia snorted then jumped when his fingers found more sensitive territory. She knew her husband. He meant to seduce. Would like to have her beg for him to bring her to her release. Would do so even if they had company which would be inevitable on such a beautifully warm day as this one. For now, they would revel in their good fortune.

The blanket he wrapped around her, covered her. He had *carte blanch* with all her body parts. Georgia let her head fall back on his shoulder while he explored, enjoying the moments. She'd been thinking about names. Wanted to call the lad, James or Seumas in the way of the highlanders. Would need to run the name by Hamilton.

"The *bairn* is due in June sometime near the beginning of the month. Believe this time I will be able to deliver the child. Doubt if I'll feel so nervous that my knees might buckle. You had me sweating bullets about the birthing of Colin. My head was spinning. When I saw you, I couldn't think straight."

"Colin's birth was not ideal. We never had a wedding night. Not a real one," Georgia mused, thinking about all that happened on the night of their wedding. She saw Chandler for the last time. Despite the fact Hamilton wished they could all forget the horrid man, he continued to remind her about him along with all his depravities. Warned her about growing lax. Whenever Harris visited, she and Ash would tell them news about the brothel. News she didn't enjoy hearing. Harris told them Bertram reminded Chandler daily about her. Coaxed him to find a way to abduct her so she could perform again.

She had a difficult time believing how easy it was for Chandler to get away with everything. The signed contracts kept him out of trouble with the law. He bought and sold women making exorbitant amounts of money. Prayed on young women as well as those who fell into desperate straits. Made money on breeching young virgin's maidenheads.

He would never change.

"Somehow, I've started thinking about Chandler…his business. Don't want to think about him or remember. Not now, while the day is so wonderful. Wish we could think of a way he would lose everything he holds dear. In London, his business is legal. The man has taken steps to ensure nothing falters. Wish I could return to those days knowing what I do now. If I was able, would never sign the contract." She held up her hands. "I know, we must remain guarded at all cost. Don't know when, if ever, he will show his face again. You know he did manage to bring Mackenzie, Mara's sister into the business. Heard Johnnie sweet talked her then used cocaine to make her more compliant."

Hamilton pressed a kiss on the nape of her neck. She shivered with the delightful contact. "Don't wish to talk about him either. Don't we have more pleasant avenues of conversation as well as activities to pursue?"

The back of his hand, brushed the underside of her breast then across the tip. Almost the moment they sat down, he had her gown undone and her chemise unlaced. With the cool air, her nipples hardened. With more stimulation they elongated. She understood he wished to suckle. They both would be in a desperate state of arousal by the time they returned home. He orchestrated the urgency to a fever pitch.

"It's almost Christmas. What do you think we should do to celebrate? We've been invited to the Frasiers for Christmas dinner. Wynnie and Connal asked us to attend the festivities the night before. Mass would be nice to attend. We would need to leave the children at home. They are far too young to be up past midnight. Bea along with Hollis will spoil them silly on the night before Christmas."

"Maybe…" Georgia turned in his arms, her breasts pushing against the fabric of his shirt. She thought she should unfasten the ties holding it together. Needed to feel the crisp dark hair on his chest against her skin. "Maybe we could use the bridal suite for a wedding night. Not the night before Christmas but maybe on New Years Eve. Do you think Connal and

Wynnie would allow us a wedding night? It is two years later but..."

"New Year's Eve?" he asked with a soft brush of his mouth against hers. "Sounds perfect. The day is not that far away. I will make arrangements tomorrow."

Georgia reached behind his head. Her fingers sifted through the soft strands of his hair. "I love you, Hamilton Adair. You tamed my rebellious heart."

"Ah," Ham placed tender nipping kisses along the outline of her mouth. "Don't ever wish to tame you, my love. I do adore your rebellious heart. Must have been why you stole my breath the first moment I saw you."

"I like the sound of those words. Don't wish to be tamed either. If not for the rebel inside me, I might not have left Chandler. Now I have you."

"I do love you, sweet. And..." His seeking hands cupped her breasts, "I'm looking forward to our first honeymoon."

"New Years Eve..."

"Yes, the beginning of a new year."

Coming Soon

Pure Phoebe

Carnoch
Present day

This day in early June was one she would remember forever. Sunshine blanketed the earth providing an unusually warm day. The near cloudless sky was cerulean blue. A soft breeze swept down from the craigs to the loch where the man she loved frolicked in the silver blue water. She no longer knew what to think. Her father had been telling her stories of the McKenna clan. Implied they were shifters. It was as if he wanted to turn her against this man, the love of her life.

Shifters didn't exist. She told herself this every time her father brought up the topic.

Her father said they turned into big black man-eating panthers. Said Cole McKenna was one and the same. Believing his tall tales was impossible. He said they roamed the highlands preying on innocent women and children. When they caught an unsuspecting soul, they would play with them then eat them. Wrapping her arms around herself she suppressed a shudder starting to wrack her body. Asking him if what her father said was true was impossible.

Looking back at the water she watched him swim with sure strokes. He couldn't be a shifter. Cats didn't enjoy water. She should join him in the cold water. He would like her company. Would tease her. A tiny shiver wrapped around her when she thought of jumping into the chilled lake. Maybe in late August she would have the nervc to jump in then play with him. With her head back and closed eyes, she soaked in the radiant sun. The heat warmed her. Her heart beat with a frenzied staccato as she felt his presence.

A shadow covered her heat. The man stood with his feet braced apart, his hands resting on his narrow hips. "Do you have sunscreen on?"

The question startled her. With wide open eyes, questioning, Phoebe MacAuliffe looked into the smiling eyes of Cole McKenna. "What? Sunscreen? Yes…" He surprised her. She babbled. Thought he was still playing in the water. Moments ago, he was far from the shore, gliding across the silver liquid. When did he turn to shore?

In the next moment he startled her anew. Cole picked her up as if she was no heavier than a feather. She shrieked. Clung to his broad shoulders. He strode with long strides toward the shimmering frigid water of the loch. "No! Don't you dare!" To keep from falling, she held on to his shoulders, nestling her cheek against the broad expanse of his chest. Caught a drop of man-warmed liquid left over from his swim. His clean male scent filled her senses.

"Yes…" Cole replied. "It's time you went swimming."

"Where are you going, Cole McKenna? You're not going to…" Phoebe had the horrible premonition she wasn't going to be given a choice in the matter. If he wanted her in the water with him for playtime, he would never allow her to hold back. He was like that. Wanted his way in all matters. Would never be denied.

"Where do you think? Found I was lonely all by myself." He was wading. The water would reach his knees soon then his hips. Would close over their heads.

A distraction would be nice. Any distraction. She was right to be suspicious of his motives. "No…no! Don't want to swim. The water is too cold." Phoebe understood her protests would never move him to change his mind.

"You will get used to the temperature. The chill will feel good against your sun heated skin." For a few beats of her heart, he stayed in the same place. "With a bit of exercise, you will warm right up."

Maybe she didn't want to remember today. "Cole!"

Cole stopped when he was thigh deep in the water. "Hold your breath!" He tossed her. She found her arms flailing as if she could fly. She couldn't. Water closed over her head just after she gulped in a huge dose of oxygen. She sputtered. Her feet found the bottom. She surged upward Letting out a screech that would do any banshee proud, she cupped her hand to send a spray of water flying toward her abuser.

He laughed. Dove. Surfaced beside her capturing her arms with his hands then pulling them behind her back, her breasts pushing against his chest. "Your mascara is running. Should we dip under again to wash more of it away?"

He pulled her tight against him. She felt his entire body pressed against hers. Felt the evidence of his need. Wasn't ready to go there with him. "You don't play fair." He touched her in so many different ways.

"Fair or not, we haven't begun to play." Cole touched with a soft brush of his mouth on hers. Nibbled across her lips. Sipped on the soft plump flesh of her bottom lip. She opened for him. He became part of her.

The melting began, scorching followed. All he did filled her with need. She both did as well as didn't wish to be strong when it came to a more intimate physical relationship with him. He held back because she understood he could sense her hesitancy.

When he lifted his head the grin on his face was still broad. "Let's swim to those rocks. We can sun ourselves in private. Explore more about each other."

Phoebe wasn't certain if she understood what his words meant. They would have privacy to explore anything they desired. Over the last few weeks, he'd been so patient with her. At first, she never said no. As he grew bolder in his sightseeing, she grew more restrained.

By the time she reached the rocks, she was panting for air. Didn't know how to pull herself up to sit on the rock. When she tried, she sank back into the water. "Cole, I can't. Is there somewhere else to get out?" Hated him seeing this weakness in her. Always wished she could be strong. The long distance swim wore her out.

"No. There isn't. Didn't think about you not being able to get out of the water." He turned his back to her. "Climb on." He looked over his shoulder. "You can. I'll get us both out. Sometimes you will need to rely on me."

With great skepticism she stared at him. She was certain her mouth gaped open. Slowly shaking her head, believing him a bit daft, she spoke her thoughts, "You're crazy. I'll just hang on here until I catch my breath then I'll swim back."

"Phoebe." He turned back to touch her chin with the tip of his finger.

"You have no faith in me. I'll piggyback you right out of the loch. No problem."

"I'm too heavy," she countered with a soft sigh. "You won't be able to carry both of us up then over the ledge."

"Hardly." He turned his back to her again. "Wrap your pretty little arms around my shoulders. Your long legs around my waist. We will be out of the water in no time at all."

She lifted her shoulders in a shrug. If he were looking, he would see her silent language. Perhaps it was a good thing he didn't sense her doubt. "Have it your way."

As soon as she followed his directions, he braced his hands on the ledge then lifted them both from the water. Once on solid ground she slid to the ground, her body rubbing against his. She heard his low groan. She'd been with Cole enough times to understand he wanted more from her. He was tolerant. Told her more than once when she told him to stop, he would.

The rocks were warm on the soles of her feet. She shaded her eyes to look back to where they swam from. Seemed so distant. She was a strong swimmer. Yet…she didn't believe she'd ever gone this far.

"How far?" Phoebe wasn't positive she could make the return trip. She sucked in a deep breath of heather scented spring air. Felt a bit of a wobble inside when she thought about later this afternoon when she'd immerse herself in the coldness again.

Sleeping well was no longer something she was able to do. There were too many things on her mind. Factors about her life to consider. Without thinking, Cole seemed to be taking over her life. She both wanted him to make decisions for her and she didn't. Her father always dictated his wishes. Cole cold never be a father figure. He meant too much to her. Last night left her sleepless, tossing the blankets as well as the pillows around on her bed. When she woke in the middle of the night, the sheet was wrapped around both her arms as well as her legs. She had trouble extricating herself from the quagmire of her bedding.

The two of them could not keep going like this. Their lives were too unsettled.   While Cole was older, he understood what he wished for in his life. She did not.

"A quarter mile…maybe less…maybe more." His smile kept that melting sensation going. "You can make it back if we decide to swim. We will be rested."

"You read my mind. However, I've a differing opinion. I'm tired."
Phoebe felt exhausted all the way to her bones.

"An open book. Come…there is a grassy place where we can sit,
stretch out. Take a nap if you like. Are you warm enough? You've got
goosebumps on your arms." He trailed the tip of his finger along one arm
causing more shivers to blossom. "Now I've made more."

She nodded. Wished she had a towel or something to put on the
ground to sit. He placed her hand in his. She followed him when he walked.
For several minutes she traipsed along beside him. As they walked inland
there were fewer rocks replaced by more grass.

"Where are we going?"

"You'll see in a minute. Hope you are pleased. It's a little surprise
for you. Seems you've been working hard at the restaurant. You haven't had
many minutes to relax." He pointed, leaning close to her. He touched her ear
with the tip of his tongue. "Over there. Beneath the tree my father planted
years ago. This is a spot he used to take mother. Believe this is where she
conceived me. Just speculation on my part. Might not be true."

"Don't get any ideas, Cole McKenna." Getting pregnant at eighteen
was not part of her almost nonexistent plans. Cole was older. Might be ready
for a family. She wasn't a wife yet. Had not been asked.

Phoebe was surprised anew when she saw a large blanket spread on
the ground complimented with a basket of what looked to be filled with food.
She saw a bottle of wine poking out between a red plaid cloth. There was a
plot here. She decided getting to the bottom of his scheme might serve her
purpose. Obvious to anyone with eyes, these items did not arrive at the island
the same way they did.

"A picnic in the middle of the loch?" Phoebe knew her voice must
sound skeptical then sarcasm coated her words. "How strange? I suppose
they swam by themselves and were able to remain dry." She was looking for
a way back which didn't involve swimming. Perhaps she was making
headway in her endeavor.

"Don't get testy." Cole cracked a laugh then continued his march to
the picnic spot. "Mother put the basket together for us. Earlier today, I
brought it over in a small boat." He had the look of a pleased man on his
face. "Believed you would enjoy a few moments together…alone…private.

I know I would. We've both been too busy to spend much time together. You have your work. I need to get father caught up in all he missed over the years he was trying to reach home, lost in the Kinnel Stones. Today is for us, for fun."

The compliment to his mother was beginning to form when the knowledge she didn't need to swim took its place. "A boat!"

"He lifted his all-male shoulders. "I like to swim. Wished to swim with you." He ran his hands through his damp hair, pushing long wet locks from his face. "You don't like to swim? Thought you to be the athletic type."

She looked at the romantic gesture. Grinned at him. "I like to swim. Today wasn't planning on freezing my bu…on freezing. Never swam this far before. Haven't been sleeping well. Too much on my mind."

Walking around her, he made a face as he studied her. Took her face between his large hands. "Your sweet little butt looks fine to me. Should I put my hand on your rump to see how cold the tender flesh is? And…if you're not sleeping well, I also have a solution for that." He slid his hands across her shoulders then down her back. They came to rest on her rump.

His audacity made her laugh. He always looked for an opening to touch her. "Cole…bite your tongue…" realized what she said. She'd made the same mistake several times before. "No, don't say the words. I know what you're thinking." She paused to inhale a swift deep breath of air. "No, you will not bite mine." The idea of his mouth on hers, warmed her again. The feel of her stomach pressed against his need fired up the dragons inside.

The last weeks since graduation, she'd been trying to keep some distance between them while he attempted to get closer. For her, he moved too fast. Wasn't use to a man sweettalking her. All she had to compare were a few stolen kisses from boys. No one had touched her as he did. In the beginning, she succumbed with no hesitation, no thoughts to the contrary, no reasons to tell him to stop. Now, she still wanted those caresses, all his kisses. Realized from the start he wanted all of her. She wasn't ready to give all of herself to any man or boy.

His long, drawn-out sigh was one, she believed, to be of frustration. His mouth was so close to hers, she thought he would kiss her. Needed a kiss before they moved on to other topics. Realized a kiss might lead to more caresses, touches in intimate places. He brought his hands back to her shoulders.

"Let's have something to eat besides each other," Cole said as he stepped away from her.

Sexually he was miles ahead of her. Cole told her he would give her time. This little maneuver told her he was growing impatient. Alone on a private island. How quaint.

Sitting down on the blanket, she curled her knees so some of her legs were beneath her. She wished she had a coverup to put on. In the tiny swim suit, she felt almost as if she was naked. A tweak here and a push there, she would be bare as the day she was born. He wouldn't disrobe her unless she told him a resounding yes. When he caressed her back, he did slip one hand beneath the bikini she wore. Reveled in her soft warm curves. Wished he dared pursue more sweet territory.

Making a different face at her, he spoke with a soft cadence to his voice. "We need to talk. Get a few things out of the way. A few ideas have bothered me. I know you've been seeing your father. Is seeing the man a good idea? He hasn't abused you again, has he? I would have you tell me if he has. You do understand, I don't think it is good for you to see him."

Cole reached into the basket bringing out one of her oversized shirts. "Mother thought of the coverup. Can't say I appreciate her consideration. Enjoy looking at you with hardly anything on. Even now when your bent over, I catch a glimpse of a rose-colored crest." His gaze roamed over her as if this was the last look he was going to get.

Hissing in a drink of air, she stiffened in an attempt to cover herself. "I'll thank her next time I see her. And…I thank you not to look at me."

"Need to look at you as much as I need to draw breath. If you reveal intimate parts of you, unwitting or not, I won't hesitate to see my fill."

Cole did have a point. She needed to take more care with her lack of apparel. "You asked me a mouthful of questions." Phoebe slipped the covering on, buttoning the front. Some of her tension vanished. The nerves that were always ready to snap, seemed to relax somewhat. "I do agree with you about father. Wasn't my choice."

"Tell me about your father? Why did he want to see you?"

Cole was right. They did need to have a conversation. He wanted her. At least she was fairly certain. She didn't know what she wanted. Well, she did want him but with strings attached. For her peace of mind, he needed to stop rushing her. Now that she wasn't going to school, her life seemed to drift nowhere. If she were to be honest with herself, she would love to go to college. Didn't know why because she had no career in mind. In high school, she disliked the class work. Never saw a purpose in most of her studies. Why did she want to subject herself to more of the same?

"Where to start?" She didn't know. "Yes. I've seen him. Not by choice. He comes to me. Am I supposed to tell him I won't speak with him?" For the moment she would tell him nothing more. The thoughts her father brought up were not to her taste. Just as everyone else in the community, she'd heard the rumors about shifters.

While she was looking across the lake, wishing she wasn't going to need to swim back when the time came, Cole poured them both a glass of wine. He sat down next to her. She sipped on the wine, allowing the liquid to glide down her throat. He didn't say anything. She didn't know what to say.

"I feel awkward," she finally told him after she set her glass down on a flat piece of ground. "Here we are, alone, with nothing to say to each other even though I've a million thoughts swirling in my head. My tongue feels tied with apprehension." She puffed in a small sip of air. "My father has made accusations about your family. Seems he is trying to rip me away from you." Phoebe was afraid to bring up the topics of her concern. While she could answer questions from Cole, she could not ask the ones foremost in her head.

"I've plenty to say. As I said earlier, a conversation is what we need. Just waiting for you to relax. Would you like some food. Don't know what mother had the cook pack. I would wager there is a little bit of everything. Sweets for your sweet tooth."

"We aren't going to be here long enough to eat much. And…" she punched his chest. "I do not have a sweet tooth. It's you who can't seem to eat enough sugar."

"Ah…but when we kiss, your teeth are very sweet as is your tongue. This afternoon we are going to get sidetracked with kissing." He chuckled when she punched him again.

"You are going off on a different tangent. I want to see what else is in the basket." She leaned over giving him a view of her rear. When she realized what she was doing, she sat. "Stop looking as if you want to devour me not the food."

"So, you say. Yes, I want to savor all your sweet flesh as well as eat my fill of the food mother packed." He brought out a sandwich. "Ham and cheese among your favorites. Eat. You'll need the energy for the return trip."

"Would rather return by boat." She sounded peevish. "Someone will come to retrieve all this. Before we leave, I'd like to sleep." She bit into the sandwich. It was made just the way she liked it. Lots of mustard and mayonnaise coupled with pickles.

"We can do whatever you like. Told mother if we weren't back by seven to send the boat our way. Father will be driving. What do you think? Can we find enough to talk about to keep us busy until seven?"

Phoebe felt certain he had other thoughts besides talking.

"Seven?" Phoebe looked at her watch even though she knew what time it was. "Five hours away?" Thought of falling asleep next to Cole. Was certain his mind was bouncing in the same direction. She loved his arms around her. Enjoyed nestling into his chest. Didn't want the next phase. Not yet. Loved a kiss or two. Liked to play with him. He wanted more. Was trying to be patient.

"A few weeks ago, you weren't hesitant to be with me in any way. You were always eager to experience new things. Now..." His voice sounded accusatory then tentative as he stalled for a few seconds. "Why Phoebe? Did I do something to frighten you? I won't know unless you speak to me. Part of the reason I felt the need to come here was to better understand your reluctance concerning us."

"No...yes...You're moving too fast for me. While I've enjoyed everything we've done, once I started thinking about the places you've touched..." Feeling the rapid rise of heat to her face, she looked to her hands. Didn't want to look into his eyes.

"Don't hide from me. Your face is a lovely shade of rose. Beautiful." He reached toward her. Set his fingers beneath her chin. Lifted.

"I can't help the blush. When I think about..." Her heart thundered out of control. She thought the organ might beat out of her chest.

"You're not ready for more than a few kisses. I understand." His long drawn in breath seemed to calm him. "You've no experience with men. Wait..." He held up his hands to stop the words she was ready to toss his way. "I'm glad you've no experience. You've just turned eighteen. I've been waiting for you to graduate from high school for what seems an eternity.

Yes, I've touched you places…your breasts…your cold wet butt… I want to give you more pleasure than you've ever imagined."

Tilting her head a bit to the side then out of nowhere, she asked, "How old are you?" Since he brought up age, she felt as if she could ask. She'd been curious since the moonlight ride. Since he touched her breasts with both his hands as well as his mouth. The night in question, she felt things she never imagined a person could experience. Would have given herself to him if he pursued. He didn't. Cole seemed to realize, even though she'd been an eager as well as willing pupil, he was moving too fast.

"Does my age make a difference?" Now, he sounded frustrated. He stared at her with a strange expression on his face. Scuffed a palm against his face. "Thought you knew my age. Yes, I'm older."

"No, I don't know. Just curious is all." She didn't understand what he saw in her. Couldn't comprehend why he would choose her instead of a woman closer to his age. A woman who could match him with her physical responses. She was too young, too shy as well as too inexperienced.

"Will be twenty-seven in two months." His words sounded stiff this time. "I am older than you, yes. The fact makes no difference to me."

Phoebe wanted to know what his thoughts were behind his words. Just as she wasn't telling him everything, he wasn't straightforward with her. If anything was meant to change between them, they both needed honest replies.

"You're nine years older than I am." The numbers sounded impossible to bridge the gap between them. Cole graduated from college years ago. Probably when he was twenty-two. Phoebe didn't know what his degree was in. He was so much smarter. His mother told her he also completed his masters in something.

"I can do the math," Cole shot back as if she said something wrong. Crease lines in his brow came together.

All she did was make a comment as to fact. This was reality. She felt as if she was swimming backward. Treading water would be an improvement over this fiasco. Never wished to make him exasperated with her.

"I understand." Decided she wasn't about to apologize for something she couldn't get a grasp about.

Closing her eyes, she found herself counting to ten. She made him angry. Never wished for that to happen. With a deep breath coupled with the need to have the conversation go in a different direction, she finished her wine. Kept her silence. Sampled more of the ham and cheese. The food rolled in her stomach. Searched for something to say that would diffuse his seething emotions.

Cole walked away. His strides filled with purpose. With his feet braced apart, he stared out over the loch. What that purpose was she didn't have any thoughts. He returned.

Said words she told herself she wouldn't. "I'm sorry. Didn't mean to irritate you. I…" Phoebe inhaled several long deep breaths of air. Smoothed her sweaty palms down her shirt. "My problem stems from the reality I don't know what I want. Besides you…that is. I do want you. But…" Seemed in problems there was always a but involved. "I don't know how to make you happy. Give you what you need."

"Those words feel good in my ears. I want you too. Will be more patient…try…can't make a lot of promises. All along, I've understood you are young. Realized before we started to talk, because of age we would have some difficulties. There are things you should know. Those things are also truths that are not mine to tell you until you've committed to me. I would need to become more certain…" As if thinking, he pinched the bridge of his nose. Changed the subject. "Do you want to go to school, Phoebe? If you do…"

Pouring herself more wine, she caught her bottom lip between her teeth. The question was a moot point. There was no reason to discuss the possibilities when there were none. "Yes. You know my grades are not good enough to get into any university."

"I could help." He sounded eager, enthusiastic. "Tutor you if you need to take a test. Help you understand if a course is difficult. I would be there for you every step of the way."

"Buy my way into the university? Bride someone? Talk to a dean? No, won't have anyone cheat for me. I'm not college material." With a heavy sigh, she went on to say. "What's the point? I don't have any idea what I would like to study. For me, attending would be a waste of money." She lifted her hands in a fitful gesture. This topic was not of her liking. She failed at school. Needed extra help just to graduate from high school. Understood the reality of college was not for her.

"Believe it's possible to take some online courses for credit without actually being admitted to the school of your choice," Cole told her appearing to worry the question overmuch. "I could help you look into the possibilities. Freshman classes are pretty general. If you did well, good grades and all, whichever school you apply to might consider you." He put up his hands. "If you would like to further your education, I would do whatever I could to help you achieve any goals you might set."

He gave her food for thought. His idea had merit. She thought of Dallas along with Rafe. One didn't have to be good at history or science or literature to be an artist. They were both very artistic. She felt a small sliver of hope. "I like photography. You know like Dallas does. Travel places. Take pictures. Maybe I could be her apprentice. She could teach me what she knows." She thought about the few times they'd been together. "Dallas likes me. Doesn't she?" In most relationships, she did have confidence. Felt a kinship with Dallas. Helped her pick out the dress for her wedding.

"Believe so. You were part of her wedding. A girl doesn't ask another one to stand by her side when she gets married unless she likes the female in question." His handsome grin returned. "I will talk to her."

"No, let me take the initiative. I need to pursue this. Dallas stops by the restaurant from time to time just to say hi. She usually gets a cup of tea along with a pastry when she comes in. Always sits at one of my tables."

"If that is what you would like, I'll stand by your side. All you need to do is tell me what you want."

She tossed her hands up then let them fall into her lap. "This entire conversation is ridiculous. I don't have money to pay for classes." She shook her head, making a face at him before pointing to him. "Don't go where I think you are about to go. I'm not taking your money. You best understand me."

His shoulders lifted in the all-male shrug of indifference she adored watching. Sometimes he quirked an eyebrow to the sky. "Didn't offer. The thought was on my mind. I have more than enough. You could pay me back after you get your first job."

"Maybe Dallas will give me an apprenticeship. If she is willing, I would only need to pay my expenses." She returned full circle. "I could learn from the best of the best." Phoebe thought her's was a fine idea. "I'll go see her first thing on Monday morning."

"Alright. We've put one issue to bed. Now on to the next." Seemed he wasn't going to let up until the discussion returned to her father. Talking about her father would be too difficult.

She tapped her finger to her chin. "Dallas put herself through college by modeling for art classes. I could do that."

"No!"

Turning on him, she was baffled by his sudden and very negative answer. "What is wrong with modeling?" Phoebe felt confused again. His incisive no gave her no room for discussion of any type. "I could model. I would be good," she decided to persist with this line. Hoped to learn what it was that had his voice so adamant.

"Naked?" he queried a gentle lift to his dark brow. "Dallas was buck ass naked when she modeled in art classes. Yes, she was paid well. Women who will sit in front of a room full of students are far and few between. They deserve the money."

"Oh…!" She could never be naked in front of a class room of people. How did Dallas manage in the situation. Supposed Dallas wanted to go to college more than she did. She made a face as if she could forget what she learned. "I…?"

He appeared relieved the issue was settled. Seemed he intended to move on to the next topic he wished to tackle. "What do you say we talk about the other problem bothering you."

"How do you know there's another issue in my head?" Shock might come close to describing how he made her feel. There were too many questions. She could never tell him the things her father told her.

"Watching you withdraw from me, for one. Every time you hesitated to come with me or looked at me with a faraway expression, I felt distance between us grow. Don't need distance. Want my Phoebe back. Need to move on with our lives in a forward direction. You know. The girl who adores an adventure. Likes to learn new things with me by her side. Was surprised today you consented to come here with me. Was positive you would tell me you were too tired." Now, he sounded more resigned than bitter or angry.

She didn't know how to bring up what her father told her about shifters. "You are right. Besides our age difference coupled with the fact I'm nowhere near your equal in any endeavor, there is something else on my mind."

"I don't like to hear you put yourself down."

"Nothing I said was false. If the words are true…"

~ * ~

"No, they are partial truths. There is no doubt in my mind if you had had support from your father, you would have achieved in school. My God, the man let you run wild! You are a free spirit. However, young girls should not be allowed to go anywhere whenever they pleased. He never took care of you. Now…" Cole raked his hands along the back of his neck. "You needed a parent when you were growing up. You didn't have one. He abused you then. I believe the man is still abusing you. Is he?"

She made a little face at him. "He hasn't hit me if that's what you're implying. When I was little, he did use corporal punishment to keep me in line. I sported a black eye from time to time. Couldn't sit after a spanking."

"Verbal abuse now since he cannot get you alone to hit. He has you frightened of me. Terrified in some way. Before the day ends, I hope you will explain." He wasn't about to tell her they weren't leaving this huge rock until she spoke to him of this fear that was tearing them apart. If his father came with the boat, he'd send him away.

This day was not going how he planned. When Phoebe mentioned modeling for the art classes, he almost exploded. His fury rose to the surface so fast, he couldn't control his reaction. Did everything in his power to keep his boiling rage behind his teeth.

He needed to discover what was bothering her. She didn't appear to wish to speak her mind. It wasn't his reaction to her statement about a way to earn enough money to pay tuition, causing her reticence. She was right. Money for tuition wasn't something she needed to consider at this beat. What had him concerned was her renewal of her relationship with the man she called father. Believed when he moved her into the McKenna keep, she would no longer find herself at his mercy. Somehow, he found a way to nestle a burr into her head. The man was playing her, using her lack of knowledge about shifters to hold over her head. He knew the issue was about people who were able to change form. He caught glimpses inside her head despite the fact he tried not to meddle.

He sifted in a long breath of Phoebe scented air. Damn, she smelled so fine. Wished he could take her into his arms then teach her more about the pleasures of the flesh. Reminded himself she was only eighteen. He'd been seeing her for fewer than three weeks. He paused for a moment to center his thoughts.

He placed her hands in his. Rubbed the backs of her wrists. Marveled about how tiny she was compared to him. "We need to be honest, Phoebe. You must tell me what bothers you so much the notions have you retreating from me…from us. You hesitate now when you use to rush forward, all guns blazing. When I ask if you want to go with me…anywhere…you hesitate. I need to understand why."

She inhaled a huge deep breath. Beneath the coverup, her beautiful jewels moved with the breath of air she stole from the sky. He wished his mother had not thought to put the shirt in the basket. Phoebe would not be comfortable in this situation wearing only her skimpy bikini. He did however appreciate the sight when there was no one else around to look at her. On a different day, they could sunbathe. He could rub sunscreen on her, touch places on her body that would entice other things.

Patience man…

With each day he grew more possessive. Would like to propose. Offering for marriage was too soon. With a growl he tried to hold back, "Talk to me about your father." Now, concerning her single parent, all he wanted to do was get to the truth. If he needed to dig all the way to China to find those truths, he would do whatever was necessary. "I didn't realize you were seeing him. When? You should have told me. I could put up a buffer. I will make the time to be there when he is accosting you."

"Not by choice," Phoebe was quick to point out. She ran her hands along her legs, appearing to think about what she should say. "He comes into the restaurant every morning for breakfast. Whenever I have a break, he expects me to sit with him, enjoy a cup of coffee while conversing. Most of the time he asks questions about me. What I'm doing. Who I'm seeing. He is there for a few hours each day." She lifted her beautiful female shoulders as if to give emphasis to her frustration. "I don't know how to tell him I don't want to talk to him. If I did get the courage, he would blame the words on you. Tell me I've no thoughts of my own. He would say I parrot your opinions. Which is in part true. I do agree with you in most things."

"Good. Your opinions as well as ideas are important to me. Don't want my woman to say what she thinks I want her to say." He turned her wrists over, bringing them to his lips. Kissed the palms. "What falsehood is he telling you? Don't allow him to put you down. Don't believe everything he says. You work hard at the restaurant. If you get time with Dallas, you might make enough to try a few online classes." Cole didn't mean to rant. Wished she would have more confidence in her abilities.

Eighteen years.

For eighteen years plus, her father beat her into the ground with verbal abuse. There were times he hit her so hard his fist would cause bruises. He managed to get her away from her father just before her graduation. Now, the man was finding new ways to torment. Cole didn't know what else he could do to combat this treatment of his daughter.

To see into her beautiful head at the moment would be preferable. He could listen to her thoughts. Didn't want to abuse this ability of shifters. At least not until her trust in him was complete as well as absolute. All shifters could see into the head of their mates. Not until she understood his ability would he allow himself to listen. Granted, he couldn't ignore the fact he'd been there a few times. When she was troubled, she reached out to him. Those instances were the ones that brought her thoughts to the forefront of his head. His instinct to protect was strong in male shifters.

Phoebe poured herself another small glass of wine. She swirled the ruby red liquid in the glass, staring at the liquid as if mesmerized. He stilled his breathing, waiting until she was prepared to speak her words. He would push if necessary. The time wasn't quite there yet. He sipped. Watched the fingers of her free hand fiddle with the hem of her coverup. The words were hard for her.

"Trust in me," his soft voice was meant to reduce the tension he saw in the set of her jaw as well as the stiffness of her shoulders.

When she looked at him, he saw moisture in her eyes. Drops on her dark lashes shimmered as bright as diamonds. Her sweet pink tongue slid across her bottom lip. He wished they could abandon the conversation for more intimate pursuits. He missed holding her close, tasting her essence, catching her sweet perfume. The plump fulness of her lips beckoned every male part he possessed. Her aquamarine eyes questioned. She could ask him anything. He would answer with all the honesty he possessed.

She tilted her head to gaze into his eyes. Touched the tip of his chin with a fingertip. "This is not easy for me to say or ask," she told him playing with one of the buttons on her shirt.

A nervous habit of hers he adored. "Don't ever be afraid to speak your mind. Whatever is in your head will never change how I feel about you."

"Yes, so you say. With this statement, you will think I'm touched in the head. People around these parts talk. Not one person I know believes the gossip is true. They call the rumors old wives' tales."

Whatever it was hovering in her mind would not be easy to speak. He stiffened a bit having a good idea about what was to come. Needing to encourage her to tell him everything on her mind. "Go on," Cole prompted. "I won't bite." He almost hooted a laugh when she looked at him with the impish face telling him she would bite him. Perhaps today they made some headway with their relationship. Phoebe had not teased since their first two outings, not since she began to distance herself form him. Not since her father began to meet her at the restaurant where she worked.

"You said that on purpose. Didn't you?" she queried with a little giggle. "I imagine my mind wandered in the same direction as yours. Before, I enjoyed the kisses as well as the tiny bites of pleasure." The single button separated from the hole. She began to fiddle with the next one in line for attention.

He caught a glimpse of the valley between her breast along with the sweet curves of both. "My words were not by chance. Now. Tell me why your father is visiting you every morning while you are working as well as why his words are disturbing you. Talking always makes a person feel better. Speaking will shed new light on the difficult problems."

His sweet Phoebe sipped in another big draught of air after that another gulp of wine. She was trying for courage, "His words are about your family. He means to make me think bad things about all of you."

Why didn't that surprise him? Her father was both a jealous as well as a petty man. "What bad things has he said? You realize my parents are not bad people. Neither am I." His heart seemed to stall out when she first spoke. This might become the beginning of his worst nightmare. Understood he would have to see this through at some time.

"Your family is the nicest ever, your mother especially. She has done nothing but treat me as if I'm a daughter, part of the family. Your father is still trying to put to rights the muddle that was his life for so many years. Still, he is always the sweetest of men." Phoebe made a soft sound in the back of her throat. Wasn't quite a sigh. The noise intrigued him.

Deciding to fish for a few compliments, Cole went on to ask, "What about me? Am I the nicest?" He didn't need to search for commendations. Meant to do so anyway. Found he was stalling. Perhaps it was Phoebe doing the wasting of time. He comprehended the major fact. Pheobe was hesitant to tell him what her father spoke. What bothered her.

Phoebe played with her thick blond braid, looking at the ends as if they held all the knowledge in the world. Her hands trembled. All her actions pointed to a person who was afraid. "You know I think you are also the nicest. Father can't change my mind about you or your parents' characteristics. I understand who they are. Realize what the two mean to you. I was with you when your father was found after being missing for too many years."

"Well then, what has he said? What has that father of yours been saying that has you withdrawing from me? It isn't just the fact I might have pushed you to hard with my attentions. Was afraid I moved too fast. Now, you tell me I have. But that isn't what has your holding yourself back. Tell me."

"This is not easy." Phoebe looked at him with wide bluish eyes. They still shimmered with moisture. "He told me all the Stuarts, the Frasiers as well as the McKennas are shape shifters. Said they all turn into giant black panthers. That they eat women and children." She let her hands fall in her lap before lifting them with an imploring gesture. "I'm not superstitious. Don't believe such creatures exist. It would be crazy to think they are real... Wouldn't it? To believe that you are one of them?"

Cole searched his thoughts for the best reply. Didn't feel as if Phoebe was ready to know the truth about his family. Wasn't about to blurt out his father was right about what he told her. To his knowledge no women or children were ever eaten. "You do have a valid point. There are creatures such as the Loch Ness Monster..." Deep inside Cole was sweating hard. He wondered what she would say or do if she discovered today shifters truly did exist. "We know Nessie isn't in the loch even though people continue to claim they've seen her."

"Kelpies," she started a list. "*Bean Nighe...* are creatures in our heritage. No one believes they are real. Do they? I don't. Nonetheless…"

"Selkies as well as *Baobhan Sith*. Don't forget the helpful *brùnaidh* also known as a brownie. I do enjoy the helpful household spirits," he told her with a smile as he added to the list of mythical creatures in Scottish lore.

Her hand over her mouth, she giggled. He meant to have a serious expression on his face. Needed to help her understand, he took the statements about shifters in a serious manner. Phoebe spoke up again. "You don't believe in any of these mythical Scottish creatures? What if I tell you I do believe? What would you say to my words of faith?" Before she drew her hand back to her lap, she reached out to him.

He was keeping something important from her. His heart thundered beneath his chest while his stomach flipped over. "I would tell you about most mythical creatures. To the best of my knowledge, they do not exist."

"Just as I told my father the same. Why would shape shifters exist if none of the others do? He insisted the families he listed could change shapes," Phoebe said as she began to put her trust in him. "Still, I have doubts. When one person is so adamant about a fact, makes another think more than once what they say might be true."

Cole was curious. More of this discussion needed to be delved into. "What did you father tell you about shifters? Did he know anything except the tiny fact they are able to change to a different form?" Her father would manufacture lies. Most people in the little town of Coronach excepted the truth of the existence of shifters. All who could change shape were careful not to do so in public. They played in the privacy of their homes or they traveled to uninhabited parts of the highlands. To his knowledge, no one reported a sighting in a very long time.

"Father told me…" She was plucking at buttons. Another popped free. If she continued, he might not be responsible for his actions. With the unveiling of her perfect little body, Pheobe was playing with fire. "I know he cannot be correct."

"What did he say?" Cole questioned while he dreaded what might come out of her beautiful lips. Unable to stop himself as well as needing to close some of the distance between them, he scooted toward her. Ran the back of his hand along her cheek then down the graceful slope of her neck. Watched her blood pump hard at the pulse point at the base. She was not immune to his touch. "Tell me how he described these so-called mythical creatures. Did he call them monsters?"

He watched her breasts heave as she sought air. Saw her fingers fumbled with more buttons. "Told me..." she sipped another piece of air. "Said, shifters were huge. They would devour anyone who got in their way or took something they thought belonged to them. They were all mean spirited. If they didn't like their children, they...they..." he watched her swallow what appeared to be a lump in her throat. "They ate their children."

Fury at her father curled in the pit of his stomach. Pushed the antagonism aside to further his cause with Phoebe. Needed to show her shifters were the opposite of mean spirited. They were gentle. Nothing he said was true.

"You don't say?" The tip of his finger slipped between her breasts then rose to her collarbone. "What else?" Distraction was always a fine tactic. With the puffy little breath of air trembling from her mouth, he understood his ploy worked.

Appearing to shoot straight to the point. "Are you a shifter. Father told me you are one. Would you show me what you look like in your other form?"

What to do now?

There was no bloody way he could answer her question with a yes or no. One answer would send her running in the opposite direction he wished her to go. The other one would be a lie. He wasn't going to lie to her. Neither could he speak the truth until she was loyal unto him alone.

Pleasure at her question bubbled up from the deepest part of him. Phoebe, the girl of his dreams, his mate, wished to see his cat. Doing so was for another time. Cole answered in the only way he could think. "How could you see something you don't believe in? If something doesn't exist, goes to reason it cannot be seen."

"I know you are possessive. Being a possessive person does not make you a shifter." She already entered dangerous territory. Where would she go next. "From some of what I heard; shifters have mates. A partner who travels through the centuries with them. Ever since I first saw you, I've felt an uncanny sensation of knowing you...we...came from another time."

"Yes, I'm possessive of you. I'm certain you've heard people say shifters are freaks of nature. If you believe I'm a shifter, could you also believe I'm a freak?" He asked too much. Said too much. Needed to backpedal before he revealed more than he should.

At her nod he continued not waiting for an answer to any of his other questions. "What do you believe?"

All the fasteners on her coverup were free. If he didn't miss a guess, she was inviting him to play. Her invitation might not stem from conscious thought. Comprehended she was nervous. Fiddling with buttons was a habit of hers when nerves took over.

Instead of answering, Phoebe started with a story. "I saw a black panther once. I was young. Maybe ten."

She must have seen the change in his demeanor because she stopped speaking showed him a questioning tilt to her head. "I didn't mean to stop you." Cole told her. "Just surprised. That's all Go on…"

"I expected some kind of scolding about how I was somewhere I shouldn't be. It's true. I was alone in the woods. Needed some private time. A lecture…you know. You tend to do that."

"Perhaps later. Would enjoy hearing what you have to say. You said you were ten?" he asked as if he meant to clarify.

"The cat was beautiful, all black and soft looking. I wished…never mind. Don't know if the animal was a shifter. He didn't tell me if there was a person just waiting to find its way out of the cat body. I wasn't frightened. Wished I could reach out then pet the cat."

"You're by far too curious. Your curiosity is one of the characteristics I enjoy. Nonetheless, you do need to temper your inquisitiveness with a good dose of common sense. You must have been a distance from our village."

She let out a throaty snort as she shook her head. "The scolding comes sooner than expected. Yes, the cat was huge. Looked at me as if I might be his next meal. It's eyes gleaming a deep silver blue. For a few seconds my heart leaped to my throat. For some reason, I felt connected in a bizarre way. Hoped the cat was friendly."

"You weren't afraid?" Cole knew she might be frightened. If the cat was his, she would not have feared him. The shifter wasn't him. He would have remembered the incident. Understood even when she was a small girl, she was his mate. He always looked after her. Knew there were times she wandered from the village. Tried to be close by when she did. Wasn't successful each time.

"Terrified. Afraid if I ran the cat would pounce on me. Horrified if I stood where I was, he would pounce on me. My feet were frozen to the ground. I could not have moved to save my life. You're angry with me. I realized I should not have been where I was. Learned my lesson. Never returned though there were a few times I watched the hills with longing. Wondered if I walked along the same path I would see another black panther."

Cole sucked in as much air as his lungs could hold. He tamped down the frustrated fury he felt for a man who was never there for his daughter. Controlling the rage, he spoke with a low calm voice. "Where was your father?" Cole had the horrible suspicion she wandered into the hills not only by herself but without explaining to anyone where she went. As he told her earlier, her father allowed her to run wild. He was unable to keep tabs on her day in and day out.

"I was lonely most of my life. Yes, I explored the hills. Found solace as well as companionship there. Father was at home drinking. That's what he almost always did starting at five in the afternoon until he passed out on the floor. If I got in his way, he would swat at me then mumble fowl words beneath his breath about women and girls who were worthless creatures." She lifted her shoulders a bit, sending her body in a pleasing display. "I didn't enjoy his company. Didn't like spending every evening in my room. If I ventured into the main room, I would always regret doing so. As you said, I ran wild." Then with some defiance in her voice. "What of it?"

Unable to resist the beautiful temptation in front of him, the tip of his finger traveled to her navel then back. Saw the quiver of her stomach muscles as he passed across the softness of her belly. Heard the tiny noise of pleasure ruffle from the back of her throat. At this instant, Phoebe wasn't withdrawing from him. She was running toward him. If he continued, she might gift him with her female body in a delightful way.

"What do you think? Are there shifters…" he paused to send his finger back to her navel then lower to the top of her suit. Traveled just above the elastic wishing to dip lower into more intimate as well as sensitive flesh. "If they exist, are they freaks of nature as some say? You never answered. Seems you distracted me with your statements about seeing a panther. What do you say? Give me an answer now." He was so tempted to slip into her head. Read her feelings about the shifters along with his blatant exploration.

If he wished it to be, he could discover the truth without her saying the words. For some unfathomable reason he needed to hear the words come directly from her to him. He hoped she would reveal her honest truths.

"Wh…what do you mean by freak?" She was having trouble talking. Her voice dropped an octave with each new pass of his fingers.

Cole continued his foray across her stomach then higher to circle each breast. Passed the palm of his hand across the hard crests of each one brushing the cloth aside for an instant with each pass. She was panting hard, breathing erratic. Her heart pounded as blood rushed through her. Touched on the out-of-control pulse point. He asked again. "Are they freaks?"

"You…you should stop. I'm sorry…" She caught her lip beneath her top teeth. He wished to do the same.

He wasn't at all sorry about this venture. It had been too damn long since he treated himself to the delights she possessed. Indeed, he was quite pleased with the passing moments. Enjoyed the few minutes she was not stepping backward from him. At this beat of her heart; she was still rushing forward. "Hmm…let me think. Freak? An accident…maybe a surprise. Freak doesn't have to mean ugly or weird. What do you think? Tell me." He began to unravel her braid. Dropped the tie onto the blanket where they sat. Spent time running her loosened hair between the insides of his fingers. The strands were still damp from their swim across the loch.

Her sweet pink tongue passed across her bottom lip. A trace of kissable moisture remained behind. Setting his hand beneath her chin, he followed the path with his thumb. Tugged on her lip so he could forage inside the warmth he found within.

"Cole," his name on her lips was a thin wail. "Please…" Phoebe brought in a long deep breath of air as he continued in the same vein.

"If shifters exist, true the first ones might have been an accident. A possible surprise to the parents. Who knows? You still need to answer me. What is your opinion?" His knuckles grazed down the long column of her neck then lower to seek more sensitive territory in the valley between her breasts.

"No…no freak…just…"

The cat was beautiful. The panther wasn't him. He couldn't keep this up. Would not seduce her until she was ready. Today they made progress toward their goals. He didn't wish to ruin the steps forward. With a sigh of regret, Cole began to fasten her shirt. "You need to keep this on unless you want me to ravish you. Right here. Right now. You must understand I'm on the verge."

Phoebe was shaking her head her eyes huge. "Thought the panther I saw was beautiful. Had a surprising urge to pet the animal. Was too terrified to get close enough to the beast in order to pet."

When I show you my cat, I will let you pet me as much as you like, anywhere you like. We can play together. Perhaps not. I might hurt you. If you were also a shifter, we would change into our cats right now. Play in the lock before father comes to retrieve us. Oh, he did wish to play with her. He would soon. Today's playtime was too short. With longing he gazed at her. With each caress he swelled more, jumped to life.

He sat back, leaning on his elbows. Crossed his ankles. Thought the view was nicer with the coverup unfastened. "Should we have some of the sweet treats mother packed? I'm hungry. Are you?" Cole felt satisfied with her answers. Realized this afternoon they made more headway than he hoped. By her actions, he understood she still wanted him. She'd backed off because of her father's whisperings in her ear.

Today he was pleased.

Exhilarated.

Phoebe closed her eyes on a soft sigh. He moved closer to her. Wrapped an arm around her. Held her close. She snuggled her cheek against his chest. Played with the dark black hair she found there. Her mind was spinning in so many directions. Against his will her thoughts were playing peek a boo with his. Time and again, he tuned her out only to find himself listening. He told himself he wasn't going to accept her thoughts into his mind. He wasn't intending to take advantage.

Didn't seem to be able to resist a peek or two.

He knew when she fell asleep. Her body as well as her mind relaxed. Tension vanished. Her breathing along with the rate of heart slowed. He absorbed her heat into his gave back as well. Discovering she was open minded about shifters, thrilled his heart. The need to tread with caution was ever prevalent in his head. However, now, he could walk more easily along the narrow precipice dividing normal folk from his world, no longer afraid of falling when she learned his truth. He felt confident given time, she would understand there was nothing to fear from a shifter. Her father would try to reinforce the opposite scenario. Now that he understood more, he could combat the hurtful innuendos the man would toss his way. With this newfound knowledge, her father became his enemy.

Phoebe, you are my mate. Given the necessary alone time together, we will sort all this out. You will understand all you mean to me. You are my heart and soul as well as my very life angel.

In this same spot almost twenty-seven years ago, he knew his mother lost her innocence as well as conceived him. Perhaps he could orchestrate the events with his Phoebe much the same way. By August she might be ready to share more than kisses along with innocent caresses. Most shifters are intimate with their mates before the wedding.

They would explore a career for her in photography. He knew without asking, Dallas would be pleased to be her mentor. He prayed she had talent in the field. If not, Dallas might be able to employ her in other ways. Perhaps teach her how to find the perfect shot. Understood sometimes innate talent was involved as it was with Dallas.

Cole slowed his breathing to match Phoebe's. As he listened to her heart, his along with hers melded together to beat as one. He heard this was true of mates. They were so in tune with each other as if sharing one heart between them their hearts beat at the same pace. He closed his eyes enjoying the beautiful solitude.

At peace with himself, he listened to the soft roll of waves lapping against the rocks. Watched a few billowy clouds ghost the sun. An eagle flew across the water searching for prey. Felt the gentle breeze slipping down from the craigs to caress his face. Smelled the heather coupled with the sweetest scent of all, his Phoebe. Sipped his wine. Sampled the chocolate confection his mother asked their cook to pack. Phoebe didn't wish to swim back. Neither did he. What he wanted was to spend as many minutes with her before they needed to return to the real world. His father would be here at seven. If she woke before the allotted time, they might enjoy a kiss or two.

Needed to put her to bed early tonight. She pulled the morning shift this week. Phoebe would need to rise early to get to the restaurant by five o'clock in the morning. When they married, she wouldn't need to work. Hoped the wedding would only be months away. Not the years, he feared.

Red wine.

Chocolate.

Phoebe…pure Phoebe.

His life was made of his dreams. *Fairytales.* Fairytales always fought with monsters, misunderstood creatures. Phoebe's monster was her father. Short of forbidding her to leave the keep without him or his mother was the only way he could keep her father from accosting her. At work she would always be vulnerable. He couldn't be with her all the time.

Ah, the lapping of the water soothed his soul. Her soft body pressed against his was heaven. Wished they could bypass all the difficulties then move on with the rest of their lives together.

He must have dozed. Phoebe was still sleeping. The sun was slipping toward the horizon. A few colors were splashed across the sky, golds, pinks, apricots. The scene breath stealing. Perhaps they could sleep here some night in the future. During the summer they wouldn't have need of a tent. Together, they would be able to watch the stars travel across the sky in a never-ending parade of brilliance.

Waking her soon might be pleasant with a several well-placed kisses. A few here. Some more there. He knew where he wished to try the flavor of Phoebe. Before his father picked them up at seven, he needed to taste her again. More than a week passed since he kissed her. Savor her essence for more than a few minutes. She was addictive. More than a few minutes might lead to other delightful encounters. He would need to hold himself back. She was untried. Her only suitor was him.

Thought to ease Phoebe into wakefulness in the most delicious means he could think of. Cole slid his hand along the inside of her thigh passing close to dark secret places he'd yet to explore. Soon he would learn all of her. Set his hand on her little butt. Slipped his fingers beneath her bottoms to encounter soft flesh. Squeezed with a gentle caress. She stirred. Rubbed her cheek against his chest. He squeezed again wishing he dared enter more intimate territory.

Restraint was the operative word.

"Cole…?" His name was uttered with a soft purr from her lips. "Cole…your hand is on my…"

"Yes, it's on your delightful butt. You fell asleep. Needed to wake you before father comes to retrieve us. Unless you've changed your mind about swimming." He grinned at her. Removed his hand from the hot spot he found. Let his fingers dance one by one along her ribs until he reached the soft, heavenly mounds he adored.

"Don't want you to stop. Touch me, please…," she begged. "It's been so long. I understand I withdrew from you but…"

"Yes, you do want me to stop. Father will be arriving soon. If he's early he could come upon a compromising situation. This time I refuse to listen to your plea. If we keep going, I might frighten you. Don't want you to push away from me again. Lovemaking needs to be eased into. Not experienced all at once." He heard her thoughts about sex with him. She'd told him earlier; she would wait until marriage. Understood the idea was antiquated. While he doubted, she would still be chaste on her wedding day, this evening was not the time to teach her about becoming a woman in truth. "If we do much more petting, I'll be deep inside your hot sweet core. You won't get what you want."

"You're so smart. Tell me what I want." Her tongue flicked across one hard little nub. She bit then nibbled across his chest. She learned how to entice every male part of him.

Under attack by her sweet pink tongue, Cole gritted out in desperation. "To be a virgin bride."

"Oh…"

Seemed she was reminded about her wishes.

"Maybe I no longer want to go to my wedding an innocent. Seems those words were spoken ages ago."

~ * ~

"Do you see the way our son looks at Phoebe? He's holding back. Tense. Jittery when he's around her. I thought the time they spent together a week ago on the rock would have washed the tension right out of him. Doesn't seem that it did. If anything, he is more reserved than before. Those two need some more alone time to hash out what's bothering them," Ruby said as she bent over to set a dish into the dishwasher. She straightened. Picked up a plate to rinse. "I don't know what to make of those two."

"He gets up every morning to walk her to work. Cole stays there until noon then he returns home to finish going over the accounts he is dealing with now. The girl works too hard at the restaurant. They don't have time just for themselves. What the devil does she do with the money she earns?" Richard asked while he continued to clear the table. "She doesn't buy things for herself. I swear she has only a couple of dresses to her name along with a few other articles of clothing.

"Cole always takes his laptop with him when he accompanies her in the mornings. Believe he's protecting the girl from Angus. The worthless bum. If I made a guess, the money she earns goes to the man." Ruby turned to point a fork in his direction. "You wouldn't know this because you were gone but Angus use to smack her around. She would wander off to the hills to get away from him. Ran wild in the streets of Carnoch too. Her life was free of restraint. Moving in here with us has been the first time her life has held any substance or control. At least she no longer fears the beatings."

"Don't suppose our son is too happy to hear about her father. He would have known about her exploits around town." Untying his apron, he poured himself a cup of coffee then sat to watch his wife finish with the dishes. "Would you like another cup?"

"No, I'm thinking another glass of wine would do me just fine. Worrying about our son is stressful. Happy I no longer worry about you." She closed the front of the dishwasher then leaned against the counter. With her arms crossed in front of her, Ruby went on to say. "Need to speak with Phoebe sometime when Cole's not around. Need to hear what she thinks about our son as well as her father. Cole would say I'm meddling. Nonetheless, someone needs to give these two stubborn children…"

"Young adults."

"Young adults need some counseling. Given our circumstances, no one should let grass grow under their feet. Take life for all it's worth when you can. That's my motto. We lost so much time we will never retrieve."

With a soft chuckle he pointed a finger at her. "Don't you go meddling in their affairs. We don't have any business…"

"Feel close to the girl. She's important to me as well as my son. A month ago, she dreamed about weddings as well as wedding gowns. We all went to Inverness to help Dallas select a gown for her marriage to Rafe. She was starry eyed as well as over the moon in love with our son. What has happened between them?" What has happened between the two of you was the important question she meant to confront Phoebe with as soon as Phoebe could find time to visit.

She was always at work. Most days she worked double shifts. Ruby felt positive she gave her wages and quite possibly most if not all her earnings to her father. There needed to be a way around her doing so. A girl needed her independence. Money gave that to her. She never asked her for anything. Doubted if she asked her son.

"I can see the wheels spinning in your head, Ruby McKenna. You are thinking she needs to be stronger. Who are we to tell her how to spend her money?"

Fists clenched tight, "Phoebe doesn't owe that son of a bitch anything. Angus owes her. I've a mind to go visit him then give him my thoughts."

"Wouldn't do any good." Richard tossed his coffee down the sink before pouring a glass of wine for both of them. "Why don't we take this," he held up the glasses he poured along with the bottle to the living room. We can relax. Play a little. Need my mind occupied with you." He sent a wicked glance down her body then back to remain on her mouth.

Ruby snorted. "You want to have your wicked way with me no doubt. Seems since you came home a few weeks over a month ago making up for lost time is all that's been on your mind."

"You have the right of it. Since I was celibate all those years, waiting to return to my wife, yes, I'd like to make up for the lost time."

"I'm pregnant. Haven't you guessed?"

"I know. How do you feel about another little shifter. By the way, the child's a boy."

Also by the Author
at
Rogue Phoenix Press

Connal's Eternal Love
Sweet McKenna Book One

A few days shy of All Hallows' Eve Connal McKenna, Laird of Clan Chaton stands on the parapets of his castle. Bonfires line the hillsides while his clan prepares for the upcoming festivities. Drawn by the whispering of the wind, Connal McKenna feels a strange restlessness in his soul. Setting out to discover the wickedness that is calling to him, he discovers his mate. With gentle words and sensuous kisses, the auburn-eyed highlander conquers his mate, the beautiful, defiant Wynnie Adair who he comes upon during an evening ride. She must ultimately put her trust in the only man who can save her from the ruthless plans of her father and succumb to his gentle coaxing.

In Brady's Arms
Sweet McKenna Book Two

Forced to run from the only home she knows, beautiful, headstrong Lillian Townsends seeks shelter in the wild highlands where the McKenna clan live. Trying to avoid a betrothal contract signed by her stepfather to an aging lord, she is desperate to find a means to sidestep the inevitable, including a marriage to the oldest son of the laird. Lilly is enamored of the young lord who pursues her with unrelenting determination flashing his devilishly handsome charms. She is hard pressed to resist.

Besotted from the first moment Brady McKenna sees Lilly, he is determined to find a means to coax her into his arms and bed. With only the promise of carnal pleasure as his mistress, Brady relentlessly pursues the woman who has unwittingly forged a place in his heart. She is like no other woman, proud, defiant and enchanting. Despite his father's advice to stay away from her, he cannot. He boldly seeks her out and makes her his own.

Nobody but Walker
Sweet McKenna Book Three

The Highland Lass...

She was brought up, adored and loved by a doting mother and father ardently protected by her brothers. She was everything sweet and innocent until she was faced with betrayal and an unexpected and out of wedlock pregnancy. When she gave her love to a man who couldn't return her passion and commitment, she was left devastated and furious. Faced with the loss of her child if she didn't comply to his demands, Crissie McKenna followed him to Belfast then on to his country home to discover he was already married.

...The Irishman

Stunned to find out his one and only encounter with the woman he wanted to love forever created a child, Walker Endicott, Earl of Briarwood, claimed his child as his only heir. Walker threatened all her previously held values even while he thrilled her senses. From the moment he first saw her to the second she ran after him begging him to make love to her, his captivating masculinity held her fascinated. In his arms she would know tempestuous passion, bitter despair, and a soaring joy that would humble them both before the power of love.

Roby's Moonlit Night
Sweet McKenna Book Four

Once she'd been a pampered child with high expectations for her future blessed with love. Then she became an innocent pawn in a terrible game of greed and power. Now, with a noose around her neck, Pippa was to hang before she had the chance to unveil the men who drove her from her home, before she had the chance to live.

Roby McKenna was a man blessed with endless charm and wit. While he searched for his eternal love across the Atlantic in a new land, he would have to come home to find her. His silver blue eyes could sparkle with amusement or harden to steel gray with displeasure. He had all the women a man could want or need. As he grew older, mistresses were not enough. A quirk of fate brought him to the gallows, a spark of destiny made him claim the condemned Pippa as his bride.

Made for Houston
Sweet McKenna Book Five

Leah Kennedy is as wary of people as she is strikingly beautiful. However, the shocking death of her father that forever changed her girlhood has left her terrified of the very love she desperately longs for. Only in the untamed splendor of the Scottish crags does she feel safe from the feelings she stirs in men and the cruel mockery of Selkirk's villagers.

Debonair, well-educated doctor Houston Stuart has turned his back on social privilege along with professional honors to set up a medical practice in the lowlands of Scotland. There, serving those who need him the most, he hopes to forget the bitter memories and disillusionment that disturb his days.

Coincidence brings the cultured doctor and this fey mountain girl together. Something as bizarre as destiny disrupts the obstacle of birth and breeding, stubborn pride and fear which has kept them apart...as each seeks to heal the other's wounds with a raw passion neither can deny and all the odds against them cannot defeat.

Say You Love Kit
Sweet McKenna Book Six

Fascinated...

When the woman stepped through the door of the pub, the sun setting her fiery red hair glowing around her delicate features, Kit Stuart finds himself captivated by the sight. The moment he sees her he knows she will be his. Convincing the fire-haired lady of that fact isn't easy. After she calls out another man's name when he kisses her that night, he is instantly enraged as well as jealous. The road they travel is fraught with secrets that neither can tell. Trust is an elusive quality that neither can give.

Intrigued...

Forced to run for her life, desperate and afraid, Aila MacDuff willingly enters into the Kinnel Stones, a mysterious place where people disappear then appear magically in different times. At the first sight of Kit, she finds herself inexplicably drawn to him. She's been told to search for her mate and that she will know when she finds him. Aila doesn't know what this man's name is or what he looks like. Nonetheless, she is certain he will be similar to her mate from one hundred years earlier. Despite the fact she is falling in love with Kit, he can't be her mate. Her mate is a shifter. Kit is not.

It Had to be Riley
Sweet McKenna Book Seven

Her anger assured retaliation...

Shawna's only concern with the contemptable scoundrel she had been forced to wed was the return of her dowry. She had not seen her husband in three years, and now Riley Stuart furiously repudiated there had ever been a marriage. He even went as far as to tell his family he'd never seen her before this day.

...Her passion promised love

In the heather clad hills of the beautiful Scottish crags surrounding the small village so near to the Mckenna keep, the ferocity of her loathing yields to the intense hunger of unquenched longing. In the powerful arms of the dark and handsome husband she thought she reviled, Shawna shivers with the honeyed torment of awakened desire and powerlessly submits to the wild, enchanting ecstasy of burning passion. Together they abandon themselves to the exquisite pleasure of the love their hearts cannot escape.

The Magic of Hawk
Sweet McKenna Book Eight

With her extraordinary silver-mauve eyes, Maisie McRae struggles with the return of her lost love. She finds solace living with her half-sister and existing on dreams. After three long years the man she once dreamt of marrying asks her to make the same foolish mistake again. Holding herself aloof from the arrogant man, Maisie refuses to let his sweettalking words seduce her into his arms.

Smitten from the first instant Hawk Frasier sees Maisie, he is determined to find a means to entice her into becoming part of his life. A missing letter keeps the unlucky couple from realizing their dreams. Defeated by her rejection, Hawk searches for a way to ignore the woman. Unable to forget the way she feels in his arms, Hawk returns from the colonies, ready to try again. Despite the chance of a second rejection, he forges ahead. Boldly, he seeks her out and makes her his own.

Roc's Steadfast Heart
Sweet McKenna Book Nine

Dallas Elaine Shaw, on a photo shoot for the magazine she works for, tumbles down an incline to find herself catapulted into the eighteenth century. Facing three men, one of those men, the one with laughing silver blue eyes commands her attention. The other two stare at her with leering, malicious intent. She finds herself rescued by the man with the intense eyes. Terrified of horses, she discovers herself riding in front of the arrogant man who saved her. In a few short minutes, he sends a multitude of sparks simmering within her.

When Roc Frasier sees the woman sprawled on the ground, he thinks he's gone to heaven. This is the woman all his dreams are made from. Her body holds the enticement of lush bountiful breasts, curved hips he could hold onto. She is his dream come true. What he doesn't understand is this woman has traveled through time. She comes to him to complete the interrupted circle of life. This woman is his soulmate. His life's blood. She wants nothing more than to leave him, to return to her time. She can't. They are each other's destiny.

Harris' Reckless Heart
Sweet McKenna Book Ten

The Highland Lass…

Harris Frasier was raised and adored by a devoted mother and father, zealously sheltered by her two older brothers. Harris is everything sweet and spicey, trusting and loyal until she is faced with what she believes is betrayal to all she holds dear within her heart. She gives her love to a man who confuses her. A man who she doesn't think can return her loyalty. Given no viable choice, Harris is forced to follow him to London then on to his home near the Dover coast to discover she is correct in all her assumptions about his fidelity. He is a womanizer. Harris cannot abide a life with a man who will not remain faithful.

…The Sassenach Soldier

Stunned to discover the woman he will love forever then into eternity believes he is a cad and a philanderer. Ashton Wolcott realizes the uphill battle in front of him will worsen before Harris will learn to trust his word. He isn't anything like the man she assumes him to be. Ash endangers all her previously held values. Even while he delights her senses, she battles misconceptions. From the moment he first sees her sunning herself naked by the loch to the moment she runs after him begging him to compromise her, his captivating masculinity holds her in thrall. Within the shelter of his arms, she will learn all-encompassing passion, loyalty, and joy and the lasting power of love.

Rafe's Every Wish Fulfilled
Sweet McKenna Book Eleven

Her life was tipped head-over-heels…

When Dallas Shaw realized her long-time friend meant more to her than she ever imagined, she panicked. With the first kiss, unexpected sparks flared between them. Because of her intensifying passions, she was relieved to receive an assignment far away from the town of Cranach so she could come to terms with the raw desire coursing within. The handsome brooding artist who'd painted her many times was a hazard of a different kind. Dallas soon found herself yielding to his mercuric enchantment.

…and so was her heart

Taught to believe in eternal love Rafe Frasier thought he would never find his mate in this lifetime. If he didn't find her, they would never meet again in the future. Once, he thought Dallas might be his mate. Yet, there was no energy between them, no spark of raw passion when they touched. After Dallas returned from an unexplained absence, he couldn't deny her intoxicating effect on him. Now Rafe would risk his life to protect the innocent beauty who had seduced him with her tender love.

FOR THE FULL INVENTORY
OF QUALITY BOOKS:
http://www.roguephoenixpress.com

Rogue Phoenix Press

Representing Excellence in Publishing

Quality trade paperbacks and downloads
in multiple formats,
in genres ranging from historical to contemporary romance,
mystery and science fiction.

www.ingramcontent.com/pod-product-compliance
Lightning Source LLC
Chambersburg PA
CBHW060352260626
47160CB00006B/2287